To Susan:

It's resistance time!

— Michael [signature]

FULL ASYLUM

FULL ASYLUM

A Novel
by Michael Isenberg

Monteferro Press
Boston

This book is a work of fiction. Names, characters, places, and incidents either are products of the author's imagination or are used fictitiously. Any resemblance to actual events or locales or persons living or dead is entirely coincidental.

Copyright © 2012-2013 by Michael Isenberg
All rights reserved, including the right of reproduction in whole or in part in any form.
Map copyright © Open Street Map Contributors
(http://www.OpenStreetMap.org) CC BY-SA 2.0
(http://CreativeCommons.org/licenses/by-sa/2.0)

ISBN 978-0-9853297-2-3
Special Edition C

10 9 8 7 6 5 4 3 2

To my father, who took me to my first James Bond movie.

CONTENTS

Prologue at Pentagon Palace 9

Part I. The Art of Paintball War 23
   1. Goodbye, Mr. Dunn 24
   2. Byte Yourself Software 32
   3. Sorry 67
   4. Paint Misbehavin' 83

Part II. A Plethora of Betas 121
   5. The Ring Recycle 122
   6. O'Hare at National Airport 140
   7. Bad Neighbors 164
   8. An Enemy of the People 182
   9. Reason Expired 209

Part III. Error of the Moon 229
   10. Southern Breeze 230
   11. Getting Unwired 255
   12. Full Asylum 290
   13. George Washington Shows the Way 316

Epilogue. Independence Day. 354

Acknowledgments 368

What enables the wise sovereign and the good general to strike and conquer, and achieve things beyond the reach of ordinary men, is foreknowledge. Now this foreknowledge cannot be elicited from spirits; it cannot be obtained inductively from experience, nor by any deductive calculation. Knowledge of the enemy's dispositions can only be obtained from other men. Hence the use of spies.
– Sun Tzu, *The Art of War*, 13.4–7

Prologue at Pentagon Palace

The neon sign was gone but the letters were still visible: streaks of dirt and smoke spelled *The Mall at Pentagon Palace*. Otherwise the reddish granite wall, like the gray November sky, was bleak and featureless. Gimbel remembered when he used to shop here, before the Third Financial Crisis and the Federal Economic Sabotage Act. Come to think of it, that's where he bought the clothes he had on. The torn jeans and faded flannel shirt had been buried in the back of his closet for a while, but today he needed something old and well padded.

Up ahead, a chain-link fence enclosed the vacant lot where a hotel had once abutted the mall. The hotel had been torn down, the materials scavenged for shantytowns and government office buildings. Gimbel maneuvered his blue Solo coupe along the fence. The tires flattened the weeds that grew through the asphalt. Gimbel did his best to dodge potholes and puddles of broken glass. He hoped that the suspension would hold up; three years ago, when he walked into the Hankuk dealership with his checkbook, he hadn't planned to navigate the broken pavement of a suburban wasteland. Back then his purchase criteria were the Solo's low sticker price and its sort-of resemblance to the Cheetah YK-2. That was the car Jon Dunn, Secret Agent Beta Eleven, drove in *Best Served Deadly*.

Dunn used it to escape the Soviet agents chasing him through the streets of Allahabad.

Finding the parking garage empty, Gimbel tried the ramp that descended to the delivery entrances. A guard shack halfway down was abandoned. Beyond that, Gimbel discovered an oasis of normal. Cars occupied what used to be a truck court. He parked next to a shiny SUV with a layer of toys covering the back seat. On the other side, a GWU sticker decorated the bumper of a car badly in need of washing.

A steel door next to the loading dock appeared to be the way into the building. The smell of wood smoke choked the air; Gimbel tried to remember if he had read anything about a fire at Pentagon Palace. On the other side of the steel door a cinderblock corridor stretched to the back entrance of a store. A sign with an arrow and the words *Pentagon Palace Paintball* pointed the way.

It was a hell of way to settle a lawsuit. But that's how Jon Dunn would have done it. Every Dunn movie had a scene where he confronted the villain in a casino or a luxury resort and challenged him to some contest—billiards usually, but sometimes blackjack, and in one bad movie from the 1970s, roller disco. The difference was that when Dunn did it, he was actually good at the game. Gimbel had never seen a paintball gun outside of a movie.

The other difference was that Cindy wasn't really a villain, or at least Gimbel couldn't bring himself to think of her as one. They had never been friends, but they had always worked well together, like the professionals that they were. Between the two of them they generally got the software to run in spite of the "guidance" from management. Lately Cindy and Gimbel had gotten along a little better than usual—when she wasn't telling him, in exasperation, to man up. He had started to relax around her—which was probably why he was in trouble now.

Instead of a casino or a luxury resort, the venue for their confrontation last night was the pool table in Kilkenny's. From there they moved to the bar, where they haggled over the terms and conditions while Andy and Bart looked on and Madame Butterfly took unintelligible notes. Three weeks from today they would play Capture the Flag on the summit of Crestview Mountain. Cindy and her friends would set up fort and defend; Gimbel would be on offense. They would settle the lawsuit in favor of whoever held the flag at the end of an hour. Upon reaching a deal, Gimbel and Cindy shook on it. Cindy's grip was bony, cool, and unyielding.

In the harsh light of day, or at least the dim light of a back corridor at Pentagon Palace, it appeared to Gimbel that the deal was *not robust*, an engineering phrase that meant *it sucked*. Negotiating in a bar was a mistake: the second glass of Glenjohnnie downgraded his bargaining skills. The contest would be four against one and paintball was their game; they had won some sort of regional trophy. The only provision favorable to Gimbel was that he had three weeks to train—starting when he opened the door at the far end of the corridor.

On the other side of the door he found the remnants of a large clothing store. The walls had been stripped to the concrete and metal fences divided the space into a check-in area, a pro-shop, an equipment cage, and a holding area. At the check-in Gimbel signed a credit card receipt and several documents saying that Pentagon Palace Paintball was not responsible for injuries, stains, faulty equipment, lost articles, parking lot vandalism, allergic reactions triggered by vending machine fare, or anything else. The woman at the desk gave Gimbel a tag identifying him as a member of Group 5 (Rental). Then she directed him to join other newbies for an orientation and safety lecture.

A young instructor with red hair over his eyes and a Pentagon Palace Paintball t-shirt introduced himself as Joe. He was a tall boy of eighteen with big feet and pimples. He talked like he wasn't used to being in charge, but could fake it by mimicking some gym teacher from his past. As long as he could keep a straight face, the imitation was passable. "Listen up, class," he said in a raised voice, with a pause after each sentence. "We work on a rotation....You must wait in the holding area until your group is called....Then you must proceed to the doorway with the black curtains....Divide into two teams and line up behind the doorway.

"When the referee dude—the referee—tells you that it's time to go into the mall, proceed through the curtains....You will be in the corridor behind the food court....One team will go left...the other team right....Exit the door at your end of the corridor and you will find yourself behind one of the counters....The match starts when the referee blows his whistle....At that point you ladies may proceed through the opening in the counter and into the mall."

The gym class stock phrase "you ladies" made Joe giggle. He took a moment to re-establish the channel to his inner grown-up.

"If you are hit, you are done for this match....You must hold your marker over your head and proceed out of the mall the way you entered....The match is over when one side has been completely eliminated or when time is called....The referee will then blow his whistle a second time and all players must leave the course and return to the holding area....Are there any questions?"

Gimbel raised his hand. "What's a marker?"

β 1 1

It turned out a marker was a paintball gun. After Joe explained that and went over some safety rules concerning barrel bags and facemasks, he directed the players to the equipment cage. The attendant issued each of them a mask, a gray jumpsuit, a bag of paintballs, and a Tilmann B-6 marker. Gimbel found an unoccupied picnic table in the holding area and laid out his gear for inspection.

The jumpsuit was faded but clean. Gimbel slid it over his clothes and zipped the front. It was only a little too big. He thought it made him look like a janitor. Next he examined the paintballs.

FULL ASYLUM

They were about half an inch in diameter, and their hard shells made them look like yellow gumballs. Gimbel snapped the cap off the plastic hopper on his marker and tried to pour the brightly colored spheres through the opening. Two-dozen paintballs clattered on the concrete floor; he had poured too fast. The sound got the attention of some middle school kids from another group. Eager to get something for free, they swarmed around Gimbel and tried to steal his ammunition. Still, Gimbel was able to recover most of it. He checked with Joe whether the paintballs were still okay to use (they were; they were undamaged) and then spent several minutes dropping them into the hopper a few at a time.

By the time Gimbel filled the hopper and donned his facemask, Joe was calling for Group 5 to line up at the door. There were a dozen in the group: several college guys, but also three women and a father with two boys aged eleven and thirteen. It was the eleven-year-old's birthday; this was his celebration. Finally there was a blond lawyer named Chris, who had just started some kind of job at the Department of Justice. Whatever it was, Chris was important enough to have the attention of the attorney general, a circumstance that he managed to bring up frequently. "Attorney General Peterson is personally helping me with the investigation," "Attorney General Peterson is helping me find an apartment," "I told Attorney General Peterson that he's going to be president someday; he didn't say 'no.'"

They divided into teams as Joe had instructed. Gimbel joined the team with fewer people, which turned out to be the one with the two boys. As he waited to enter the mall, he alternated between adjusting his mask and checking out the other players. The mask fit badly over his glasses. The other players all looked alike in their jumpsuits and facemasks. Except for the two kids, Gimbel wondered how he would tell which ones were on his team.

Finally Group 4 (Self-Equipped) finished its match and cleared the floor. Gimbel's group paraded through the doorway between the black curtains, removed the barrel bags from their markers, switched off the safeties, and advanced to a counter where pretty women in green uniforms used to serve two-entrée plus fried rice Chinese combos for $8.95 each. The referee blew his whistle. Gimbel and the others ran past the counter and fanned into the atrium.

When they got out into the open, Gimbel halted.

The Mall at Pentagon Palace had been metro-Washington's first super-sized, super-luxury fashion hub. Its Grand Opening, coming in the last weeks of the 1980s, had been an Event. The scale of the building and the vast choice of merchandise had epitomized the morning-in-America capitalism of that decade. Suspended in the atrium, beneath the glass ceiling, an American flag the size of a house had signaled that shopping was patriotic. Catwalks with ornate white railings had bordered the rows of clothing boutiques, shoe stores, hair salons, and restaurants. The tiers of retail were iconic, like the decks of a steamship chugging down the Mississippi. In the food court on the ground floor, carts with green awnings had dispensed a coffee drink that was new to the United States: the *latte*. Back then, affluent young women had relaxed under real palm trees and sampled the foamy beverage. Nearby, teenage girls had shown their purchases to their friends and plotted how many more stores they could assault before mom arrived in the minivan.

It was a more prosperous era, before the Financial Crises. But when Wall Street crumbled, the market for high-end apparel dried up and Pentagon Palace went the way of hundreds of other American malls. At first a trickle of luxury shops closed. Then Gracie's Department Stores went bankrupt and signs with the half-moon Gracie's logo came down all across the country. Robbed of their anchors, the malls saw a drop in the number of shoppers entering their doors. Without sufficient traffic to sustain the stores, the dripping faucet of closings became a fire hydrant. Heavily mortgaged owners accepted whatever sources of rent they could find: dollar stores, Halloween outlets, psychic medicine clinics. The owners of Pentagon Palace converted the whole mall into a paintball arena.

The warm open space was now a post-industrial ruin. Plywood replaced half the glass panes in the ceiling; the other half were so grime-laden that a dim grayish haze was all the light that penetrated from outside. The catwalk lighting was stripped, its gentle radiance replaced by the cold glare of industrial floodlights. Even under this harsh illumination the atrium appeared dark, thanks to the dirt that coated the walls. The tables and chairs were gone from the food court, but the coffee carts remained, turned on their sides and scattered among the trunks of dead palm trees. Pads wrapped the carts and tree trunks to provide safe cover for play-soldiers with paintball guns. The American flag remained, tattered but still there, watching gallantly over hundreds of not-so-perilous fights.

No one can stand in the open for long in a paintball arena. Within seconds, Gimbel felt something strike his left shoulder and the match ended for him. He never saw where the pellet came from. At least it didn't hurt; he had heard that paintballs hurt. Following Joe's directions, Gimbel raised the Tilmann B-6 over his head and marched back to the hallway like a soldier surrendering. He removed his mask and restored the safety and the barrel bag to his marker.

Back in the holding area, he examined the stain on his coveralls. Jon Dunn had been hit by a paintball in a training exercise at the beginning of *Blueprint for Terror*. It left a powdery purple patch on his black commando sweater. The splotch on Gimbel's jumpsuit wasn't purple and didn't look like paint. More than anything else, it resembled egg white, except it was greasier, at least until it dried. Then it looked like bird crap.

He did better his next time out. He made it to one of the coffee carts and spied an opposing player taking cover behind a palm tree.

Standing behind the cart, Gimbel got several shots off before his opponent gave him a stain on his right shoulder to match the one on his left.

In the third match, his marker jammed. Gimbel raised it over his head and abandoned the course before anyone fired a shot at him.

In the fourth match, a sniper hiding in the catwalks took Gimbel out with a single shot. The pellet hit the top of his mask. Grease oozed through the vents into his hair and onto his glasses. It was difficult to see his way back to the entrance through the smeared lenses, but he would have to wait until he was off the floor before he could clean them; Joe had warned them never to remove their masks while on the floor.

He found some paper towels at the equipment cage, cleaned his glasses, and looked around the holding area. Chris lounged at one of the picnic tables, bragging to a pair of college guys. "I think the third one I hit was the biggest threat. I already got him in the previous match, so he knew I was up there in the catwalk. If I didn't do something quick, he could have shot me. It was him or me. Sure, the railing protected me, but he could get lucky. I stayed cool though. I aimed carefully. I pulled the trigger. Whoomp! Right in the back of the head. That little boy wouldn't put *me* in danger anymore."

"He was just a kid," said one of the college students. "Chill out, bro."

"Hey, I got a reputation to uphold. I always win."

Gimbel joined the birthday boy and his family at their table. They looked dejected, slumped in white-splotched coveralls.

"I think the boys are frustrated," their father said. "That guy Chris keeps sniping at them from the catwalk. Three times in a row now."

"What are their names?" Gimbel asked.

"Bobby and Jeff. I'm Stu."

FULL ASYLUM

"Gimbel O'Hare."

They shook hands. "Jeff's the birthday boy," Stu said. "I wish it were more fun for him."

"Take a look at this," Gimbel replied, passing his facemask across the red planks of the table.

Stu examined the crusty stain on the top of Gimbel's mask. "He got you too, I see. That jerk ruins it for everyone."

A bright burst of red and yellow got their attention. It appeared on a TV screen that hung from the ceiling in one corner of the holding area. Gimbel recognized the opening sequence of the latest Jon Dunn film. The fireball was the first clip in a montage from the movie. Several more explosions followed, the last one erupting from the center of the Eiffel Tower. The structure swayed and toppled onto the Champs de Mars, breaking cleanly into three pieces. There were also scenes of a car chase, two SCUBA divers wrestling underwater, and a man and a woman kissing in the living room of a hotel suite. Upon completion of the montage, the scene shifted to a TV studio where an attractive thirtyish woman in a swivel chair conducted an interview.

"I'm here with Grant Casey, and those of course were scenes from *To Die or Not to Die*, his latest outing as Jon Dunn. Grant, I believe you're the eighth actor to play Secret Agent Beta Eleven."

"The ninth, actually," Casey replied in a crisp British accent. He was a rugged-looking man with a dimple in his chin. His thick black hair was cut neatly and parted on the right. The lines of a tuxedo enhanced his broad shoulders.

"Tell us about your next adventure."

"We started filming *Error of the Moon* last month at Consolidated Studios in Hollywood and we'll soon go on location in Geneva, Santa Fe, and Washington, DC. I can't tell you the plot, but I assure you it will be quite topical."

"Of course no Dunn film would be complete without the Dunn Ladies. I hear you have a lovely co-star."

"Lana Wong has been cast in the role of Su Mi. It's been a pleasure to work with her."

Casey began a story about a practical joke Lana played on the set. As he spoke, a publicity still appeared on the screen. Lana wore a white karate uniform with a black belt. The photo was taken in some sort of gym—apparently during a martial arts demonstration. Lana stood barefoot on one leg. The other was extended in a high kick, her foot only an inch from the head of a short, liver-spotted man, obviously her *sensei*.

"Of course," said Casey, finishing his story, "it's not just Lana. It is a pleasure to work with all of my co-stars."

"You're gracious to say so."

"Any actor would say the same."

"You'd be surprised how many don't. Tell me, Grant. You've had a great deal of success in your career, yet you've avoided letting it go to your head. How have you managed to remain such a nice guy?"

"He wasn't very nice when I met him," Gimbel complained.

"You met Grant Casey?" Stu was impressed. "When was that?"

Gimbel regretted bringing it up. He had had this conversation enough times in the past few weeks to know better. But it was too late now. "I was on TV last month."

Stu's eyes widened. "I *know* you," he said. "You were on the *Sorry* show. You're Little 'n' Cuddly."

"That's me. Little and cuddly and so tired of people calling me that."

The excitement of being two degrees of separation from Grant Casey prevented Stu from registering the hint to change the subject. "You're right," he said, "Grant Casey wasn't nice to you. But he did have a point about your walk. You scurry all hunched over, like a beetle. You walk like some old movie comedian. Charlie Chaplin, I think."

"I don't walk like Charlie Chaplin."

"No?"

"No," said Gimbel. "I walk like Groucho Marx."

Stu was suddenly sympathetic. "I'm sorry," he said. "I just realized I'm being callous. It must have been an ordeal for you, having to defend yourself like that on national television."

"I'm not that defensive about my walk."

"No, I meant the accusations. Personally, I thought they were frivolous."

"Thank you," Gimbel replied.

"That woman...what was her name?"

"Cindy."

"Right. Cindy. As far as I'm concerned, she was completely out in left field. I thought what you said to her was very funny—and not offensive at all." He stretched for something else to say. "How did it finally end up between the two of you?"

"I'm afraid our little episode of *Sorry* wasn't the end. She's suing me now."

Gimbel was spared the need to explain further: Joe came through the holding area, calling for Group 5 to line up for the next match.

Back on the mall floor, Gimbel watched for snipers. Immediately after the whistle blew, he spied one dashing up a stalled escalator and onto the catwalks. When he was sure the sniper was looking the other way, Gimbel sprinted to a java wagon. This time he was careful to stay under cover, popping his head up just long enough to fire at another player before ducking into the shelter of the cart. He succeeded in marking one of the college guys. For the first time Gimbel thought this was something he could be good at—like writing software or pissing off his boss. His burst of confidence soon died. He aimed for another of the college guys, but the other guy fired first. The pellet hit Gimbel on the exposed skin of his hand. It turned out that paintballs hurt after all. Back in the holding area, he tried curling his fingers. Pain shot up his tendons, enough to convince him it was time to turn in his equipment.

Half a bag of paintballs remained; he gave them to the two boys. Then he collected the marker, mask, and jumpsuit and headed over to the equipment cage to return them. On the TV in the corner, the interview with Grant Casey was still in progress. It reminded Gimbel of what Casey had said to him. "In your case, Mr. O'Hare, wanting to be Jon Dunn is just ridiculous. Who ever heard of an international superspy who walks funny? Face it, Mr. O'Hare. You are the un-Dunn."

Gimbel halted mid-scurry. "We'll see who's undone," he said. He straightened, changed direction, and walked casually to the pro-shop. There he invested in a new bag of paintballs—and a pair of gloves. Stuffing the credit card receipt in his pocket, he returned to the holding area to dress up again like a bandit janitor.

He rejoined Bobby, Jeff, and their dad. "I got an idea how to ruin it for that sniper jerk," he told them. "Kids, hang back a little. You'll know when it's okay to move."

When the match started, Gimbel hung back as well, taking cover behind a food counter while Chris advanced towards the motionless escalator. Chris would be in range for only a moment; to stop him, Gimbel would need to take him out in that moment. Once Chris reached the first steps, the glass balustrade would protect him. Gimbel waited patiently. When the enemy was within steps of the escalator, Gimbel aimed, squeezed the trigger, and scored a direct hit. Chris stared at his coveralls in disbelief. "That will put a stain on his reputation," Gimbel said.

Free from the menace of overhead fire, and now outnumbering the opposition six to five, Gimbel's team advanced across the floor, Bobby and Jeff taking the flanks.

Gimbel bounced rapidly from cart to cart like a pinball caroming between bumpers. He crouched behind a cart two-thirds of the way across the floor. Stretching upward to peer over the top, he saw the muzzle of an enemy marker peering back at him. Above it, dark plastic lenses stared at Gimbel with as little feeling as a surveillance camera.

Gimbel dropped to the floor, rolled onto his back, and aimed upwards. In a moment the other player would clamber over the top and have a clear shot at Gimbel from the high ground. Gimbel had to shoot first. For now, he saw only empty catwalks and dark store windows above the top of the cart. Then something moved. His adversary popped into sight, marker pointed at Gimbel's chest. Gimbel tried to squeeze his trigger but pain shot from his earlier injury. He heard the thump of a paintball gun and then another, but they didn't come from above. The player overhead had fresh egg-white stains on each sleeve. Bobby and Jeff stood on each side of the cart, their markers still pointed at the opposing player.

The referee blew his whistle. For the first time, Gimbel was still on the floor when the match ended.

"We're gonna have cake now," Jeff said to Gimbel. "You can have some if you want."

β 1 1

Back in the holding area, Chris sat at a picnic table and sulked. Across from him, the two college students complained about their post-graduation prospects. "I planned to take a year off and travel Europe," said one. "But then I got this letter from Washington Metro Bank. It said the government repackaged my student loan and sold it to them. Now they expect me to pay it back."

"That's bullcrap," his friend replied. "What are you going to do?"

"What can I do? I have to look for a job."

"That reeks. You shouldn't have to work just because you owe money to some greedy bank. It's like being a slave or something."

"Banks suck, bro."

The first student talked about his job search. No luck so far. "It's Big Business," his friend said. "They want the job market to suck. That way they don't have to pay as much. They can keep more for themselves."

"Big Business sucks."

Chris was about to suggest that they make up their mind about what upset them: working or not working. But a melody distracted him. Across the holding area, birthday candles flickered on a cake with chocolate frosting. Their orange glow lit the face of one of the Annoying Kids. Next to him, his brother belted out "Happy Birthday" while two men harmonized. All four looked cheerful and relaxed, despite their paint-covered jumpsuits.

"Enjoy yourself, Mr. O'Hare," thought Chris. "We'll see if you're still singing when the Department is through with you."

β 1 1

Gimbel walked out to the parking lot with Bobby, Jeff, and their dad. The kids were in much better spirits than they had been earlier. They were roughhousing a bit, trying out some moves they had seen on UWL wrestling. At one point Bobby put Jeff in a headlock and Stu had to intervene.

Their SUV was parked close to Gimbel's Solo. As the kids strapped themselves into the back seat, their father stood by the driver's side door and wished Gimbel well. "I hope everything works out with your lawsuit," he said. "Something like that has got to turn your whole life upside down."

Gimbel watched them drive away. *My life was upside down before that*, he thought. It had been upside down ever since the night Liza had come to his apartment and they watched *The Future Is Just Beginning*.

That was almost two months ago.

PART I
The Art of Paintball War

The art of war is of vital importance....It is a matter of life and death, a road either to safety or to ruin.
 – Sun Tzu, *The Art of War*, 1.1–2

CHAPTER 1

GOODBYE, MR. DUNN

Sight hateful, sight tormenting! Thus these two,
Imparadised in one another's arms,
The happier Eden, shall enjoy their fill
Of bliss on bliss; while I to Hell am thrust,
Where neither joy nor love but fierce desire,
Among our other torments not the least,
Still unfulfilled, with pain of longing pines!
– John Milton, *Paradise Lost*, Book IV

Goodbye, Mr. Dunn. You have interfered with my plans for the last time."

Dr. Arsenic gestured for the two guards to take Jon Dunn to the shark tank. As they took hold of Dunn's arms, the doctor continued, "It was very foolish of you to rush in here after Miss Kane with no plan. Clearly you have forgotten your *Art of War*."

"Remind me," Dunn replied in his Eton accent.

"Sun Tzu said, 'The general who wins a battle makes many calculations in his temple ere the battle is fought.' My calculation is that you fought your last battle, Mr. Dunn."

The guards led the prisoner out of the control room and through a rock-lined corridor to the giant aquarium sunk in the floor. Three evil-looking fins patrolled the surface. Dunn and the guards approached the water's edge. The sharks swam towards them as if they knew it was suppertime. The guard with the big wart on his cheek reached out to push Dunn into the water, but Dunn grabbed his arm and twisted it behind his back. He swung the man between himself and the other guard just in time to shield himself from the bullets spraying from the second guard's Uzi. The man with the wart shuddered and died. Blood spread over his black commando sweater. With his free hand, Dunn removed the corpse's pistol and, with a single shot, killed the man with the Uzi. He released the corpse he was holding; it fell in the water. Fins glided towards it and the water boiled with red foam.

Dunn put the safety on the pistol and shoved it into his waistband. He took the Uzi from the other corpse, placed the strap over his shoulder, and ran back down the corridor. Snapping a fresh clip into the weapon, he burst through the control room door. The technicians never knew what hit them. A geyser of sparks erupted from the control panel as stray bullets punctured it. Dunn approached the big stainless steel armchair in the center of the room where Dr. Arsenic was shouting orders. "Kill him! Kill Dunn you fools!" Three more guards in black commando sweaters fired at Dunn from behind. He turned and shot all three. But when he pivoted back toward the armchair, Dr. Arsenic was already at the other exit, pushing Sugar Kane roughly through the doorway.

Flames swept the control room. Dunn dodged several fires as he raced to the other door. He got there in time to see Dr. Arsenic and Sugar Kane disappear around the corner at the end of the hall. Dunn ran after them. He pushed the Uzi aside on its strap, drew the pistol, removed the safety, and carefully turned the corner. The corridor dead-ended at a large copper door with a big wheel in the center. Standing in front of it, Dr. Arsenic pressed a nine-millimeter automatic against Sugar Kane's temple.

"Don't come any closer, Mr. Dunn."

"I don't intend to," Dunn replied calmly. He fired a single round into the center of Dr. Arsenic's forehead. The supervillain crumpled onto the stone floor. "Goodnight, sweet prince," said Dunn.

"Oh, Jon!" sighed Sugar Kane. But her relief was short-lived. A loud explosion shook the corridor. Rocks and dirt rained from the ceiling. "Come on!" yelled Dunn as he turned the copper wheel. The big round door swung open like the entry to a bank vault, revealing the hatch of Dr. Arsenic's escape pod. Moments later, Jon Dunn and Sugar Kane were strapped securely in the pod as it shot towards the ocean surface in a suggestive column of bubbles.

The pod emerged into the air and bobbed several times. Through the porthole, Jon Dunn and Sugar Kane saw a ball of fire erupt from Dr. Arsenic's private tropical island, lighting the night sky. They blinked. "He always did think he had a bright future," Dunn said.

A gravelly and very British voice crackled on the radio. "Alpha One calling Beta Eleven. Alpha One calling Beta Eleven. Come in, Beta Eleven. Jon, are you all right?" Sugar Kane reached for the microphone, but Dunn took her hand and stopped her. He put his arm around her, kissed her, and said, "Our future is just beginning."

"Oh, Jon!"

Then the music played and the credits rolled across the screen. The song was one of the slow, romantic ones where the singer reveals how much she loves agent Beta Eleven:

> The future is just beginning.
> I'll spend every moment with you.
> I've known many guys
> Who promised me lies,
> But I know you love me true.
>
> The future is just beginning.
> The past was just chapter one.
> Your kiss makes me feel
> Like I'm finally real.
> You're the best there is, Jon Dunn.

Gimbel and Liza watched the credits to the end. They sat on the sofa in the living room of Fox Hunt Apartments, Building 32, Unit 2A. On the glass-and-chrome coffee table, the LCD screen of a Byte Yourself control pad glowed dimly. Gimbel reached for the pad and slid his finger across the screen. Overhead, half a dozen compact fluorescent coils radiated a warm orange and then a stark white. They revealed a sea of wall-to-wall beige acrylic. There were no plants, no natural wood grains, no hint of life, not even in the man and the woman seated on synthetic upholstery.

Gimbel pressed an icon on the control pad; the television turned off. He looked at Liza. He had become fond of her during the month they had been dating. She was smart and down-to-earth and knew about current events. Although she dressed severely—tonight she wore an Oxford shirt and corduroy pants—her clothing could not disguise her cuteness. The spiky bangs of her pixie haircut jutted over her forehead. Her pretty lips pouted like the mouth of a porcelain doll. They made Gimbel want to take the relationship to the next level. *Next level. What am I being so polite for? There's a more direct word for what I want.*

"Did you like the movie?" he asked.

"Oh, yeah," she replied. "Sitting in your living room watching television on a Friday night is so much better than going out somewhere."

"We could go out for a walk."

"I think it's too cold."

A few more taps on the control pad brought up the time and temperature display:

Friday, Sep 17 10:17 p.m.
Fairfax, VA, Temp 66°F

Not too cold.

They walked along the road that circled Fox Hunt Apartments. Several cars drove by. Gimbel figured the occupants were on the way home from the restaurants in Washington. Liza didn't say much. He usually didn't bore her with talk about his work, but now he struggled to fill the pauses. "I'm going to see Beverly—she's my boss—I'm going to see her about it Monday morning. I think the idea will get us back on schedule. Maybe I'll get some recognition for it. Cindy keeps saying that's important for me, professionally."

They passed a dumpster and arrived back at the parking lot by Gimbel's building. He didn't want her to leave yet so he led her around back to the pond at the center of the complex. They sat without talking on a bench at the edge of the water. Looking at the ring of three-story buildings, Gimbel was surprised by how many of his neighbors were still awake; he was usually asleep at this hour. Gimbel and Liza watched the lights from the apartments and the disk of the full moon dance on the water. He imagined himself and Liza in a native village on a tropical island.

He took off his glasses with a nerdy flourish, leaned towards her, and kissed her. "Our future is just beginning," he said.

"Don't," she replied angrily. She stood abruptly.

He put his glasses back on. "What's the matter?"

"I don't understand how you can watch those movies."

"I like them. They're fun."

"They disrespect women."

Gimbel was puzzled. "I always thought the Jon Dunn movies were ahead of their time in portraying strong female characters. Think about the movie we just saw. What was disrespectful?"

"Every woman in it was either evil or stupid."

"Sugar Kane was a naval architect."

"That proves she was stupid. It's like a cover up. Why else would they have to give her a profession like that?"

Gimbel tried to break the circular reasoning. "Maybe because she was smart."

Liza crossed her arms and started to walk away. She walked quickly; Gimbel hurried to keep up.

"I really am trying to understand this. Give me some examples."

She stopped, turned, and put a hand on her hip. He had invited her to trash the movie some more and she obliged. "You want examples? Start with naval architecture. To convince you that Sugar Kane was smart, they put her in a male-dominated profession. Why couldn't they have made her a social worker or a women's studies professor instead of a ship designer?"

"Because it was a movie about submarines?" Gimbel knew that was the wrong thing to say before Liza reacted. He apologized. "What else?"

"See-through blouses. Every outfit Sugar Kane owned had a see-through blouse."

"It was the 1970s. A lot of women wore see-through blouses. Anyway, I liked that part."

"That's just my point, Gimbel. You objectify women, just like Dr. Arsenic and Jon Dunn did. For Christsake, Gimbel, they fought over her. A woman isn't a piece of property subject to dispute about ownership."

"You make it sound like a bad thing," he said wistfully. "Sometimes I wish women would fight over me, especially if they're wearing see-through blouses. How come women in see-through blouses don't fight over me, Liza?"

"Probably because you're the kind of man who would want them to."

Gimbel didn't have an answer to that.

There were some stones by the water. He found a flat one and skipped it across the surface of the pond without saying anything. Then another. He wasn't sure if Liza felt bad about arguing with him, or was just bored, but after he skipped several more, she joined him. She picked a stone that was too round; there was a plop as it sank into the water, shattering the moon's reflection. "Try a flat one," Gimbel offered, picking one for her. "Also, give it some spin." He held her wrist gently to demonstrate.

Liza threw the stone the way Gimbel showed her. He couldn't see where it went, but it must have been a good throw; he heard the water ripple each time it bounced. "Spin is key," he said. "A spinning stone gathers more hops."

For several minutes they took turns skipping stones without speaking, until all the flat ones were gone. After searching unsuccessfully for more, Liza said, "You know about physics. How come the stones have to be flat?"

"When the stone hits the surface, the weight has to be spread over a large area so it doesn't sink."

"Can anything flat skip? What about a brick?"

"Probably not. It would be hard to throw it fast enough."

"Cars go fast but they can't skip."

"They might, if they had flat bottoms. And maybe some kind of flywheel for spin."

On the way back to her car, they passed a few late-blooming tiger lilies; the flowers palely reflected the moonlight. Gimbel broke one off and handed it to Liza. She smiled at him for the first time since the movie ended. "Oh. That's sweet," she said. "You make it hard to stay mad. I like that about you."

Gimbel pushed for more. "What else do you like?"

"The way you talk. It's normal. It's not…" She reached for the right word. "It's not affected." Grinning mischievously, she added, "I'm not too fond of your walk though."

He took the tiger lily from her and tried to put it in her hair. But the sides were cut short and the flower fell to the ground. Gimbel picked it up and carried it the rest of the way to the parking lot for her. The evening hadn't gone as planned, but it wasn't a total loss. It was as close as he had gotten to an intellectual conversation since he finished grad school. Besides, it was healthy that he and Liza could disagree.

Standing by Liza's car, a mud colored hybrid, they made a date for next weekend. Liza would pick the movie this time. He was about to kiss her goodnight when a man and a woman appeared from around the corner, robbing them of their privacy. The new arrivals weren't worried about privacy at all. They were clad in bathing suits; they must have come from the hot tub in the clubhouse. They walked with their arms around each other, pausing frequently for rather moist kisses. In between, the woman's gaze locked with the man's in a look that telegraphed gratitude, devotion, and smut. Whatever had gone on in that hot tub, it wasn't an argument about movies.

By the time the bathing suit couple disappeared into a building, Liza was already in her car with the seatbelt fastened and the engine running. As she pulled out of the parking space, Gimbel noticed he was still holding the tiger lily. He called after Liza, "You forgot your flower!" But the mud-colored hybrid had disappeared around the corner. Gimbel stood alone in the parking lot, holding out a flower to no one.

CHAPTER 2

BYTE YOURSELF SOFTWARE

Sir, I lack advancement.
— William Shakespeare, *Hamlet*, 3.2

T hank God it's Monday."
Gimbel drove past the sign with the red and black company logo and the slogan *Get Unwired* and approached two rectangular glass buildings that sparkled green in the morning sun. They stood beside a small man-made pond; it seemed there was an unwritten rule in Northern Virginia: all new developments had to have a pond. This one was different from the pond at Fox Hunt Apartments. Instead of benches scattered around the grassy banks, there were picnic tables. Also, there was a fountain.

The road split. A second sign directed visitors to their destinations:

⇦ Building 1
    Byte Yourself Software Corporate Office
    OSD Operating Systems Division
Building 2 ⇨
    BAD Business Applications Division

Gimbel took the right fork and parked by Building 2, BAD. It was early and there was only one other car in sight. Across the parking lot, at the entrance to the other building, a red Cheetah coupe with a black convertible top stood out against a backdrop of green glass and shrubbery. It was too far away for Gimbel to read the vanity plate, but he knew what it said: TINA LEE. The CEO had beaten Gimbel to the office again.

β 1 1

9:00 a.m. Time for 'stenics. Gimbel saved the file he was editing, locked his workstation, and headed back to the parking lot.

Ever since the government established the Healthy Office Program "to promote best lifestyle practices among America's sedentary population," fifteen minutes of calisthenics were mandatory each workday. The BAD engineers assembled on a concrete terrace at the edge of the pond. A black rubber mat cushioned knees and feet from the impact of elementary exercise.

Gimbel looked for someone he knew and saw Desmond "Brownie" McCoy in the back row. "How was your weekend?" Gimbel asked him.

"Too short, man."

"Brownie—get some new jokes."

Brownie checked out Gimbel's t-shirt. "What's the selection today?"

Gimbel straightened the fabric to give him a better view. "The public key encryption algorithm," he said.

"You're the geek t-shirt master," Brownie replied.

"Too bad you're the sysadmin. If Addison hadn't decided you were technically a manager, you wouldn't have to follow the dress code. You could wear geek t-shirts too. Or in your case, tie-dye."

Instead of tie-dye, Brownie wore a dingy dress shirt. A doublewide necktie with a brightly colored psychedelic pattern hung beneath his white beard. A three-inch tiepin shaped like a peace sign held it in place over his generous stomach. As for his hair, Brownie kept it off his collar as the rules required, but only by tying it into a ponytail, which he twisted upward and secured with bobby pins. He adhered to the letter of the management dress code, but subverted its spirit.

Standing with the other managers on a wooden platform, Addison Reed, the division president, watched the neat array of four hundred resources. No doubt he was counting how many wore ties. He raised a bullhorn to his mouth. "Come on, people, remember the Byte Yourself slogan. Get unwired! Stretch those forearms!"

Gimbel dutifully stretched his arms. Next to him, Brownie groaned as he raised his arms to shoulder height. His shirt came loose from his pants, and the hair on his flabby pink mid-section poked through the gaps.

"Okay. Touch your toes!" said Addison. "One…two…three…" Gimbel's boss, Beverly Dix, exercised on the platform with the other managers. Every chemically treated hair in her platinum-blond coiffeur stayed in place as she reached for the tips of her pumps.

Two women hurrying across the parking lot grabbed Gimbel's attention. Although Cindy Valence and Daphne Kellogg were often together, they seemed to have little in common. Cindy was born with ones and zeros in her veins: her code was always on time and bug-free. No one knew what Daphne did. Her co-workers had nicknamed her Madame Butterfly because of her colorful blouses and the way her attention wandered, like a butterfly flitting from flower to flower in the summer sun.

"You're late," Gimbel said when they reached the exercise terrace.

"Had to take my car into the shop," Cindy replied.

"What went down with your *coche*, man?" Brownie asked.

"Some idiot wrecked it on the way to paintball. Hint: his name is Andy and I'm dating him."

"How did it happen?"

"What a silly question," Madame Butterfly interrupted. "He asked her out and she said yes."

"No, I meant the accident, man."

"Oh, you should have been there. Cindy, Andy, Bart, and I were in the car. You know how when the light turns green, you're supposed to check the traffic before you start moving? You want to make sure that the car coming down the cross street really stops?"

"Yes."

"Well, that's the car Andy was driving."

"The car coming down the cross street," said Brownie. "Bummer."

On the platform, Addison announced the next exercise. "Push-ups!" Gimbel prostrated himself on the mat and began to work his arms and shoulders. Brownie balanced on his stomach and pretended to swim. Madame Butterfly started on toe touches. Gimbel asked if anyone was hurt in the crash.

"No," Cindy replied. "But there's a dent in my bumper, my radiator grill is broken, and the other car is going to need a new door."

"Why didn't Andy drive his own car?" Everyone in the department had heard about Andy's new Cheetah YK-8.

"He didn't want to," said Cindy.

"Why not?"

"Because there was a thirty percent chance of rain."

They moved on to jumping jacks. Brownie's bouncing belly reminded Gimbel of a question he wanted to ask. "Is it possible for a car to bounce across a pond like a stone? I thought that if you put some sort of shield on the bottom, and installed a flywheel…"

"No way, José," Brownie interrupted. "The surface tension of the water couldn't support anything that heavy."

Cindy's jumping jacks were flawless. "It's not surface tension," she said. "It's lift." She spoke evenly, without any sign of being out of breath. "The stone actually breaks the surface. The water provides an upward force. It's the same force that supports a water skier on the ocean or an airplane in the sky."

"We should listen to her," said Gimbel. "She started life as a mechanical engineer."

"Why the switch to software?" Brownie asked.

"In this economy, I took what I could get," Cindy replied with resignation.

They started on quadriceps stretches. Each engineer stood on one leg and stretched the other by bending it backwards and grabbing the ankle. Cindy noticed that Madame Butterfly was doing jumping jacks. "Daphne," she called loudly, to get her attention. "We're on quadriceps."

"Well you should be ashamed of yourselves," Madame Butterfly replied. "Doing drugs in the workplace!"

"Quadriceps aren't drugs. They're—never mind. Keep doing what you're doing."

"What about the water?" Gimbel asked. "Is there enough lift to make a car bounce?"

"Probably," said Cindy. "The atmosphere provides enough lift to make a spacecraft bounce if the re-entry angle is too shallow. Water is denser than air. But do the math. If the equations come out, then it will work."

"Why don't you just try it?" Madame Butterfly asked. "Equations take up a lot of paper and I wouldn't want you to waste any."

"Primo idea, man," said Brownie. "We could jury-rig my old Solo hatchback with a satellite dish and a salad spinner. Haul ass into the Potomac and see what happens."

Madame Butterfly called shotgun, but no one volunteered to sit behind the wheel.

β 1 1

Gimbel liked to offset the healthy effects of 'stenics with a stop at the cafeteria for toaster pastries. This morning's selection was blueberry cinnamon. He scarfed them down and headed to Beverly's office.

BAD had hired Beverly Dix as a programmer. She did not remain one long enough for anyone to find out if she was good at it—Addison promoted her to manager after three weeks. He said it was important for Byte Yourself to demonstrate its commitment to the advancement of women.

She was on the phone when Gimbel arrived. As he stood in front of her desk, wondering whether to stay, she talked into her slender headset without acknowledging his presence. "No, I went to Kilkenny's with my girlfriends...we gabbed until 8:00...wine spritzers....Oh, I don't know...Addison was there, but I didn't get a chance to talk to him....I'll ask him out the next time I see him....I have tickets for the Kennedy Center. I'll ask him to come with....Hang on a sec, I have another call.

"Oh, Hi Addison. Let me get rid of someone."

"It's him. I'll ring you back."

"Addison? What's up?...No, it's not done yet....Yes, I know it was supposed to be done last week....We lost three days because of a bug in the Toolbox....I did talk to Tina. She can't spare any more resources from OSD....She said there's no budget for new hires....Okay, I'll update you close-of-business."

Beverly pushed the off button on the phone and turned to Gimbel. "What do *you* want?" she asked.

"Sorry," he said. "If this is a bad time…"

"Don't be so serious, O'Hare. I was making a funny."

Gimbel didn't get the joke so he just came to the point. "I think we're making a mistake building the BAD Toolbox," he said.

"What's the mistake?"

"Building it."

The powdery makeup that coated Beverly's face revealed no signs of enthusiasm; her penciled eyebrows were expressionless. "Thank you for your input," she said. She launched an explanation of the inevitability of building a toolbox. "Every piece of software we write has certain features in common: scroll bars, database connections, animated icons depicting furry animals."

Gimbel tried to interrupt. "I know all this."

But Beverly ploughed ahead. "By creating a library of these objects, and making it available, there is no need for each programmer to reinvent the wheel."

"The whole thing reinvents the wheel. I was talking to some of the programmers over in OSD and they told me they already have a toolbox. I checked out their source code and it has everything we need. We could start using it tomorrow."

"And after that, since we won't have jobs anymore, we'll finally have that big chance to move to Neverland and fight pirates all day."

Her sarcasm caught Gimbel off guard. He thought his idea was a no-brainer and he had not planned how he would sell it to Beverly. He tried anyway. "Of course we'd have jobs," he said. "There are more openings than the company can afford to fill on the other teams. They desperately need our help." He tried to anticipate Beverly's concerns. "Even management help."

"Of course, we won't need computers in Neverland. We'll have to sell them. I'm sure someone at Consolidated Software would be interested."

"The BAD Toolbox is full of bugs. It's holding up every programmer who uses it—which means every programmer in the division. The OSD Toolbox has been debugged already."

"I suppose Brownie is the logical person to unload the computers. He'll have to stay behind. No Neverland for Brownie. Do you want to give him the bad news or should I?"

"This is our best chance to get back on schedule."

"Look, Gimbel. I know you spent a lot of time in grad school getting some kind of advanced degree, but let me explain to you how things work in the non-fantasy world. Criticisms about management direction have to be aired before an issue is decided. Once the decision is made, every-fricking-body in the organization has to be on the same page, or else we all really will need to sell our computers and find something else to do. The decision to build a BAD Toolbox has already been made, and I expect you to support it. Do I make myself clear?"

"Perfectly. I *am* supporting it. But what if, after it's made, it becomes obvious that the decision isn't working?"

"Then you have to make it work."

He wasn't ready to give up yet. "I still think using the OSD code is a good idea. May I mention it to Addison Reed?"

Gimbel thought Beverly would be sick. Her pallor gave a greenish tinge to her platinum-blond hair and he was sure the next sentence out of her mouth would have at least five swears in it. But then she smiled, as if an idea struck her. Her shoulders relaxed; her face returned to its original color. "We have an open door policy in this company," she said. "You have a right to talk to Addison if you wish."

"What's the best way to reach him?"

"Policy bars me from trying to stop you. It bars me from retaliating against you. But it doesn't say I have to help you." Gimbel bit his lip to hold the anger on the inside. "One more thing," said Beverly. "I don't want you to chat with anyone in OSD again without my say-so."

β 1 1

Cindy rolled the chair back from the monitor and pronounced her verdict. "This will work. It's our best chance to get back on schedule. Maybe I'll get to spend some evenings with Andy instead of debugging in the Test Nest."

The group was gathered in Gimbel's cube. Cindy sat at the desk while Gimbel stood behind her, looking over her shoulder at the

OSD code on the screen. Occupying the guest chair, Madame Butterfly played with the toy car Gimbel kept on his desk—a midnight blue Cheetah YK-8. She mimicked the sound of an engine as she ran the car along the plastic laminate and crashed it into the fabric-covered partition.

"I'd like a few more evenings off, too," Gimbel said. "But management buy-in is still standing in our way."

"I'll talk to Beverly," Cindy replied. "She'll listen to me."

"What if she doesn't? There's no point in both of us being on her blacklist."

"Then we're back to Addison."

The programmers tried to figure out the best way to reach him. They considered and rejected e-mail (too easy to ignore), instant messaging (Addison wasn't logged in), "accidentally" running into him in the hallway (he mostly stayed in the executive suite), asking a question at an All Hands Meeting (the next one was seven weeks away), searching for him on a social network site (it turned out he had a SoshNet account, but the last post was over six months old), and saying it with flowers (Madame Butterfly's contribution). Gimbel began to understand why Beverly was not afraid to let him talk to Addison. The division president was impossible to reach.

They were beginning to reconsider the flower idea when they noticed Brownie leaning in the entrance to the cubicle and laughing at them. "You young people are clueless."

Gimbel picked up a rubber stress ball from the desk, tossed it to Brownie, and said, "Then clue us, O Ancient One. What are the new passengers on Spaceship Earth missing?"

"You're too plugged in, man," Brownie replied. "You have e-mail, IQPhones, IM, and SoshNet, but it never occurs to you to pick up a phone and actually talk to someone." He whipped the stress ball back at Gimbel, hitting him in the arm.

Chastened, Gimbel switched places with Cindy, punched some buttons on his speakerphone, and brought up the company directory on the LCD display. He found Addison's name and pressed the dial icon.

"Executive suite," said a voice on the other end of the line. "Ms. Maxwell speaking." The voice was a little cranky.

"Wrong number." Gimbel hung up quickly.

"What did you do that for?" Cindy demanded.

"I didn't know there was going to be an admin," he replied defensively.

"Addison is president of the division. Of course there's an admin. Call her back and just ask to speak to Addison."

"I don't think she'll put me through. Admins exist to keep people like us away."

"Christ, Gimbel," Cindy said impatiently. "Man up."

Cindy, Brownie, and Madame Butterfly looked at him with expectation. Gimbel took a deep breath. "Okay," he said. "I'll do it."

He hit the redial button.

This time Ms. Maxwell sounded annoyed instead of cranky. "Who is this?"

"This is Gimbel O'Hare with the BAD Toolbox Team. I'd like to speak to Addison Reed, please."

"Toolbox Team? That's Beverly Dix's department. Why doesn't she call herself? There's such a thing as hierarchy, you know."

Gimbel hesitated. Cindy raised her hand as if to slap him. Gimbel held up an index finger, signaling Cindy to wait a moment before inflicting bodily harm.

"Ms. Maxwell," he said, trying a mixture of flattery and authority, "I see you know the organization. As you pointed out, quite correctly, I work for Beverly Dix. By definition then, if I need to talk to Mr. Reed, it is in support of a task that Beverly delegated to me. I would therefore very much appreciate it if you put me through."

The phone went silent. Gimbel's colleagues leaned over his shoulder to see the LCD display: Was the call still connected? A man's voice came out of the speakerphone. "This is Addison Reed. What can I do for you?"

Gimbel explained who he was, why he was calling, and how sorry he was if he had interrupted anything. "Don't apologize," said Addison. He actually seemed interested in the idea of sharing code across divisions, even after Gimbel told him, as fairly as he could, about Beverly's opposition. Addison asked how many resources would be saved (he always said "resources" instead of "software engineers"). Gimbel provided an estimate and then Addison said, "This is just the kind of idea I've been looking for."

"Thank you, sir," said Gimbel.

"What I'd like you to do is put it in writing. Boil it down to a paragraph and send it to me in an e-mail. I'll take it from there."

β 1 1

Gimbel spent the next hour and a half composing a single paragraph:

To: AReed@ByteYourself.com
From: GOhare@ByteYourself.com
Cc: BDix@ByteYourself.com
Date: 20 September
Subject: Replacement of BAD Toolbox

Mr. Reed:

I propose that we abandon work on the BAD Toolbox and use the OSD Toolbox instead. By leveraging software that the Operating Systems Division has already written, we can save work for the Business Applications Division. Eliminating redundant work frees up resources to program other parts of the Business Applications. I think this is the best way to get the development of Business Applications back on schedule and beat our competitors to the market.

Respectfully,
Gimbel O'Hare

Gimbel compared the e-mail with what he had learned in business writing class and decided it was okay. The word *resources* was a nice touch. He clicked the send button and the mail server delivered another entry to Addison's inbox.

Gimbel heard Cindy moving on the other side of the partition; she was locking desk drawers and zipping her coat. "Kilkenny's bound?" Gimbel called over the wall.

"Per usual."

"Can I come?"

Cindy stood on her toes to see over the barrier. "Sure," she said. "But you never come with us. What's the occasion?"

"We have something to celebrate."

β 1 1

"Hamburger," said Gimbel. "Medium well."

The bartender looked annoyed. "We're pretty busy tonight, buddy. Are you sure you want to do this?"

"I'm celebrating."

Gimbel's colleagues, Andy and Bart, had his back. "Bur-ger! Bur-ger! Bur-ger!" they chanted. Although Cindy was concentrating on an e-mail on her IQPhone, she managed to join half-heartedly. In contrast, Madame Butterfly showed great enthusiasm, although she was chanting, "Gargle!" Some strangers at the bar rounded out the chorus.

The bartender folded. "I'll get the manager," he said, resigned. The customers cheered.

When he arrived, the manager read the government-mandated disclosure to Gimbel. "The surgeon general has determined that the consumption of beef and beef products has been linked to heart disease, certain forms of cancer, E. coli, salmonella, lack of sensitivity to the feelings of others, and in rare cases, acts of economic sabotage." Gimbel signed the acknowledgement and liability waiver and presented his certificate of low cholesterol. The manager returned to his office for a quick certificate check in the online government database; after that, the order went to the kitchen.

While he waited for his food, Gimbel studied the decorations on the wall behind the bar. They included a colorful map of Ireland, a Notre Dame pennant, a frosted glass mirror with shamrock decals in the corners, and, inexplicably, a black velvet cityscape of Bangkok. Mounted above the mirror, an enormous TV played UWL wrestling. Gimbel wished someone would change the channel: Jon Dunn never watched wrestling. Still, the others seemed to be enjoying the insult-slinging in the ring.

"I WON'T HAVE TO DO AN AUTOPSY TO KNOW YOUR CAUSE OF DEATH!" the Coroner shouted. "EVERY ONE OF THESE GOOD PEOPLE IS GOING TO SEE IT FOR THEMSELVES!"

He wore a black robe and black hat with a curled brim, like the Munchkin coroner from *The Wizard of Oz*. Behind him stood his girlfriend, Brenda Biggs. She was a large woman with frizzy hair and wore a baggy gray sweatshirt and sweatpants. The Coroner faced down Kong, a 6'5", 350-pound muscleman in monkey fur bikini briefs. Suzie Winsome, a perky blonde in a bright blue, low-cut spandex top, accompanied the ape-man. The cameras had a clear view of her surgically enhanced breasts. In the middle of the ring a tiny, irrelevant referee tried to keep the Coroner and Kong apart.

"NO, I WON'T NEED TO DO AN AUTOPSY ON YOU, KONG!" the Coroner continued when the shouts of the crowd died down. He jabbed his finger in Kong's direction. "I'M READY TO FILL OUT YOUR DEATH CERTIFICATE NOW." He reached into his robe and pulled out a parchment scroll labeled *Certificate of Death*, along with a comically large feather pen. The Coroner bellowed, "AND THE CAUSE OF DEATH—" but the crowd interrupted again. "THE CAUSE OF DEATH IS MASSIVE INTERNAL INJURIES DUE TO SEVERE PUMMELLING!"

A loud growl from Kong silenced the crowd. "CORONER SPEAK FALSE!" he boomed in a deep voice. "CORONER NO PUMMEL KONG. KONG PUMMEL CORONER!"

"KONG SAYS—" replied the Coroner, "KONG SAYS THAT HE WILL PUMMEL ME. BUT I THINK THAT KONG DOESN'T KNOW WHAT THE WORD *PUMMEL* MEANS. I CHALLENGE YOU, KONG, TELL ME WHAT *PUMMEL* MEANS. I FORFEIT THIS MATCH RIGHT HERE AND NOW IF YOU CAN TELL ME THE DEFINITION OF THE WORD *PUMMEL*!"

Kong bowed his head in shame. The crowd sighed sympathetically. "Awwwww" traveled around the arena like the Wave. Suzie leaped to her big man's defense. "KONG MAY NOT KNOW A LOT OF WORDS FROM THE S.A.T.," she said. "BUT AT LEAST HIS GIRLFRIEND ISN'T F.A.T.!"

Meows came from the crowd.

"WHAT DID YOU CALL ME?" cried Brenda Biggs.

"DO I HAVE TO SPELL IT OUT FOR YOU?" (Actually, she already had). "I SAID *FAT*!"

Brenda lunged at the smaller woman, nails outstretched. The Coroner stopped her and held her by the waist. Fortunately for Suzie, his arms were long enough to encircle Brenda's considerable girth. "ARE YOU GOING TO LET HER GET AWAY WITH THAT?" Brenda asked him.

"KONG, TEACH YOUR GIRLFRIEND SOME MANNERS," the Coroner demanded, "OR I'LL LET BRENDA GO AND SHE'LL DO IT FOR YOU."

"SUZIE RIGHT," said Kong. "CORONER GIRLFRIEND FAT. GROUND TREMBLE WHEN BRENDA WALK."

Brenda twisted to break free, but the Coroner was too strong for her. Suzie corrected her boyfriend. "BRENDA DOESN'T WALK," she said. "BRENDA WADDLES."

"I'VE HAD ALL I'M GOING TO TAKE FROM YOU," the big woman shouted. "YOU AND ME. RIGHT HERE! WE'RE HAVING IT OUT ONCE AND FOR ALL!"

"WHAT ARE YOU GOING TO DO? SIT ON ME?"

"YOU JUST WAIT AND SEE! WHEN I'M DONE WITH YOU, YOU WON'T EVEN BE ABLE TO WADDLE!"

Andy and Bart took advantage of the commercial to check the baseball scores on Andy's IQPhone. Seeing Gimbel left out of the conversation, Cindy asked him how Liza was.

"I don't know," Gimbel replied between bites of hamburger, "I can't figure out where that relationship is going."

"I'm sorry. What brought this on?"

"She says I don't respect women."

Cindy scoffed. "You respect everyone, Gimbel. That's probably not the problem."

"What do you think the problem is?"

"Knowing you, you're *too* respectful. Man up. Be more aggressive. Like Jon Dunn."

"Any other advice?"

"Yes. Stop walking like Groucho Marx."

On the TV, the UWL was back. Kong, the Coroner, and the two women were gone and a ramp descended from an enormous dark archway. Red neon letters *UWL*—Universal Wrestling League— topped the arch. "I don't understand," said Gimbel, "Aren't Suzie and Brenda going to fight?"

"They'll probably get around to it next week," Andy explained. "Wrestlers really don't do that much wrestling."

FULL ASYLUM

"Ladies and gentlemen," said the announcer in a voice that could have heralded the apocalypse. "Tonight we introduce a new force to the world of women's wrestling. From the heartland of America, at 6'3", 239 pounds, UWL is proud to present the perfect combination of sweet and tangy: Cheri Tarte, the Crimson Crusher!"

Clouds of red smoke filled the archway. The neon letters flashed. An ominous beat of kettledrums maintained the suspense. Then the crimson billows cleared to reveal a giant papier mâché pie. Slowly, a woman rose out of its center, like Venus rising from the ocean. But unlike the goddess that graced Botticelli's painting, this woman was more clothed (slightly) and more muscular (significantly). Her hair came into view first, long red hair the exact color of cherries. A red leotard matched her tresses; laces crisscrossed the open neckline and strained against her breasts. A wide belt and matching bracelets showed off her waist and arms. She stood perfectly still as the stage lift raised her out of the pie. When her red boots finally came into view, the announcer repeated, "Ladies and gentlemen, Cheri Tarte!"

The Cheri Tarte theme played over the PA system. Although it was an original composition by the UWL music department, it sounded like the soundtrack of a glam metal video from the early 1980s, the kind where leather-clad musicians abused their instruments while a wholesome-looking girl on roller skates winked at the camera. In time with the start of the music, Cheri Tarte came to life. She bounded down the ramp, jumped the ropes, and landed in the ring. Raising a sinewy arm and pumping her fist above her head, she shouted, "WHICH OF YOU BITCHES IS GOING DOWN FIRST?"

β 1 1

It was almost 11:00 when the party at the bar broke up. Andy and Bart stayed behind to watch the ballgame just getting under way in Seattle. Cindy was spun up about an e-mail from one of the second shift test engineers—something about a bug in the word processor application. She returned to work, taking Madame Butterfly with her.

As he lay in bed, Gimbel thought about Cindy. She was cool towards Andy in the bar: she buried herself in her IQPhone and hardly interacted with him at all. Earlier, during 'stenics, she had complained about what he did to her car and called him "some idiot I happen to be dating." Was that relationship about to crash? It was strange that she told Gimbel to be more like Jon Dunn with women; it was strange that she thought about what he was like with women at all. He wondered if she wanted him to be more like Jon Dunn with *her*. Maybe he could be the idiot she was dating. Not that it mattered. He was with Liza.

Unable to sleep, Gimbel booted the computer in his spare bedroom to check his news feed. *SoshNet—The Social Networking Site* appeared at the top of the screen. There wasn't much of interest. Two of his high school classmates had sent him pal requests. Gimbel recognized one of them as the guy who used to aim for his glasses during dodgeball. The other he didn't recognize at all. He selected the thumbs down icon on both requests. Liza was logged on. They made small talk by IM for a while. After she went to bed Gimbel moved to the living room to watch TV.

One Dies Every Minute was made in the late 1960s, at the time of the first Apollo flights. Like every film in the series, it began with a quiet country road and the chirping of crickets. An explosion, followed by a crash of music, suddenly ripped the peaceful scene. As the TV screen turned orange and yellow, a midnight blue Cheetah coupe—it was a YK-3 in those days—appeared from the center of the flames. The car sped toward the viewer while an electric guitar played the Jon Dunn theme. The car hurtled closer. In moments it filled the screen and kept on coming and the camera centered on one of the headlamps. Then the white light faded and the first scene appeared through the round opening.

FULL ASYLUM

Launch Control, Kennedy Space Center. Engineers in white short sleeve shirts sat behind rows of consoles. The giant screen at the front of the room showed a Saturn V rocket. Wisps of steam coiled from the rocket's colossal engines. "T-minus five seconds," said the launch director over the PA system. "Four...three...two...one...liftoff. We have liftoff." On the screen, smoke and fire shot from the rocket. The spacecraft boosted off the pad, slowly at first, then building speed. The launch director continued counting. "T-plus three seconds. The Explorer has cleared the tower. Congratulations, gentlemen, you're on the way to the moon."

Three astronauts, identical in their space suits, sat side by side in the vibrating capsule. "Roger that," one of them replied over the radio. "All systems go."

"T-plus ten seconds."

Suddenly a buzzer sounded and there was a close up of a red light flashing on one of the consoles. An engineer reported, "I have a variance in the LOX pressure, it's—" But no one heard him finish. There was a deafening noise as the rocket burst into a white-hot fireball. In the control room, stunned silence fell on the engineers as the knowledge that three astronauts were dead sunk in. After a moment, the launch director picked up the red telephone. "Get me the president," he said.

The scene shifted to a large wood-paneled office. Another man talked into another red telephone. Admiral Bradley Trumbull, code name Alpha One, was head of the Crown Security Service. "Yes, Defense Minister," he said into the receiver. "Yes, Defense Minister. We'll give the Americans every cooperation. Good night, Defense Minister." He hung up the phone and barked at an intercom. "Miss Early, where's Beta Eleven?"

"Los Angeles, sir," his secretary replied through the speaker. "He's helping the CIA interrogate the computer programmer suspected of intercepting the NATO communications. I believe he's working her now."

Another office. This one was modern, with Scandinavian furniture and stainless steel paneling. Jon Dunn embraced a woman on the sofa. She broke off his kiss reluctantly. "If you keep that up, Mr. Dunn," she said, "the system will go down on you."

"If it does," he replied, "I should inspect your input port."
"Oh, Jon! That's a program I could sign up for."
"Speaking of programs," he said casually, as if it were of no importance whatsoever, "where do you keep the one you used to intercept the NATO communications?" Her eyes darted to the Danish modern desk. Before she realized her mistake, he pinned her and cupped his hand over her mouth. "Thank you, darling. You've been most cooperative. I ought to get you a diamond bracelet. But these will have to do for now." He held up a pair of handcuffs. He cuffed her to the metal arm of the sofa, and then tied her bra around her mouth as a gag. "Sorry, darling. I have slight trust issues."

He put on his shirt and carefully knotted his necktie in front of a mirror. Then he searched the desk and found a large reel of computer tape in the top drawer. He tucked the tape under his arm, kissed the struggling woman on the cheek, and said, "Don't bother to get up, darling. I'll say goodbye to Boris for you." Dunn walked out of the office into a large computer room. Lights flashed and tapes spun on the rows of electronic equipment. Boris, a heavyset man with a shaved head, sat at a Teletype in front of a curtain. Seeing Dunn emerge from the office, he drew a pistol and aimed at Beta Eleven. "The tape, Mr. Dunn," he said. "Give me the tape with the program on it."

"Gladly, old boy." Dunn tossed it to Boris. Reflexively, Boris dropped his gun to catch the spinning tape. The pistol fired on impact, launching a bullet at one of the fluorescent lights. It flickered out in a burst of sparks. Dunn grabbed the curtain, revealing a plate glass window behind it. He pulled the fabric over Boris's head and punched him hard. Boris reeled backwards and crashed through the glass. As he disappeared from sight, his screams grew faint. Dunn approached the window and looked down. Twenty stories below, he saw a beige station wagon with wood paneling on the sides. There was a large opening in the roof rimmed with jagged pieces of metal. Boris was inside, lying dead on top of the curtain. He still clutched the tape. "Well," said Dunn, straightening his tie, "he certainly fell for that."

FULL ASYLUM

The camera zoomed towards the reel of tape. Streams of blood flowed across it. Sucked into the hole at the center, the viewer was swallowed by the opening credits. Silhouettes of naked women swam through the red-tinted ocean, their conical breasts rebounding with each stroke. The silhouettes twisted, dove, and shot upwards. They dodged torpedoes and turned somersaults. Then they dissolved.

β 1 1

The lamb was sure to go.
And everywhere that Mary went,
Its fleece was white as snow,
Mary had a little lamb,

Cindy cursed. "Why the hell is it backwards?"

She sat at Gimbel's workstation in the Test Nest. Next to her, Madame Butterfly studied the monitor. "I think the screen is upside down," she said. "I can fix it." She reached for the plastic frame of the flat panel display.

"Daphne, the problem is the software, not the screen," Cindy said sharply. "Don't touch it."

"Oh, Cindy, that's just silly. How can I touch the software? It's inside the computer."

Test Nest II took up the entire second floor. It looked like any other computer room on the planet. There were raised floor tiles, fluorescent lights, racks of servers, and rows of PCs. Blackout curtains covered the windows; there was no doubt that given the opportunity, the losers at Consolidated Software Services would use high-powered telescopes to spy on Byte Yourself's engineers. The stakes were that high.

But there was no need to worry that anyone at Consolidated might steal the piece of software displayed on Cindy's screen. It was a mess. She had patched it the best she could, but somewhere she had used the wrong pointer. As she scanned the lines of code and tried to find the error, Brownie approached. His white beard hovered over the monitor. "Gimbel!" he said cheerfully. "You sure have changed."

The best way to deal with Brownie's jokes was to ignore them. "Hi, Brownie," Cindy said without looking up. "Gimbel's at diversity training. He said I could use his workstation until 3:00."

"Are you going to last that long? You look ready to crash."

"Tell me about it."

"That blouse looks like the one you wore yesterday. Did you sleep in it?"

"I wish."

"You wish you slept in it?"

"I wish I slept. I was here all night."

"Bummer."

"On the plus side," Cindy said, "I found out why the word processor crashes every time a document goes over fifty thousand words. Some idiot programmed an array instead of a stack. Hint: his name is Andy and I'm dating him."

Brownie clasped his hands under his chin. "Ah, workplace romance."

"I replaced the array but now I can't get the stack to work."

Her IQPhone rang. She picked it up from the desktop and glanced at the screen. "I got to take this," she said. "It's my mechanic."

The effect of the estimate for repairing her front bumper was not unlike that of pouring gasoline onto a fire and then fanning the flames in the direction of a warehouse full of acetylene, thereby starting a second fire that was bigger and hotter than the first fire. She yelled into the phone, "How much labor? If I had the tools I could do it myself in half that time!...No, I don't authorize it. Get back to me when you can knock off an hour and a half!"

"Crook," she muttered as she hung up.

FULL ASYLUM

Cindy resumed scanning the code on her screen while she complained to Brownie about boyfriends, auto mechanics, and data stacks. "Got it," she said suddenly. She typed in the correction and restarted the program. The screen blinked and then turned blue. Cindy shook the mouse and struck the keys but nothing happened. The workstation was dead.

β 1 1

"Daphne," said Addison, "please tell me in your own words what happened when Gimbel finished diversity training and returned to the Test Nest."

The Incident Investigation was underway in the Executive Conference Room. Perched on top of Building 1, the spacious executive suite had the best view on the Byte Yourself campus. Through the oversized picture windows, Gimbel could see sunlight frolicking on the surface of the pond. Beyond the rectangle of Building 2, a carpet of treetops stretched to the Blue Ridge Mountains, where low-flying clouds snaked among the peaks. Inside the conference room, the brushed aluminum table was made from a piece of an actual airplane wing. The decorator had explained that aeronautical furniture suited the leaders of a company that was taking off at jet speed.

It was not how Gimbel imagined his first visit here. He had always thought that after several years of steady contributions to the company, he would be promoted to technical lead for some important project. Then he would come to the executive suite on a regular basis to brief senior leaders on its progress. Instead, he was here to explain why he should continue to be allowed to contribute.

He sat alone on one side of the table facing off against Beverly, Cindy, and Madame Butterfly. At the foot of the table, Diaphanous Van Dyke of the HR Department took notes in a spiral-bound steno pad. He was a scrawny man with a silk suit and a tenuous blond goatee.

Addison presided at the other end. He clearly enjoyed being the Decision Maker. He listened carefully to Madame Butterfly's testimony, but had difficulty making sense of it. When Madame Butterfly finally seemed to be making progress, the late arrival of Brownie McCoy interrupted her and she had to start over again.

Addison consulted the report in front of him, "It was a little after 3:00 when Gimbel returned from diversity training. Is that correct?"

"That's right," replied Madame Butterfly. "Brownie and Cindy and I were sitting around the computer with the cover off."

"I understand it had crashed."

"Oh, no. Brownie put the cover on the table very gently."

"No, I meant the computer."

"That was already on the table."

Brownie tried to help things along. "Yes, the computer crashed," he said. "Blue Screen of Death, man."

"Blue Screen of Death?" Addison repeated. "What's that?"

"It refers to the blue screen that appears in those situations. You would recognize it by the apparent absence of any brain activity within the computer."

Gimbel knew Brownie well enough to pick up on the suggestion that Addison was familiar with the absence of brain activity: the patented Brownie McCoy stealth attack on authority. Cindy gave Brownie a sharp look that was half exasperation and half pleading. Obviously she picked up on the insult as well.

Addison took back control of his meeting. "Let's get to the part where Gimbel arrived," he said. "What happened then?"

"Gimbel saw Brownie poking inside the computer with a probe and he asked what was wrong. Cindy answered, 'It keeps going down on me. Brownie thinks the power supply is flaky.' Then

Gimbel said to Cindy, 'While he's checking the power supply, I should inspect your input port.' That's when Cindy got mad."

"Why do you think Cindy got mad at Gimbel?"

"Well, there was no sense in getting mad at Brownie. He didn't say anything."

It made sense to Mr. Van Dyke. He circled *didn't say anything* in his notes.

"What happened then?" Addison asked.

"After Gimbel said, 'I should inspect your input port', Cindy replied, 'I don't *think* so.'"

"And what did you think of that?"

"I didn't think so either. Brownie said the problem was the power supply."

Beverly tried to move things along with a leading question. "Daphne," she said, "If there was no problem with the input port, why do you think Gimbel brought it up? Do you think he meant something prurient?"

"Prurient?"

"You know, dirty."

"Oh no, it wasn't dirty. They vacuum the Test Nest every night."

Addison looked through the papers, but there was no mention of vacuuming. He found the part where Cindy said, "I don't think so," and picked it up from there. "Now according to the report, you and Cindy then left the Test Nest. On your way out, you turned to Gimbel and said, 'Degenerate.'"

"That's right."

"If you didn't think Gimbel was talking about something dirty, why did you say that?"

"I was helping."

"How did that help?"

"Well, I figured if you couldn't get electricity from the power supply you could get it from degenerate."

Addison suddenly felt the need to call a fifteen-minute recess.

During the break, Gimbel remained alone in the conference room. Addison was first to return, with Beverly holding on to the sleeve of his suit jacket. "You had a lot of presence," she said. "You really got a clear story out of Daphne. I have to confess, I have trouble doing that."

Addison removed his sleeve from between Beverly's fingers. He looked concerned as he smoothed the wool. "Beverly," he said, "communicating with the people who work for you is an important part of your job. I hope you're not telling me that you can't handle it."

She backpedaled. "Oh yes, I communicate fabulously with my team. *Fab*-ulously. I have just this tad bit of trouble with Daphne. I wouldn't even mention it, except, like you say, it's such an important part of my job. Perhaps you could give me some mentoring. We could grab some drinks tonight and..."

"Tonight is quite out of the question, Beverly. Board meeting."

Beverly checked the calendar on her IQPhone. "I'm open Friday night," she said. But by then Addison had noticed Gimbel in the room and started small talk with him. "Very nice suit."

"Thank you, sir." Everyone knew about Addison's clothing obsession. Gimbel was grateful he had left his t-shirts at home today.

"October fifth is good, too," said Beverly.

"The shoes are shined, I see. So many men neglect their shoes."

"Also the sixth."

"Aren't you the young man who sent me the idea about replacing the BAD Toolbox?"

Jerking her head up from her phone, Beverly blanched. She stopped throwing out dates for cocktails and started a hasty explanation. "I'm sorry about that, Addison. I know how snowed you are. I didn't mean for Gimbel to be a nuisance, but I had to follow the open door policy."

"Not a problem," Addison replied. "I think Gimbel has a very interesting idea. Byte Yourself Software is a technology innovation leader. We should always encourage our resources to think outside the box."

Beverly reversed herself. "Absitively," she said. "Where would we be if Tina hadn't thought outside the box when she thought up IROSS?"

"What's the next step?" Gimbel asked.

"I got your e-mail," Addison replied. "Beverly and I will get together and discuss it. I guarantee you that something will come of it."

As they talked, the others gradually returned from break, mostly carrying cups of coffee. The cup in Mr. Van Dyke's manicured hand exuded the scent of artificial hazelnut flavoring. The meeting reconvened and Brownie was first up. His story went more quickly than Madame Butterfly's. He confirmed her version of events, adding that "I should inspect your input port" was a line from a Jon Dunn movie. When it was her turn to tell the story, Cindy added tears at key points. Beverly reached over and squeezed her hand.

"Mr. O'Hare," said Addison. "We've heard from your three colleagues. Do you disagree with anything they told us?"

"No, sir," Gimbel said. "That's how it happened. I'm very sorry I said I should inspect Cindy's input port."

"Why did you say it?"

Gimbel didn't know the answer. Maybe the line was in his mind because he had just seen *One Dies Every Minute*. Maybe Cindy's advice to be more like Jon Dunn had encouraged him. Maybe he was just feeling rebellious after diversity training. The only thing he knew for certain was that he had meant it as a joke and that's what he told Addison. Then he added, "I never would have said it if I realized Cindy would be offended." As he spoke, Mr. Van Dyke scribbled his words in the steno book.

MICHAEL ISENBERG

After the two sides rested their cases, Addison said "I need to talk to Beverly alone. If the rest of you could wait outside for a few minutes…"

β 1 1

They sat in fuzzy blue armchairs in the windowless reception area. Behind the closed door of the conference room, Beverly spoke angrily; they could hear her voice, but not Addison's. Whatever she was saying, it couldn't be favorable to Gimbel. She had been giving him the silent treatment ever since his e-mail to Addison.

Gimbel looked around the reception area. On one side was a pair of walnut doors with brass placards that said *Addison Reed, President, Business Applications Division* and *Freddie Hanscom, President, Operating Systems Division*. Across the room, the brass placard on another door said *Tina Lee*. There was no title and no need for one. Her story was one of the legends of high tech, like Steve Jobs visiting PARC or Bill Gates dropping out of Harvard.

Eight years ago, when she was chief programmer for Consolidated Software Services, Tina had an idea for the first operating system designed specifically for the networked home. She put together some slides and pitched the idea to Consolidated's chairman, Isaac Ross. He rewarded her with a lecture on how she was thinking like a programmer. "If you want to be a leader, you need to take the thirty-thousand foot view," he said. "You can't confine your thinking to interesting technical problems. You have to consider how the Home Network Operating System would be positioned in the global marketplace. Consolidated provides the operating system for ninety-seven percent of the world's computers. So a new system competes primarily against existing Consolidated products. It is not apropos for expanding our market share."

"If we don't develop this," Tina replied. "Another company will. Then we'll have no market share."

"You're going to have to offer more enticing bait than that if you expect me to bite, missy." Isaac got up from the conference table to indicate the meeting was over. As he approached the connecting door that led to his office, Tina yelled after him. "Bite yourself, Isaac Ross!"

She walked out of the conference room—and out of Consolidated. Two weeks later, she incorporated Byte Yourself. She lured the best engineers from Consolidated with technical challenges and stock grants. Inspired by dreams of wealth, they dove into their task. They begged forgiveness from family members for missed Little League games, forgotten birthdays, and in the case of one programmer, late arrival at her own wedding. After eleven intense months, they surfaced with Byte Yourself IROSS—the Intranet Ready Operating System Software—Version 1.0.

Within five years, IROSS replaced Consolidated's OSViews as the world's most popular operating system. Seventy percent of American homes got unwired with a Byte Yourself router and control pad. Even offices and factories started installing the systems. At age forty-nine, Tina Lee became the world's richest self-made woman. Besides a pricey chunk of Byte Yourself stock, she owned a football team and a yacht. Gustav Klimt's *The Kiss* added color to her living room wall. Right wing pundits praised her for demonstrating that, in spite of the economic downturn, success was still possible in America, if only you worked hard. On the other side of the aisle, environmental organizations recognized the potential for IROSS to reduce energy use; one conservation group presented Byte Yourself with its Greenest Product of the Year award. When asked in an interview how she became so dedicated to the environment, Tina replied, "I didn't. I just wanted to save money for my customers."

Consolidated Software's loss of market share hit its bottom line hard. Isaac had some consolation, though. He always knew that his operating systems monopoly would not last forever and he had leveraged his outsized stock valuation to diversify. Consolidated Oil and Consolidated Aircraft generated considerable revenue, albeit not as much margin or equity growth as the software business. When he merged several smaller companies into Consolidated Studios, and thereby acquired the rights to the Jon Dunn character, the *Sorry* TV show, and the Universal Wrestling League, Isaac promised to demonstrate that "an entertainment company can be profitable without swimming in the steaming puddle of puke that is popular culture. Under enlightened management, a studio can, in time, be an instrument for bringing about a more educated, refined, and cooperative society."

Isaac's other consolation was that Byte Yourself's next venture was not going as well as IROSS did. Tina had announced that she would compete with Consolidated in business applications like spreadsheets, word processors, and accounting software. She promised that the new products would integrate seamlessly with the Byte Yourself network and thereby revolutionize enterprise computing the way IROSS revolutionized the wireless home. She established a new division—the Business Applications Division—and hired Addison Reed to run it.

Addison had been the program manager for spreadsheet software at Consolidated. When Tina offered him a division of his own, he was reluctant. He told her that he could only be successful if she gave him a free hand. "I have my own ideas about how to run things," he said.

"Why else would I hire you?" Tina replied.

β 1 1

Cindy caught Brownie's eye and whispered, "Where's the bathroom?" Brownie pointed to Addison's office. "He's got his own throne."

"Will it be all right?" Cindy asked.

"Provided you leave the toilet seat up."

Cindy still seemed reluctant so Brownie encouraged her. "Check it out. There's a shoe shine machine and a full-length mirror."

Convinced, Cindy slipped into Addison's office.

"I'm impressed," Gimbel said. "Even Tina doesn't have her own bathroom."

"Addison's got lots of things Tina doesn't have: his own bathroom, a reserved parking spot, a twelve-foot-high picture of himself in the lobby."

Gimbel objected to the way Brownie characterized the division president. He conceded the private bathroom and the picture in the lobby were over the top, but Brownie was being completely unfair about the parking place. "Tina has a reserved spot."

"No she doesn't."

"I see her red convertible parked next to the door of Building 1 every day."

"That's just because she's the first to arrive, man."

While they were speaking, Madame Butterfly expelled several fake-sounding coughs, as if she had something important to say. "Daphne," Gimbel said, "is there something on your mind?"

"Did you know that the sexual harassment complaint was Beverly's idea?" she replied.

"No, I didn't. When did that happen?"

"Right after Cindy got mad at you. She was having a bad day. The software wasn't working and she had a fight with her mechanic. When we left the Test Nest, we went to Beverly's office. Cindy complained for a while. Then she thanked Beverly for listening and got up to leave. But Beverly told her to sit down again. She said Cindy would never get ahead in the workplace if she didn't stand up for herself. Then Beverly called Mr. Van Dyke. While we were waiting for him, she said to make sure you didn't know it was her idea. So I'm making sure."

"That's very thorough of you," Gimbel replied. "Beverly will be grateful."

When Cindy returned from the bathroom, Madame Butterfly looked pleased with herself. Beverly's voice inside the conference room was quieter now. At one point, Addison came to the door and asked Mr. Van Dyke to join him and Beverly inside. Mr. Van Dyke trotted happily to the conference room to be of service. Then the door closed again. Gimbel wondered why they needed the HR man. It was a bad sign; he was certain that Beverly had persuaded Addison to fire him and now they were filling out the paperwork. Gimbel tried to persuade himself that getting fired would be the best thing that could happen.

He didn't always think that. He remembered the little jolt of excitement he used to feel when he arrived at the Byte Yourself campus in the morning and saw the company logo on the road sign. It was like reaching a bucket list destination at the end of a long journey—which in a way it was. He had spent years at the University of Virginia writing a graduate thesis about the weaknesses of encryption algorithms. Byte Yourself gave him the opportunity to use what he learned to take down the bad guys.

The company had attracted the attention of hackers. They breached home networks and launched attacks on the company's servers. Tina's response was the Encryption Research Team.

She asked Gimbel's thesis advisor to recommend talented cryptanalysts. He gave her several names, including Gimbel's. A week later Gimbel entered a Byte Yourself conference room and shook hands with the engineer who would interview him. The word around UVa was that Gimbel should prepare for a grilling, but Gimbel thought the questions were pretty basic. The engineer asked whether it was possible for him to hack into his neighbor's home network and change the channel on his TV, set his thermostat to a hundred degrees, or read his e-mail.

"Not easily," said Gimbel. "The network traffic is encrypted."

FULL ASYLUM

"How does that work?"

Gimbel explained the basics of public key encryption. The explanation must have been satisfactory, because Byte Yourself invited him back for a second interview. Tina conducted this one herself. "As you know," she said, "a sufficiently fast computer can decipher a coded message, even without a key. When Byte Yourself began to catch on, no such computers were available. But the hardware is catching up. The newest Veron Supercomputers can decode a message in a few hours—and it won't be long before a garden variety PC can do the job. The industry needs a new generation of encryption technology and there is tremendous profit potential for whoever holds the patents. I want that to be Byte Yourself Software."

She explained the org chart. The Encryption Research Team was divided into two groups: the Makers and the Breakers. The first group developed new algorithms, the second tried to crack them. Tina hoped that the competition would reproduce the excitement and sense of mission that the company had experienced while writing IROSS.

She offered Gimbel a position as a Breaker and he accepted. At age twenty-seven, he had *arrived*. He worked for the most successful company in the world, at the cutting edge of his chosen field; many of his classmates had to accept work doing something else. He had the best equipment available: Byte Yourself purchased a Veron 8 massive parallel processing supercomputer for the exclusive use of the Breakers. He had stock grants. He had a new car that kind of looked like a Cheetah YK-2. In spite of the housing shortage, he even lucked out on an apartment.

The competition between the Makers and the Breakers exceeded Tina's expectations. Once or twice she dropped by the Test Nest late at night. The energy and noise levels made it seem like a party was going on. The team members started placing bets on the fate of each new algorithm—first bottles of beer, then bottles of wine. By the time the Makers came up with Algorithm 299, the stake was a case of champagne.

Algorithm 299 beat the Breakers. Gimbel and the others worked around the clock for a month trying to decode it. They ate and slept in the office. In the end, they failed. They invested in a case of *prestige cuvée* and carried it noisily to the Makers' war room. The two teams drank it together. Algorithm 299 was re-christened *Crypt Yourself* by the Marketing Director. He announced it would come free with all copies of IROSS, version 3.0 and above.

Then the government stepped in.

Bill Peterson was deputy director of the FBI. He chaired an investigative committee that concluded Crypt Yourself would make the FBI's fight against economic sabotage more difficult. If sabos had access to it, the government would be unable to read their electronic communications. The committee recommended that the president use his authority under FESA—the Federal Economic Sabotage Act—to prohibit the sale of any software product containing Crypt Yourself.

Tina expected the Peterson Report. Peterson's predecessors had made similar recommendations about earlier algorithms. In the past, the software industry had always stuck together and defeated the recommendations. But in thinking that the industry would stick together this time, Tina hadn't counted on the spitefulness of Isaac Ross. On the last day of the annual World Software Exhibition in Las Vegas, he held a press conference to announce that, in a "demonstration of good corporate citizenship," he would support the Peterson recommendations.

The president was swayed. He invoked FESA and banned sales of Crypt Yourself. The headline in the *Washington Courier* was *Ross Bytes Back*.

Tina disbanded the Encryption Research Team. The twin towers of the Veron supercomputer sat unused in a corner of Test Nest I like a pair of abandoned skyscrapers. Some of the team members left the company. Most, including Gimbel, wanted to stay. Tina transferred them to the Business Applications Division. She hoped that the transfers would end the resource shortages that were Addison's perennial excuse for missed deadlines.

She was destined to be disappointed, but she was not alone. When Gimbel moved to Building 2, he thought the only change to his life would be where he parked his car. But the Toolbox project had neither the excitement nor the intensity of Crypt Yourself. The software was low tech and Gimbel found it hard to adjust to BAD culture. Political correctness and the Addison Reed Cult of Personality grated on him. Judging from the complaints of his colleagues, the culture grated on them as well; it certainly didn't bring out the best in them. They just didn't own the work. There were a few exceptions, like Cindy, but most of them came in, put in eight hours of perfunctory effort, and went back to their real lives. When things went wrong, they shrugged and said, "I get paid either way."

β 1 1

Addison summed up the results of the Incident Investigation. "I have a pretty good idea of what happened here," he said. "Gimbel, Cindy, I'm sure you're eager to hear my judgment." He was keeping them in suspense and being a jerk about it. "My main responsibility in this matter is to the stockholders of Byte Yourself Software. That responsibility is twofold. First, I have to ensure that the organization functions smoothly and that we can all do the work for which we were hired. We all know how important that is, given how far behind schedule we are." He aimed a cutting look at Beverly. At least he was an equal-opportunity jerk.

"Second, I have to keep us on the right side of the Department of Justice." He looked at Gimbel. "Termination of the employee responsible is certainly one option. However, if I can retain a valuable resource, and still satisfy all the legal requirements, that is my preference. Gimbel, do you understand why your behavior was unsuitable for the workplace?"

"Yes, sir," said Gimbel.

"Why not?"

Gimbel shifted uncomfortably in his seat. He had already admitted that he had offended Cindy and that he shouldn't have done it. It embarrassed him that Addison continued to press the point in front of Gimbel's teammates. "My remark was unsuitable because it was of a sexual nature and was offensive to Cindy," he said.

"And what else?"

Gimbel blushed. *Is it my imagination or is Addison actually enjoying this?* "It created a hostile environment in the workplace."

"Very well," said Addison. "I'm satisfied that you can talk the talk. Now we're going to see if you can walk the walk. I instructed Beverly to work with Mr. Van Dyke to put together a performance improvement plan for you. There will be a goal for you to demonstrate sensitivity to the feelings of others. Beverly will help you determine the best way to meet this goal and review your progress at your next performance appraisal. Also, I want you to apologize to Cindy."

"That's fair," Gimbel replied. "Cindy, I'm really—"

"No, not here. I made arrangements for you to appear on the next episode of *Sorry*."

Gimbel waited for Addison to say he was kidding. When he realized that wasn't going to happen, he asked, "Couldn't I just be fired?"

CHAPTER 3

SORRY

Never apologize, never explain.
  – Benjamin Disraeli

Live from New York, Consolidated Studios presents *Sorry*, the show for people with a lot to apologize for. I'm your host, Jim Roberts. Tonight we have three apologies from the Washington, DC, area—including the apology the entire nation has been waiting for.

"Ernie Stevens seemed to have it all: successful law practice, supermodel wife, vacation home in the islands, and, for the past six years, he has been attorney general of the United States. But it wasn't enough for him. A Labor Day 911 call about a domestic disturbance at the Stevenses' Georgetown mansion, and it all came unraveled. Since that fateful call, fifteen women have come forward to confess extramarital affairs with the nation's top cop. The attorney general is with us tonight, ready to apologize to the people of America—and his wife.

"But first, the Chevy Chase Polluter. This Maryland retiree was caught dumping plastic bottles in the regular trash instead of the recycle bin. Then, workplace Romeo or copy machine cad? A software engineer from Fairfax, Virginia, sexually harasses a colleague—and you won't believe where he stole his lines from."

Jim Roberts stood at a podium as he faced the audience and the TV cameras. Behind him, images of Attorney General Stevens, an elderly woman, and Gimbel O'Hare flashed in sequence on a giant TV screen. On each side of the host, shorter podiums were unoccupied, as were the three seats at the desk to his right.

"Now let's meet tonight's panel of judges. Our first judge is the distinguished chairman and CEO of Consolidated Industries. Please welcome Mr. Isaac Ross!"

The Consolidated jingle played over the PA system as a jowly man with a brush haircut descended a spiral staircase behind the desk. Reaching the bottom, he waved to the audience before lowering his bulk into the seat on the left. Jim Roberts said jovially, "Consolidated Industries is, of course, the parent company of Consolidated Studios. I guess that means you're my boss, Isaac. I better watch what I say tonight."

"If you don't, we can discuss it at your next performance appraisal," Isaac replied. The audience didn't laugh.

"Next, the newest, and so far undefeated member of the Universal Wrestling League Vixens, Cheri Tarte, the Crimson Crusher!" Cheri Tarte's glam metal theme song played as she descended the stairs. The audience had been silent after Isaac's joke. At the sight of Cheri Tarte's trademark red leotard, they recovered. Woohoos erupted as she treated them to a double bicep pose before taking the middle seat. Isaac's eyes narrowed behind his oversized glasses.

"You're now 3-and-0 in the UWL," Jim Roberts said to Cheri Tarte. "How do you feel about that?"

"NOT AS GOOD AS I'M GOING TO FEEL ABOUT 4-AND-0!"

"At this rate, you will soon be going against Brenda Biggs for the women's championship."

"BRING HER ON! IF YOU'RE WATCHING, BRENDA, I WANT YOU TO KNOW YOUR DAYS AS WOMEN'S CHAMPION ARE NUMBERED!"

When the crowd stopped cheering, Jim Roberts continued, "Sounds like Isaac isn't the only one I'll have to be careful around tonight.

"Our last judge is the star of the most successful franchise in movie history. Ladies and gentlemen, it is my very great honor to introduce to you, from Hollywood, California, Grant Casey. Grant Casey *is* Jon Dunn!"

The tall actor, dressed in a tuxedo, emerged at the top of the staircase. The Jon Dunn fanfare played. The greeting for Grant Casey was different from the greeting for Cheri Tarte. There were no whistles and no rebel yells, just sustained and respectful clapping by an audience on its feet. After Casey took his seat and the audience members returned to theirs, Jim Roberts asked him about *Error of the Moon*. "This is your fourth outing as Jon Dunn, isn't it?"

"Fifth, actually. We commence filming next week. Incidentally, I am not the only cast member in attendance tonight. The studio has just announced that Cheri Tarte will play the henchwoman to the villainess Iona Klimt."

Cheri Tarte turned to Grant Casey. "GUESS I'LL BE KICKING YOUR SKINNY ASS SOON!"

"I shall certainly look forward to our scenes together, madam."

With the judges introduced, Jim Roberts set up the first apology.

It was trash TV—literally. A flock of seagulls circled over a mountain of garbage. Periodically a bird eyed a treat and dived to recover it. An announcer read statistics about the amount of waste the United States produced every year. "If we don't recycle aggressively," he warned, "the America we leave our children will be a giant continental garbage dump stretching from Atlantic to Pacific. But this woman, Phyllis Bentel of Chevy Chase, Maryland, just didn't care."

An old woman in a green tracksuit carried a trash bag to the curb in front of a small ranch-style house. The yard was neat, albeit bare. Sinister chords played. Then a new face appeared on the screen. The Bentels' next-door neighbor explained that she became suspicious that Mrs. Bentel was not recycling properly. She looked through the Bentels' garbage and sure enough found three plastic containers—two iced tea bottles and one diet soda bottle.

The scene returned to the studio where Jim Roberts introduced the first guests. Mrs. Bentel stood at the podium on his left. On his right, a representative from Citizens Allied for the Environment spoke first.

"Citizens Allied views this case with the utmost gravity. Recycling is not something that is optional. It is not something that you can do now and then to feel good about yourself before you get back to your real life. It is the centerpiece of environmental stewardship."

Gimbel stood at the video monitor in the green room and watched with interest, hoping to get a sense of what to expect when it was his turn at the podium. Next to him, a dapper man in a worn three-piece suit watched the screen through thick, yellowish glasses.

"I can't believe this is happening," said the dapper man. A few minutes before, Gimbel had watched him kiss his wife as she left the green room for the studio. "Phyllis and I always tried to be good people. We took our kids to church every Sunday and paid our bills and didn't make noise that would bother the neighbors. We must have bothered them anyway somehow, 'cause the thing with the bottles happened. We didn't know how we were going to pay the fine. Our accounts never recovered after the Third Financial Crisis. Then this man called and said he was from the TV station and said he'd pay the money for us if Phyllis came on the show."

On the screen, the man from Citizens Allied intoned the final bars of his hymn to recycling.

"Now, Mrs. Bentel," said Jim Roberts. "It's time to apologize. Are you sorry for what you did?"

"I didn't mean to do the wrong thing with the trash," she said. "I'm sorry. I just...we got these directions from the city...and they were so confusing."

"Judges, it's your decision. Do you accept Mrs. Bentel's apology? Isaac, we'll start with you."

Isaac Ross sneered. "I don't think Mrs. Bentel is apologetic at all. If she were, she wouldn't be trying to blame the city. What's confusing about it? You put the plastic bottles in the blue bin. Any idiot can do that."

Mrs. Bentel tried to explain. "But there were all these numbers on the plastic. Sometimes I couldn't see them and I didn't know if I was supposed to recycle or not."

A few members of the crowd hissed. "You've had your turn, Mrs. Bentel," said Jim Roberts. "Please let Isaac finish."

"You're so typical of the public, Mrs. Bentel," Isaac continued. "You just refuse to understand how important this is. If only you were more educated about the danger to the planet, you wouldn't be so cavalier with your soda bottles."

Someone in the crowd shouted, "Apologize again!" Other members of the audience took up the cry, "Again! Again! Again!"

In the green room, Mr. Bentel yelled at the monitor, "Stop it! Can't you see you're scaring her?" But of course, the studio audience couldn't hear him.

Isaac wagged his finger as he continued to lecture Mrs. Bentel. In the audience, tiers of angry faces yelled insults at her. A tear of sweat slid down her temple.

She started, "I'm so..." Then her eyes rolled up and she fell to the floor.

β 1 1

Mrs. Bentel was going to be okay. She had only fainted. An extended commercial break allowed the studio doctor to examine her and then she was moved back to the green room. When the show returned, Gimbel stood at the podium on the host's left. The right hand podium was empty.

Jim Roberts made a brief announcement concerning Mrs. Bentel's condition. Then he introduced the next segment. "Before we begin," he said, "this case contains material of a sexual nature which may not be suitable for small children. Households with small children may wish to switch to another channel at this time.

"This is a story of workplace sexual harassment, a civil offense that is deeply humiliating to its victims. But there is nothing civil about it. In this case, the victim requested that, to be spared further humiliation, she might remain anonymous. She will therefore appear by pre-recorded video only."

An image of Cindy appeared on the big screen. Shadows hid her face and an electronic scrambler altered her voice. She once again told the story of how her PC had crashed and Gimbel had offered to "inspect her input port." It was the same basic story she had told in the Executive Conference Room, but this time there were new details. According to Cindy, Gimbel had stood "uncomfortably close" and "leered."

When the video ended, the lights came up and the host said, "Now, Mr. O'Hare, it's time to apologize. Are you sorry for what you did?"

"Cindy," Gimbel said, "I hope you're watching, because I really want you to know how sorry I am. You're one of the best programmers it's been my privilege to work with, and I never wanted to do anything that would offend you. I also want to apologize to the rest of the Byte Yourself team. I know this incident has been very disruptive, and I'm sorry for that as well."

It wasn't a bad apology and the audience applauded. Jim Roberts turned to the judges, starting with Isaac again.

"I don't accept Gimbel's apology, for the simple reason that he hasn't learned his lesson regarding sexual harassment. He talks about it as a matter of professionalism. He is sorry because Cindy is a good programmer—as if it would be all right if she were a bad programmer. But it's not all right under any circumstances because what sexual harassment is really about is the violation of women. Consider the phrase 'inspect her input port.' That's a synonym for penetrating her vagina. It would not be too extreme to say that in this case, sexual harassment is rape by other means. Women should be protected from that—in the workplace and anywhere else they go."

This time the applause was louder.

"SPEAKING OF PENETRATION, ISAAC," said Cheri Tarte, "DON'T YOU THINK YOU SHOULD PULL OUT THE IRON ROD THAT'S STUCK UP YOUR ASS?"

The applause turned to cheers. Isaac's face grew dark, but he stayed calm. "If respect for women makes me uptight, so be it."

"Respect for women, MY ASS!" Cheri Tarte shouted. "We just heard Gimbel tell us he respects the professional accomplishments of a woman in his office, and you said it was irrelevant. Then *you* told us that women need to be protected. So of the two of you, who really respects women?

"We're all in show business. We know what happened here. Gimbel told a joke that went wrong. It happens to all of us. It sounds funny and edgy in the script meeting, and then during the performance, it's flat and tasteless. You know, like jokes about what you'll discuss at someone's performance appraisal."

Isaac could no longer keep silent. "You better start worrying about your own performance appraisal, missy," he sputtered.

"I'm just saying, lighten up, Isaac. If you don't know the difference between a pussy joke and a workplace rape, I hope I never go with you to a comedy club. I vote to accept Gimbel's apology. Look at him. He's so little 'n' cuddly."

When the laughter subsided, Grant Casey got his turn. "It's appropriate that I'm the deciding vote," he said, "because there's an aspect of this case that nobody else mentioned. 'I better inspect your input port' is a line from a Jon Dunn movie, albeit one from before my time. Mr. O'Hare, I suspect you see yourself as the Jon Dunn of software, the cool Casanova of the keyboard who's so good at what he does that no woman can resist him."

"Actually, quite a lot of women resist me," said Gimbel with a self-mocking, angelic smile.

"But you want women to be unable to resist you. Give it up, Mr. O'Hare. It isn't real. Jon Dunn is a fictional character. How many Jon Dunns do you know in real life? You wouldn't want to know a man who blows up every building he walks into. Anyone who thinks he's Jon Dunn in real life is going to end up in an insane asylum. Besides, in your case, Mr. O'Hare, wanting to be Jon Dunn is just ridiculous. Who ever heard of an international superspy who walks funny? Face it, Mr. O'Hare. You are the un-Dunn. Of course, there's nothing wrong with that. And that's the lesson you need to learn: be yourself. Until you learn that lesson, I do not accept your apology."

β 1 1

Gimbel left the TV station immediately after his appearance. He stopped in the green room long enough to grab his jacket and check on Mrs. Bentel (she was awake). Then he went straight to Penn Station, still in his studio makeup. Ever since Consolidated cast Grant Casey in *The Merchant of Malice*, Gimbel had wanted to meet him. Now the meeting had occurred and consisted of Casey telling a national audience that Gimbel was flirting with insanity. Gimbel wanted to put as many miles between himself and that humiliation as possible.

Because of his rapid exit, Gimbel missed the history made that night. After listening to Attorney General Stevens, the judges decided he was not contrite enough. They did not accept his apology, and neither did Mrs. Stevens. The attorney general of the United States resigned on the spot. For the first time in the annals of the Republic, a cabinet member gave up his post on the set of a game show.

β 1 1

Grant Casey strode gracefully into the office and closed the padded soundproof door behind him. "Good morning, sir," he said.

"Good morning, Beta Eleven," Melvin Arbuthnot replied. "Sit down."

The sound engineer interrupted. "I'm getting feedback."

It was the first day of filming for *Error of the Moon*. The set that represented Alpha One's office had been pulled out of storage and assembled on the sound stage. A canopy of lights, booms, and wires hung over the wood-paneled walls.

FULL ASYLUM

The director conferred with the sound engineer. After a moment, the director returned to his chair and shouted "Action!"

"Good morning, sir," said Dunn.

"Good morning, Beta Eleven," said Alpha One. He sat at his massive oak desk in front of a painting of a fox hunt. "Sit down."

Dunn sat in one of the leather wingback chairs in front of the desk. A small gentleman moldered in the other one. "You know Sir Brandon Pringle, Chancellor of the Exchequer," Alpha One said.

"Chancellor," said Dunn. Sir Brandon grunted.

"What do you know about economic sabotage?" Alpha One asked Dunn.

"It's a new category of crime since the Financial Crises," Dunn replied. "The Americans call it E.S. Individual saboteurs are referred to as *sabos*. After the Third Financial Meltdown, the G-20 powers responded with appropriate measures to expand the money supply and re-regulate out-of-control markets. Although there were some initial signs of their effectiveness, in the long run, the global economy did not improve. Eventually, governments around the world realized the reason. Their political opponents deliberately harmed their efforts: scared off investors, cut jobs, and even committed acts of vandalism.

"The sabo threat is particularly severe in the United States, where Congress responded by passing the Federal Economic Sabotage Act. The act, also called FESA, gave the government the powers necessary to combat the problem. One provision of the act prohibited criticism of government economic policy. There was a constitutional challenge to this, but the Supreme Court upheld the provision on the basis of the governmental interest in safeguarding the integrity of interstate commerce.

"To enforce the law, the government created an elite civilian military unit. The Coordinated Response Emergency Economic Protection Squad reports directly to the attorney general. Although its acronym should be pronounced CREE-TWO-P-S, certain elements of the public have taken to calling the unit members CREEPS, and this pronunciation has, regrettably, caught on. This new force has made significant inroads against the sabos; however, it has not been able to eradicate them entirely. I think that's all, sir."

"Yesterday afternoon," said Sir Brandon, "the Advanced Missile Corporation filed for bankruptcy. Seventy-eight thousand people around the world are filing for unemployment compensation as we speak, fifteen thousand of them in England."

Alpha One pressed a button on his desk. The fox hunt painting slid into the wall, revealing a large flat panel display. On the screen a photo sprang into view. It depicted a short, middle-aged woman in a fashionable red and black business suit. She had short dark hair and large dark eyes and was smoking a cigarette in a long black holder. Sir Brandon continued, "Iona Klimt, head of Klimt Defensive Software Corporation—KDS. Born in Soviet Russia, 1967. Emigrated to the US in the 1980s during the last days of the Cold War. Estimated net worth: 12.6 billion dollars."

The picture morphed to an office park. There was a pond with a fountain and two green glass buildings. "KDS headquarters. Just outside Washington, DC. The company is...was...Advanced Missile's largest competitor."

"Iona Klimt is one of the leaders of the information revolution," said Dunn. "Do we suspect she is engaged in economic sabotage?"

"That's for you to find out," said Alpha One. "You leave for America as soon as you draw your equipment from Double-G Branch. That's all, Beta Eleven."

"Cut!" yelled the director. "Get ready for close-ups."

"I don't know about this one," his assistant said. "Iona Klimt seems lame. All these years we made movies about supervillains plotting to destroy the world. Now they're plotting to lay people off?"

"That's what Isaac wants. He says E.S. is the crime of our time. Isaac's the boss."

"Everybody's going to know she's supposed to be Tina Lee. Aren't you worried about getting sued?"

"We have the right to satire a public figure, but I asked the lawyers to go over the script anyway. Then Isaac told me not to worry about it. He said he would take care of Tina Lee."

β 1 1

The judges had ruled against him, but Gimbel was still employed. Addison had let him off easy.

It didn't make sense. When the economy was good, companies forgave first offenses such as Gimbel's. It was too hard to replace a software engineer. But today there were thousands of engineers out of work in greater Washington. Addison could have fired him and found a replacement in a matter of hours. It would be easy for Addison, who looked at resources as interchangeable to begin with. At first, Gimbel had thought that Addison was so impressed with Gimbel's Toolbox idea that he decided Byte Yourself needed Gimbel O'Hare. But Addison hadn't pursued the idea further and Gimbel remained uneasy.

The episode on *Sorry* didn't make sense either. How had Addison gotten him on the show on such short notice? Gimbel saw Brownie in the Test Nest the day after the broadcast and asked his opinion. Brownie reminded him that Addison used to work at Consolidated. He probably still knew people there. "He must have been well-liked, man. Usually when someone leaves, Isaac Ross sees to it they're persona non grata—especially if they go to work for a competitor."

"Isaac's a vindictive bastard, all right" Gimbel replied. "We saw that with Crypt Me."

"I'll tell you this—I wouldn't want to be Cheri Tarte right now."

The discussion with Brownie did nothing to soothe Gimbel's anxiety. Gimbel wasn't a Buddhist; he didn't know much about karma. But he knew he had gotten something he didn't deserve and it was only a matter of time before the universe figured that out and took something back.

The universe didn't keep him waiting.

Gimbel had asked Liza to join him in New York. But *Sorry* aired live on a Tuesday evening and Liza couldn't get away from her job at HHS early enough. She promised she would stand by him, if not literally, at least in spirit. She might have kept that promise too, if she hadn't watched the broadcast with her friends. They were concerned about her. She didn't deserve this embarrassment. She could do better than the "copy machine cad."

That weekend, Gimbel took her to a cozy trattoria near Dupont Circle. The pinot noir paired well with the *petto di pollo alla Cologero*. The rich sauce, earthy wine, and flickering candles combined to make Gimbel feel warm, happy and, for the first time since *Sorry*, relaxed. Liza seemed to be in a good mood; she chatted happily about work, friends, and politics. She was more reserved on the drive home, but it was a thoughtful rather than an angry reserve. When they got to her building, they lingered in the Solo. Gimbel was close enough to her to smell her hair. She had washed it with some sort of herbal shampoo and it smelled fresh. When he turned to look at her, she was looking back.

He was about to kiss her when she said, "Gimbel, we've been out a few times now. I think you're sweet. You're obviously very smart, so I'm sure you can figure out where I'm going with this."

The night was definitely taking a turn for the better. "Yes, I think I know where you're going," he replied. "Should we go up to your apartment?"

"No," she said. "Let's do this right here."

"In the car? What if your neighbors see us?"

"I'm sure they won't see anything they haven't seen before."

"Your neighborhood is different from mine."

"A thing like this should be done quickly. Like pulling off a bandage. It doesn't pay to be gentle."

"I thought women like it slow, but if you want it fast and rough, I'll oblige. Should we take off our clothes, or can't you wait?"

"Take off our clothes?" Liza asked, confused. "What are you talking about?"

"I'm talking about sex. What are you talking about?"

It took her a moment to comprehend the misunderstanding. "Breaking up, Gimbel. I'm breaking up with you. It's over."

This never happened to Jon Dunn.

β 1 1

The letters around the edge of the seal spelled *United States Senate*. Beneath the circular disk, the nineteen members of the Judiciary Committee presided from their high-backed chairs. Bill Peterson, the president's choice to be the next attorney general, sat alone at a felt-covered table and faced the committee. Photographers knelt on the floor in front of him and jostled each other for the best shot. In spite of efforts to hide the TV cameras behind apertures in the wood paneled walls, the hearing room looked more like a television studio then the sanctuary of a deliberative body. The cameras captured Peterson's opening statement and transmitted it across the country.

"This hearing is not legally necessary. Article II of the Constitution requires the Senate's advice and consent to the appointment of officials. But due to the need for the federal government to respond quickly to the Third Financial Crisis, the Federal Economic Sabotage Act gave the president emergency fast-track authority to appoint members of the cabinet and other officials of the United States. What FESA did was provide advice and consent in advance—like a pre-approved credit card."

The senators laughed. Peterson picked up a water glass from the black felt, took a sip, and continued. "Nevertheless, as you heard on the news, I insisted on a straight up-or-down vote by the Senate on my nomination. I told the president that I would not take the job without one.

"The war on economic sabotage is still with us. We see nightly images on our TV sets of the suffering of the unemployed. The ranks of the homeless grow monthly. Nothing can be more important to Americans than to crack down on the sabos who, solely for political and financial gain, obstruct the efforts of the federal government to create jobs and build homes.

"For the last five years I've been on the front lines of this war. As deputy director of the FBI, I led investigations leading to the arrest of hundreds of sabos. I also worked hard to deny sabos the tools they needed to disrupt our economy. I froze bank accounts. I authored the so-called Peterson Report that led to a ban on sales of the Crypt Yourself software. Through all this, I unfortunately had the opportunity to see firsthand the devastation caused by E.S. I've seen empty office buildings and shuttered factories. I've seen entire families living in cars and homeless shelters.

"I've also seen that, in our commendable eagerness to ease this suffering, we've taken some constitutional shortcuts. Fast-track appointment authority was one. Suspending Miranda warnings was another; we stopped informing alleged sabos of their right to remain silent and have an attorney. Dozens of suspected sabos have been held in prisons for years without benefit of trial, or even having charges filed against them. When I was at Harvard Law School, I learned that these constitutional shortcuts are not the American way. That is why I am here today. We need to get back to our founding documents. We need to get back to the Constitution and the Bill of Rights. We need to start by restoring the power of the Senate to advise and consent.

FULL ASYLUM

"While I was waiting for this hearing to start, I had an opportunity to study the Seal of the Senate on the wall behind you. At the center is the American flag. Above is a red cap, like the ones that were worn during the French Revolution. The red cap, also called the Phrygian cap, symbolizes liberty. Below are the fasces. Those are the axes that you see on the bottom wrapped in bundles of sticks. The fasces symbolize authority. The seal reminds us to maintain a balance between liberty and authority. But since the Financial Meltdowns we've had only the fasces; we forgot the red cap. If you choose to confirm me as attorney general, I promise you that my highest priority will be to restore the balance. The authority of government is necessary for our safety as citizens. But the liberty of the individual is our birthright as Americans."

The eruptions of noise that greeted Peterson's last line were the cheers of the audience and the banging of the chairman's gavel.

β 1 1

Chris Molson congratulated the attorney general on his confirmation.

"Thank you," Bill Peterson replied. "And welcome aboard."

"After your speech, the *Courier* called you a presidential contender. I think they're right."

Peterson was non-committal. "First things first," he said. "Let's see what we can do about economic sabotage."

They shook hands and sat down.

Peterson's office was modest—just big enough to fit the antique desk and a few guest chairs without crowding. Behind the desk, sheer curtains were drawn over the bulletproof windows, blurring the details of nighttime Washington. Anyone looking in from outside would see only shadows in the attorney general's office.

"Tim Becker told me you really wowed him at the interview," Peterson said. "But I'd expect nothing less from a Harvard man.

When I was there, I learned firsthand what a tough school it is. Found a place yet?"

"Not yet. I went apartment hunting three nights this week. But there are no vacancies and nobody's building."

"Well, vacancies can be created. In fact, perhaps we can find you an apartment and help the investigation at the same time."

"I appreciate that, sir. I'm eager to settle in so I can get to work."

"I can understand that. It's a big case for a young man just out of Harvard. You'll have plenty of help, though. Some of our best lawyers are on the team. What do you think our chances are?"

Chris hesitated. "Sir, the problem is going to be probable cause. We'll need some kind of smoking gun to convince a judge to issue a warrant."

"I've got what you need," Peterson said. "I'll e-mail it to you. In the meantime, take a look at this." He handed a manila folder across the desk. "That's your surveillance target."

Chris opened the cover and studied the photograph inside. The man in the picture needed to visit a barbershop. His black hair was shaggy and several locks had fallen over his forehead. The mouth and chin were determined, but the glasses spoiled an otherwise nice face. What sort of burrow dweller would pick those frames? *Subterranean nerd.*

Chris turned the photo over and read the document underneath:

Byte Yourself Software Corp.
Personnel Record
Employee Name: Gimbel O'Hare

CHAPTER 4

PAINT MISBEHAVIN'

Nothing in life is so exhilarating as to be shot at without result.
 – Winston Churchill

Every Jon Dunn movie followed a formula and *Error of the Moon* was no different. After Dunn got his orders from Alpha One, he went to see the Crown Security Service's equipment officer, code name Double-G. This sobriquet stood for guns and gadgets. His curvy assistant was called Double-D, for two obvious reasons.

Double-G wore a tweed jacket and an old school tie. "Now pay attention, Beta Eleven," he said. "We've put together a rather impressive motorcar for you."

"This way, Mr. Dunn," said Double-D. Her white lab coat grew tight across her breasts as she pointed to the car.

"Late model Cheetah YK-9 coupe," said Double-G. "Three seventy horsepower BK-V8 engine with supercharger. Automatic traction control and global positioning system are standard equipment. Bulletproof glass, rotating number plates, and E.M. pulse generator, naturally. Missile defenses are the same as on your last car. I hope you take better care of this one, Beta Eleven. Your last car had the best defenses technology can provide, and you drove it into a wall."

"You'd be surprised at how few options a driver has when he's being chased down an alley at two hundred kilometers per hour," said Dunn. "My assistant has installed a new feature to prevent you from driving into a dead end alley in the first place. Dual radars in the headlamps scan for obstacles on the road in front of you."

"Interesting," said Dunn. "Perhaps Double-D can give me a closer look at her headlamps."

"Try to be a grown-up, Beta Eleven," said Double-G. "Now this, I'm especially proud of." He handed Dunn a small piece of paper. It was smooth, like the backing for a sticker, but punctuated with an array of tiny bumps. "Miniature video cameras," Double-G explained, with a tad too much excitement. "They transmit a high definition image that you can view from your car on this screen here. Range ten kilometers. The cameras peel off and adhere to any smooth surface."

"Is this smooth enough?" Dunn asked. He pressed one of the dots onto the skin of Double-D's neckline, just above her cleavage.

"Oh, do be a grown-up, Beta Eleven."

β 1 1

It was happy hour at Kilkenny's, but not in Cindy Valence's booth. The high backs of the green vinyl seats, the brass railings on the seat backs, and the circle of light from the Tiffany lamp isolated the three women from the rest of the room. On the wall, a photo of James Joyce watched forlornly. Beverly sipped wine spritzers and Cindy downed Dublin Margaritas, but these festive beverages couldn't dispel the gloom. Only Madame Butterfly was cheerful. She had somehow obtained a children's placemat and now she matched wits with the word search puzzle.

"I never did ask Addison to the Kennedy Center," Beverly said. "I told him I had tickets, but he said he hoped they weren't for any time soon because I needed to work overtime until the project is back on schedule. Typical male. He thinks that you have to have a penis to finish a project."

It was so obvious that Beverly expected to shock Cindy with the word *penis*, but Cindy wasn't going to give her the satisfaction. "No, you don't have to have a penis to bring in a project," Cindy replied. "Just a brain." But it was no fun insulting Beverly; the insults went past her.

"Of course there's no way I'm working that night, so now I got an extra ticket. You want to come with?"

"No, thanks."

"It would be a gas—just us gals. It's that new musical *Don G*. They took the story from Mozart's *Don Giovanni* and set it to music."

"Because there's no music in Mozart's version." But sarcasm went past Beverly too.

"Don Giovanni is Don Juan. He's a man who—"

"I know who Don Juan is. Jon Dunn in a ruff. It's almost an anagram."

"—he's a man who sexually harasses women."

"Oh, that *is* a gas."

"The songs are teriff," Beverly said. "There's a big production number in Act I when Don G's victims swear vengeance."

"Do they get it?" Cindy asked, not really caring.

"Absitively. In the end demons drag him down to hell."

"So it really is about sexual harassment," Cindy said. She looked over to see how Madame Butterfly was doing with her word search. "Daphne," she said, "There's no such word as *injusta*."

"Sure there is," Madame Butterfly replied. "That's the word you use when you do things really fast."

"Huh?"

"You know, like when you say, 'I'll be done *injusta* second.'"

Beverly wasn't done talking about sexual harassment. "I can't believe Addison let Gimbel keep his job," she said. She lowered her voice in imitation of Addison's. "I told Gimbel to apologize on *Sorry* and he did. The judges didn't accept it, but that's neither here nor there."

Cindy stared at her drink.

"What gets me is the way men always stick together," Beverly continued. "I know I'm supposed to support Addison, but I think you were swindled royally."

Cindy tilted her head to drain her glass. "That's it. Swindled," she said. She peered into the darkness and waved the waitress over.

The waitress was a healthy blonde in a green uniform with a nametag that said *Pam*. Seeing the empty glasses she asked, "Would you like a top off?"

"Certainly not," said Madame Butterfly indignantly. "You should be ashamed of yourself, suggesting such a thing in a family restaurant."

Cindy said, "I was swindled."

Beverly mouthed an apology. "Cindy," she said, "I don't think Pam can help you."

"Who else would help me?" Cindy looked up at Pam. "I was swindled," she said again. She handed her empty glass to the waitress. "That was almost all margarita mix. Bring me another one, and this time don't swindle me on the tequila."

Madame Butterfly watched closely as Pam made a notation on her pad. "Pam, what's that you're writing?" she asked. "DM?"

"That stands for Dublin Margarita. I write the initials to save time."

"Well isn't that clever. What's that you wrote after? ET?"

"Extra tequila. That way we'll make sure the bartender doesn't swindle your friend again."

"You sure know a lot about those Dublin Margaritas," said Madame Butterfly. "Have you been to Dublin?"

"No," Pam replied. "The guys that come in here don't tip enough to pay for airfare."

"Well that doesn't make sense. If they don't tip enough, they should have plenty of money left for airfare."

Pam looked to Beverly for guidance, but Beverly shrugged.

"Anyway," Madame Butterfly continued, "it's too bad you've never been to Dublin. I heard it's the biggest city in the world."

"Where did you hear that?" Beverly asked.

"Brownie McCoy. He said it's doublin' every day."

Pam dashed back to the bar.

Beverly asked Cindy if she was listening to what she was saying before Pam came over.

"You were saying us 'gals' need to do something. What do you want me to do? Want me to sue the company? I could sue the company."

"You'd lose. Addison covered his ass pretty well."

Beverly let the silence go on until Cindy felt uncomfortable. Then she came to the point. "You *could* sue Gimbel O'Hare."

"What for? Gimbel doesn't have any money."

"He's three months away from his third anniversary at Byte Yourself. Then he'll be vested in the stock plan. He'll have gobs of money."

"I don't know, Beverly. I just want to put this behind me and focus on my job."

"Listen to yourself. This is what holds us gals back. Do you think men get ahead in the company just by focusing on their jobs? No way. They stick together. They *play ball*." Cindy didn't pick up on the hint; Beverly made it more explicit. "You're management material, Cindy, I'm sure of it. I may make you team lead soon. But not if you give up when things don't go right the first time. If you can't stand the heat, go back to the kitchen. Do I make myself clear?"

"You're clear, Beverly. You're transparent. And you're full of it. You don't give a damn about helping my career. I know what happened. Gimbel went over your head and told Addison to abandon the BAD Toolbox. Now you want to make his life miserable and you need my help."

Suddenly Cindy lost her train of thought. She was drowsy and just a little nauseated. Maybe the bartender had been more generous with the tequila than she thought. She held her head between her hands and tried to remember how many refills she'd had. Beverly wanted something. Where did she go? Cindy realized her eyes were closed and forced them open. Beverly sat across the table, holding her wineglass and watching Cindy with a concerned look. The oversized buttons on her aquamarine blazer looked like globules of chocolate; they didn't help Cindy's nausea any. *God, she's a bitch.* Out loud, Cindy said, "Okay, Beverly, be a bitch. We'll both be bitches. I'll sue Gimbel and we'll swindle his shares if I win and you'll pay my lawyer if I lose."

"Thanks, Cindy. I'll remember this."

"Just remember to make me team lead."

Beverly raised her wineglass. "A toast," she said. "To remembering. And to dragging Gimbel O'Hare down to hell."

β 1 1

The morning the summons arrived, Gimbel called in sick. A sweaty man with crumbs in his mustache had delivered it to the apartment while Gimbel was shaving. It was wrapped in a light blue folder and demanded an answer to a complaint of sexual harassment brought by Cynthia M. Valence (Plaintiff) against Gimbel O'Hare (Defendant).

He didn't remember dragging himself to the living room sofa, but it must have happened because the TV was playing and Gimbel was watching it. The Jon Dunn marathon lasted all day. It was after dark when the idea came to him. He was about an hour into *Bitterweed*. The CSS suspected that Hector Bitterweed operated a rubies-for-opium smuggling ring. Alpha One sent Beta Eleven to investigate.

At the top of the stairs, a vase of flowers brightened a circular marble tabletop. Dunn broke off a carnation and threaded it through the lapel of his tuxedo. Then he descended the half-circle staircase that swept into the gaming room. He crossed the floor to the ornate bar.

"Glenjohnnie, neat," he told the bartender.

Carrying the single malt, Dunn approached the billiards tables. They were arranged in rows under an enormous crystal chandelier. Admirers bunched around the center table where Bitterweed lined up his next shot. Dunn joined them and edged his way to the front. He captured a spot next to Bitterweed's mistress, Penny Short, a stunning woman in a copper-colored evening gown.

Seeing the intruder across the table, Bitterweed lay down his cue. "A newcomer," he said. "Have we met, Mr....?"

"Dunn, Associated Industries."

"Ah, Mr. Dunn. Your reputation precedes you—as does that of your firm." The drug smuggler walked around the table to shake hands.

"Yes, I believe I knew your associate," said Dunn. "Mr. Hashasheen."

"His untimely death was a great loss to me. I should very much like to meet the man who killed him."

"Perhaps I know him. Any message if I see him?"

"Mr. Hashasheen was transporting a rather valuable gem for me at the time of his death. I am determined to recover it. Perhaps his killer could guide me to it."

"A gem like this one, perhaps?" Dunn reached into the pocket of his satin-striped tuxedo pants, extracted an enormous ruby, and tossed it onto the billiards table. It hit the green felt with a thud. Penny Short moved closer to get a better look. Bitterweed fingered the jeweler's eyeglass that hung on a gold chain around his neck. He screwed the glass into one eye and inspected the stone.

"Exactly like that one," he concluded. "It seems, Mr. Dunn, that we have unfinished business."

"And if I refuse to enter into a transaction?"

"Then you will not get out of this room alive. Cast your eye to the stairway, Mr. Dunn."

Beta Eleven had already seen them. Two sharpshooters with red berets and sniper's rifles had taken position on the landing. Penny Short gasped.

"Such a crude way of conducting business, though, would be most unfortunate, Mr. Dunn," Bitterweed continued. "I would prefer a more civilized negotiation."

"And that would be...?"

"A contest. A game of billiards with this ruby as the stakes."

"And if I win?"

"A very unlikely scenario, Mr. Dunn. You see, in addition to being a successful international jeweler, I am one of the world's leading billiards players. Nevertheless, we should agree to all the terms and conditions in advance. What is your price?"

"A drink with Ms. Short."

Gimbel turned off the DVR. "A drink," he said, "is exactly what I need."

An hour later, showered and dressed in a sports jacket, Gimbel scurried into Kilkenny's. "Glenjohnnie, neat," he told the bartender.

The four of them were there, as usual. Andy was at the pool table lining up a shot while the others stood by holding cues, except for Madame Butterfly. She insisted she could play much better with a bridge and couldn't understand why her friends didn't do the same. "Three ball in the side pocket," said Andy.

Carrying the single malt, Gimbel approached the pool table. Cindy saw him first. "You told Beverly you were sick," she said scornfully.

"I got better," he replied, "and we have unfinished business." He reached into the inside pocket of his blazer, extracted the summons in its blue folder, and tossed it onto the pool table. It hit the green felt with a hollow sound.

Cindy realized what it was and said, "My lawyer told me that if you have any business with me, you should conduct it through him."

"Courtrooms and lawyers are such a crude way of conducting business. I would prefer a more civilized negotiation."

"And that would be…?"

"A contest. A game of eight ball with my Byte Yourself shares as the stake. That's what you want, isn't it? If you win, I sign them over to you and you keep them all instead of sharing them with a lawyer. If I win, you drop the lawsuit."

Cindy and her friends stepped out of earshot to confer. They spoke animatedly for several minutes, during which Gimbel finished his whiskey. When they returned, Cindy said, "I accept your offer, with one small change. Not eight ball. Paintball."

"Accepted," Gimbel replied. "Shall we?" He gestured to the bar. "We should agree to all the terms and conditions in advance." Climbing onto a bar stool, he ordered Dublin Margaritas for Cindy and Madame Butterfly, a refill on beer for the guys, and a second Glenjohnnie for himself. Madame Butterfly took a blank book out of her purse; the fabric cover matched her floral blouse. "Pam taught me how to take notes using *initials*," she said with excitement. She poised her pencil as Gimbel and Cindy opened negotiations.

β 1 1

Buoyed by his success in defeating the sniper jerk during his first visit to Pentagon Palace, Gimbel returned the next day—Sunday—and every evening that week. By Friday he could generally hit two or three of the opposition while ending unscathed himself. He was also getting to know the regulars. There was a computer programmer who, it turned out, worked at Byte Yourself. There was the waitress Pam; Gimbel recognized her from Kilkenny's. And there was Joe, the redheaded instructor who gave the safety lecture the first day. Joe had a second job somewhere else. He was evasive about it, though.

A couple times Cindy and her friends came in to train. They exchanged strained "hellos" with Gimbel, and then, like prizefighters, retreated to their corner of the holding area. Since they were self-equipped while Gimbel was still a rental player, their paths did not cross inside the arena.

That might change soon. When Gimbel returned his coveralls Friday night and noticed there wasn't a stain on them, he decided it was time to move up. He had been asking the regulars about their equipment and he already knew what he would buy: the Tilmann G-9 Destroyer was an electropneumatic marker with a spool-valve mechanism. It had a sleek black design that, if it weren't for the clunky agitating hopper, would resemble US military issue. The Destroyer had a muzzle velocity of three hundred feet per second, the maximum allowed by the National Simulated Weapons Regulatory Agency—the NSWRA—which had been established to prevent sabos from misusing toy guns.

His first battle with the Destroyer was disappointing, though. Half his teammates were picked off early and Gimbel got trapped behind a coffee cart with the two that remained. Several of the opposing players circled behind them while two others had a clear shot from the second floor railings. The match ended in a carpet bombing of paint. When the referee finally and mercifully blew his whistle, Gimbel's jumpsuit looked like printed leopard skin. Clearly the level of play was higher now.

The other team followed Gimbel's into the kitchen corridor, laughing and high-fiving. The leader lowered the top of a camo hoodie to reveal a thicket of red hair. It was Joe. "*Dude*, you got *lit up!*" He rubbed it in, but he was so good-natured about it Gimbel couldn't get mad.

"It's a trifle embarrassing," Gimbel said.

"You know your problem? No game plan. You get half your team clustered together like that and it's over. Paintball is about strategy."

"Well, Sun Tzu is never around when you need him."

"Is he that Korean dude Pam goes out with?"

"No, he was born about twenty-five hundred years too early to date Pam. His loss. Sun Tzu was the dude that said, 'the general who wins a battle makes many calculations in his temple ere the battle is fought.'"

"Well, I'm not Jewish so I don't know about temple, but we make plans in the holding area before the battle is fought. You can join us."

Gimbel spent the next week studying the Art of Paintball War at the picnic table of Master Joe. He learned the techniques for creating a game plan, the fine points of choosing terrain, the importance of speed, and the methods for drawing an enemy out. Joe made him draw maps of the mall from memory, showing the location of every coffee cart, the exact number of steps on the escalators, and the places where a player could slip through broken doors and store windows to emerge suddenly on the other side of the playing field.

The lessons in strategy got Gimbel thinking about *The Art of War*. All Gimbel knew about Sun Tzu's classic textbook was the handful of quotations he had learned from Jon Dunn movies. He looked up a translation on the web and read it several times. The master's advice to "mask strength with weakness" proved useful one evening when he got matched up against Cindy, Madame Butterfly, and their boyfriends. He relived his first day out, standing stupidly in the open. Within moments, Andy and Bart took him down. Gimbel made a show of limping out of the mall. He hoped he hadn't overdone it.

Joe needed a sniper. Gimbel volunteered, thinking that the skill would serve him well in his contest against Cindy. After several days of target practice—he used the third floor of the garage as a firing range—he consistently hit the target from a hundred feet. Although that was not the full range of the Destroyer, he struggled to be accurate from further away. Joe explained that paintball rifles, to be affordable, are not machined to precise tolerances. A true paintball sniper's rifle would be priced out of the market.

When Joe was satisfied with Gimbel's aim, he assigned him to the catwalks. Gimbel had fun occupying the high ground, picking off the opposing players. Remembering Bobby and Jeff, however, he never shot at children. Generally Gimbel was safe up there, although he did enjoy the occasional second-story firefight when an opposing sniper got past his teammates and up the escalator.

The only difficulty with the catwalks was getting to them. Gimbel was an exposed target during the dash to the escalators. Looking for another way around, he tried the door to Gracie's Department Store. At first, the door gave a little. But then it snapped shut, as if someone on the other side wanted to bar Gimbel from entering. Gimbel let go of the door handle and listened. Was someone breathing on the other side? Before he could be sure, a paintball hit him between the shoulder blades and he had to abandon the field of engagement.

Afterwards, Joe made fun of him for being eliminated so easily. Gimbel asked whether there was anyone in Gracie's.

"I hope not," Joe replied. "Didn't you know? The roof collapsed two years ago. Not safe, dude."

FULL ASYLUM

β 1 1

Pentagon Palace Paintball had shut its doors for the night, but Gimbel and Joe lingered in the holding area. They sat with their legs stretched on a picnic bench while the UWL played on the TV in the corner. Suddenly Joe exclaimed, "It's your girlfriend!"

He was pointing to a close-up of Cheri Tarte. Gimbel had never really noticed her face before; it was hard to notice anything other than her body. Now, thanks to the selectivity of a zoom lens, he saw that her features were quite alluring. A superior smile curled a pair of juicy lips. The eyes were green—not the pale, muddy color that people call green, but the icy sparkle of a polished emerald. Their clarity transmitted the world without prejudice, distortion, or pity.

"Tonight—will the Crimson Crusher end Brenda Biggs's five-year reign as Women's Champion? At 6-and-0, the latest addition to the UWL Vixens is still undefeated. Earlier, we caught up with her backstage."

A room with gray cinderblock walls. Cheri Tarte wore tights and a sports bra. She lay on her back on a padded bench and held a barbell loaded with eight steel plates that had *45 lbs* embossed on each. At the head of the bench, Bulldozer spotted Cheri Tarte and counted reps. "Eight...nine...ten." Cheri Tarte's arms shook as she raised the weight. "Eleven. Come on, one more." This time the barbell stopped halfway. "You can do it!" Another push, another stop. Bulldozer wrapped his hands around the bar. The two wrestlers guided it the rest of the way together. "I'm calling it twelve," he said. "That was all you at the end."

A head and shoulders shot. She sat in a studio in front of a blue background. *Cheri Tarte—Women's Championship Contender* was written on the lower right of the screen. "I was on the basketball team in college," she said. "Afterwards I wanted to do something related to health and fitness. I got a job in the administrator's office at a big hospital. This was right after the government took over health care. The hospital was overrunning its budget and we were supposed to contain costs. We did a lot of unnecessary testing—MRIs that were unlikely to find anything and so on. At the same time, we had patients dying while they waited for operations they really needed, like coronary bypasses. I went to my boss with some ideas to improve things, but he said, 'Don't worry about it. You get paid either way.' I realized that I would never be allowed to excel working in a bureaucracy. The whole structure rewarded mediocrity, and that's not what I'm about.

"That's when I started hitting the gym in a big way. I was always athletic, and I just wanted to see where I could go with it. And it brought me here."

Bulldozer's shaved head appeared next. "We didn't know what to make of her at first. The Vixens are all great athletes, but also very feminine. Now here's this woman who's over six feet tall and can bench press four hundred pounds. So in the beginning there was this kind of awkwardness backstage. But now she's just one of the guys."

Cheri Tarte and Bulldozer stood in front of a squat machine. Bulldozer playfully slapped Cheri Tarte on the back of the head. Cheri Tarte punched him in the arm. Bulldozer conjured a mock expression of pain.

"They all say that now," Cheri Tarte said. "'You're one of the guys.' I know they mean well, but it's a strange thing to say. How would they react if I told them they were one of the girls?"

"Femininity is very important to me." She spoke over a black-and-white video of herself leaning towards a mirror, applying eye shadow with a brush. "A guy is horny all the time and a woman can use that if she knows how. If she just washed her hair, or lays her hand on his arm, or 'accidentally' brushes him with her boobs, he'll do anything she wants. Femininity is power."

"And now," said the announcer, "the battle for the Universal Wrestling League's women's championship is about to begin."

Brenda Biggs and Cheri Tarte waited impatiently in opposite corners of the ring. They were both big women; the canvas strained under their weight. The wardrobe department had traded Cheri Tarte's usual red leotard for a green-and-black camouflage bikini. It showed off her definition, abs more eight-pack than six-pack. A taut red braid bisected the triangle of her back muscles. If Cheri Tarte was an anatomy textbook, Brenda Biggs was Mother Earth, fertile and immovable. A blue leotard covered the three spheres of her midsection. Her frizzy black hair was pinned in the style of a sumo wrestler.

The bell rang. Cheri Tarte walked to the center of the ring. Brenda moved quickly for her size; she ran at her opponent, her arm extended to knock her over. The collision had no effect: Cheri Tarte took the blow in the chest and remained standing. Brenda picked up speed, reversed direction on the ropes, and ran back towards the center. She jumped, her legs stretched in front of her, and sailed towards Cheri Tarte in a flying kick. Her feet found their target in the center of Cheri's back.

"Damn, your girlfriend is strong," said Joe. "Brenda flew at her at full speed and she didn't budge."

"Stop calling her my girlfriend."

"Gimbel has a crush on the Crusher. Gimbel and Cheri sitting in a tree. You know they're coming to Washington next month. You two could go on a date."

"I'm sure she's forgotten all about me."

"She's a big girl. She might be too big for you."

In his imagination, Gimbel compared Cheri Tarte's size to his own. "Too big for me? No such thing."

"Seriously though," Joe said, "the UWL is going to be at the Horizon Center on the twentieth. Do you want to go, dude? I could get tickets."

"I'll be there," Gimbel said, hoping he didn't sound too eager.

Brenda Biggs ran up behind Cheri Tarte and pulled her braid. The she went for the pile driver. She grabbed Cheri Tarte by the crotch and shoulders, picked her up, and slammed her head first into the canvas. As Cheri Tarte jerked in agony, Brenda dropped on top of her, grabbed one of her legs, and pinned her to the canvas. The referee counted, "One, two."

Cheri Tarte kicked out and the combatants returned to their corners for the next attack.

This time it was Cheri Tarte who picked Brenda up. As the crowd cheered, she held her opponent over her head and carried her full circle around the ring. Straightening her elbows, she raised Brenda just a little higher before throwing her down forcefully. She took a running jump over Brenda's twisted body, sprinted to the corner, and scrambled up the turnbuckles. Her red braid whipped in a circle as she flipped backwards off the post and landed with her breasts smothering Brenda's face.

The referee made it to ten. The UWL had a new women's champion. Cheri Tarte, the Crimson Crusher, leaped up the ropes in one corner, leaned out towards the audience, and spread her arms in victory. Then she ran across the ring and repeated the celebration in the opposite corner. The announcer and the Coroner pulled the ropes apart to enter the ring. The Coroner helped his girlfriend Brenda stand and guided her to the locker room. She limped and her cheek was bruised but she was on her feet. The announcer met Cheri Tarte at the center of the ring and held the gold champion's belt up high. Cheri Tarte took the belt from him and waved it to the crowd.

"Now that you've climbed to the top of the Vixen ladder, what's next for you?" the announcer asked.

Cheri Tarte answered without hesitation. "BRING ON THE MEN!"

β 1 1

> We are not fit to lead an army on the march unless we are familiar with the face of the country—its mountains and forests, its pitfalls and precipices, its marshes and swamps.
> – Sun Tzu, *The Art of War*, 7.13

Pentagon Palace Paintball was closed on Thanksgiving. Gimbel took advantage of the day off to learn with whom, in Sun Tzu's words, "lie the advantages derived from Heaven and Earth." Traffic was light on the interstate as he drove to Crestview Mountain. He was sorry he had not flown home to Chicago to spend the holiday with his parents, but with nine days until his showdown with Cindy, he couldn't afford a break.

As the Solo climbed the mountain road, vistas of the Shenandoah Valley appeared in breaks between bare trees. Clusters of miniature houses dotted greenish-brown pasture. The road ended at a gravel parking lot. Leaving his car behind, Gimbel hiked the short trail to the summit. Dry leaves crackled under his army boots.

He emerged from the woods at a mountaintop clearing about the size of a baseball field. It spread down the hillside like an apron until the forest swallowed it up again. A cluster of boulders grew from its center. Gimbel sat on one of the cold stones and studied the terrain.

The valley below was majestic in the mist, but Gimbel was too preoccupied to admire the view. A week from Saturday, Cindy and her friends would be stationed here. The rocks would provide them with cover; Gimbel would have none. He would not be able to fire on them from the shelter of the trees: at a distance of two hundred feet, his opponents would be out of range. There were four of them, so they could post sentinels in every direction. Gimbel would have no way to approach without being seen. Clearly the advantages of heaven and earth lay with Cindy. Gimbel swore never again to negotiate the rules of a contest while drunk.

He spent three hours surveying the battlefield. He walked around the clearing and then explored the woods. There were quite a few paths. That at least was something he could use. But the Destroyer marker was not going to cut it. He knew what he needed. He wasn't sure if it existed, but he knew whom to ask.

MICHAEL ISENBERG

β 1 1

Two hours later, Gimbel was back in the world of strip malls, carpet-like lawns, and cavernous houses. "Welcome to Casa McCoy, man," said Brownie as he opened the door to the cavernous house he shared with his wife. It was just Gimbel, Brownie, and Mrs. McCoy for Thanksgiving dinner. Mrs. McCoy was a rotund woman in a granny dress; she tied her long gray hair in a bun. As she arranged the flowers that Gimbel brought, she told him how happy she was he could come. The McCoys' son, a junior at Duke, was spending a semester abroad. Gimbel would be their surrogate child for the day.

The McCoys' dining room table was set with rough terra cotta plates. Bottles of homemade turnip wine communed with bowls of cornbread stuffing and cranberry relish. The spicy smoke of incense blended with the aroma of roast turkey. On the walls, framed posters of moons, sunbeams, and kaleidoscope patterns duplicated an acid trip in sunset colors. A reproduction of Peter Max's *Liberty Head* watched sternly as Brownie carved the bird.

Brownie McCoy registered for college too late to protest the Vietnam War. That didn't stop him from becoming a campus radical. In the age of Reagan, he wore tie-dyed t-shirts and spurned shoes. He marched against the Contras in Nicaragua and the Pershing missiles in Europe. He earned his nickname during a kitchen experiment involving organic flour, cocoa, and hashish. There were rumors of other experiments in Brownie's kitchen, but the campus police never could link him to the bombing of the engineering building. In any case, no one was hurt.

Perhaps his extracurriculars were the reason it took Brownie seven years to earn his degree. After graduation, the Debs Institute, the big socialist think tank, hired him as a junior researcher. The Institute put him to work assembling statistics about corporate tax loopholes. One day it occurred to him that he was overqualified. He had the computer skills to get a job in industry that would pay three times what he made at the Institute. He could donate a third of his salary to pay for a less skilled, but still qualified, researcher, and both Brownie and the Institute would be better off. Later he learned that free market economists called this *comparative advantage*.

During his first years in industry, he discovered that free market economists were right about other things as well. It turned out that the bosses weren't monsters—at least most of them weren't. The workers weren't oppressed either. Most of them, including Brownie, lived pretty well. He soon stopped donating to the Debs Institute.

Although he was a hippie for the Right now, he continued to defy the Man when he thought the Man needed defying. These days, the Man's main offenses were FESA, 'stenics, and the BAD dress code.

The dress code didn't apply to Casa McCoy, though. Brownie had let his hair down and replaced the dingy shirts and doublewide ties that he wore around the Test Nest with a t-shirt and jeans. The t-shirt said *Thankful...for capitalism* on the front and *"for it made all hands industrious"* on the back.

When Gimbel asked about it, Brownie explained, "Thanksgiving is all about capitalism." He slid another slice of turkey onto the serving platter. "The Pilgrims were communists, man. When they started Plymouth colony they agreed to joint ownership of land, tools, and stuff. Whatever crops grew they would split equally. Trouble was, when it was time to work, the Pilgrims split. They starved, man."

Mrs. McCoy had heard this speech every year since Brownie broke with the Debs Institute. "Are you ever going to pass that turkey?" she said. Brownie handed the platter to Gimbel. As Gimbel loaded his plate with white meat, Brownie continued. "So then they tried something different. They divided up the lands and the tools, and they told everyone they could keep whatever they grew on their own land. Now everyone was working for himself. Suddenly it was like Foodstock. They had more than they could eat. That's why they invited the Indians over."

Brownie offered the gravy boat to Gimbel. Several mushrooms floated in the thick brown sauce; Gimbel eyed them suspiciously. "Anything you want to tell me?" he asked.

"I think you already know. The Pilgrims and the Indians gave thanks to God and everybody stuffed themselves."

"No, I meant about the gravy."

"It's cool, man. They're normal 'shrooms, not tripping 'shrooms."

"I didn't know the story about the Pilgrims," said Gimbel. "At least, not the way you told it."

"They don't teach it in school."

"But it was four hundred years ago. How does anybody know it?"

"They wrote it down, man. Governor Bradford kept a journal. He wrote that the change 'made all hands industrious' and that 'much more corn was planted than otherwise would have been.'"

"People work their butts off when they feel ownership. That's how I felt when I was on the Encryption Research Team."

"Not how you feel now, huh?"

"The BAD Toolbox." Gimbel sighed. "I didn't think it could get worse, but now that Cindy is team lead, all she does is give me orders. Lots and lots of orders."

Brownie dabbed gravy from his beard with a faded cloth napkin. "If Cindy is giving you orders," he said, "it's because she knows you can get things done."

"So it's in no way payback?"

"Don't be too hard on Cindy. If you ask me, she thinks the whole lawsuit is out of control. She's not the type, man."

"What type?"

"The type to go crying to a lawyer."

"Then why did she do it?" Gimbel asked. Then he answered his own question. "Beverly."

"Beverly's bad news, man. She's been bad mouthing you ever since you sent that e-mail to Addison. I'm sure she put beaucoup pressure on Cindy. Beverly's her boss and Cindy's young like you are. It takes experience to know when to tell the boss to get bent. I think Cindy is relieved you agreed to fight it out with paintballs instead of legal briefs. Which reminds me, how did it go at Crestview Mountain?"

Over barley tea and pumpkin pie, Gimbel described the terrain and explained his problem to Brownie. They finished their desserts and folded their napkins. "Best dinner I had today," said Brownie to his wife. "Excuse us, dear." He stood and gestured for Gimbel to follow him.

At the bottom of the cellar stairs was a metal door with a keypad that looked like the ones at Byte Yourself (Gimbel thought it probably once *was* one of the ones at Byte Yourself). Brownie entered a code and a lock clicked open.

A famous psychiatrist once said that every man secretly wanted to be Jon Dunn. Gimbel always suspected that Brownie secretly wanted to be Double-G. When he saw what was on the other side of the door, he was sure of it.

They might have been back at Test Nest II—if a herd of irritated cattle had stampeded through the place. There were the same raised floor tiles, fluorescent lights, racks of servers, and PCs. But the equipment was scattered randomly. Wires hung from the electronics. A row of metal cabinets lined the back wall. Through half-open doors, Gimbel could see piles of dusty circuit boards stacked precariously on shelves. The surface of a workbench was almost invisible beneath its load of disassembled electronic equipment, wire cutters, probes, soldering irons, and a partly eaten sandwich.

Multicolored physics equations were penned on a whiteboard. One formula had a box around it:

$$F_{lift} = Const \times \rho U^2 \alpha l_x l_z \quad (L \& L, \ 1959)$$

Brownie led Gimbel through a bead curtain into another room. This one contained a firing range that ran the length of the house. At one end, paper targets hung from the ceiling. At the other, a gun rack held an array of firearms, not all of them legal. Brownie removed a deadly looking weapon from the rack and handed it to Gimbel.

"Paintball sniper's rifle," Brownie said. "Muzzle velocity of three hundred feet per second meets NSWRA regulations like any legal marker, but with far greater accuracy. Laser sight, naturally."

"Looks like a real gun. Where are the hopper and cartridge?"

"Internal. That's what gives it the realistic look. I stopped a mugger with it last summer."

"There are no muggers on Crestview Mountain. What's the capacity?"

"Ten rounds. The breach opens with this lever." Brownie pointed to the catch.

"Ten is not going to be enough."

"Ten is going to be more than you need, man. Try it out."

Brownie opened a metal box and removed a pair of paintballs from their foam rubber niches. "You need custom ammunition," he said, handing the spheres to Gimbel. "These are machined to one one-thousandth of an inch." Gimbel loaded the marker, switched on the laser sight, and aimed the red dot at the center of the target. The house was almost a hundred feet long. At that distance, Gimbel could hit the target with his Destroyer, but he needed luck to hit the bull's-eye. He squeezed the trigger. Bull's-eye. He tried again. Another bull's-eye.

"And I thought you just *looked* like Santa Claus," he said.

"It's not a Christmas present. I want it back when you return from the field."

"Of course. Now how much do you know about the Cheetah YK-8?"

β 1 1

It was dark when Gimbel returned to Fox Hunt Apartments, but the floodlights of a helicopter, hovering just overhead, generated a bubble of light around his building. He eased the Solo along the driveway. When he came around the final curve he saw half a dozen Humvees scattered around the parking lot. One of them blocked the road. In front of it, a pair of soldiers held up their hands for Gimbel to stop. Gold embroidery spelled *CREEPS* on their black baseball caps.

Gimbel shifted the car into park and stepped out onto the pavement. He was glad the paintball rifle was in the trunk, out of sight. He asked the two soldiers what was going on.

The older one seemed to be in charge. "Federal business. Nothing you need to worry about."

"I need to get to my apartment."

"No one can go in or out just now. Please return to your vehicle, sir, and you'll be able to proceed in a few minutes."

Just then the door to Gimbel's building swung open and two more soldiers emerged. They wore body armor, helmets, and goggles. They shoved a man in handcuffs roughly onto the path. He was short, with a neat black mustache and round glasses. Gimbel recognized Mr. Lazuli, the accountant who rented the apartment above his own. "I didn't do anything!" Lazuli shouted. "Please tell me what this is about."

The soldier who had been talking to Gimbel turned towards the prisoner. "It's about harming the people of the United States of America," he said. "Ricardo Lazuli, I have a warrant for your arrest for violations of the Federal Economic Sabotage Act. You have the right to remain silent. Anything you say can be used against you."

So the attorney general wasn't blowing smoke when he promised to restore the Miranda warnings.

"Economic sabotage?" Mr. Lazuli pivoted his head from one CREEP to another, desperately looking for an answer that made sense. "How?"

"You conspired with your clients to keep badly needed tax dollars out of the hands of Uncle Sam."

"But I'm a tax accountant. I'm supposed to do that. My clients pay me to find deductions."

"We got a confession. Put him in the Humvee."

They crammed Mr. Lazuli into the back seat and secured the door. Humvees absorbed soldiers from every corner of the parking lot like wet vacs sucking up a spill. The helicopter switched off its lamps and rotored away, leading a convoy of speeding vehicles.

Gimbel stood alone in the dark and deserted driveway. The commotion of the CREEPS operation had vanished. As far as the public could see, it had never happened.

β 1 1

Inside, where the public could not see, was a different story.

Gimbel passed his own floor and climbed another flight to see if Mrs. Lazuli was okay. She was no doubt in shock at the arrest of her husband. Gimbel rehearsed what he would say to her when he knocked on her door.

But there was no door on which to knock. The metal rectangle lay on the floor just inside the apartment, a dent in its center from the impact of a CREEPS battering ram. Through the empty doorway, Gimbel saw a broken floor lamp and an overturned coffee table. Evidently the usually gentle tax accountant had put up a fight.

FULL ASYLUM

Gimbel knocked on the doorframe. "Hello? Mrs. Lazuli?" Inside a baby cried. It must have been Mimi. Gimbel entered the living room. "Anybody here?"

A paper streamer had been hanging over the entry to the dining room. It was torn now. The letters *Happy Thanks* hung on one side, *giving* on the other. The crying seemed to be coming from the room beyond the banner. Gimbel looked inside and found devastation.

The CREEPS must have arrived just as the Lazulis sat down to dinner. The turkey was still uncarved. It lay upside down on the floor, grease soaking the beige carpet. Next to it was a centerpiece in the shape of a white-bonneted pilgrim woman. Someone had stepped on her, crushing the black honeycomb paper that had been her skirt. A dark red Chianti stain marred the wall. Glass shards and tangled wicker littered the floor nearby. The window was broken; cold air blew into the apartment. Mimi lay wearing a turkey costume in a basinet by the wall. Googly eyes and a yellow beak decorated the hood, fuzzy red wattles hung from the neck. She was normally a quiet infant, but now her cries had the volume and persistence of a fire alarm.

Two chairs were still upright. Mrs. Lazuli sat stiffly in one of them and stared. A pin with metallic red and yellow leaves decorated her gravy-stained black dress. She gasped periodically, the way people do when they're all cried out. Her American Dream had become the American Nightmare.

Gimbel approached and gingerly placed a hand on her shoulder. Mrs. Lazuli looked up. Seeing a friendly face, she stood and threw her arms around Gimbel. She leaned her head on his chest, her wiry black hair pressed against his jacket. Gimbel wrapped his arms around her—one neighbor holding another badly in need of comfort. Slowly, Mrs. Lazuli came out of her trance. "Mimi," she said. She let go of Gimbel and picked up her daughter from the basinet. In the security of her mother's arms, the baby stopped crying.

Eventually Mrs. Lazuli spoke. "Gimbel, I don't understand any of this. When I woke up this morning, I felt nothing but love: our first Thanksgiving as a family." She returned the baby to the basinet. Kneeling by the turkey, she tipped it back onto the carving board and carried it to the galley kitchen. Gimbel began putting overturned chairs back on their feet.

Mrs. Lazuli returned to the dining room to watch her daughter fall asleep. "We waited so long to have Mimi," she said. "You know, when Ricardo and I came to America we had two suitcases and a hundred dollars. Ricardo worked for his uncle then, helping with the international accounts. It took him years to be certified as a CPA, and then, after his uncle died, years after that to get his own practice off the ground."

She shuttled to the kitchen with bowls of stuffing and gravy. Most of the food ended up in the disposal. Gimbel carried two bags of broken dishes and torn decorations to the dumpster. He swung by his apartment to fetch some brown paper and a roll of duct tape. While he patched the broken window, Mrs. Lazuli washed dishes. She got as far as a colander and couldn't go on. She sank onto the linoleum and just sat there, muttering, "Where's the pilgrim woman? I need the pilgrim woman." Gimbel retrieved the crushed paper centerpiece from the dining room; Mrs. Lazuli cradled it in her lap. He finished the dishes for her. Then he took the tablecloth and napkins to the laundry room and swiped his credit card to start the wash cycle. The stains on the wall and carpet would have to wait until Mrs. Lazuli bought some paint and rug cleaner.

β 1 1

"HEY, KONG! HOW MANY RATS DID YOU KILL TO MAKE THOSE PANTIES?"

Cheri Tarte taunted Kong from the archway. Bulldozer stood behind her, enjoying the show.

"CHERI TARTE SPEAK FALSE," Kong shouted back from the ring. "KONG NO WEAR RAT FUR. KONG WEAR MONKEY FUR."

"YOU ARE WHAT YOU WEAR, MONKEY MAN."

"THEN CHERI TARTE BIG COW IN LEATHER BRA!"

She lifted her breasts with two hands and released them; they jiggled a little. "AT LEAST I GOT SOMETHING TO FILL OUT MY BRA. THAT'S MORE THAN I CAN SAY FOR YOUR SORRY PANTIES!"

"CHERI TARTE THINK SHE MAKE KONG MAD SO KONG FIGHT HER. CHERI TARTE THINK SHE CAN PLAY LIKE BOY."

"OH, I CAN PLAY LIKE A BOY, ALL RIGHT. HEY, KONG, I GOT SOMETHING OF YOURS."

A cheerful tune played on the PA system. It shocked the spectators when they recognized it—the theme song for Kong's girlfriend Suzie Winsome. Suzie appeared through the archway wearing a gold lamé vest, tight pants, and heels. Her blond hair swung as she sashayed. When she reached Cheri Tarte she put her arm around the bigger woman's waist.

"Remember me, Kong?" Suzie said. "Your ex-girlfriend?"

Kong bowed his head. "Ex?"

"What can I say? You just weren't man enough for me."

She turned her head towards Cheri Tarte and stood on tiptoe. Cheri Tarte lowered her mouth towards Suzie. Their kiss was long and passionate. The giant overhead screen showed a close-up of their locked lips; the crowd loved it. Kong's look of sorrow turned to fury. He leaped over the ropes and ran down the runway towards Cheri Tarte, Suzie, and Bulldozer. "I SHOW YOU. I SHOW YOU WHO MAN ENOUGH. I KILL YOU, CHERI TARTE!" he roared.

Bulldozer stepped between Kong and Cheri Tarte, stretching his arms to hold them apart. "NOT NOW," he yelled in a deep, gravelly voice. "THREE WEEKS FROM NOW IS THE TIME TO SETTLE THIS. THREE WEEKS FROM NOW DURING OUR PAY-PER-VIEW SPECIAL, LIVE FROM WASHINGTON, DC. THIS IS WAY TOO BIG TO WASTE ON BROADCAST TV. SAVE IT FOR AN AUDIENCE THAT WILL SPEND SOME MONEY!"

β 1 1

Gimbel was spending too much money.

He worked at the computer in his spare bedroom, paying bills online. He eyed the declining balance apprehensively as he typed the amounts into boxes next to each account: rent, student loan, credit card. The last one was high. The cost of daily trips to Pentagon Palace added up. On top of that, the National Health Quarterly Supplemental Premium was due. There wouldn't be any money left over to put into savings this month. After paying to travel home for Christmas and buying gifts for his parents, there wouldn't be anything next month either. He still had six weeks until he could cash his Byte Yourself shares—if he didn't have to sign them over to Cindy first. Even if he lost on Saturday, he'd still be okay as long as he kept his job. But with the performance improvement plan hanging over his head, there was no guarantee of that.

The knock at the door surprised him; Gimbel didn't expect anyone. Other than the man who delivered the summons, no one had come over since Liza's last visit, over two months ago. His first thought was that Liza had returned. But the banging on the door was rapid and loud; someone was desperate to see him. Liza had never been desperate to see him.

The peephole lens made Mrs. Lazuli look shorter and squatter. She stood on the landing, holding Mimi in one arm. Gimbel turned the lock and opened the door.

"They froze our accounts!"

Clearly she had cried a great deal during the last few days. Her eyes were moist and red-rimmed. Usually a well-groomed lady, unruly strands of hair now escaped from her coif; she still wore the gravy-stained dress from Thanksgiving. Gimbel offered her a chair and a cup of tea. After a few sips, Mrs. Lazuli told the whole story.

FULL ASYLUM

Her husband was the breadwinner for his family. He managed the finances carefully to ensure his wife and daughter would be taken care of if anything ever happened to him. But now, as part of the prosecution, the Department of Justice cut off access to all the Lazulis' joint accounts. The rent was due tomorrow and Mrs. Lazuli had no money and no income. She tried to reach her husband for advice; the CREEPS wouldn't let her see him.

"I didn't know who else to turn to," she said. "I asked Mr. Willow in the management office for an extension on the rent. He told me absolutely not, that we had already caused enough problems with the raid. He said that if I didn't pay on time he would evict me." Mimi whimpered.

While Mrs. Lazuli waited, Gimbel returned to the spare bedroom. He logged back in to the Washington Metro Bank site and transferred funds out of his savings account to cover the check he was about to write. "Pay to the Order of Fox Hunt Apartments. For: December Rent—Lazuli." He entered the amount, signed his name, returned to the dining room, and pressed the check into Mrs. Lazuli's hand.

"I don't want to get you into trouble," she said. "Mr. Willow will know it's from you."

"Let him know."

β 1 1

Hold out baits to entice the enemy....If his forces are united, separate them.
– Sun Tzu, *The Art of War*, 1.20–23

"Any sign of him?" Cindy asked.
"No," Andy replied.
"Nothing over here," said Bart.

They had their own flag: four white letters arranged in a square on a blue background—ABCD for Andy, Bart, Cindy, and Daphne. It was mounted on a flagpole at the center of the rock fortress; it flapped in the December wind. Next to the flagpole, Madame Butterfly sat and played jacks. The ball bounced unpredictably on the uneven ground and she seldom got past onesies.

Cindy, Andy, and Bart spread out along the rocky perimeter, standing watch. They had not seen Gimbel since they left the parking lot twenty minutes ago after reviewing the rules. Madame Butterfly had brought the little book with her notes, but it wasn't a lot of help. *IYAH, YAD* clearly stood for *If you are hit, you are done*, but it took a while to figure out that *WHTFATEOAHW, ROWTOPASS* meant *Whoever has the flag at the end of an hour wins, regardless of whether the opposing players are still standing.* They also inspected each other's weapons. Gimbel's rifle was unusual, but legit. The laser sight might give them some trouble, but judging from what they observed at Pentagon Palace, Gimbel was too inexperienced to use it.

It was peaceful on the mountaintop. The birds had flown south for the winter; the only sounds were the fluttering of the flag and the bouncing of the rubber ball.

A siren demolished the peace. Waves of noise rose and fell. "Damn, it's my car alarm," Andy said.

"Are you sure it's yours?" Cindy asked.

"I know what my car alarm sounds like. I better go see what it is."

"Don't go anywhere," Cindy ordered. "Gimbel's trying to split us up."

"If he did anything to my car..." Andy left the threat unfinished.

A minute went by. A minute is a long time, but Cindy would not let Andy abandon his post. The regular sequence of long and short electric shrieks continued for a second minute, then a third.

Andy was visibly agitated. Finally, Cindy said, "Take Bart with you."

"Bart should stay here and guard the flag."

"I got a defensible position. You won't. Bart goes with you."

As the two men walked across the open ground, Cindy covered them with her marker and scanned for signs of Gimbel. Only when Andy and Bart disappeared into the woods did she exhale. Then she began a series of long patrols around the perimeter of the fortress.

β 1 1

Andy and Bart emerged from the woods and crunched the gravel of the parking lot beneath their boots. The siren was louder here. Andy's red Cheetah was parked beside Gimbel's Solo. He pressed the unlock button on his key fob. That should have turned the alarm off.

It didn't.

"Try starting the engine," Bart shouted over the siren, which was beginning another series of shrill arpeggios.

Andy wrenched the door open, jammed his key fob into its slot, and stabbed the starter button. The engine came to life but the alarm didn't die.

"Look under the hood."

He released the catch and raised the hood. But as he stared stupidly at the engine, he didn't know what to do next. At work, when a problem wouldn't go away, he rebooted the computer. Maybe if he disconnected the battery...

"Hey, there's something under the car," said Bart.

Andy bent down and peered between the front wheels. Sure enough, there was a metal object the size and shape of a shoebox. He got on his knees and pulled the box out from under the car. The noise grew louder; it came from a speaker on the side of the device.

There was a keypad and an LED on the top, but no power switch. "Get the crow bar out of the trunk," he yelled to Bart.

Five blows were enough to silence the fake alarm. By then it was nothing but bent aluminum casing and busted printed wiring board. Andy was catching his breath when he heard Gimbel yell, "Cindy!" He tossed the iron bar onto the broken electronics as he and Bart ran back to the woods.

β 1 1

> He who is skilled in attack flashes forth from the topmost heights of heaven.
> – Sun Tzu, *The Art of War*, 4.7

Gimbel straddled the branch of a tree and spied on Andy and Bart. Anxiety distorted their faces as they emerged from the shelter of the rock fortress, crossed the clearing, and disappeared into the woods, towards the parking lot. His time was limited, but before he acted, he had to see what Cindy would do.

She patrolled the rocks. She walked a little, paused, scanned for the enemy, and then walked a little more. When she was on her second trip around the redoubt, her back to Gimbel, he dropped from the tree. He ran down the mountain, across the open ground towards the fortress. Once in range, he went down on one knee, shouldered his marker, and aimed. Through the sight, he saw the red dot of the laser at the center of Cindy's back. The sound of the car alarm stopped. Andy and Bart would return in a moment. Gimbel had to fire now. He began to squeeze the trigger.

This wasn't right. Twenty-nine movies and Jon Dunn never once shot anyone in the back. Gimbel released the trigger. Sun Tzu would completely disapprove of the risk he was about to take. Cindy's commercial marker may not be accurate at this range, but there was always the chance she would get lucky. He did it anyway.

FULL ASYLUM

"Cindy!" he yelled. She did a 180 and ran across the fortress to face Gimbel. Crouching behind the rocks, she opened fire. The sound of her automatic pumping paintballs across the field resembled playing cards in the spokes of a bicycle wheel. The globules burst harmlessly around Gimbel, leaving a mess of broken shell and a sticky residue on the grass. Only the upper half of Cindy's mask and her camouflage hat poked above the rocks. Gimbel took his time. He breathed deeply, looked through the sight, and aimed the red dot at the mask, right at the center of Cindy's forehead. He squeezed the trigger and felt the hollow thump of the marker. An egg-white stain replaced the red dot. Brownie had been right. Ten rounds were more than Gimbel needed.

There was no referee, no witness at all other than Madame Butterfly, happily absorbed in her game of jacks. If Cindy wanted to cheat and continue firing as Gimbel ran into the range of her marker, there was nothing to stop her. Afterwards it would be her word against his.

But she didn't cheat. She leaned her marker against the rocks and stood motionless while Gimbel clambered over them, grabbed the flag of ABCD, and scrambled over the other wall. He ran across the open field, the flag streaming behind him like a cavalryman's banner. He reached the woods just as Andy and Bart emerged at the opposite side of the clearing. As Gimbel disappeared among the trees, the last thing he heard was Madame Butterfly yelling, "Twosies!"

β 1 1

> Dangerous faults which may affect a general...a hasty temper, which can be provoked by insults.
> – Sun Tzu, *The Art of War*, 8.12

The leaves rustled. Andy tiptoed through the brush, marker held in front of him. He pivoted from side to side like a cartoon hunter stalking rabbits. A short distance away, Bart did the same. Fifteen minutes to go, acres of foliage to search. They had as much chance of finding Gimbel as they did of passing a camel through the eye of a needle after finding the needle in a haystack. Nevertheless, they would play the game to the end.

Andy's text message ringtone—the Cheetah jingle—jarred the quiet forest. He jerked the IQPhone off his belt.

From: Gimbel O'Hare
Received: 1:46 p.m. Sat Dec 4
You guys really suck at this.

"Laugh all you want, asshole," Andy said. "It's your funeral." If Gimbel was using an IQPhone, he was broadcasting his position. Andy tapped Gimbel's name on the screen and selected *Locate*. A moment passed and then a dialog box popped up: *No GPS location found for Gimbel O'Hare*.

The Cheetah jingle played again.

From: Gimbel O'Hare
Received: 1:47 p.m. Sat Dec 4
You don't really think I'd have the GPS turned on, do you?

"Bite yourself, Gimbel," Andy shouted. He hurled his phone at a pine tree. It bounced off the trunk and disappeared into the underbrush.

"God damn it!"

FULL ASYLUM

β 1 1

The general who is skilled in defense hides in the most secret recesses of the earth.
 – Sun Tzu, *The Art of War*, 4.7

Gimbel laughed and returned his IQPhone to his coverall pocket. He sat on the ground in a stand of mountain laurel. The dark rubbery leaves around him absorbed the light and hid him from view. Next to him the enemy flag, now furled, rested beside his sniper's rifle. Gimbel glanced at his Chromega watch (the same brand Jon Dunn wore). 1:48 p.m. There was nothing he needed to do now but run out the clock. He stretched his legs and rolled his head back. Patches of blue dappled the sky. The day had been cloudy, but now the sun broke through. 1:53 p.m. Gimbel daydreamed about the scene in *Bitterweed* where Dunn defeated the villain at billiards, pocketed the ruby, and had his drink with Penny Short. He ordered a Tequila Sunrise for her and a Glenjohnnie, neat, for himself. 2:00 p.m. Gimbel won. He returned to the parking lot and drove to the nearest bar for a Glenjohnnie, neat.

β 1 1

She stood tall, arms folded, expression grim. Cheri Tarte wore green camouflage pants and a black stretch top. The muscles of her bare arms and shoulders were full and round. They were muscles capable of doing violence.

No view appeared through the window behind her, just a plain blue wall. Computer graphics would fill in the scenery later: a daytime panorama of the National Mall with the Washington Monument in the foreground and the Capitol Dome behind it. It wouldn't occur to most moviegoers that, to have such a view, the building would have to be located in the middle of the Reflecting Pool.

The director yelled "Action!"

"Mrs. Klimt will see you now."

The business card that Dunn handed the secretary identified him as an acquisitions manager. But his athletic figure suggested he worked a job less sedentary than that of a bureaucrat in the Ministry of Defense; the cut and fabric of his gray business suit suggested that his compensation was better as well. The secretary smiled invitingly at him as she ushered him into the office. She was tall, with sleek black hair down to her shoulders. The short silk dress that clung to her hips seemed more suitable for a cocktail party than an office, yet somehow it suited her. Dunn followed, admiring her backside.

The office décor was executive modern minimalist. Blond wood paneling and LCD displays covered the walls. To one side a bar stood behind a fence made of taut aluminum cables. Cheerful pendant lamps brightened the surface of the bar. Dunn walked across the white marble floor, skirting the sunken Zen garden with its raked white sand and towers of black stones.

Iona Klimt reigned behind a blond wood desk with curves that evoked the helm of a starship. On seeing Dunn, she stood and extended her hand to him. She was a short woman; the tall Cheri Tarte, standing guard at the window behind her, made her look even shorter. The black-haired secretary provided the introductions. "Welcome to Washington, Mr. Dunn," Mrs. Klimt said with a Russian accent. She told the secretary to pour Mr. Dunn a drink.

The secretary walked smartly to the bar. She slid a bottle of vodka out of the freezer and filled two square crystal shot glasses with viscous liquid. Returning to the desk, she smiled at Dunn again as she handed one glass to him and the other to Mrs. Klimt. Then she slipped out of the office.

Dunn raised his glass. "*Nazdrovia!*" he said diplomatically.

"Cheers," Mrs. Klimt replied.

They emptied their glasses and placed them on the desk. "Excellent," said Dunn. "Especially when properly chilled." He inquired as to the brand. "Romanov?"

"Of course," Mrs. Klimt replied. "Now. Mr. Dunn. What can Klimt Defensive Software do for the M.O.D.?"

"As you know, the bankruptcy of Advanced Missiles has had widespread repercussions throughout the defense industry. Dozens of weapons programs have ground to a halt. The minister is particularly eager to get the Falcon Missile back on schedule. We are seeking a new contractor to develop the guidance software."

"Guidance software is our, how do you say, claim to fame. I assume we are looking at about three hundred and fifty thousand lines of code?"

"Closer to four."

"*Da*, my company will be quite interested in bidding on this project."

"Well then, the Ministry will send you our RFP in a few days."

Dunn picked up the shot glass from the desk and studied the smooth surface. "Pity about Advanced Missiles," he said nonchalantly. "I don't suppose you have any insight into where it went bad."

"If I had that sort of insight into my competitors," Mrs. Klimt replied, "this business would be far easier."

Dunn rubbed the glass with his finger, as if removing a smudge. "Then you don't suspect economic sabotage."

Iona Klimt swiveled in her high back black leather chair and looked out the window. "Not as far as I know," she said.

"That is most fortunate. My government would take a rather severe view of anyone who purposely interfered with the development of the Falcon."

"You would be right to do so," said Iona Klimt, turning back to face Dunn again. "Goodbye, Mr. Dunn. It was nice to have met you."

She pressed a button on her desk and the secretary returned to escort Dunn out of the office. When the door closed behind them, Mrs. Klimt turned to Cheri Tarte. "Take these dirty glasses away," she said. "They are quite unsightly."

The shot glasses disappeared into the henchwoman's fists as she turned her muscular back to her boss and exited the office. Iona Klimt dialed a telephone. "The British suspect something," she said into the receiver. "Are you sure there have been no leaks?...We had better be on the safe side. It is time to terminate our relationship with the Banker."

Cheri Tarte re-entered the office as Iona Klimt returned the receiver to the cradle. "Did you examine the glass?" the executive asked.

"We found this." Cheri Tarte pressed a button on a remote control. A picture of Jon Dunn's shot glass appeared on the center LCD display. She held down another button and the image zoomed to an extreme close-up. A small hemispherical object was stuck to the side of the glass. "It's a tiny video camera," Cheri Tarte explained. "We neutralized it."

"Look after Mr. Dunn," said Mrs. Klimt. "Traffic is very heavy this time of day. I am concerned he will be in an accident."

PART II
A Plethora of Betas

When sorrows come, they come not single spies, but in battalions!
– William Shakespeare, *Hamlet*, 4.5

CHAPTER 5

THE RING RECYCLE

He that cursed love, he alone,
Could jealously use the spell of the ring
For the eternal humiliation of all nobility:
The courage of heroes he would steal from me.
   – Richard Wagner, *Die Walküre*, 2.2

Victor Shepherd zipped the cover of his black roller bag. He carried it across plush bedroom carpeting, through the hall, and down the stairs. Although the house was one of the newest in Fort Wayne, the old-fashioned oak banister always made him think of a country store. The foyer had dark blue wallpaper with tiny white flowers on it. Leaving the roller bag next to his laptop case, he entered the kitchen. His wife, wearing a bathrobe, stood at the counter packing jelly sandwiches into reusable lunch bags; the school didn't allow peanut butter or disposable sacks. His son and daughter composed text messages on their IQPhones while their neglected cornflakes grew soggy. Victor kissed his wife. "I should be in Washington before lunch," he told her. "I'm meeting with the government all afternoon, then we're getting dinner. I won't check into the hotel until late."

"The usual place?" his wife asked.

"Barnett Crystal City. It's like I'm stuck in a do-loop. But I got to rack up those points if we're going to Florida this winter."

She kissed him on the mouth. "What's the matter?" she asked. "You seem tired."

"I'm fine. It's just not the same," he replied.

"You mean peddling radios isn't the same as building a fighter jet?"

"Uh-huh."

"What happened to the F-38, Dad?" his son asked.

"Didn't I tell you? The funding got cut. Congress decided to buy more of the old-style fighters from Consolidated."

"But the new ones were going to be faster with the latest missiles. They were so much cooler."

"Well, son, Congress doesn't really consider cool. Maybe they will when you get elected. The real tragedy is that Consolidated planes aren't just uncool. The workmanship is crap. Even the coffee makers are unsafe."

The taxi outside honked. "Call me when you get to the hotel," said his wife.

"You want to make sure I'm safe and sound, huh, sweetie?"

"Always, Victor," she said quietly.

The children squirmed when their father kissed the tops of their heads. "Dad!" his daughter whined without looking up from her IQPhone. Returning to the foyer, Victor picked up his bags and left his house through the front door. He descended the steps between the hydrangea bushes and followed the path to the waiting taxi. He tossed his bags onto the back seat and leaped in after them. "Airport," he said.

β 1 1

"I can't see the ring," Gimbel complained. "I have to turn my head all the way to the side."

"You'll thank me when the show starts," Joe replied. "We're in the front row by the runway. All the wrestlers will come right by us."

Gimbel and Joe sat in premium seats on the floor of the Horizon Center. Groups of spectators filed in behind them. The many families with children surprised Gimbel; what he saw of the UWL on TV wasn't suitable for underage viewers. Some of the children wore their own costumes and championship belts. There were eleven-year-old Kongs in fake monkey fur briefs and ten-year-old Cheri Tartes in camo training bras.

The last couple weeks had been tense. Gimbel had no way of enforcing his victory in the paintball match. If Cindy wanted to renege on their deal and proceed with her lawsuit, Gimbel had no remedy.

He was disappointed that Brownie wasn't happier for him. When Gimbel returned the sniper's rifle, Brownie said, "So you won. Do you think Beverly is going to give up?" Then he grumbled that Gimbel had let the fake car alarm get destroyed.

On top of that, Mrs. Lazuli and Mimi had disappeared. Gimbel wanted to make sure they were all set with the January rent. The door to their apartment had been replaced after the CREEPS raid, but when Gimbel knocked on it, no one answered. He tried several more times over the next few days and got the same result. There were no lights in their windows and no footsteps overhead. Mr. Willow at the management office was no help. The Lazulis were gone.

The gloom lifted somewhat today. Gimbel received a letter from Cindy's attorney informing him that she was dropping all claims related to the sexual harassment incident. She had behaved honorably, just as she had when she put down her marker. It was also Gimbel's last day of work for the year. He was already packed for tomorrow's flight to Chicago. Christmas with his parents would make up for the Thanksgiving he missed. He was overdue for some fun.

He was also overdue for some junk food. BAD had implemented Phase II of the Healthy Office Program—the diet phase. Hamburgers, deli meats, and toaster pastries disappeared from the cafeteria. Lentil salads, tofu stir-fry, and bran flakes took their place. Of course, there had been no sugary sodas since they had been outlawed, but now the diet varieties disappeared as well.

The company had also installed a video camera. Gimbel didn't understand that part. It wasn't as if anyone was going to steal paper napkins. The napkins were so small that they were wholly inadequate for protecting pants from food stains. According to placards on the dispensers, the napkin size had something to do with conserving the earth's resources. Although, how stained pants helped save the earth, Gimbel had no idea.

He finally learned the reason for the camera one day last week when he brought a sandwich from home. That afternoon, Beverly summoned him to her office. When he arrived, she was waiting for him, as were a nurse in a white uniform and a security guard with a gun. They explained that Gimbel had been captured on video eating ham and cheese and that government policy now required him to receive a lecture on the principles of good nutrition. The lecture took two hours, the low point being an animated video depicting an epic struggle of good and evil between Gary W. Grain (the W stood for *whole*, or maybe it was *wholesome*) and Lippy the Loathsome Lipid. After that, Gimbel refrained from bringing food from home. Sometimes he brought napkins.

Fortunately, the Horizon Center wasn't an office. It was beyond the reach of the Healthy Office Program and its concessions stands were out of sight of the cafeteria cam. Before the show, Gimbel loaded up on hot dogs and artificially butter-flavored popcorn. During the early matches, Joe brought him up to speed on the history of the UWL. Since Gimbel had only been watching for a few months, he didn't know that Titan used to be a bad guy before he was good guy, that Kong dated Brenda Biggs before he hooked up with Suzie Winsome, or that the Coroner once lit Bulldozer's shorts on fire. Joe was on his feet cheering when Boulder made his entrance. Gimbel stood too, if only to avoid an elbow to the head from the short woman clapping wildly on his other side. Joe returned a high five from Boulder. For the fourth of fifth time that evening, he said to Gimbel, "I met him once and got his autograph. He was really nice."

"How did you meet so many of the wrestlers?" Gimbel asked.

Joe blushed. His skin turned the color of his freckles, momentarily hiding them. Then he said, "That's a secret."

During intermission, Gimbel brought the empty popcorn tub and his other trash to the disposal bins by the entrance. He carefully separated plastic, aluminum, and "waste", and then went straight back to his seat. The Kong vs. Cheri Tarte showdown would be the first fight after the break, and he didn't want to miss it. The intermission went on for some time. After half an hour had passed, Gimbel found himself trying to explain his t-shirt to Joe. "Obviously the two guys with the stethoscopes are doctors. They look very similar, almost as if they're twins, except one is much older than the other. So you see, it's the twin pair-of-docs."

"I still don't get it," Joe replied. "If one is older than the other, how can they be twins?"

"That's the paradox."

"I see the pair-of-docs. But where are the twins?"

What had begun as a conversation about Einstein's Theory was turning into an Abbott and Costello routine. Before it could degenerate further, the big event started.

It was clearly the event the crowd was waiting for. The spectators grew louder as they advertised their allegiances with hand-lettered signs. Slogans like *Crimson Crusher: Crush his Skull, King Kong: Crown Her,* and *Cheri Tarte, Marry Me* filled the

FULL ASYLUM

Horizon Center. Cheri Tarte was the favorite—signs favoring her outnumbered Kong's two to one. Joe wouldn't tell Gimbel whom he was going to root for. But he must have had a preference because he brought a sign with him; it lay rolled up under his chair.

Kong entered first. He treated the crowd to a Tarzan yell as he swung through the archway on a rope decorated with plastic vine leaves. Landing on the runway and bounding into the ring, he pumped two beefy arms in the air to rile the crowd. "TONIGHT," he shouted, "TONIGHT KONG TAKE BACK GIRLFRIEND FROM MEAN LADY."

"DREAM ON, APE MAN," yelled Cheri Tarte from the archway. Suzie stood behind her. The entire crowd stood now, cheering and stamping their feet. Joe reached under his chair, picked up his poster, and removed the rubber band. Cheri Tarte and Suzie strutted towards the ring. A cameraman backed down the runway ahead of them. The red light on his videocam indicated they were on the air. The two women slapped hands with the spectators, especially the children. Creepy middle-aged men, apparently there by themselves, threw business cards and paper airplanes at the women. One of the airplanes landed by Gimbel's feet. He picked it up. *I love you, Cheri Tarte*, followed by an e-mail address, was written on it in black marker.

When Gimbel looked up from the page, Joe was holding up his poster and grinning. It said *Little 'n' Cuddly* in green letters above an arrow that pointed to Gimbel.

"Put that away," Gimbel protested.

But it was too late. Cheri Tarte saw it and stopped. "I *know* you," she said. "You were on *Sorry* with me."

She put one arm around his shoulders and waved to the camera with the other. Bending her knee, she pressed her hip into his side. Gimbel was enjoying this now. Even with her knee bent, he only came up to her chin. Fifteen thousand people chuckled as they looked into the overhead monitor and saw Gimbel lean his head on her breast. He smiled angelically. Cheri Tarte turned around and gave him a bear hug, lifting him a foot off the floor.

"I'm very sorry about this," she whispered. Then she licked his ear, set him gently on his feet, and resumed her jog to the ring.

"What did she say?" Joe shouted over the noise of the crowd.

"'I'm very sorry about this,'" Gimbel replied, drying his ear with his sleeve.

"What are you sorry about?"

"Nothing. That's what Cheri Tarte said."

"What's she got to be sorry for?"

"I don't know. Maybe for embarrassing me."

"Or maybe she's going to lose."

β 1 1

A hundred feet above Gimbel and Joe, Isaac Ross leaned back in his armchair. He sat alone in the darkened skybox. The only sources of light were the arena beyond the glass doors and the screen of the notebook computer in his lap. *Since the time of the ancient Greeks,* he typed, *philosophers have identified two types of social structure: the cooperative society and the competitive society.*

> Through most of history, the competitive society has predominated. But a competitive society is like a sick body. A body would not survive if the lungs and the heart competed with each other to pump blood or provide oxygen. Similarly, a society would not survive if those best suited to drive trucks competed with programmers to write software, or those best suited to write software competed with philosophers to make decisions. We saw the end game, the final illness of the competitive society, in the excesses that led to the three Financial Meltdowns. The poverty, homelessness, and psychological stress that we now see all around us are the

inevitable result when society is run by those who put profit and gain above enlightenment and compassion.

If a competitive society is a sick body, then a cooperative society is a healthy one. Although a true cooperative society has never existed, we know from Plato's *Republic* what it would look like. Each member of the cooperative society knows his or her place and has a role to play that is suited to his or her natural abilities. In a healthy body, all the parts work in harmony. Similarly, in a healthy society, all citizens work in harmony. In a healthy body, all operations are coordinated under the control of the brain. Similarly, in a healthy society, all operations are coordinated under the control of the *philosopher-king*. This extraordinary individual makes the decisions that are beyond the ability of the lesser citizens. A truck driver does not have the enlightenment to decide, for example, the best health care plan or the best way to fund his or her retirement. A software engineer does not have the compassion to ensure that society's wealth is spread in a fair and equitable manner. Only a naturally enlightened and compassionate person is suited to be the brains of a healthy society.

The philosopher-king makes the rules for society, or to put it another way, the existence of rules presupposes the existence of the philosopher-king. It is therefore illogical for the philosopher-king to be constrained by the rules set down for lesser people. Illogical, and also unnecessary. Regardless of the rules, the philosopher-king will always act in the best interests of the cooperative society. If those interests require the philosopher-king to arrest an innocent man, rig an election, or conceal his true intentions behind a mask of falsehood, then it is not only permitted for him to do so, it is a moral imperative.

Isaac reread the last paragraph and frowned. *This won't do. The masses are not ready for the truth.* He deleted the final sentence and replaced it with a mask of falsehood.

Glare from the corridor suddenly rendered Isaac's screen unreadable. He jerked his head and saw the silhouette of an usher in the open doorway.

"Excuse me, Mr. Ross," said the usher.

"Leave here at once," Isaac yelled. "I am composing a major philosophical work and must not be interrupted."

"I'm sorry, sir, but—"

"Are you still here? Is the only way to get rid of you to arrange for you to cash an unemployment check? Because one e-mail from me is all it would take."

"Of course, sir, but you asked me to notify you when the Kong–Cheri Tarte match was about to begin."

"I know that. I don't need some minimum wage ticket checker reminding me what I told him myself. I want to see that match, so don't you dare forget. Now leave."

"Yes sir. By the way, sir, the Cheri Tarte–Kong match is about to begin."

"It took you long enough to come out with that. I waited two months for this. If I missed it, I'd send that e-mail before you could get out of this room. Now get out of this room."

Isaac slammed the cover of his laptop. He left the computer on an end table and walked through the glass doors to the balcony. Looking over the railing, he saw Cheri Tarte climb over the ropes into the ring. The match hadn't started yet; that idiotic usher was lucky.

Isaac wished he could have been at the script meeting today so he could have seen the look on Cheri Tarte's face when she found out what was in store for her. But of course, as CEO his presence would have been suspicious. When intermission ran long, Isaac wondered whether he'd be getting a call, but his IQPhone remained silent. Apparently the lawyers took care of everything as planned. Two months of waiting were about to pay off. The Christmas sweater was a nice addition to the script. Taking a little dig at the churchgoers always gave Isaac a lift.

He descended the four steps and settled into one of the stadium seats. His oversized head sunk between his shoulders, and he scanned the audience like a buzzard searching for carrion. The fans were on their feet, cheering and waving signs. From Isaac's vantage point, their voices merged into one loud drone. *Morons*, thought Isaac. *All this racket over some steroid addicts bludgeoning each other. Starting tonight your enthusiasm will serve the cooperative society.*

β 1 1

"KONG WAIT NO MORE. CHERI TARTE GIVE KONG GIRLFRIEND BACK NOW."

"JUST TRY AND TAKE HER. I'LL HAVE YOU EATING CANVAS BEFORE YOU GET WITHIN TEN FEET."

Standing behind Cheri Tarte, Suzie Winsome put her hand on her hip and stuck out her tongue at her ex. The audience laughed.

Kong lunged at her. "AFTER KONG BEAT CHERI TARTE, KONG TEACH SUZIE RESPECT," he bellowed.

"I'LL TEACH YOU RESPECT," Cheri Tarte replied, moving to block Kong's advance on her girlfriend.

The little referee stepped between the combatants. "We're doing this by the book," he said. "Both of you go to your corners and don't come out until you hear the bell."

The fight about to start, Suzie slipped out of the ring. Kong began lumbering to his corner, but a shout from Cheri Tarte interrupted him. "WHAT THE HELL DO YOU THINK YOU'RE DOING?"

He turned around to discover that she wasn't yelling at him. She was looking out at the audience. The crowd was as confused as Kong appeared to be. Silence muffled the arena for the first time since Cheri Tarte made her entrance.

"YEAH, I'M TALKING TO YOU. WHAT THE HELL DO YOU THINK YOU'RE DOING? I'M GOING TO STOP THIS RIGHT NOW!"

Cheri Tarte grabbed hold of the top rope and sailed out of the ring feet first. A spotlight followed her as she ran up an aisle. As she reached the exit at the end, it became clear at whom she was yelling. A plain woman was standing in front of the trash bins. She wore a red Christmas sweater and held a plastic soda bottle.

Cheri Tarte grabbed the woman by the ear and dragged her back towards the ring. The woman stumbled as she struggled to keep up. "YOUR TYPE MAKES ME SICK," Cheri Tarte yelled. When they reached the bottom of the aisle, Cheri Tarte lifted the woman and pushed her under the bottom rope into the ring. The woman rolled to a stop as Cheri Tarte climbed in after her. "I AM SO GOING TO KICK YOUR ASS," she yelled at the woman, and then, to the audience "DID YOU SEE WHAT SHE WAS GOING TO DO?" Like the people around them, Gimbel and Joe exchanged puzzled glances.

The woman lay on her back on the mat. Her sweater was decorated with a green Christmas tree with puffball ornaments in primary colors. Cheri Tarte ground her boot on the Christmas tree, grabbed the soda bottle, and displayed it to the audience. "THIS WOMAN WAS GOING TO PUT A RECYCLABLE BOTTLE IN THE REGULAR TRASH!"

The audience burst out laughing.

"KEEP LAUGHING AND I'LL KICK ALL YOUR ASSES."

Two stagehands lifted a waste bin into the ring as Cheri Tarte continued. "EVERY YEAR AMERICANS PRODUCE 250 MILLION TONS OF TRASH. DID YOU HEAR ME? I SAID

TONS! DO YOU KNOW HOW MUCH 250 MILLION TONS IS? ENOUGH TO FILL 850 SKYSCRAPERS THE SIZE OF THE EMPIRE STATE BUILDING. SO UNLESS WE WANT ALL OUR BUILDINGS FILLED WITH GARBAGE, WE BETTER RECYCLE." She released the woman from beneath her boot and walked over to the trash bin. "YOU SEE THIS? THIS IS A MULTI-USE WASTE DISPOSAL BIN! IT'S SO EASY EVEN YOU CLOWNS CAN USE IT."

The spectators became restless at being called clowns. A few of them booed.

Cheri Tarte ignored them and went on with her demonstration. "THERE ARE THREE OPENINGS. THIS FIRST ONE SAYS *WASTE*. THAT'S FOR ANYTHING NOT RECYCLABLE—AND YOU BETTER NOT HAVE VERY MUCH OF THAT. THE NEXT ONE SAYS *ALUMINUM*. ALL YOU DRUNKS OUT THERE, THIS IS WHERE YOU PUT YOUR BEER CANS."

"Start the fight!" yelled the short woman next to Gimbel.

"THIS LAST OPENING SAYS *PLASTIC*. IF YOU'RE TOO MUCH OF A WUSS FOR A REAL DRINK, HERE'S WHERE YOU PUT YOUR SODA BOTTLE."

Cheri Tarte grabbed the woman off the mat by the collar of her sweater. She yanked upwards, pulling the woman to her feet, but also pulling the sweater off. The woman wore a white bra underneath. She was unusually fit for a random audience member, with a path of defined abs leading into her jeans. Cheri Tarte shoved the plastic bottle in her face. "NOW WHERE DO YOU PUT EMPTY SODA BOTTLES?"

A man drinking a diet soda in his ringside seat stood up and yelled, "I'll show you." He hurled the half-full container at Cheri Tarte but missed. Lemon-lime flavored liquid splashed on the canvas.

"WHERE DO YOU PUT THIS?"

"The plastics slot?" she asked meekly.

"LOUDER," Cheri Tarte ordered. But by now, several more plastic projectiles were incoming.

"The plastics slot!"

"DON'T LET ME CATCH YOU PUTTING IT IN WASTE AGAIN!"

The entire audience jeered now. Gimbel looked uneasily around him. Several children chanted, "We want a fight, not a class at night." Gimbel saw the anger contorting their faces. If rationality is what makes us human, these children had no humanity in them. He looked up into the balcony. The tiers were too steep. He imagined that if someone slipped and tumbled into the row in front, he would start a human avalanche. It would pour over the railings like a swollen river over a dam, drowning Gimbel and everyone else on the floor below. The crowd was no longer a collection of individuals; it was a fluid.

A bottle whacked Cheri Tarte on the temple. Her head snapped to one side as it took the impact. Then a box of nachos hit her in the center of the chest. Melted cheese oozed into her cleavage. Kong put his arms around Suzie Winsome to protect her from the rain of trash. A half dozen uniformed security guards entered the ring and surrounded Cheri Tarte. They escorted her back to the arch. On her way in, men had thrown their e-mail addresses at her. On her way out, they threw their garbage.

β 1 1

"THIS IS BULLCRAP!"

Cheri Tarte sat at a table in the bar of the Barnett Crystal City hotel. A red spot swelled on her temple where the soda bottle had hit her. She picked up her beer and pressed the frosty mug against the swelling. Back in the Horizon Center, she had needed a half hour under the shower to get the stink of cheese out of her breasts.

After that she put on one of Brenda's baggy gray *Property of the UWL* sweatshirts. Anything dressier seemed like too much work.

Behind the bar bottles of vodka and scotch, lit from the bottom, shone like Christmas lights. On a TV above them, a news clip replayed the impact of the soda bottle.

"Ouch, that must hurt," said an anchorwoman.

"Cheri Tarte gave new meaning to talking trash," her male partner replied.

"TOTAL BULLCRAP!" Cheri Tarte repeated.

Kong and Bulldozer commiserated with her. The woman who had been the cause of the commotion joined them. She had replaced her red Christmas sweater with a t-shirt. Kong looked very civilized in a white linen suit, bow tie, and two-tone shoes. Although he did not normally wear white after Labor Day, Washington was, after all, *the South*. His hair was slicked back and methodically combed. "It was your performance on *Sorry* that did it," he said. He waved an empty martini glass at the waiter. "You should not have advised Isaac to extract an iron staff from his rectum."

"I was in character," she replied. "I get paid to do that."

"You're always in character. That's why you committed yourself to this asylum known as the Universal Wrestling League: the real world can't handle you. Personally, I find it expeditious to get out of character as rapidly as practical upon exiting the ring. Faux monkey fur is rather itchy."

The wrestlers fell silent as a waiter laid out a fresh martini for Kong and another round of beers for the others. When the waiter was out of earshot, Bulldozer asked Cheri Tarte, "What happened after we left the script meeting?"

"I told them I wouldn't do it. They said they had a contract with me and I better. Then I called my agent and she called my lawyer. They told me not to say or do anything 'til they got there. It took them a while to arrive and then a while after that to go over the contract. By then the show had started. When we couldn't find a loophole, we tried to negotiate. We were still going at intermission."

"So that's why intermission ran long."

"When we didn't get anywhere on terms and conditions, I offered to go on for free if they went back to the original Kong vs. Cheri Tarte script."

"Why would you do that instead of crying all the way to the bank?"

"You never did get me, Bulldozer. I'm the chick that mixed it up with Kong. Not the recycling chick."

"At least it's over," said Bulldozer.

"No, it's not," Cheri Tarte replied. She buried her face in her hands.

"What do you mean?" Bulldozer asked.

Cheri Tarte raised her head. "They got a whole series of eco-messages planned for me: community gardening, carbon footprints, even vegetarianism—like any of us are vegetarians."

"I'm so sorry."

Someone shouted from the bar, "Hey, Sweater Lady." The wrestlers looked up. A foreign businessman in a dark suit and a loose tie approached holding out a pen. "Sweater Lady, can I have your autograph?" She took the pen and signed *Joy* in angry letters on the back of a cardboard coaster. The businessman then asked Bulldozer for his autograph. Bulldozer grunted as he reached for the pen. Unlike the other three, he had fought tonight; he was sore. After Bulldozer signed, the businessman returned to the bar. He didn't ask Kong for a signature because he didn't recognize him; he didn't ask Cheri Tarte because he did.

"Just merry great," said Joy. "I work for years to become a Vixen and now I'm the Sweater Lady. When I get home I'm going to burn that merry sweater. What's wrong with recycling anyway? It's good for the environment."

"That's not entirely clear," Kong replied. "Recycling aluminum is good for the environment. Recycling other commodities sometimes uses more resources than it saves."

"So we shouldn't recycle?"

"I didn't say that. I'm a recycling agnostic: I'm not smart enough to know. The market is." Joy looked out of her depth, so Kong explained. "If we left trash removal up to the private sector, then the market would drive us to recycle—if it made sense. We would just do it without a bunch of silly recycling evangelists preaching on TV about 'the centerpiece of environmental stewardship.'"

"Well I don't see why my career should suffer because Cheri Tarte had a fight with Isaac."

"Put a sock in it," Bulldozer bellowed. Some of the bar patrons looked up at the disturbance.

"Bulldozer expresses himself rather crudely," said Kong. "But I must, nevertheless, agree with him. You're a newcomer to our UWL family, Joy, so perhaps you do not yet appreciate how we operate. We band together and help each other out."

"You didn't always," said Cheri Tarte bitterly.

"She's got you there," Bulldozer agreed.

Kong sipped his martini. "I confess to planning one or two practical jokes when Cheri Tarte joined our company."

"One or two? I lost count how many times I 'somehow' was given the wrong time for the script meeting and got in trouble for missing it."

"It wasn't just script meetings," said Bulldozer. "You missed a couple flights, too."

"Well, you were rather unlike the other Vixens," Kong said. "We did not know what to make of you at first."

"Hey, remember when you hid her clothes?"

"*I* remember," said Cheri Tarte. "When I got out of the shower, my clothes were gone, the towel shelf was empty, and there was nothing to wear but a giant rubber condom."

"I went to great lengths to steal that costume from the set of a prophylactic commercial."

"She didn't wear it though," Bulldozer said. "Instead she came out of the locker room buck naked and popped you in the eye."

"Makeup had a dickens of a time covering that shiner."

"That was the turning point," said Cheri Tarte.

"Yes, I did develop some respect for you after that," Kong replied.

"You developed respect for her right cross." Bulldozer laughed heartily.

"My right cross did the trick," said Cheri Tarte. "That was the last practical joke."

"In point of fact," Kong said, "it was the second to last."

"Did I forget one?"

"You never knew about one. Do you remember when you were interviewed and demonstrated the bench press?"

"Sure I remember. Four hundred and five pounds, twelve reps. Or eleven anyway. Bulldozer gave me the twelfth."

"What you may not be aware of is that the measurements inscribed on barbell plates are not particularly accurate."

"What do you mean?"

"They're all supposed to be forty-five pounds, but since variation is natural in all physical systems, some are a little lighter and some a little heavier."

Bulldozer guffawed. "We used the scale in the men's locker room to pick out the heavy ones."

"The plates that actually made it to the bar were approximately five percent overweight."

Weightlifters are skilled at multiplying by forty-five. Cheri Tarte did the math in her head. "So you're saying I actually lifted 423 pounds?"

"426, to be precise," said Kong.

"And what made you decide to tell me after all this time?"

Kong became serious. He looked Cheri Tarte in the eye and said, "It seemed like a good time for you to know that you're stronger than you think."

β 1 1

"I just checked in. It was the dinner that wouldn't end."

Victor cradled his IQPhone between his neck and shoulder as he unpacked his roller bag. The bright lights of National Airport created glare on the window.

"I don't think we're going to get the deal."

He opened the dresser drawer and placed three pairs of folded boxer shorts inside. Then he removed the Gideon Bible and placed it on top of the dresser. Somehow it didn't seem right for the Holy Scriptures to share a drawer with his underwear.

"What?...I'm a little tired....Nothing....It's a lot of work just to *not* sell a couple dozen radios."

He carried his shaving kit into the bathroom and unpacked it. "What's doing in Fort Wayne?...Again? What was his excuse this time?...Sabos took it! Tell him that if he loses another jacket he's going to pay for it out of his allowance."

He removed the last items from the roller bag. He left a pair of red plaid pajama bottoms on the bed; he would need those later.

"I'm just going to go down to the bar for a drink and then hit the hay....What am I going to have? Glenjohnnie, neat." Something his wife said made him laugh. "Right," he replied. "That's me. Dunn, Associated Industries."

CHAPTER 6

O'HARE AT NATIONAL AIRPORT

Ay, now am I in Arden, the more fool I. When I was at home, I was in a better place, but travelers must be content.
 – William Shakespeare, *As You Like It*, 2.4

Joe removed another suitcase from the bellman cart and slid it into the luggage compartment of the bus. The big UWL motor coach loomed in the semi-circular driveway of the Hotel Barnett. As soon as all the wrestlers boarded, and the last bags were loaded, the bus would emerge from under the *porte cochere* and drive the few blocks to National Airport. A crowd waited on the sidewalk across from the hotel entrance, hoping to get a glimpse of Kong, Bulldozer, and the others as they pushed through the revolving door. As Joe loaded the luggage, excited children speculated about the owner of each suitcase.

When the cart was empty, Joe wheeled it back into the lobby and waited for an elevator. He leaned on the bellman cart and ran a hand through his red hair. Carrying the suitcases for an entire wrestling team had required many trips, but now he was down to the last load. It was worth it. He had gotten three new autographs. The only one he missed was Cheri Tarte. She wasn't in her room. It was too bad; he was looking forward to showing her signature to the guys at Pentagon Palace. Granted, it wasn't as cool as it would have been before last night.

FULL ASYLUM

A chime sounded and one of the elevator doors slid open. Joe scooched the cart to one side to allow several wrestlers to exit. Most wore baseball caps and sunglasses. Apparently they were under the delusion that these disguises would prevent the public from recognizing them. No doubt the public would take them for an ordinary group of Washington, DC, tourists in which the men happened to have an average weight of two hundred and fifty pounds and the women happened to have an average bra size of 38DD.

One man—clearly not a wrestler—remained on the elevator. He wore a suit jacket and a dress shirt, no tie, and a pair of red plaid pajama bottoms. He was unshaven and his hair was uncombed. He blinked a few times, as if he had just arrived in bright sunshine instead of the dimly lit lobby of the Hotel Barnett.

"You getting off, dude?" Joe asked. The bellboy later told the lieutenant from the CREEPS that he thought the man, or as he called him, *the Dude*, was on drugs. That's why Joe noticed him right away, and also because of the pajama bottoms.

Joe's inquiry brought the Dude out of his trance. He exited the elevator. As he crossed the lobby, Joe watched to see where he went; he disappeared behind the Christmas tree. Joe pushed the empty bellman cart slowly past to get a better look at what he was up to. He was holding up an IQPhone and taking pictures surreptitiously. *The Dude's a spy!*

The Dude aimed his camera at Joe. Seeing the surveillance target looking back at him, he said, "Bellboy, please bring my bags down to the lobby."

"I'll need to know your room number," Joe replied.

"Exactly," the Dude said knowingly, as if Joe had given him the correct response to the recognition signal. He put the IQPhone in Joe's hand. "Get this to HQ immediately." Then he disappeared in the direction of the gift shop.

Joe wondered what that was all about. He looked at the IQPhone and saw the name of the owner on the display: Victor Shepherd, Fort Wayne, IN. It was a good thing Mr. Shepherd hadn't stuck around. The union steward had given Joe strict instructions that no one should see what he was about to do.

Back on the twenty-sixth floor, he wheeled the last load of luggage—the bags from Kong's room—into the elevator. The door slid closed. Alone inside, Joe pulled the red emergency stop button to make sure that no one entered until he was done. He turned the biggest suitcase over and pulled up on the outer panel. He heard the rip of Velcro as the panel came free, revealing a thick 8 ½ x 11 envelope. Joe picked it up. It felt like there were bundles of cash inside, but he couldn't be sure. Of course, he knew better than to open it: he had been given strict instructions about that too. Joe hid the envelope under his uniform jacket and replaced the panel on the suitcase. Then he pushed the emergency stop back into position.

β 1 1

For forty-five painful minutes, the security line inched along the black- and rust-colored stone floor of Terminal C. Gimbel knew it was forty-five minutes because he checked the Chromega during every one of them. The stink of urine pervaded the airport. All along the concourse homeless people dozed on tattered blankets or asked the passengers for spare change. It was hard to ignore their pleas—with the line barely moving, Gimbel couldn't just walk away. After he had exhausted the change in his pockets, he avoided eye contact by staring upwards. The vaulted ceiling reminded Gimbel of the nave of a cathedral. He thought that was appropriate with so many passengers praying they'd be home for Christmas.

A murmur spread along the security line. Travelers faced the large windows and pointed. A few took pictures. Gimbel turned to see what they were looking at. Next to an airplane a bus discharged its passengers; the UWL logo was painted on both vehicles. The wrestlers climbed the stairs to board their flight. In the terminal, passengers argued over whether the tall gentleman in the white suit was Kong. Cheri Tarte swaggered next to him; she seemed more cheerful than she was when she apologized to Gimbel last night.

At last Gimbel reached the front of the line. He slipped into the privacy booth where a TSA inspector waited inside. The inspector closed the curtain. He was an elderly man with crooked yellow teeth. "Please remove your clothes," he said to Gimbel. His breath smelled of onions.

Gimbel removed his overcoat and handed it to the old man. As the inspector sifted the pockets and felt up the lining for hidden objects, Gimbel unbuttoned his shirt. He took off each item of apparel in turn and passed it to the inspector. At last he stood naked under the fluorescent lamps and curled his bare feet away from the cold floor. The inspector reached into a cardboard box, pulled out a surgical rubber glove, and snapped it over a gnarled hand.

The cavity search was unpleasant, but Gimbel had nothing to hide. Dressed again, he exited the booth and approached the baggage inspection station. He now saw why the line moved so slowly. A short brunette security guard made small talk with every passenger about the items in their carry-ons. She wore a blue security uniform and work boots and a rectangular ID hung from a lanyard around her neck. It displayed her name, Dora Jarr, in block letters beneath her picture. She confronted an old lady in a green jogging suit across the inspection table. Several plastic bins, a computer, an air horn, and the contents of the lady's purse were spread out on the table. The guard questioned the lady about some photos she found in the purse.

"This is Randy," the grandmother explained. "He's my daughter Susan's oldest. And this is Mitchell, my son Terry's middle child. He does very well in school. Barry plays Little

League. I went to one of his games, but the other team didn't show up."

Gimbel suddenly realized he knew the old woman. It was Mrs. Bentel, his co-contestant on *Sorry*. Clearly she had recovered completely from her on-air fainting spell. Gimbel fumed as Mrs. Bentel went on about Mindy who plays the flute and Brad who's into computers. Finally she came to the end of the stack of snapshots. Dora Jarr continued her search.

"What's this?" she asked, fingering a circular metal object.

"Oh, that's a compact."

"Is it gold?"

"Yes. My husband gave it to me on our last anniversary."

The guard opened the compact and sniffed the contents. "This powder looks suspicious to me. I'll have to confiscate it. It might be anthrax."

Mrs. Bentel protested politely. "Please let me keep it. It has great sentimental value to me."

"If you don't cooperate with the security procedures, I'm going to call the police."

"May I speak with your supervisor please?"

"That's it! I warned you." Dora Jarr beckoned to a nearby policeman. After a brief conversation he handcuffed Mrs. Bentel. She started to say something, but then her eyes rolled up and she fell to the floor. The policeman summoned the paramedics over his radio while Dora Jarr tossed the gold compact into a gray plastic bin. The compact joined an heirloom fountain pen ("You could stab someone with that"), three silver necklaces ("You could strangle someone with those"), and a bottle of Moche perfume ("You could start a fire with that").

FULL ASYLUM

β 1 1

The hotel gift shop carried the usual collection of mass-market paperbacks: romances, a few business books, and lots of spy novels. Gold letters on brightly colored backgrounds proclaimed, "*Bitterweed*—a Jon Dunn thriller by Ethan Fielding," "*One Dies Every Minute*—the Dunn classic," and "*Error of the Moon*—soon to be a major motion picture starring Grant Casey as Jon Dunn, Ethan Fielding's Secret Agent Beta Eleven."

Victor Shepherd studied the covers for some time. Finally, he picked up a copy of *Blueprint for Terror* ("The International Dunn Bestseller!") and skimmed a few pages. One page got his attention. Horror shot up his spine and purged the drowsiness from his eyelids. Still holding the novel, he ran out of the store. "Sir!" the cashier yelled after him from her candy-ringed platform. "Sir! You have to pay for that, sir!" But the man in the plaid pajama bottoms kept running until he reached the revolving door. He pushed through at full speed, causing an elderly couple that was already in the door to stumble. A taxi waited in the driveway. He tossed the book into the back seat and leaped in after it. "Airport," he said.

β 1 1

The line stood still for several minutes while the paramedics arrived, examined Mrs. Bentel, and wheeled her away on a gurney. Finally Dora shouted, "Next!"

A stylish woman in a pinstripe business suit approached the table. Dora asked her to take off her shoes.

"These are very nice," she said as she turned them over in her hands. "The leather is so soft. Where did you get them?"

"They're Italian. I got them in Italy."

"I wish I could go to Italy, but the TSA doesn't pay very well. Did you go to the Coliseum?"

"Is this question really necessary?" the businesswoman snapped.

"If you don't cooperate with the security procedures, I'm going to call the police."

The businesswoman cooperated—she saw what happened to Mrs. Bentel and she didn't want to miss her flight. She was trying to squeeze in one last meeting before the holiday. After recounting her Italian sojourn day by day, the conversation returned to the shoes.

"I can't get over how pretty they are. You said you bought them in Milan?"

"Yes."

"They're even my size. Can I try them on?"

The businesswoman nodded reluctantly. The guard sat down and took her time unlacing her black work boots. The fit of the Italian pumps was excellent. After walking back and forth across the security area a couple of times, the guard said, "You know, these heels are really very sharp. You could stab someone with them. I'm afraid I'm going to have to confiscate them."

The businesswoman started to protest, but thought better of it. She skulked to her gate in her stockings.

"Next!"

Gimbel stepped up to the inspection table and came face to face with Dora Jarr.

β 1 1

"If you don't cooperate with the security procedures, I'm going to call the police."

Gimbel had no carry-on bags. He had dropped his car keys and his cell phone in his checked luggage and given away his spare change. He thought he had nothing on him that would instigate a conversation with Dora Jarr. But when she noticed his Chromega watch she said, "There are an awful lot of dials and buttons. You could be trying to bring a time bomb onto a plane."

"There's a time bomb on these planes," someone shouted from behind Gimbel. Gimbel pivoted. A man in red plaid pajama bottoms ran towards the inspection station. Shoving Gimbel aside, he spoke urgently to Dora Jarr. "My name is Jon Dunn. I must speak with your supervisor. This airport must be evacuated forthwith. There are bombs on these planes."

"Sir," said the guard, "You must calm down. No one is allowed in this area until they've been strip-searched. If you do not return to the privacy booth immediately, I'm going to call the police."

The man waved a paperback novel. "I know their plans," he said. "There is no time for the privacy booth." He vaulted over the inspection table, dropping the book in the process. Clearing the table, he ran towards the gates. Dora reached for her air horn and pulled the trigger.

β 1 1

The private jet climbed out of Andrews Air Force Base. Inside, Attorney General Peterson spoke into the telephone. "Thanks, Chris," he said. "Where do we stand on your probable cause problem? Did the e-mail I sent you make it go away?…That's terrific.…I have to protect the source, I'm afraid. Let's just say it's someone who will make sure we nail the bastards.…When will you be ready to pull the trigger?…That's too late. My political advisor here says it's got to be April." He nodded to the man seated opposite him. They shared a silent chuckle—Chris's protests were audible over the handset. "Get it done, Chris," Peterson said.

He replaced the receiver in the base built into the table beside him. Two crystal glasses stood next to the phone, one of ice water, the other of whiskey. A chime announced that the fasten seat belt sign was off and it was permitted to move about the cabin. Peterson opened the buckle of his safety belt and looked out the oval window. He could see his own office on the top floor of the Department of Justice building. Next door, at the National Archives, he observed crowds of tourists in heavy overcoats lining up to see the Declaration of Independence and the Constitution.

His political advisor guessed his thoughts. "I was correct about the Constitution, was I not, Bill?"

Peterson swiveled in his caramel-colored armchair to face the other man. "It's touching that the public cares so much about our founding documents," he said, "but yes, you were right. The political mapmakers are aware of me now, and I have you to thank. You came up with the idea for my speech in the Senate."

"You're not just on the political map, Bill. I took the liberty of commissioning some polls. You're the most popular politician in the country."

"I saw the reports. It's pretty thin support. Most people don't know enough about me to have a negative opinion."

"Then we'll just have to educate them as to what a caring and effective leader you are. There will be plenty of opportunities between now and April."

Peterson picked up the whiskey glass and sipped thoughtfully. He had the sort of lean build that looked good in expensive open-collared white shirts and neatly pressed slacks, which is what he wore now. A profile in the *Washington Courier* said that he looked like an older version of the actor who played Jon Dunn in the 1990s. "It's going to be a challenge to have everything in place by April," he said. "Are you sure that's the right time?"

"Absolutely," his advisor replied. "Just over eighteen months before the election. We can't wait longer than that to announce your candidacy."

"How's the war chest?"

"Coming along nicely. In fact, you received a significant donation this morning from the Hotel and Restaurant Workers Union."

"That's excellent," said Peterson.

"It will buy a few commercials."

"No, I meant the scotch. Are you sure you won't have some?"

An electronic buzz interrupted them. A red light flashed on the telephone. Peterson answered and listened to an agitated voice on the other end. "Is anyone hurt?...That's good. I'll be there in a few. Make sure there's no problem about landing." He hung up and said to his advisor, "One of those opportunities we talked about is knocking on our bulkhead. Let's show the public what a caring and effective leader I am." He pressed the button for the intercom. "Turn us around," he instructed the pilot. "Take us to National."

The plane banked as Bill Peterson refastened his seat belt.

β 1 1

"We are on an active taxiway," Marge said over the PA system. "All passengers must return to their seats and fasten their safety belts."

"THAT MEANS YOU BRENDA," Bulldozer shouted.

"I have to pee," Brenda Biggs protested as she continued down the aisle to the aft lavatory. "It's not like we're going anywhere."

The flight attendant insisted. "It is a violation of federal regulations to disregard instructions from a flight crew."

"*Federal* regulations? Sorry, I didn't know." She hurried back to her seat. Marge surveyed the cabin, her eyes narrowed. The wrestlers were arranged in neat rows and columns. Her partner, a pretty blonde named Nicole, sat in the jump seat, absorbed in a paperback romance. Marge's thin lips turned upwards; order had been restored to the world.

Two rows in front of Brenda, Titan stretched his legs. The tallest member of the UWL, he always occupied the first seat behind the buffet table to enjoy the extra legroom. The table was bare now, but the flight attendants would lay out a spread once they were in the air. Titan took a deep breath and inhaled the aroma of coffee and plastic. Next to him, Suzie Winsome said, "We've been sitting here for an hour and that flight attendant hasn't told us a thing. Does anyone know what's wrong with the plane?"

"There's nothing wrong with the plane," said Kong. He sat in 23D with a martini glass in one hand and a book in the other. Cheri Tarte dozed in the window seat next to him. "It's not the plane at all. It's a sabo threat."

"Oh, bullcrap," said Bulldozer. "Why do you think it's a sabo threat? Did you get some news on your IQPhone?"

"No, my IQPhone is not working."

"Then how do you know?"

"Because my IQPhone is not working. Standard procedure for a federal operation. Jam all cellular frequencies to prevent sabos from communicating with each other or remotely detonating explosives. The other reason I know is by looking out the window. It's not just us. This whole airport is stopped."

Bulldozer looked. Planes were lined up on the taxiways, but none of them moved.

Joy was worried. "If there's a sabo threat, shouldn't we be getting out of here?"

"We're the only ones on this plane," Kong reassured her. "We're much safer than the ladies and gentlemen on commercial flights." He gestured to the airfield with his martini glass. "They're surrounded by strangers, any one of whom might be a sabo. So unless you're secretly a saboteur, Joy, I'd say we're in the safest place in the airport. Do you have anything you want to confess?"

Joy relaxed. "Not me. But Bulldozer looks twitchy."

"Very funny," Bulldozer snorted. "So what are we going to do?"

"I'm going to pee my pants if they don't let us get up soon," Brenda complained.

"I for one am going to take advantage of the perquisites of not flying commercial," said Kong. "I'll wager that, in addition to being the only stranger-free zone in town, this plane is the only place in the airport that still has beverage service." He reached overhead and pressed the fight attendant call button.

At the front of the cabin, Nicole told Marge, "I'll get it." She walked down the aisle to row twenty-three, where Kong handed her his empty glass. "Another gimlet, please," he said.

"Certainly, sir." Her freckled nose wrinkled as she flashed a smile at him.

"Take it easy, big guy," said Bulldozer as Nicole returned to the galley for limejuice and gin. "We don't want anyone crock-faced during the show tonight."

"I assume that metaphor refers to my degree of sobriety rather than your own ugly mug. Because there's nothing we can do about that flattened nose of yours before we get to Tulsa."

"You asshole."

Nicole interrupted. "Your drink, sir." She handed the pale green liquid to Kong.

"Thank you."

She lingered in the aisle. "I'll bet you could drink a lot of these, being a big guy. You wouldn't get drunk at all."

"Size does have its advantages."

"What book is that? It looks old."

He told her about the leather-bound Victorian novel, Benjamin Disraeli's *Henrietta Temple*. "It's considered a classic," he said, "yet I doubt it's much different from that brightly colored soft cover you have." Flattered that he noticed what she read, Nicole flirted with him for several minutes. He was about to offer her backstage passes when a curt voice on the PA system interrupted them. "Nicole, please return to the galley."

"Don't get too close to these guys," Marge told her when she got to the front of plane. "You don't want them to forget that we're the authorities here."

From his seat, Kong called out to his teammates. "We mustn't disappoint the good people of Tulsa, Oklahoma. And since we're stuck here, who's up for some rehearsal?"

"Yeah, right," Bulldozer said sarcastically. "Let's have a smackdown in the aisle. 'Cause that flight attendant's just itching to tell us about federal regulations against powerslamming when the seat belt sign is on."

"I was thinking of rehearsing *dialogue*." He closed Disraeli, placed the small volume in the seat back pocket in front of him, and removed the script for tonight's show.

The other wrestlers followed suit, reaching into seat pockets and carry-on bags. A few had to get bags out of the overhead compartments. Marge removed the PA system handset from its cradle, but the wrestlers were back in their seats before she could switch it on.

"Suzie, start at the top of page 19," Kong said.

"I made a big mistake, running off with Cheri Tarte. Kong, I'm so sorry. Please take me back."

"Kong miss Suzie."

"That's so sweet. I missed you, too, babe."

"Wait, Kong not finish. Kong miss Suzie. But Suzie mean to Kong. Suzie say Kong not man enough. Kong not know what Kong will do."

Loud sirens interrupted the rehearsal. A CREEPS Humvee led two unmarked trucks across the tarmac. All had blue flashing lights.

"They're coming right towards us," Joy cried. "The sabos must be after *this* plane. What should we do?"

But the trucks kept going. Rows of men with military postures and black body armor sat in the backs. Rifles stood ready at their sides. The three vehicles disappeared behind the terminal C gates. The sirens stopped, but the wrestlers could still see the reflection of blue lights flashing on the blacktop.

"We should continue where we left off," said Kong.

"Kong not know what Kong will do."

"I'll tell you what to do," Brenda Biggs interrupted. "Forget about this cheap tramp."

"YOU STAY OUT OF THIS, BRENDA," shouted Suzie.

"Someone should keep you away from Kong. You had no right to hurt him the way you did. I'm gonna smash your baby face right now."

"Brenda," said Kong. "It's flat. It's perfunctory. I'm not believing."

"I can't help it. I still have to pee."

"You're the toughest Vixen in the UWL. It says so in the script. Act like it. You're not going to let a full bladder stop you. Show us real anger."

"I'M GONNA SMASH YOUR BABY FACE RIGHT NOW. I'LL SHOW YOU WHO'S THE TOUGHEST VIXEN IN THE UWL. I AM. I'M IN CHARGE HERE. IF I TELL YOU TO STAY AWAY FROM KONG, THEN DAMMIT, YOU'LL STAY AWAY FROM KONG. AND IF I WANT TO PEE, THEN DAMMIT, I'M GOING TO PEE."

She leaped out of her chair and ran down the aisle.

"Now I believe it," said Kong. The flight attendant, shocked by the revolt, said nothing.

Bulldozer looked out the window. "There's a plane coming in."

β 1 1

The plane rolled to a stop and the door opened. Attorney General Peterson bent in the entry and surveyed the scene in front of him. He now wore a jacket and tie and was pulling on a blue woolen overcoat. Across the apron, a large passenger jet waited at the end of a jetway. Through the jetway window Peterson could see a crowd of people gathered at the doorway to the airplane. Staircases had been pushed up against the other entrances. CREEPS stood guard all around. A Humvee and two trucks with flashing blue lights were parked nearby, along with several news trucks, their antennas telescoping into the cold gray sky.

Peterson bounded down the steps of his plane as the flight attendant closed the door behind him, sealing the cabin against the December chill. News cameras and flashbulbs followed the attorney general as he jogged across the tarmac; the skirts of his coat waved in the breeze behind him. He mounted the flimsy metal staircase to the jetway and opened the door. People crammed the small space inside. Most of them were shouting. It reminded Peterson of the trading pit at a commodities exchange. Troops in bulletproof vests guarded the airplane door, trying to keep the crowd away. Airline maintenance men unpacked tools. Down the jetway, CREEPS questioned the flight crew and gate attendant. Reporters with their IQPhones in record mode sought statements from anyone who would talk to them. When they saw the attorney general enter, they pushed towards him while shouting questions. "Mr. Peterson, do we know who the suspect is?" "Mr. Peterson, is this a sabo attack?"

The crowd parted for Peterson as he approached the senior officer. "What is the situation?" he demanded.

"A single suspect is inside the plane, sir. Male Caucasian, mid-to-late thirties. Wearing a suit jacket and pajama bottoms," the officer replied.

"How did he get in?"

FULL ASYLUM

"He pushed his way past the gate attendant when she unlocked the door to let the flight crew board. Then he ran down the jetway and boarded the plane. The plane was empty except for a maintenance man. The suspect shoved him into the jetway and locked the bulkhead behind him. He must have jammed the door mechanisms—we can't get any of them unlocked."

"Get them open."

"A workman is on his way with a blowtorch. We're going to cut our way in. It might take a few hours, but we'll get inside."

Peterson wondered whether it would be too late in a few hours. "Is the suspect armed?" he asked.

"We questioned the flight crew and the maintenance man and they told us they didn't see any weapons. We can't know for sure, though."

"Do you know where he is inside the plane?" Peterson asked, looking thoughtfully at the aircraft.

"The forward galley."

Peterson walked to the bulkhead and tried to peer through the porthole. The shade was drawn.

"I suggest you step back from the bulkhead, sir," the officer said. "If the suspect is armed, it's not safe."

"How do you know he's in the galley?" Peterson asked, without moving. "You can't see him."

The officer jerked his head in the direction of a soldier with a listening device pressed against the fuselage. "We can hear him. He's doing some sort of mechanical work. We hear him hammering something metal, and also an electric drill."

"Where did he get the tools?"

"The maintenance man had them."

"Do you hear anything else?"

"Yes. He's humming."

"He's humming? What's he humming?"

The soldier passed a set of headphones to Peterson. Holding a speaker against one ear, Peterson listened to the whine of a power tool. Then the whine stopped and, sure enough, the suspect was humming. Peterson recognized the tune.

It was the Jon Dunn theme.

β 1 1

The turbulence caused the screwdriver to slip. Dunn retrieved it from the cockpit floor and tried again. He removed the last screw and wedged the point of the screwdriver between the edge of the faceplate and the housing. Gingerly, he pried the faceplate open to reveal the interior of the bomb. The numbers on the LED display continued their relentless countdown. Two minutes. Dunn took a deep breath through the oxygen mask and studied the intricate arrangement of wires; it reminded him of the capellini at the little trattoria in Siena. He fished in the toolbox for a pair of wire cutters. The hammering on the cockpit door had stopped. Clearly air was becoming scarce in the main cabin.

Gimbel sat on the floor of the inspection area reading *Blueprint for Terror*. He had found it under the table where the man in the pajama bottoms had dropped it. Gimbel marked his place in the book with his boarding pass and stood to stretch his legs. Beyond the inspection station the gates were still deserted, as they had been since the TSA evacuated the gate area and ordered all passengers back to the security line. The sky was growing dark beyond the windows. Gimbel could no longer see the river. He looked at his Chromega, which, for the time being, was safe from Dora Jarr. Four hours had passed since the man had jumped the table. At least Gimbel would be first in line when the gates re-opened. He wondered when that would be. He could see the overhead monitors in the gate area, but they were too far away to make out the flight numbers and estimated departure times. He sat down again, cross-legged, and resumed reading.

Dora Jarr sat in a black plastic chair opposite him. She held the gray bin in her lap. Rifling through its contents, she found something shiny: Mrs. Bentel's compact. Dora pulled it out of the bin and admired the polished gold cover. She turned it over several times and fumbled with the latch. The color of the makeup inside delighted her. She dabbed some on her cheeks and studied herself in the mirror.

β 1 1

Brenda Biggs's trip to the lavatory was like the Battle of Lexington—a small skirmish, but one that started a revolution.

The wrestlers used the restroom when they wanted. Each time, the flight attendant ordered them to return to their seats, but they ignored her. They were all starving; they were used to eating every four hours. Eventually Bulldozer yelled, "HEY! HOW 'BOUT SOME FOOD BACK HERE?" Nicole started to get up from the jump seat, but Marge stopped her with a gesture and a sour look. When no one responded to him, Bulldozer repeatedly pressed his call button. Finally Marge came over the PA system. "We regret the delay in our food service. As we could be cleared for takeoff at any time, service items have to remain stowed. We will set out the buffet once we are airborne. We apologize for the inconvenience and request that all passengers stop pressing their flight attendant call buttons."

Bulldozer stood and advanced towards the galley. "THE FLIGHT ATTENDANT SAYS THAT WE HAVE TO STOP PRESSING THE CALL BUTTONS. WELL I SAY IF SHE WON'T TAKE A CALL, THEN SHE'S GOING TO TAKE A FALL." Several more wrestlers joined him in the aisle. Marge pushed the beverage cart into their path. Bulldozer hoisted it off the floor and heaved it into an empty row of seats. Ice cubes and miniature liquor bottles scattered.

Brenda and Bulldozer leaped into the galley. While Brenda held Marge by the wrists, Bulldozer opened the refrigerator door. "Do something," Marge yelled to Nicole.

Nicole didn't move from the jump seat. "We're on an active taxiway," she said. "Federal law requires me to remain in my seat with my seatbelt fastened."

Bulldozer reached into the refrigerator and pulled out a ham with one hand. With the other, he pulled the PA system handset toward him, stretching the spiral cord. "DINNER TIME!" he said into the handset. "WHO WANTS HAM?"

"OVER HERE!" Titan yelled. "I'M OPEN."

Bulldozer tossed the ham at Titan, but it went wide and hit Suzie Winsome in the head. "YOU SON OF A BITCH!" she yelled. Wrestlers jumped out of their seats into the aisle like hockey players clearing the bench. Soon all the seats were empty, except in row twenty-three, an island of calm amid the storm. Kong sipped his gimlet and watched the riot as if it were theater. Cheri Tarte still slept in the window seat, or pretended to. If anyone had paid attention to her, they would have noticed a smile on her face.

Suzie Winsome picked the ham up off the floor and threw it back towards the galley. It bounced off Brenda Biggs's cheek, leaving a greasy spot and causing her to loosen her grip on the flight attendant. Marge twisted free and pounded on the cockpit door. "Let me in," she yelled. "They're out of control back here."

β 1 1

The workman knelt in the jetway. He held the blowtorch steady as the flame cut into the aircraft door. Sparks scattered where the flame bit the metal; a blackened incision marked its progress. A squadron of CREEPS stood alert, ready for action the moment the door opened. Attorney General Peterson and the reporters stood behind them. Acetylene and oxygen hissed as they flowed into the torch.

Suddenly a loud pop signaled that the lock had broken free from the bulkhead. It dangled from the fresh opening in the metal. The workman took off his safety goggles and wheeled the tanks out of the path of the soldiers. The soldiers pulled their night vision masks down over their faces. Their commander made a cutting gesture across his throat. In response, an electrician shut off the external power to the plane. The suspect would now be in the dark.

The commander counted down from three with his fingers. When he reached one, a soldier pulled the aircraft door open and the squadron burst into the cabin. In a moment, one of them yelled, "Secure!" Reporters and cameramen ran through the bulkhead with less discipline than the soldiers. One of them would win a Pulitzer Prize for the iconic photo of Attorney General Peterson's silhouette framed in the aircraft door, the bright light behind him contrasting with the still darkened cabin.

The fluorescent lights flickered on and Peterson surveyed the cabin. Three soldiers guarded a man wearing red plaid pajama bottoms. Handcuffs held his arms in place behind his back. The suspect introduced himself to Peterson. "Dunn, Associated Industries. You are perfectly safe. I disarmed the bomb." Unable to move his hands, he gestured to the galley floor with his chin.

Peterson followed the gesture and saw the dismembered corpse of an aircraft coffee maker. Among the twisted bits of metal he could distinguish a filter, a heating coil, and a coffee pot. But there was no dynamite, no fuse, and no timer. It was just a coffee maker.

β 1 1

The Department of Justice seal hung on the podium beneath a bouquet of microphones. The transparent screens of a teleprompter spread out from the sides of the podium like wings. A throng of reporters waited for the attorney general to make his appearance. Cameramen stood behind tripod-mounted units or moved about with video cameras on their shoulders. Beyond the podium, on the other side of security, CREEPS swept the gate area to ensure the suspect had not left anything harmful behind. They searched under seats and rummaged through trash bins.

Attorney General Peterson emerged from a privacy booth that had been converted to a surrogate green room. He stepped up to the podium where Dora Jarr was waiting. Although she was a little taller now in her Italian high-heeled shoes, the attorney general still towered over her. Under the vaulted ceiling of the concourse, a line of police held passengers and homeless a hundred feet away. After the long day, it was hard to tell which were which. They all craned their necks to see what was happening.

"Ladies and gentlemen," said Peterson. "I am happy to report that today's bomb scare was a hoax. The alleged perpetrator is in custody. We have identified him as Victor Shepherd of Fort Wayne, Indiana. Mr. Shepherd is showing symptoms of an unbalanced mental state. He has been taken to Walter Reed hospital for observation and his family has been notified.

"I can say that he is not a known sabo. We have learned that he spent last night at the Barnett Hotel in Crystal City. Most of what we found in his room was normal enough. He apparently had been reading the Gideon Bible while he was there. It had been removed from the drawer and sat on top of the dresser. We are currently following up to determine if Mr. Shepherd had ties to religious extremist groups. We are also concerned by the discovery of a laptop computer with plans for the F-38 fighter jet. The documents aren't classified, but they're not for the general public either; they're what the military calls Distribution D. We will release more details during the coming weeks, as the investigation unfolds.

FULL ASYLUM

"The airport will remain closed for tonight while we finish securing the gate area. All flights have been cancelled until tomorrow morning.

"I realize that the events of today disrupted holiday plans for thousand of travelers. Nevertheless, I hope that some good will come from them. When I was at Harvard Law School, I learned the importance of civility. If nothing else, today's events underscore the need to restore civility to our national debate. I appeal to those of you in the media and in the blogosphere who are critical of the administration to exercise greater caution before you speak. As we saw today, your words have consequences.

"Finally, I would like to recognize the real hero of today. Dora Jarr is the security guard who raised the alarm when the suspect jumped the security line. Her quick thinking prevented what might have been a serious national tragedy." Peterson turned to the guard and reached down to shake her hand. "Ms. Jarr," he continued, "in recognition of your heroism, I have arranged a transfer for you. Starting tomorrow you will be stationed at the Department of Justice building."

"Department of Justice building?"

"Yes, in the city. It will be a great improvement for you. You will no longer have to commute to the airport, no longer have to search carry-on bags."

"No carry-on bags?"

"No. The folks coming to work at the Department of Justice usually just carry briefcases with laptop computers and a few papers."

"So they don't bring a lot of shoes and jewelry?"

"Just what they're wearing. Think of it, you won't have to deal with a lot of rude strangers either. You'll get to see the same people everyday. In a few weeks, everyone will know you."

"Know me?"

"Yes. We're very friendly at DOJ. Why do you look so disappointed? This is a great honor for you. I won't take no for an answer."

β 1 1

Gimbel laughed as he listened to the car radio. Dora Jarr's days of confiscating suspicious yet expensive carry-on items were over. His Chromega watch was the last thing she would ever try to steal.

Gimbel had watched Dora paw through her bin of other peoples' property until a phone call told her to clear the inspection area. Furious that he had lost his place at the front of the line, he stood behind the row of police and watched technicians set up the podium and cameras for the attorney general's press conference. He stayed until the word *canceled* appeared next to the entries on the flight monitors. After claiming his suitcase from the carousel, he tried to reschedule his flight on his IQPhone, but he couldn't get a signal. Then he started driving.

The skies cleared just outside the beltway. Now, as he traveled the dark Maryland countryside between Frederick and Hagerstown, stars filled Gimbel's windshield. There were more of them than he ever saw amid the lighted windows and street lamps of Fox Hunt Apartments. On the radio, the press conference ended and an announcer provided commentary.

"Although he gave the credit to security guard Dora Jarr, there is no doubt that the real hero of today is Attorney General Peterson. He showed real leadership in the decisive way he took charge of the operation. He reminded many observers of Mayor Giuliani after September 11. Although Peterson has long been known to beltway insiders, there is no doubt that after today he is a national figure.

"Today's sabo attack affected many people, among them the athletes of the Universal Wrestling League. The UWL team waited aboard their private plane for six hours before deboarding and returning to their Washington-area hotel. Tonight's show in Tulsa, Oklahoma, has been canceled. The revenue loss to parent company Consolidated Studios is estimated at $1.6 million. In a related story, following the departure of the team from the aircraft, a maintenance crew found flight attendant Marge Dennis in the forward lavatory. She was tied up with what appeared to be the handset cord from the public address system. A TSA spokesman said that when questioned by police, Ms. Dennis merely kept repeating, 'It is a violation of federal regulations to disregard instructions from a flight crew.' Since she made no specific complaint, no charges will be filed."

Gimbel pressed the scan button on the radio. Entertainment was returning to the airwaves after a day of special news broadcasts. The radio skipped from rock and roll to C&W to sports to a Spanish channel. Finally Gimbel heard Christmas carols and stopped the scan. On the radio, the choir of a famous cathedral sang of mistletoe, chestnuts, and traveling home.

CHAPTER 7

BAD NEIGHBORS

NEIGHBOR, n. One whom we are commanded to love as ourselves, and who does all he knows how to make us disobedient.
— Ambrose Bierce, *The Devil's Dictionary*

"What do you mean, he can't drink?" The director sat at the head of the table in the windowless conference room. Various assistants were scattered among the other chairs. Laptops, three ring binders, and IQPhones lay in front of them on the laminated tabletop. It was a meeting where real work was being done.

"That's what Isaac said in his e-mail," the head writer explained. He read out loud, "I just previewed the footage from the office scene with Iona Klimt. Remove the part with the vodka, along with any alcohol in the rest of the script. In a nation where twelve thousand people die every year due to driving under the influence, Consolidated Studios will not present the public with a role model who imbibes alcoholic beverages. Especially when Beta Eleven is going to get in a car in the next scene."

The director blinked. "Oh, for Pete's sake," he said. "Whoever heard of a teetotaling Jon Dunn? What's Isaac going to do next, make us take out the sex?" After the laugh traveled around the room, he added, "Let's not give him any ideas. For now our problem is to figure out what to do with the office scene."

FULL ASYLUM

"Can we push back?"

"You saw what happened when Cheri Tarte tried it. Anyone else want to be the spokesperson for recycling?"

The silence was awkward as the team considered that fate. Finally, one of the assistant writers asked, "What if we stick in a close-up where Dunn refuses the vodka? Minimal refilming and Isaac would love it."

"It's bad enough that Dunn can't drink," said the head writer. "Do we have to call attention to it?"

"Now hang on," the director said. "There are no bad ideas in brainstorming. Let's pursue this." He turned to the assistant writer. "What's the line? What does Dunn say when he refuses the drink?"

Everyone stared at each other around the conference table. Then the assistant writer blurted out, "I can't think of one! Jon Dunn would never refuse a drink!"

The head writer took a sip from his water glass and realized he had an idea. "Here's what you do. Take out the part where you actually see the vodka bottle. Redub the dialog so that Dunn and Iona are toasting with spring water."

"That's good," said the director. "Figure out what brand he would drink. Something European."

"Won't it seem strange that they're drinking water out of shot glasses?" the assistant writer asked.

"Maybe we'll start a trend. After all, we put 'Glenjohnnie, neat' on the map."

"Wouldn't it be easier to take the toast out entirely?"

"We can't," the head writer explained. "We need the video camera on the shot glass to set up the car chase in the next scene. Its discovery is what causes Mrs. Klimt to send Cheri Tarte after Dunn."

"Speaking of the car chase, what have you got for me?" the director asked.

"Over here," said the stunt coordinator. He and the head writer led the director to a rack on the wall that displayed several neat rows of sketches. The black and white charcoal drawings had the streamlined images and sharp contrasts found in comic books.

"So we're in Washington, right?" the director said as he scanned the storyboard.

"Yep. You're gonna love this. We got so many cool things in here." He giggled.

"Don't tell me what I'm going to think of it. Just show it to me."

The three men walked the wall. The first drawing showed Dunn getting into his Cheetah coupe. In the next he switched on the dashboard display to see the image broadcast from the shot-glass camera he left in Iona Klimt's office.

The third picture was a close-up of the display. Wavy lines shot across it, but there was no image.

In the next drawing, the Cheetah emerged from a parking garage onto a city street.

The car stops at a light.

A second car, with the KDS logo stenciled on the side, drives up behind Dunn.

Dunn views the driver of the second car in his rearview mirror. It is Cheri Tarte, her muscular shoulders stark in black and white.

Dunn pulls into the intersection, against the light. A car swerves to avoid him.

Cheri Tarte follows. Trying to avoid her, two other cars crash head-on. The word *crash* sprawls across the drawing in bold letters.

Dunn turns left onto Constitution Avenue. Six more cars, all with the KDS logo, are waiting for him at the intersection. They join the chase.

Eight cars speed by the White House.

A gunmen leans out the passenger side window of one of the cars and fires at Dunn's Cheetah.

FULL ASYLUM

The bullet bounces off the armored glass of the Cheetah's rear window.

Dunn and his pursuers speed past the panda enclosure at the National Zoo. One of the pandas does a double take.

Dunn leads the convoy up the steps of the Capitol building. Two of the KDS vehicles don't make it. They roll backwards down the steps.

"The National Zoo isn't between the White House and the Capitol," said the director.

"It isn't?"

"No. It isn't near either building. Don't you check these things?"

The cars speed past the Capitol portico. Two men, apparently congressmen, are talking in front. One of them loses his toupee in the slipstream of the passing cars.

The cars drive back down the steps towards Maryland Avenue.

A Capitol policeman sits in a squad car munching a sandwich. Seeing the speeding cars, he speaks into a handheld radio microphone.

A dozen police cars stream out of a garage.

"I think I got the idea," said the director, skipping ahead through the drawings. "What's happening over here?"

"That's where they blow up the Jefferson Memorial."

"Let's go to the end."

Two hundred cars chase Jon Dunn as he speeds towards the Washington Monument.

He turns left onto the driveway that circles the obelisk.

Cheri Tarte speaks into a walkie-talkie.

The pursuing cars split up. Half follow Dunn onto the driveway. The other half turn right and start circling the driveway in the opposite direction.

Dunn sees a hundred cars coming straight at him.

He turns right onto the grass, towards the monument.

The cars moving in opposite directions on the driveway crash into each other. A fireball rises from the two hundred car pile-up.

Cheri Tarte's car speeds towards Dunn from the direction of the monument.

Dunn presses a button on his dashboard. A missile fires from the front of the car.

Cheri Tarte swerves. Her car goes up on one set of wheels as the missile passes underneath.

The missile hits the monument. Another fireball.

The monument sways and then topples onto the National Mall, breaking cleanly into three pieces.

Ten cars crash into the fallen tower.

No longer being chased, Dunn drives casually towards the Franklin Roosevelt Bridge and the road out of town.

"Isn't that cool?" said the stunt coordinator.

The director sighed. "Been there. Done that. There isn't a single original idea in the entire sequence. Dunn drove up the Spanish Steps in Rome in *The Future is Just Beginning*. A bystander lost his toupee during the helicopter chase in *The Merchant of Malice*. And Dunn toppled the Eiffel Tower in *To Die or Not to Die*. It even broke into three pieces."

"This is different. It's the Washington Monument."

The director gave him a look of disbelief. "Try again," he said.

"It's an *homage*." He used the French pronunciation with the silent-h and the accent on the second syllable.

"It's a cop-out. Anyway, lack of originality isn't the only problem. Do you know the most popular Jon Dunn stunt of all time?" he asked patiently.

"Most popular?"

"Yes. Most popular. When we had the fiftieth anniversary celebration for the Jon Dunn franchise, we surveyed the fans.

Who's their favorite Dunn Lady, their favorite Dunn villain, and so on. And we asked their favorite stunt. Guess what the answer was."

The stunt coordinator went over various scenes in his mind. "When the cruise ship crashed into the pier in *Bitterweed*?"

"No."

"When the space station fell from the sky and was skewered by the Empire State Building in *Blueprint for Terror*?"

"No, it was at the beginning of *Best Served Deadly*. Dunn escapes from the Russian aircraft carrier in a motorboat. As he speeds away, an oversized flag unfurls from the stern. Audiences cheered when they saw it was the Union Jack."

"That was it? The British flag?"

"That was it."

"Wasn't *Best Served Deadly* made in like the 1950s?"

"Sixties."

"They didn't even have CG back then."

"No." The director chuckled. "No computer graphics in the '60s. They couldn't put hundreds of vehicles in a car chase or blow up national monuments. Instead they had to come up with something actually fun. With nothing but a motorboat and some red, white, and blue cloth, they created a scene that is still the fan favorite half a century later."

The director returned to the conference table and stood by his chair. The stunt coordinator and the head writer resumed their seats. "We're going on location in Washington in April so we can catch the cherry blossoms," the director said. "The car chase is the last scene we're going to film. That gives you three months to come up with something else. Remember, keep it simple and make it fun."

β 1 1

The sky was clear when the Cheetah YK-9 pulled into the Byte Yourself parking lot. The bright sun created thousands of tiny white-hot reflections on the windshields of cars and the gently rippling waters of the pond. It was a warm morning, but the bare trees and brown grass promised that winter would soon return to Northern Virginia. No water flowed from the fountain pipe that poked the surface of the pond.

The midnight blue YK-9 glided slowly towards Building 2. The price sticker still decorated the window. Rotating at a speed well below its capacity, the 370 horsepower engine merely whispered, hinting at its power. The shiny black tires ground sand into the asphalt. Finding an open parking space, the car curved to a stop.

"A YK-9!" Andy exclaimed as he emerged from his own YK-8 two spaces away. "That's the car that's going to be in *Error of the Moon!*" The passenger doors of Andy's car swung open and Bart, Cindy, and Madame Butterfly stepped out. Andy walked over to the other car and stepped up to the driver's side. A motor whirred, the window slid downwards, and he found himself face to face with Gimbel O'Hare.

"Somebody vested in the stock plan," Cindy said sourly.

Gimbel opened the door and stepped out of the car. He wore a new blue suit with neatly creased trousers and expensive black leather shoes. A perfect dimple marked his necktie just south of the four-in-hand. Cindy wondered why she had never noticed his compelling eyebrows and realized she had never seen them before. The eyeglasses that had hidden them were no longer there.

"When did you get the car?" Andy asked.

"Just now. I picked it up on the way here."

Andy walked around it, admiring the lines. He asked Gimbel for permission to sit in the driver's seat. From the passenger side, Gimbel demonstrated the GPS and then steered Andy to the hood release so they could check out the supercharger. They were just closing the hood when Beverly drove into a nearby space and eavesdropped suspiciously. "That's a sharp car," Andy was saying.

"The suit's sharp too," said Madame Butterfly.

The programmers started towards the entrance to Building 2. Gimbel strode gracefully: no more Groucho walk. Calling after them, Beverly asked Cindy and Daphne to remain behind.

"You guys go ahead," said Cindy. "We'll catch up."

The three men reached the building just as Brownie McCoy arrived and joined them. "Hey, Brownie, how are you today?" Andy asked.

"Can't complain," Brownie replied. "Wouldn't do any good." Noticing Gimbel's sartorial transformation, he said, "Primo threads, man. Do you have a job interview?" The glass door of the lobby closed behind them.

Beverly remained outside with Cindy and Madame Butterfly. With the males out of earshot, she said, "Daphne, what the hell are you doing?"

"I'm talking to you," Madame Butterfly replied.

"No, before that. I heard you compliment Gimbel O'Hare on his suit."

"Well I couldn't compliment his t-shirt. He wasn't wearing one—"

"Has our gals' pact completely slipped your mind?"

"—or if he was, it was on the inside. But then I still couldn't compliment him on it."

"Did you forget that you drank a toast to dragging Gimbel down to hell?"

Cindy intervened. "The pact was for the lawsuit, Beverly. We lost."

"No thanks to you."

"No thanks to me. But we still lost. What else do you expect me to do?"

"I expect you to be persistent."

"Persistent at what, exactly?"

A pair of software engineers passed on their way to the entrance. They were engaged in a heated discussion over which actor was the best Jon Dunn. Beverly gestured for Cindy and Madame Butterfly to follow her to a more secluded section of the parking lot. Then she said, "Persistent in what we set out to do. Keep the pressure on O'Hare. Keep him in the dark. Give him menial assignments. Sooner or later he'll slip up and give us a reason to fire him. Or he'll quit."

"We'll lose a good programmer."

"He's one programmer. What's the big diff?"

"The big diff is that the rest of us will have to put in more overtime to take up the slack. When you drew up the schedule, you forgot to take Christmas vacations into account. Now we're further behind. We need all hands on deck. This isn't the time to make anyone's life miserable."

"He made you miserable—or isn't that important anymore? You accused him of sexual harassment and I took you seriously. I went out on a fricking limb with Addison for you. I'd hate to have to tell him you weren't serious after all."

"Of course I was serious. But as team lead I have to consider other things besides my own feelings."

"Well, be sure to consider how you got to be team lead."

A luxury sedan cruised past. Beverly's head swiveled towards it automatically. "Oh, crap," she said. "That's Addison. I need to see him. Daphne, no more compliments for Gimbel O'Hare."

As Addison backed his car into his reserved space, Beverly ran to catch up with him. Her high heels tapped a rhythm on the pavement. Cindy turned to Madame Butterfly. "Daphne," she said, "when you make a deal with the devil, read the fine print. And also the main provisions."

β 1 1

When Gimbel returned home that night, a light in the apartment upstairs surprised him. It was the first sign of life at the Lazulis' since before Christmas. Gimbel went to the third floor and knocked on the door.

A man opened the door a crack and eyed Gimbel suspiciously. He was in his mid-twenties and had blond hair. Gimbel thought he looked familiar.

"Uh, I'm looking for Mrs. Lazuli," said Gimbel.

"There's no Mrs. Lazuli here," the man replied brusquely as he started to close the door.

"I'm sorry," said Gimbel. "This was her apartment. I don't suppose you know what happened to her?"

"No, I just moved in. Mr. Willow said that the people who used to live here were sabos."

"Did she leave a forwarding address?"

"Don't know. Sorry. Mr. Willow might have it, but if they're really sabos you should stay away from them."

"Forgive me, I should introduce myself. Gimbel O'Hare, Byte Yourself Software. I live downstairs." He extended his hand.

The man's wariness morphed to affability. "Nice to meet you," he said, returning Gimbel's handshake. "I'm Chris Molson." He opened the door the rest of the way. "C'mon in."

Entering the living room, Gimbel was greeted by the odor of fresh paint. Cardboard boxes, many of them open, were scattered around the floor. A young woman in jeans and a checked shirt unpacked legal books from one of them and shelved them in a bookcase. She was slim, pretty, and wore a bandanna around her honey-colored hair. She extended her hand and said, "Lacey Briefs."

"Uh, polka-dotted boxers?" Gimbel replied, confused.

"Lacey Briefs is my name."

"Oh, I'm so sorry—I thought it was a word game." He took her hand. "Gimbel O'Hare."

"Pleased to make your acquaintance."

Gimbel noticed a paintball marker leaning against the fireplace and realized where he had seen Chris before. Chris was the sniper who kept shooting the two kids during Gimbel's first outing at Pentagon Palace. He studied Chris's face for signs of recognition but found none. If Chris remembered him, he was doing a good job of hiding it.

"Where are you from?" Gimbel asked.

"Most recently, Boston," Lacey replied. Her accent suggested that she began life someplace more southerly. "We graduated law school last year and started work in the Department of Justice."

"We've been living in a hotel for months," Chris complained. "It took us forever to find this place." He unpacked a box of electronic equipment. Gimbel saw a Byte Yourself router, a control pad, and a tangle of CAT 5 cable.

"I'd be happy to help you with that stuff," Gimbel said.

"I can get it," Chris replied. There was an edge to his voice. Gimbel wondered if Chris thought the offer made him look bad in front of his girlfriend. "I'm glad we finally found a place, though," Chris continued, "if only so I can have my own paintball equipment again." He picked up the marker. "I'm sick of rentals."

Chris pointed the marker at Gimbel, who noticed the barrel bag hung loose instead of covering the muzzle. Gimbel thought back to the safety lecture on his first day of paintball and counted the number of violations. There were at least three.

"Thanks anyway on the electronics," Chris said, lowering the marker and leaning it against the fireplace again. "If there's anything I can ever do for you, let me know."

β 1 1

It was like a combination of gunfire and air raid sirens.

Gimbel awoke abruptly. He didn't sit up straight like a TV character waking from a nightmare. Instead, he lay tensely under the covers and tried to figure out what the noise was. He was cold and his muscles were tight. He thought he should grab the emergency kit he kept in the closet and then evacuate the apartment. But he didn't move.

He fixed on the clock. Red numbers came into focus. 12:17 a.m. Gimbel's brain came into focus at the same time. There were no bombs falling and no bullets whistling. There were only drums and a bass guitar. Rock music was playing in the apartment upstairs.

He hoped it would stop soon. When it didn't, he tried to go back to sleep, but trying to sleep never works. He put his head under the pillow, but the thumping of drums pursued him even there. He turned on the light and searched a box in his closet for his noise-canceling headphones. They helped a little, although he could still hear the drums. He got back into bed and turned out the light. The headphones were bulky and forced him to lie on his back instead of his side. When he was still awake half an hour later, he removed the headphones, put on his bathrobe, and headed upstairs.

The music was louder on the landing by Chris and Lacey's door. Gimbel had to knock six times before there was a response. Eventually the peephole darkened and Gimbel heard Chris's voice saying, with some surprise, "It's my neighbor. I'll call you back."

When Chris opened the door, Gimbel could see that there were fewer boxes on the floor. The stereo was hooked up and pumping out music. "You told me earlier to ask if I needed anything," Gimbel said, trying to sound friendly. "Well, it's almost 1:00 a.m. and I need something. Please turn the music down."

"I'm not going to watch you sleep!" Chris shouted angrily over the music. He slammed the metal door shut.

β 1 1

"Your mouth is open," said Brownie McCoy.
"It's called a yawn, Brownie," Gimbel replied.

"Up late partying, I hope."

"Just up late. My neighbor played his stereo until 2:00 a.m."

"Bummer, man."

"Every night for a week now."

The Toolbox team was getting settled in the conference room. Cindy connected her laptop to the overhead projector. Andy and Bart pored over the TV listings on an IQPhone. "Here it is," said Bart. "UWL Wrestling. 8:00 p.m. Channel 37. 'Live from the Megadome in Las Vegas. Brenda Biggs and Suzie Winsome fight over Kong. Cage match: Titan vs. the Coroner. Cheri Tarte talks about saving water with fewer flushes.' Sounds like a good one."

"Anyone seen Beverly?" Cindy asked.

"She's probably putting on her makeup," Bart replied.

"That'll be at least half an hour," said Andy. "Cindy, did you ever see her without it in the lady's room or someplace? Because I think if you scraped it all off, her head would be like the size of a golf ball."

Before Cindy could tell her boyfriend to stop being an asshole, Beverly's arrival ended the conversation. She took the seat at the head of the table and asked Gimbel to close the door. Cindy pressed the F4 key on her laptop and a five-foot high Gantt chart appeared on the screen at the front of the room. "Cindy and I put in some OT last night to come up with a new schedule," Beverly explained.

Brownie texted Gimbel: *I bet that means Cindy made the schedule while Beverly made personal phone calls.*

Beverly continued. "I realize it's aggressive but I have confidence this team can step up to the challenge."

The software engineers studied the horizontal bars on the screen and read through the columns of start and end dates. Gimbel spoke first. "It's not aggressive," he said. "It's impossible."

"That word isn't in our vocab," Beverly replied. "Addison is counting on us."

"But look at what you have in the spring. We're supposed to deliver the first of May, which, by the way, is a Sunday. But the first time we test the Toolbox with the application software from the other teams is April 11. If there are any disconnects, we won't have time to fix them. There's got to be an earlier round of integration and debugging some time next month."

Beverly snorted.

"I looked at that," said Cindy. "The Toolbox won't be ready until April. An additional round then would push the schedule out a month. Beverly said we have to hit May 1."

"You'll just have to make sure there aren't any disconnects," Beverly said.

There are always disconnects, Gimbel texted Brownie.

"This is the schedule," Beverly said. "We have to find ways to meet it. Now give me some ideas."

"I got an idea," said Brownie. "Let's smoke a bunch of weed until we're completely baked."

"How will that help us meet the schedule?"

"Meet the schedule?"

Beverly decided it would be best to move on to the next agenda item. Cindy clicked an icon and several paragraphs of single-spaced legalese appeared on the screen. "I got an e-mail from Legal," said Beverly. "They got to find fault with us to justify their existence. Their hoop-of-the-week is code headers. Apparently some of our copyright and proprietary data assertions are wrong. When you start a new file, you should use the code header that you see on the screen. But the files that already exist are going to be a bother. I need a volunteer to go through all of them and make the fixes."

After a moment, Andy said what all the engineers thought. "That's a menial job. It'll take days. Can't we get a co-op to do it?"

"No," said Beverly, "We won't have a co-op until summer." Since there were no volunteers, Beverly made a pretence of trying to decide who would get the assignment. "Sorry, Gimbel," she said at last. "You're the stuckee."

The other members of the team jotted Beverly's decision in their notebooks. They all wanted to have a record that Gimbel was the stuckee and not any of them. On Gimbel's IQPhone, another text message popped up. *Your mouth is open.*

β 1 1

Gimbel closed the washing machine door and swiped his credit card through the reader. Jets of hot water were visible through the window as they poured into the washer and stirred the detergent.

He sat down in a white stackable chair in the corner of the laundry room. The running water and motor of the dryer drowned out the music coming from Chris and Lacey's apartment, making it seem quiet. Gimbel lifted the lid of his laptop and opened another Java file. He had already written a macro that identified all the files with the correct header. Unfortunately there is only one way to be right and hundreds of ways to be wrong; now he had to deal with the incorrect files one at a time. He highlighted the proprietary marking on the screen, pasted the correct one in its place, and saved the file.

After the team meeting, Gimbel had gone to Beverly's office to beg for a different assignment. "An admin could take care of the code headers," he said. "You're going to need every programmer you have for debugging."

"I need *good* programmers for debugging," she replied.

"What's that supposed to mean?"

"It's supposed to mean that you've been fricking useless lately."

Gimbel felt like he was drowning. The last five months had been challenging, but there had been one piece of psychological driftwood that had kept him afloat: he was very good at his job and he knew it. Whatever disagreements he had with Beverly, she had never disputed that. Until now.

As the doubts poured over him, Beverly took advantage of the opportunity to hold him under. "I've been looking over your productivities. Your E-SLOC is down, you were late two days last week, and you yawn during team meetings—when you're not actually catching some Z's. I can't rely on you for debugging. I should warn you that I'm thinking of putting you back on performance improvement plan. In the meantime, let's see if you can redeem yourself with the code headers."

Gimbel knew all too well what another performance improvement plan would mean. At best, it would hold back his advancement in the company. Gimbel was already frustrated in his career. When Addison had guaranteed that something would come from his idea about leveraging the OSD Toolbox, Gimbel thought that he was finally moving up in the world. But nothing came of it. Addison never mentioned it again and at this point it was OBE. Overcome by events. The BAD Toolbox was too far along.

At worst, another performance improvement plan would put Gimbel on the path to unemployment. On the way home, Gimbel heard on the radio that the monthly unemployment report was due tomorrow; analysts predicted it would show another four hundred thousand jobs lost in January. This was a bad time to be without an income. *I shouldn't have spent my windfall on the Cheetah.* He remembered how desperate Mrs. Lazuli was when she came to him, teary-eyed and disheveled, for help with the rent. He wondered what happened to her after she disappeared.

A laundry basket pushed through the swinging door. Lacey followed it inside. She noticed Gimbel sitting in the corner but said nothing. She set the basket down on the linoleum and opened the dryer. The odor of fabric softener and lint greeted her. She unloaded bras, tank tops, and men's briefs and folded them. Gimbel focused on his laptop screen. The silence was uncomfortable.

Lacey broke first. "He's all-fired mad at you," she said as she removed a gray DOJ t-shirt from the dryer.

"I imagine he is," Gimbel replied.

"After what happened today, he's fixing to report you as a sabo sympathizer. You best not go around complaining to Mr. Willow anymore."

"Well, Mr. Willow isn't going to do anything, so you can tell Chris that he's going to get what he wants."

"He always does." She didn't seem happy about that.

"What about you?" Gimbel asked. "Do you get what you want?"

"That's none of your business, Gimbel O'Hare," she replied with too much formality.

"I just thought you seem like someone who should get what she wants, that's all."

For the first time since she entered the laundry room, Lacey's face softened. But only for a moment. Then she said, "I have to be somewhere," grabbed the full basket, and disappeared from the laundry room. The door swung on its hinges like the saloon door in a western.

β 1 1

Open. Paste. Save. Repeat.

The window in the spare bedroom was a black rectangle. Gimbel sat at the computer, the noise-canceling headphones clinging to his ears. Heavy metal still filtered through. The upside was that, unable to sleep, he made rapid progress with the code headers. The work was boring and his mind wandered. *Lacey's accent is sexy. Is she happy with Chris? What did she mean when she said he wanted to report me as a sabo sympathizer after today? What happened today?* Gimbel took a break from code headers and opened his browser to the *Washington Courier* website.

FULL ASYLUM

There had been another sabo attack. Late this afternoon, a man had broken away from his tour group at Boulder Dam, connected a laptop to an isolated network port, and uploaded a virus that shut down the turbines. The suspect was in custody. When questioned by dam security he identified himself as Jon Dunn. The *Washington Courier* website had dramatic nighttime video of a helicopter flying low through the canyon along the Colorado River. The circle of the helicopter's floodlight made for a striking effect as it skimmed the churning black waters. Ahead, the concrete wall of the dam shone under the arc lights. When the helicopter seemed on the verge of crashing into the wall, it pulled up suddenly and landed gently on top of the structure. A ribbon at the bottom of the screen said, *Cyber warfare experts arriving at Boulder Dam.* Gimbel recognized some of the men emerging from the helicopter; he met them once at a conference he attended during grad school. He also recognized their guide—it was Lacey Briefs, dressed in a blue DOJ windbreaker. *She said she had to be somewhere.* A news anchor explained that the cyber experts would try to determine the origin of the virus before technicians would be allowed to re-image the computers. In the meantime, the electricity would remain off in Las Vegas and rolling blackouts would continue in L.A. Attorney General Peterson released a statement that the CREEPS had arrested several suspected sabos in Nevada and Arizona in addition to the man captured at the dam and that interrogations would begin upon arrival of the suspects' attorneys.

Gimbel looked at the clock at the bottom of the screen. 3:07 a.m. Less than four hours until he had to get up for work. He removed his headphones. The rock beat that had become the accompaniment of his life grew louder. *I have got to get some sleep.*

CHAPTER 8

AN ENEMY OF THE PEOPLE

> They have called me an enemy of the people, so an enemy of the people let me be!
> – Henrik Ibsen, *An Enemy of the People*, 5.1

Grant Casey opened the double doors. Behind him a hallway led to nowhere. In front a movie set represented the living room of Jon Dunn's hotel suite. Clusters of sofas and chairs floated on oriental rugs. Antique lamps, vases of flowers, and a telephone graced the end tables. To the right a set of vertical blinds hung in front of a row of windows. The windows looked out onto a bare wall painted blue. To the left a large, ornate mirror hung on the wall behind a baby grand piano. The lid of the piano was propped open, as if ready for a concert.

"Okay, Grant," said the director. "We're rolling. Walk over to the windows and look at the view, starting on the right." Following the director's instructions, Casey crossed the set and admired the blank wall. "You see the Capitol Dome. It's all lit up. Move your head slowly to the left. Now look down. There's the Jefferson Memorial. Traffic is streaming across a bridge into the city. Keep scanning to the left. Now you see the gap desecrating the landscape. You were there when it went down but you're shocked anyway. When you left the hotel this morning the Washington Monument dominated the city. It's gone. There's a patch of black sky instead.

"You're doing fine. Walk over to the mirror. Check your suit and tie. Looking good. The suit's neatly creased. No one would know you were just in a car chase. And cue the phone."

The phone rang. Dunn answered. The voice at the other end was irate.

"I send you to Washington to investigate economic sabotage and instead you commit it!" Alpha One growled from across the ocean. "Have you any idea how seriously the Americans are taking the destruction of the Washington Monument? It's only by the grace of the Foreign Office and the century-long special relationship between our two countries that American Marines aren't parachuting into Piccadilly as we speak. As it is, the US government is seeking reparations to cover the rebuilding of the Monument. Do you know what that will cost the beleaguered British ratepayer?"

"When the monument was completed in 1884," said Dunn, "it cost $1,188,000. Adjusted for inflation, that comes out to approximately $37 billion in today's currency, which would be a enormous burden to the Exchequer unless..."

"Unless?"

"Unless we could show that an American company, Klimt Defensive Software, was behind the attack on me that led to the destruction of the monument."

"And how will we show that, Beta Eleven?"

"Are you familiar with a Swiss banker named Gerhard Gremwiltz, sir?"

"I was. He was assassinated this afternoon."

"About an hour after I left KDS's offices. Herr Gremwiltz's bank was one of the creditors that forced Advanced Missile Corporation into bankruptcy. I don't believe his murder was a coincidence, sir."

It was then that Dunn noticed the light under the bedroom door. He dropped the telephone receiver into a vase of flowers and drew his .45 caliber Glückenspiel revolver from his shoulder holster. On the telephone, Alpha One was still talking.

"Very good, Beta Eleven. You leave for Geneva tomorrow. I want you to look further into Herr Gremwiltz's dealings. Beta Eleven? Beta Eleven, are you there? Beta Eleven!"

The carpeting on the stairway muffled Dunn's footsteps as he approached the bedroom. He reached the landing and drew himself up beside the door. He held the Glückenspiel in one hand and silently turned the doorknob with the other. In a single motion, he flung open the door and dropped to a firing position. The muzzle of his pistol rotated like a radar dish in search of a target.

Dunn recognized the woman in his bed, the secretary from Iona Klimt's office. She sat propped up against the pillows, the blanket drawn over her breasts. Her bare shoulders suggested she had nothing on underneath. "I assure you, that I'm quite disarmed," she said as she looked him up and down. "You can put the gun away, Mr. Dunn."

"It hardly seems fair," Dunn replied.

Confusion flickered in her dark eyes. "What? Putting your gun away?"

"No, I meant the name. You know mine, but I don't know yours."

"It's Mona," she said. "Mona Lott."

"You certainly will," said Dunn under his breath.

"What was that?"

"I said it's certainly a thrill—to see you again." He sat down on the bed and caressed her face with his gaze. A strand of black hair hung over her eyes; he gently brushed it aside and tucked it behind her ear. He leaned towards her slowly until their lips met. They kissed for a long time.

"Cut," the director yelled. "Grant, go get changed for the next scene."

Casey got up from the bed and stepped off the set. Wardrobe and makeup followed him through the jungle of cables and equipment until they reached his trailer. The secretary actress emerged from under the covers. She did have clothing on, if a body stocking counts. A production assistant brought her a light robe to preserve her modesty until Casey returned.

FULL ASYLUM

The director continued giving orders. "Bring the camera forward a bit more for the next scene," he said. "Tell Cheri Tarte she's up. Now where's that notebook?"

The stunt coordinator approached. The head writer was at his side, carrying a three-ring binder; he handed it to the director. It contained the revised storyboard for the car chase. The director scowled as he flipped through the pages. Finally he sighed. "You didn't hear a word I said."

"We did," the head writer replied, snatching the notebook back. "You said keep it simple."

"Show him what we did at the monument," the stunt coordinator said.

The head writer turned to a page near the end of the book and held it up. The director said, "I see the pursuing cars splitting into two groups to circle around the monument in opposite directions. It's the same thing you showed me last month."

"No it's not," said the stunt coordinator defensively. "In the original version there were two hundred cars."

"So?"

"Now there are only one hundred cars."

The director looked unimpressed. The head writer tried to bail out his colleague. "We also took out the explosion at the Jefferson Memorial. And you were right. The thing with the toupee was way too much like *The Merchant of Malice*. So a hat blows off instead."

"Gentlemen, these are cosmetic changes. It's still the same car chase. Redo it. I'll say it again: simple and fun." The head writer and the stunt coordinator skulked back to their offices.

Grant Casey had returned from his trailer. A blue silk bathrobe replaced his suit and tie. The robe was short; Casey's contract required the studio to film at least one scene that would flatter his solid thighs.

Casey and the secretary actress resumed their places on the set.

"Action!"

"That feels so good."

The black-haired secretary lay face down on the bed. With one arm, she supported her head on a pillow. With the other, she held a crystal glass containing a clear liquid. Dunn sat on the edge of the bed, massaging her bare back. His short silk bathrobe flattered his solid thighs.

"You're even better than the masseur at my hotel in Geneva."

"Oh, when were you in Geneva?" Dunn asked.

"About two weeks ago. Mrs. Klimt took me along on a business trip."

"What was the trip for?"

"I don't know exactly. I had to set up a lot of meetings with a man named Gremwiltz."

"The banker! How is old Gerhard?"

"Okay, I guess. We're supposed to see him again next week."

"He might have to cancel. I better make sure this massage lasts you a while." Dunn manipulated her shoulder muscles with renewed intensity. "Tell me," he said, "Did Mrs. Klimt and Mr. Gremwiltz discuss a company called Advanced Missile Corporation?"

"I wasn't in the meetings, but it sounds familiar."

"Can you remember where you heard it?"

"No. Wait, I know. It was on a list."

"A list?"

"Yes. I was arranging Mrs. Klimt's portfolio before one of the meetings and there was a sheet of paper torn from a yellow legal pad. It had the names of several companies in the defense business. Advanced Missile was at the top."

"What happened to the list?"

"I don't know. The next time I saw the portfolio it wasn't there."

"Mona, this is important. What were the names of the other companies?"

She took a drink from the crystal glass and tried to remember. "There was Cargill Marine and Electreon of course. Maybe four or five others."

Mona's mood changed abruptly. Her shoulders slumped and her arm flopped onto the bed, spilling her drink. Burying her face in the pillow, she sobbed, "How you must hate me."

Dunn laid his hand on her back to calm the convulsing of her shoulders. "I could never hate you," he said.

"You don't understand. They sent me to get information out of you. Instead, I told you everything."

"If it's any comfort, you may have saved thousands of jobs." He gathered her long black hair to one side and kissed the back of her neck. He removed the empty glass from her hand. "Let me refill that for you." A bottle of spring water stood on a tray on the dresser. As Dunn unscrewed the cap, he said, "You know it's not safe for you to go back to them. I can get you out of the country."

He felt a hand on his shoulder and assumed that Mona had come up behind him for more comfort. But when he turned to kiss her, he found himself eye to eye with Cheri Tarte. Before he could react she drew back her fist and punched him in the jaw. Then she spun him around and grabbed him in a bear hug. Her triceps bulged as she squeezed his body. Dunn couldn't breathe.

"Can we leave tonight?" Mona asked as she rolled into a sitting position on the bed. "Both of us together?" She saw the intruder and screamed. Dunn flexed his thighs and tried to throw his attacker, but she was immovable. He smashed the bottle of spring water on the corner of the dresser. Shards of glass mixed with streams of water. Dunn jammed the broken end of the bottle into Cheri Tarte's thigh. Her thick leather pants took most of it. The wound was superficial, but it got her attention. She released him long enough to swat the bottle out of his hand. Taking advantage of the break from Cheri Tarte's embrace, Dunn sucked oxygen. But then she resumed her grip, tighter than before. Dunn was lightheaded, the edges of his vision turning black. He aimed his fists at Cheri Tarte's hips, but before they could connect he lost consciousness. His body hung limply over her arms like a used bath towel. She relaxed her grasp and Dunn dropped to the floor—like a used bath towel.

"Cut," said the director. "Take care of makeup and then we'll go right in to the next scene." Cheri Tarte placed a hand on Casey's back. "You okay, Grant?" she asked.

"Brilliant," he replied, without moving from the floor. "Always a pleasure to work with professionals such as yourself. They never neglect to pull their punches."

"I wouldn't want to mess up that Cary Grant face of yours."

"It's almost an anagram," Grant Casey replied.

As Cheri Tarte started to walk off the set Casey asked her, "Are you going to the Academy Awards?"

Cheri Tarte looked back over her shoulder and said, "I have plans that night." Whatever they were, she seemed to be looking forward to them. She continued walking and passed the two cosmetologists coming the other way. One of the new arrivals knelt by Casey, lifted his chin, and applied black and blue greasepaint to his jaw. A gaffer lowered a lamp so she could see what she was doing. The secretary actress wriggled under the covers and once again sat propped up on the pillows. The other cosmetologist applied white powder to her face.

Dunn opened his eyes. Painfully, he pulled himself to his feet. There was a full-length mirror near the bathroom door. Dunn rubbed his back as he stepped toward the mirror to assess the damage. Several strands of hair hung loose over his forehead and there was a bruise where Cheri Tarte punched him, but otherwise he was up to snuff. "That was a gripping experience," he said as he brushed the stray locks back into place with one hand. In the mirror, he saw Mona posed on the bed behind him. "How long was I out?" he asked. She didn't answer. He turned around and saw that she was staring straight ahead; her vacant eyes neither moved nor blinked.

He approached the bed and placed two fingers on Mona's carotid artery to check her pulse. When he touched her, her head flopped to one side. Her neck was broken. She was dead.

FULL ASYLUM

β 1 1

Daylight was dying as Gimbel approached his apartment building. The crocuses poking through the mulch were closing shop for the night, their petals curled like sleeping babies. Some sort of treelike shrubs grew behind them. He wondered if they were bougainvillea. In the books, Jon Dunn always went to places with bougainvillea. But then, they were usually places in the tropics. Suburban apartment complexes in Northern Virginia probably didn't use bougainvillea.

He had spent his Sunday at Byte Yourself. He was now on the test team. Even Beverly admitted that Gimbel was overqualified for the job, but she said that was where she needed to apply her resources. Then she gave him a speech about teamwork. Gimbel's contribution to the team would consist of sitting at a workstation in Test Nest II for eight hours at a stretch and following the instructions in a script:

>   Select a cell on the spreadsheet.
>   Enter formula =2+3.
>   Press the Enter key.
>   Verify that 5 appears in the cell.
>   Enter formula =2−3.
>   Press the Enter key.
>   Verify that −1 appears in the cell.

The scripts went on like that for hundreds of pages. When Gimbel pointed out that testing could be automated, Beverly said that she didn't trust the automation tools. He automated the scripts anyway. They ran in the background while Gimbel surfed SoshNet.

Back home, Gimbel entered his apartment. Glancing down his hallway, he noticed the bedroom door at the opposite end was closed. It had been open when he left for work. He slipped off his shoes and stole noiselessly down the hall until he reached the kitchen. Quietly, he sorted through a drawer, searching for a utensil that could double as a weapon. He wished he still had his sniper's rifle; the best he could come up with now was an eggbeater.

The bedroom door wasn't quite latched. Gimbel nudged it open with his toe. Surveying the room, he saw pastel-colored fabric on his bed; it didn't belong there. He aimed the eggbeater at it and cranked the handle. The blades whirled furiously. The fabric was a pair of pajamas. They covered the lithe body of Miss Lacey Briefs. She sat on the bed with her chin resting on her bent knee as she daubed nail polish on her toenails. The lavender color matched the flowers on her pajamas. A curtain of honey-colored hair hid her down-turned face from Gimbel. He lowered the eggbeater. "That's a dangerous-looking weapon," said Lacey without taking her eyes off her toes. "You wouldn't want anyone from the Department of Justice to get a look at it."

"Not a problem," Gimbel replied, whirling the blades one last time before putting the eggbeater down on the dresser. "Not a problem unless the Department of Justice has started regulating the soufflé business. Don't think that I'm not happy to see you, but how did you get in?"

"Mr. Willow. I told him you said it'd be all right."

"That was rather irresponsible of him. You might have been planning to rob the place. Lucky for me, all you wanted was to rest in my bed and paint your toenails."

"Oh, I'm not here to rest," she said, her Southern accent sexier than usual.

"What about Chris?" asked Gimbel.

"Now Chris isn't here now, is he?"

Jon Dunn would have kissed her at that point, but then Dunn was accustomed to returning to his room and finding women in his bed. Gimbel O'Hare needed time to get used to the idea. "He's still your boyfriend," Gimbel said.

"I have recently arrived at the realization that Christopher Scott Molson is an asshole. He indicated to me that his idea of a romantic evening is to dress up in black like a Gestapo agent and play Nazi interrogator. Looks like I need to begin anew in the romance department."

Gimbel wondered if Chris and Lacey were engineering a trick at his expense. The Nazi interrogator story was plausible, of course. During the last couple weeks, Gimbel had heard plenty of slammed doors and raised voices in the apartment upstairs; Chris and Lacey certainly acted like they were fighting. Although that could be part of the trick.

He knew what Jon Dunn would do: dive in. "Well then," he said, "we should celebrate new beginnings. Don't go anywhere." He left the bedroom and rummaged in the kitchen. When he returned he held two glasses of ice in one hand. But what got Lacey's attention was the dusty bottle he held in the other.

"How did you *get* that?" she asked, impressed and excited.

"I've been saving it for a special occasion. I bought it before it was illegal." He twisted the red cap off. The gentle hiss of carbonation greeted them. Gimbel poured the brown liquid into the glasses, waited for the heads to go down, and poured again. Lacey watched eagerly.

"Here you go," he said, offering her one of the glasses. "Vintage Volta Cola. Here's to genuine sweetness."

She replaced the nail polish brush in the container, twisted it shut, took the glass from Gimbel, and lifted it to return the toast. "To Volta Cola," she said.

"No, I meant you," he replied as he sat down on the bed.

Lacey's amber-colored eyes glowed, either from being compared to genuine sweetness or from the last rays of the sun filtering through the Venetian blind. She sipped from her glass and then put her free hand on Gimbel's shoulder. Gimbel looked down at it. Lacey set her glass on the nightstand and took Gimbel's chin in her hand. She tilted her head and kissed him on the mouth. Her lips tasted like Volta Cola. This was the pure cane sugar stuff—no nauseating and legal artificial sweeteners. Emboldened by the liqueur, he returned her kiss.

He was about to unfasten the top button of her pajama top when Lacey abruptly pulled away. "I expect he's seen enough," she whispered. Out loud she said, "It's considerable hot in here." She stood up and crossed the room. She reached up to the heating vent over the door and pulled the lever to close the louvers. Gimbel watched her, puzzled. The heat wasn't on.

As she returned to the bed she turned on Gimbel's clock radio and rotated the dial until she found a classical station. "Chris never lets me listen to this," she said as a Mozart concerto filled the room. It was one of the manic ones in a minor key where the listener can imagine the violinists desperately sawing their bows to keep up. Lacey sat down cross-legged on the mattress and invited Gimbel to sit opposite her. "Now listen up," she said. "There's a camera with a microphone hiding behind the vent in your heating duct and another one in your living room. Chris has been spying on you. Don't you fret though, he can't hear us over this music."

Gimbel absorbed this revelation. "Mr. Willow didn't let you in, did he?" he said.

"No," she replied. "You can't fault Mr. Willow. Chris has a key. I took it when he wasn't looking and I'm going to have to return it."

Gimbel realized that Chris didn't go to all this trouble because of complaints about his stereo. "This is official, isn't it?" he asked. Lacey nodded. "Do they think I'm a sabo? Am I an enemy of the people?"

"I know it's for an investigation, but I don't know what all they're investigating," Lacey said. "What I do know is that it has something to do with Byte Yourself Software. The attorney general has a personal interest in this case."

"Whose attorney is interested?"

"The attorney general."

"A general? Why is the Pentagon interested in Byte Yourself? We're not a military contractor."

"No, not a general. The *attorney* general." Seeing the blank expression on Gimbel's face she tried again. "You must know who the attorney general is. Bill Peterson? The head of the justice department?"

"Oh, of course, the attorney general. Sorry, I zoned for a minute. I haven't been sleeping much. It does a job on the memory, but I'll be okay after some shuteye."

"Poor baby. Although with Chris playing that old stereo night after night, I'm not the least little bit surprised." On the radio, the music changed as the second movement started, a beautiful andante with rising notes that made Gimbel think of longing. He looked at the woman seated on the bed opposite him. The silk fabric of her pajama top clung to her nipples; clearly she was not wearing a bra. "Want me to leave now so you can get some sleep?" she asked.

"No, stay and talk to me. I feel like I don't know you very well. Whenever I saw you, Chris was always there and he did most of the talking."

"Except that one time in the laundry room."

"Except that one time in the laundry room. But then we talked about Chris."

"Chris does tend to dominate the conversation, even when he's elsewhere."

"I asked you about you in the laundry room but you told me it was none of my business."

"Then try again, Gimbel O'Hare. Maybe I'll be more forthcoming this time."

"You told me that Chris always gets what he wants. I asked you if you get what you want."

"That's what you asked. And that's when I decided it was time to start. If it hadn't been for that old question of yours, I would have gone along and played Nazi interrogation and trembled just right when Chris said, 'Ve have vays of making you talk.'"

The visual was disturbing. Gimbel changed the subject. "What about outside the romance department? Do you get what you want?"

"Only when I work for it. But that makes me appreciate it more. I never could get Chris to understand that. Everything was always handed to him.

"I grew up in a small town south of here. My momma and daddy never had much besides each other and us kids. I was bucking at the halter to someday make a career for myself. I went through college and law school all on my own. I worked my ass off for scholarship A's, and what the scholarships didn't cover I made up during the summers, working at a factory in my town."

"What did you manufacture?" Gimbel asked.

"Cigarette butts."

It never occurred to Gimbel that someone makes cigarette butts. But on reflection, he supposed someone must.

"But it all paid off. I moved to DC and hired on at DOJ. I'm bird-dogging a big case now. Anyway, you see I did get everything I wanted. Or almost."

"What's missing?"

"You'll laugh."

"I won't. I promise."

"I never dated a really sophisticated guy. You know, a Jon Dunn type. Someone who wears linen suits in summertime and drinks from martini glasses." Suddenly she was embarrassed that she had opened up. She blushed and said, "Anyway, do you get what I was trying to say about hard work? Did you ever work hard for something and get it?"

"Once," Gimbel replied.

"What happened?"

"The Department of Justice took it away from me."

Lacey looked into his eyes. "Maybe the department can make it up to you," she said as she unbuttoned her pajama top.

"The vent's closed," said Gimbel. "Chris can't see that."

"Oh, this isn't for Chris," she replied, "This is all for you." She leaned forward and kissed him on the mouth, harder this time. Gimbel fell backwards on the bed with Lacey stretched on top of him. Her naked breasts were firm; they pressed against his shirt. By the time the third movement of the Mozart concerto began to play, Gimbel wasn't thinking about music.

β 1 1

"And the Oscar for Best Gaffer goes to...Guy Smith, Three Koala Studios."

Guy walked down the aisle to the stage accompanied by the Three Koala theme song and the audience's applause. His denim vest, tool belt, and work boots were out of place among men in tuxedos and women in evening gowns. Accepting the gold statuette, he stepped up to the podium. Behind him, two life-size replicas of the trophy in his hand guarded an ornamental art deco fence. "You know," he said with an Australian accent, "a few years ago, nobody thought there'd be an award for us gaffers."

On the TV at the foot of the bed, Guy Smith explained that this wasn't just his victory; all gaffers were winners. Lacey rested her head on Gimbel's bare chest as he poured out the last of the Volta Cola. Her hair was tousled, as were the bedcovers. On the floor, silk pajamas mingled with Gimbel's pants and the broken pieces of his clock radio. "What's a gaffer?" she asked.

"Lighting," said Gimbel as he handed her a half-filled glass. "The gaffer takes care of all the lighting for a movie."

"They give an award for that?" Lacey asked skeptically.

"Well, there's skill involved. But in any case, it's Everyone Wins a Prize Night."

On the television, the presentation of awards paused for a musical number. Men in top hats and tails twirled their canes as they sang "Hurrah for Hollywood."

"Are they still doing that old song?" Lacey asked.

"They updated the lyrics," Gimbel replied. "In the mind of Hollywood, that makes it practically avant-garde." He turned up the volume so she could hear better.

> Hurrah for Hollywood.
> We're always doing good in Hollywood.
> We lecture you on global warming
> While we're performing,
> And sabos better beware...

"Sure," said Lacey. "I bust my britches going after sabos and Hollywood takes the credit."

"Those bastards. You know, I saw you on video arriving at Boulder Dam after the sabo attack. I didn't see anyone from Hollywood there to help you."

"I'm an unsung hero."

"Did you learn anything at the dam?"

"The department thinks that the attack is linked to the bomb scare at National Airport. There have been other attacks as well that didn't make it into the news. But we can't find any connection among them except that all the suspects claimed to be Jon Dunn. None of them had any ties to sabo groups. Most had families to care for and never showed any interest in politics. We think someone is doing this to them. We're calling him, or her, the Betamaker because he's making a bunch of Beta Eleven's. My job is to find where he's at."

"The Betamaker doesn't stand a chance."

The Oscars went to commercial. Gimbel flipped through the channels. He paused when he saw Bulldozer and the Coroner facing each other across a wrestling ring.

"WHEN I'M FINISHED WITH YOU," the Coroner said, "THEY WON'T BE ABLE TO TELL YOU FROM A DEAD FISH AT PIKE'S PLACE MARKET." The Seattle audience cheered the mention of a local landmark. Hearing someone sneak up behind him, the Coroner turned just in time to see Titan swing a folding chair at his midsection. The Coroner went down like he had been dropped from the Space Needle.

"You don't really watch this wrestling show, do you?" Lacey asked.

"Just for the soliloquies," Gimbel assured her. He tapped the control pad and the scene returned to Masonic Hall. A split screen appeared. Six people waited eagerly to see which one of them would win the next award. "Hey," said Gimbel. "What's Isaac Ross doing there?"

"And the Oscar for Most Socially Responsible Studio goes to...Isaac Ross, Consolidated Studios!"

With great dignity, Isaac rose from his chair and walked slowly up to the stage. He accepted the award and parked himself at the speaker's podium. He removed several printed pages from the breast pocket of his tuxedo, smoothed them on the podium, and adjusted his glasses.

"As the CEO of Consolidated Studios, I thank you for this prestigious and important award. By honoring social responsibility, the Academy of Motion Picture Arts and Sciences demonstrates its recognition of the values of the cooperative society. These values inform every production released by Consolidated Studios. I seek, through the media of film, television, and the Internet, to demonstrate the role that every individual is to play in the world—whether by chronicling the struggles of interspecies couples in Consolidated's documentary, *My Stepmother is a Goldfish*, or using the bully pulpit of the Universal Wrestling League to publicize the benefits of recycling. Later this year Consolidated will release *Error of the Moon*, the thirtieth installment in the Jon Dunn saga."

At the mention of Jon Dunn, a rope dropped from the catwalk above the stage. A man in a black commando sweater rappelled down the rope and landed stealthily behind the decorative fence. Unable to see the alpinist behind him, Isaac continued his speech.

"Without giving anything away, I can tell you that this will be the most socially responsible Dunn to date. Grant Casey is the first Jon Dunn who has never used tobacco products in any of his appearances. In *Error of the Moon* we will push the envelope. We will see much more responsible attitudes towards the consumption of alcoholic beverages along with a newfound respect for women. Don't worry, though, there will still be plenty of swashbuckling and derring-do."

The audience laughed. Isaac smiled as if the laughter was intended for his little joke and not the antics of the commando behind him. The man in black crouched behind the decorative fence. Although he could see clearly through the grillwork, he used a portable periscope to peer over the top. Completing his reconnaissance, he set the periscope down and vaulted over the barrier, landing right behind one of the life-size Oscar statues. He grabbed the statue from behind and clasped his hand over its mouth to prevent it from crying out. Removing a knife from his belt, the commando stabbed the statue through its non-existent kidney. The knife slid easily into the gold-painted Styrofoam. The man guided the statue noiselessly to the floor before sneaking up on the second statue and slitting its throat.

"It is my fervent hope," Isaac went on, "that by transforming Jon Dunn into a role model for the cooperative society, we can give back to the community that has done so much for Consolidated Studios and the motion picture industry." Suddenly he felt an arm flung across his throat and the point of a knife pressed against his neck. Standing behind Isaac, the man in the commando sweater whispered something in his ear and began guiding him off the stage. The camera zoomed to a close-up, just the heads of the two men. Isaac looked genuinely terrified, as if he thought the man with the knife would really use it.

Then another weapon appeared in the scene. Someone pressed a gun against the temple of the man in the commando sweater. "Permit me to introduce myself," said a quiet voice off camera. "Dunn, Associated Industries." The camera zoomed out to reveal the owner of the voice. The audience applauded; it was Grant Casey. He was dressed in a tuxedo and continued to hold the gun with one hand while he knocked the knife out of the commando's hand with the other. With Isaac out of danger, two security guards in brown uniforms rushed onstage and took hold of the commando. He shouted something as the guards manhandled him into the wings, but it was unintelligible over the cheers of the audience.

"Thank you, Grant," said Isaac. "It looks like not everybody supports the cooperative society."

Laughter from the TV mingled with the opening bars of Beethoven's Fifth Symphony. It was Lacey's ringtone. She searched the clothes on the floor for her IQPhone, answered it, and held a brief conversation. Then she hung up and started typing on the screen. Looking over her shoulder, Gimbel saw she was surfing a travel site. "Going somewhere?" he asked.

"Gimbel," she replied, "I'd be beholden to you if you drove me to the airport. I'm on the next flight to Los Angeles."

"What happened?"

"That scene with Isaac Ross happened. It wasn't in the script."

β 1 1

"How come Grant Casey just happened to be there?"

Bill Peterson presided at the head of the table. The flags of the Department of Justice and the United States of America flanked the marble fireplace behind him. Men and women in business suits crammed the conference room. Around the table, a ring of older faces competed to appear attentive. A larger ring of younger attorneys girdled the wood-paneled walls. Seated beneath oversized portraits of Peterson's predecessors, they resembled the minor saints that trimmed the bottom of medieval paintings. They clutched notebooks and laptop computers that just might contain a piece of information their bosses at the conference table need.

Peterson put on his I'm-in-charge face. "I don't believe it's a coincidence that Jon Dunn happened to be on hand for an attempted abduction," he said.

One young face seemed out of place at the conference table. For the first time, Lacey Briefs had been invited into the inner circle. "Mr. Casey's presence in the wings was no coincidence, sir," she explained. "It was part of the show. He was fixing to come onstage and pose like Jon Dunn as soon as Mr. Ross finished his speech. When the attack occurred, Mr. Casey thought quick-like and stepped in. Good thing, too, on account of if he hadn't the kidnapper might have got clean away with Mr. Ross."

"Why was he armed?" Peterson asked.

"The gun was a prop, sir. Part of the act."

Peterson shifted in his blue leather chair. "Play the end again," he said, tapping the glass-topped table rapidly with his index finger. The chief of staff, Tim Becker, pointed a remote at a projector extending from the ceiling. The climax of Sunday night's near-abduction played out again on a screen above the door. "Pause it," said Peterson. He stood up and walked around the table to get a closer look. A few imitative staffers joined him. Peterson crossed his arms and looked up at the screen. He stared thoughtfully at the frozen image. A pair of security guards shoved the man in the commando sweater off the stage. His eyes were narrowed, his mouth open in mid-cry. "What's he saying there?" Peterson asked.

"I interrogated the guards about that," Lacey replied. She read tonelessly from a spiral notebook. "The suspect said, 'He's an imposter. I'm Jon Dunn.'"

"So this is definitely an agent of the Betamaker?"

"Yes, sir."

"Where is the suspect now?"

"He's at Walter Reed with the others."

"I think that covers everything," said the attorney general. "Thank you, Miss Briefs. The taxpayers got their money's worth sending you to L.A."

He passed through the double doors as the screen ascended into the ceiling above him. The crowd of lawyers followed, jockeying to get a word with the AG. As Lacey approached the exit, Tim Becker intercepted her. "Miss Briefs, a word in my office, please."

Lacey didn't have long to wonder why Becker wanted to see her. His office was a few steps away. The stark white walls and stacks of legal briefs contrasted with the dark paneling and ceremonial neatness of the conference room. Becker sat down at his desk and gestured for Lacey to take one of the wooden chairs opposite him.

"What's your next step?" Becker asked.

"Data mining," Lacey replied. "We've had attacks in Washington on December 21, Las Vegas on February 3, Los Angeles on February 27, and several others, as you know. I want to correlate those dates and places with the movements of known sabos. Maybe someone we have our eye on was in town."

"Sounds like a fishing expedition to me. We need to focus our resources on something more concrete."

"What do you have in mind, sir?"

"I'm transferring you to the US Attorney's Office in Fort Wayne, Indiana."

An hour ago, Becker told Lacey to sit at the grown-ups' table. It seemed then that her career was about to take off. Now something tightened inside her as she saw her prospects slipping away. Like any federal employee, Lacey's prestige depended on the proximity of her office to senior officials. In Fort Wayne, she would be five hundred miles away.

Becker continued. "A man from Fort Wayne, Mr. Victor Shepherd, committed the first attack, the one at the airport. I want you to look into his background and see if you can figure out what set him off."

"With all due respect, sir, we investigated Mr. Shepherd already."

"And we still don't know a damn thing. A traveling engineer calls his wife from his hotel room as if everything is perfectly normal. A few hours later he decides he's Jon Dunn and locks himself in an airplane to disassemble the coffee maker. I'm convinced that finding out why is the key to solving the Betamaker case. There are still plenty of leads to pursue."

"Like what?"

"Like the religious extremist angle. There continue to be reports in the media tying Mr. Shepherd to fundamentalist groups."

"The sole basis for those reports was that Mr. Shepherd had removed the Gideon Bible from his dresser drawer. We don't know why he did that, but as far as our investigation has discovered, he was strictly a Christmas-and-Easter Christian."

"What about the military drawings in his laptop?"

"All related to his job. That's also how he knew about the coffee maker."

"What about the coffee maker?"

"As a routine measure, I sent it to the lab. I didn't expect them to find anything, but they did. The wiring was faulty. We checked out a few more Consolidated planes and it turned out to be a common problem. The FAA had to order a recall. It was just a matter of time before one of these units caught fire. Metaphorically at least, Mr. Shepherd was right when he told the guard that there were time bombs on these planes."

"Well that's just another reason you need to go to Fort Wayne. I want to find out how much Mr. Shepherd's employer knew about this."

"Do you ever watch hockey, sir?"

"Hockey?"

"Yes. A famous player once said that he doesn't skate to where the puck is—he skates to where it's going to be. You're asking me to skate to where it's already been."

Tim Becker interrupted. "This isn't a hockey game, Miss Briefs. It's a federal case. The boss is determined to pursue this line of inquiry."

"May I speak with him?"

"The schedule is full this week. I'm afraid that will not be possible. Please stop by HR this afternoon. They have the paperwork for your relocation. You'll find that the moving allowance is quite generous."

Becker rose to indicate the meeting was over. Lacey started walking to the door. She moved slowly. After a few steps she turned and asked, "Have I done something wrong, sir?"

"Of course not, Miss Briefs. You've done excellent work and that's why the boss is giving you this opportunity. Don't look so glum."

β 1 1

Gimbel stood on his balcony and watched the semi pull out of the parking lot. The bright yellow-and-blue moving company logo on the side of the van contrasted with the gray clouds above. Lacey followed the truck in a red sports car. She glanced at the GPS to verify it had begun tracking her progress towards Indiana. Through the sloping rear window, Gimbel could see stacks of clothing, cardboard boxes, some pillows, and an oversized stuffed panda. The two vehicles disappeared around the corner. Gimbel heard an engine grind noisily as the truck began its slow crawl up the hill.

As the sound of the engine grew fainter, Gimbel once again wondered whether he had been responsible for Lacey's unwelcome relocation. After she told him about the surveillance cameras in his heating ducts, Gimbel faced the same problem that plagued intelligence agencies since the invention of spying: how to use the information they gathered without exposing their sources. He came to the same conclusion that spies do: protect sources from retaliation by using information sparingly. He left the cameras undisturbed behind the louvers.

Unfortunately he was obligated to make one use of the information he got from Lacey: he needed to warn Byte Yourself that it was under investigation. Gimbel wavered about this. Beverly had given him another menial assignment, this time to rewrite the disaster recovery plan. "Addison says we should be proactive," she explained. "He wants to be certain that the systems could be rebuilt and the software recovered if anything ever happens to the Test Nest." Gimbel's feelings of resentment led to fantasies about giving Beverly his resignation. But he knew he couldn't afford to quit. And as long as Byte Yourself deposited his salary in the Washington Metro Bank every two weeks, Gimbel had to be loyal to the company, regardless of whether the company was loyal to him. Beverly wasn't the company anyway. He wrote an e-mail about the Department of Justice investigation and sent it anonymously to Tina Lee. He used a dummy mail server to cover his tracks.

Standing on his balcony three weeks later, Gimbel realized he could no longer hear the engine of the moving van. Lacey was really gone. Ordinarily a Saturday afternoon in March brought some of his neighbors out to sit on their balconies or go for a walk. But today was too cold and gray. On the undeveloped property on the other side of the parking lot, the tall grass stood perfectly still. The scene was without sound, without motion, and without color.

Gimbel reentered his apartment through the sliding glass door. It had been fun having Lacey around, practically living with him, the last few weeks. He would miss her. But he could still solve the mystery of her departure. He believed the answer was somewhere on Chris's computer network. "Let's see if I can get unwired into your LAN," Gimbel said. He logged into his own computer and brought up a list of available wireless networks. The list was arranged by signal strength. The first two entries read,

Ohare   Secured Wireless Network
ChrisAndLaceyNet   Unsecured Wireless Network

"You should have let me help you, Chris," Gimbel said. "You made this too easy."

β 1 1

Gimbel didn't sleep that night. Getting into Chris's network was easy enough, but the Department of Justice VPN proved to be a challenge. As Gimbel peeled the layers of encryption, he subsisted on energy drinks and nutrition bars. When he got stuck, he checked SoshNet to clear his head. Joe had posted a picture of himself grinning widely as he received a paintball trophy. Brownie McCoy asked if anyone knew where he could score a five hundred-pound flywheel. The UWL offered a preview of tonight's show in Orlando. There was a picture of Cheri Tarte standing in the ring explaining a graph that predicted the imminent depletion of the earth's oil reserves. The Jon Dunn fan page featured a new album showing Grant Casey and Lana Wong arriving in Geneva.

Gimbel wouldn't have been able to sleep anyway. Although no music came from upstairs—the stereo belonged to Lacey—Chris spent the night dragging heavy objects across the floor. No doubt he was rearranging what was left of his furniture. The feng shui must have given him considerable trouble, because the redecorating continued through the next day and didn't stop until after 1:00 a.m. Monday morning. It was shortly after that when Gimbel broke through the VPN and started sifting Chris's DOJ e-mail.

It took about half an hour to find what he was looking for:

To: Christopher_S_Molson@justice.gov
From: Timothy_E_Becker@justice.gov
Date: 2 March
Subject: Compromise of Byte Yourself Investigation

Mr. Molson:

I reviewed the surveillance video you sent me. I disagree with you that Miss Briefs compromised the Byte Yourself investigation. There is no evidence for that on the tape. Nevertheless, it does show she has become overly friendly with the surveillance target. Since this is not her case, I assume it was a coincidence, but a coincidental friendship still poses an unacceptable risk. I'm therefore going to transfer her out of harm's way.

Of course we know from our other source that the investigation *was* compromised. He'll take care of damage control. Your job is to keep to the timetable and pull the trigger in mid-April as planned. The boss is counting on you.

Tim Becker
Chief of Staff

The reason for Lacey's transfer was now clear, but Gimbel wanted to know more about the investigation. He yawned as he searched the inbox for other entries with *Byte Yourself* on the subject line. There were hundreds of e-mails to review.

    The upward lurch of his head woke Gimbel. The clock in the corner of the monitor said 3:47 a.m. He had been asleep for two hours. Above the time, Gimbel glimpsed a subject line he recognized: *FW: Replacement of BAD Toolbox*. He wondered if he had bumped the mouse while he was sleeping and switched to his own e-mail account. But it was Chris's inbox all right. Gimbel clicked on the e-mail. Text unfurled on the screen.

    To: Christopher_S_Molson@justice.gov
    From: William_J_Peterson_III@justice.gov
    Cc: Timothy_E_Becker@justice.gov
    Date: 20 October
    Subject: FW: Replacement of BAD Toolbox

Chris:

Does this help?

Bill Peterson
Attorney General

    To: AReed@ByteYourself.com
    From: GOhare@ByteYourself.com
    Cc: BDix@ByteYourself.com
    Date: 20 September
    Subject: Replacement of BAD Toolbox

Mr. Reed:

I propose that we abandon work on the BAD Toolbox and use the OSD Toolbox instead. By leveraging software that the Operating Systems Division has already written, we can save work for the Business Applications Division. Eliminating redundant work frees up resources to program other parts of the Business Applications. I think this is the best way to get the development of Business Applications back on schedule and beat our competitors to the market.

Respectfully,
Gimbel O'Hare

Needless to say, finding his own e-mail in the Department of Justice system came as a shock. *What is going on?* Gimbel brought up a search engine and typed *Bill Peterson* into the box.

CHAPTER 9

REASON EXPIRED

BEGRIFFENFELDT. Sir, can you keep a secret? I must unburden myself—
PEER GYNT. What is it?
BEGRIFFENFELDT. Promise me that you will not tremble.
PEER GYNT. I will try not to.
BEGRIFFENFELDT (takes him into a corner and whispers). Absolute reason expired at eleven o'clock last night!
– Henrik Ibsen, *Peer Gynt*, 4.13

As he entered the conference room, Brownie uttered his usual Thursday morning greeting: "Over the hump."

The team waited for Cindy. A disconnected cable snaked across the tabletop by her empty seat. "I'll poke her," Beverly said as she typed a text message into her IQPhone.

Around the table, the team filled the downtime. Gimbel closed his eyes to shut out the fluorescent lights. Brownie drew dollar signs and peace symbols on a pad of paper. At the far end of the table, Bart prepared to flick an origami football between Andy's fingertip goalposts. With Andy and Bart otherwise engaged, and no Cindy to keep her company, Madame Butterfly amused herself by shining a laser pointer through the fabric of her sleeve, bringing a red glow to a bright printed petunia. A beep from Beverly's IQPhone announced a reply to her text. "Cindy's making a couple status updates to the schedule," Beverly said. "She'll be here in a few and then we'll start."

"Three points!" yelled Bart.

Beverly tried to start a conversation. "Has anybody heard if the Department of Justice has any leads on the Oscar Night attack?"

"There was a piece in the *Courier* this morning," Brownie said as he penciled in a shadow behind one of the dollar signs. "They got nothing."

"It's been three weeks," said Beverly. "You know what the problem is? The White House. They won't give Peterson enough authority to let him really crack down on E.S. The guy in the Oval Office hasn't got the estrogen."

Andy looked up mid-flick. "We'll be rid of him soon enough."

"Election in nineteen months," said Beverly. "Brownie, who do you like for president?"

"They're all fasci-zoids, man."

"You just say that because you're a closet sabo," said Andy, laughing. "Who do you like, Beverly?"

"I actually like Bill Peterson."

"He screwed over Byte Yourself pretty good," said Brownie.

"I thought you would like Peterson," Beverly replied. "He made that big speech to the Senate committee about liberty."

"Actually, he said we need to balance liberty with safety. Benjamin Franklin warned us against that. He said we'd end up with neither."

Madame Butterfly shut off the laser pointer. "Benjamin Franklin?" she said. "Wasn't he president during World War II? That was in the 1800s or something. The country is a lot different now."

"World War II was in the 1940s, man, and Benjamin Franklin died in 1790."

Madame Butterfly did the math. "Well that proves my point," she said. "The country *is* different. Nowadays we would never let a dead guy be president."

Beverly steered the conversation back to a more sensible topic. "Addison says Peterson is the guy to watch. He's the only one in Washington who's really going after E.S. I don't know a lot about him, though."

Gimbel opened his eyes. "Peterson, William J., the Third," he said. "Born at Walter Reed Hospital in Washington, DC. Father, William J. Peterson Jr., six-term US senator from Connecticut. The younger Peterson earned a BS in criminal justice from Yale and a JD from Harvard Law. Goes by the name the 'Attorney General.' Heads a large organization, the 'Department of Justice,' also known as the 'Department.' While it bills itself as the 'primary federal criminal investigation and enforcement agency,' it is presumed to be a front for other, less beneficial activities."

"Presumed by who?" Beverly asked.

"Me. The DOJ has a large base of operations on Pennsylvania Avenue. It is a massive stone building, taking up the entire block between 9th and 10th Streets. Whatever the Attorney General is up to, that will be the center of it. I think that's about all, sir."

"In case you haven't noticed, O'Hare, I'm a ma'am. And why are you talking like that?"

"Talking like what, sir?"

"Ma'am. Talking with a British accent."

"How else would I talk?"

"Talking like an intelligent person would be a welcome change."

"An intelligent person," said Gimbel, "might suspect a link between this man Peterson and the attempted kidnapping of Mr. Ross on Oscar Night."

"Of course there's a link. The DOJ investigation is the link."

"Right, you want me to investigate the DOJ. Excellent."

"No, the Department of Justice is investigating the...never mind." She massaged her temples between her thumb and forefinger. "The only thing I want you to investigate is how to recover the Test Nest from a disaster."

"I understand, sir."

"Ma'am."

"I understand. Our department can't have any *official* involvement—at least, not until I discover something concrete. I'll be discreet, of course. I believe I have a lead at Fox Hunt Apartments."

Cindy entered. "Sorry I'm late," she said as she connected her laptop to the video cable. "Did I miss anything?"

"You really didn't," Beverly replied. "Start the meeting."

Gimbel stood up and walked to the door.

"Where are you going?" said Beverly.

"I'm going to draw my equipment from Double-G branch."

"What equipment?"

"You certainly don't expect me to investigate a dangerous character like the Attorney General without night vision goggles, underwater breathing apparatus, and automobile-mounted guided missiles."

"I don't expect you to investigate anyone, O'Hare."

"Right. This investigation doesn't exist—officially." He winked at her.

"Gimbel, sit down!"

"Put in an order for night vision goggles for me too," Madame Butterfly said. "I don't need to breathe underwater."

Gimbel returned to his chair. Cindy ran through the tasks on the overhead screen and described the status of each. "As you can see," she said in summary, "we're exactly where we should be. So is the application team. That puts us on track to begin integration April 11 as planned. That'll be the real test."

Beverly adjourned the meeting. Gimbel raised his hand. "Should I draw my equipment now?"

β 1 1

"One round-trip first-class ticket from National Airport to Boston. Car rental on a Cheetah YK-9. Hotel bill for one night in the Grand Suite at the Barnett Royal Waterfront in Boston. Another hotel bill from the Barnett Roadside Motel in Concord, New Hampshire—for the same night."

"I assure you, Ms. Lee, I did not green light any of those expenses," said Beverly.

The brushed aluminum desktop that separated Beverly and Addison from Tina was made from a piece of the same airplane wing as its big brother in the Executive Conference Room. Tina's aerodynamic chair conformed to the jet travel theme. The five-foot-tall CEO sat on her seat like a gift that was too small for its box; she had vetoed plans for office furniture custom-designed to her proportions. "I don't need to look bigger," she had told the decorator. "Everyone already knows I'm in charge." Her red business suit and black bowl haircut was as much a company trademark as the corporate logo.

"There's more," she told Beverly, brushing a strand of black hair aside to see the expense report through her oversized glasses. "One admission ticket to Massachusetts Garden Arena for a performance by the Universal Wrestling League. Dinner at Le Poisson Juridique, consisting of a bowl of clam chowder, a two-pound lobster, a glass of Glenjohnnie, neat, and a bottle of méthode champenoise. He tipped generously too. All charged to your department. Now, Beverly, what were you trying to tell me?"

"I was trying to say that I did not okay these expenses."

"You better not have," said Addison. "Except for the night at the Barnett Roadside, none of these expenses falls within policy."

Beverly blushed at Addison's reprimand; the contrast made her platinum blond hair appear paler.

"Who submitted these expenses?" Beverly asked. "Did they give any explanation?"

"A very detailed explanation," Tina replied. She tossed two copies of a document across the desk. Each copy consisted of several printed pages stapled together. "Nourish your retinas on this," she said.

Beverly and Addison reached for their copies. "Trip Report," Beverly read aloud. "Purpose of Trip: Surveillance of William J. Peterson III, a.k.a. the 'Attorney General.' Employee Name: Gimbel O'Hare." At the sight of Gimbel's name, Beverly detoured into another explanation, but Tina cut her short. "Keep reading," she said. "It gets better."

Beverly and Addison read silently while Tina turned her attention to her ultra-slim monitor.

> I began my reconnaissance of the "Department" with a call at its Washington base of operations late on the afternoon of Thursday, 24 March. Pretending to be a tourist, I parked on the 10th Street side and walked slowly around the building. Although there are a number of entrances, I found them to be heavily guarded. I gained access to the lobby on Pennsylvania Avenue where Ms. Dora Jarr confronted me. I previously encountered Ms. Jarr at National Airport; during said encounter she attempted to expropriate one (1) Chromega timepiece. On that occasion, I learned she was a resourceful and avaricious opponent. At the Department of Justice building she asked me for identification. I provided a Virginia motor vehicle operator's license with the Gimbel O'Hare cover. Ms. Jarr carefully examined the license and then typed on a computer. After a moment she informed me that I was not "in the system" and would therefore not be permitted access to the building.

FULL ASYLUM

During my encounter with Ms. Jarr, I observed that she permitted several agents of the Department to enter after they flashed a specialized badge. As I returned to my car, I considered the best way to obtain a Department badge.

Having previously established a connection between Mr. Christopher Molson and the Attorney General, I tracked Mr. Molson to Kilkenny's Eating and Drinking Pub, Fairfax, Virginia, with the intent of stealing his badge. Mr. Molson met three (3) unidentified Caucasian males at this location.

The four (4) men ordered a pitcher of beer from a healthy blond waitress, Pam. They then played several (several) games of billiards. I took cover behind a painted wooden leprechaun, and therefore remained unseen as I observed the target and awaited an opportunity to pilfer his badge. I expected that one of the men would attempt to pass information to Mr. Molson during the course of the evening. I soon learned, however, that the Department of Justice had employed a different means of communication. Strategically placed television screens provided the vector for delivery of secret instructions to the Attorney General's henchmen.

A message arrived during my stakeout. It consisted of orders for members of the Department to gather in Concord, New Hampshire. An attractive woman in a tangerine blazer delivered this message via the television. She sat in front of a drawing of a domed building. "Although not yet a declared candidate for president, Attorney General Bill Peterson is acting like one. Channel Five News has learned that the Attorney General will address a political rally Saturday afternoon on the steps of the New Hampshire State Capitol. New Hampshire will be, of course, the site of the first-in-the-nation presidential primary early next year. When asked if his appearance in the Granite State signaled his entry into the race, the Attorney General said through a spokesman that he had no announcement to make at this time but would address the question during his speech."

It was clear from this message that to continue my investigation, I needed to infiltrate the New Hampshire conference. I flew to Boston the following day, Friday, planning to spend Friday night in the Barnett Royal Waterfront before driving to New Hampshire on Saturday. Shortly after I checked into the Barnett hotel, however, it became clear that word of my arrival had leaked. A woman who identified herself only as "Housekeeping" arrived at my door. I believe this was a false name; a subsequent search online failed to turn up any known Department of Justice operative who employed that alias.

Ms. Housekeeping was a particularly nasty sort. She wheeled a cart that held several types of chemical weapons in spray bottles. It had a compartment for brooms and mops; no doubt she intended to use the handles to beat me or visit worse tortures on me. She even brought stacks of towels to clean up my blood after she finished. Thinking quickly, I grabbed one of the spray bottles from the cart and pointed it at her face. "I'm not afraid to use this," I said. "Tell me what the Attorney General is planning." Unfortunately I was not able to get any information out of Ms. Housekeeping. She was visibly afraid to talk. I was more determined than ever to find out what the Attorney General was doing that put that kind of fear in people.

Following my interrogation of her, Ms. Housekeeping ran away and disappeared into a lift, leaving her odious cart behind her. I realized that the hotel was no longer safe, but I thought it best to wait for cover of darkness before leaving the city. As there were still several hours until sunset, I passed the time with an early dinner at Le Poisson Juridique followed by a performance of the Universal Wrestling League at the Massachusetts Garden Arena. The show was quite

FULL ASYLUM

informative; Kong is back together with Suzie Winsome and Cheri Tarte castigated Joy the Sweater Lady for telling her nephew to stand up to schoolyard bullies. Apparently, the correct course of action for children who are bullied is to tell an adult. By intermission it was dark enough that I believed I could travel safely out of town. Realizing that I was exposed to attack while on the road, however, I attempted to minimize my exposure by maintaining speeds above ninety miles per hour. Unfortunately my precautions were for naught; once again, agents of the Department had discovered my plans.

They attacked me about twenty miles north of the city. Apparently they hoped they could frighten me into surrender by chasing me in cars with flashing blue lights and loud sirens. There was one car initially, but when I accelerated to escape it, several others joined the chase. I eventually lost them by exiting the highway onto a secondary road. The road was curvy, which provided many opportunities when I was briefly out of sight of the pursuing vehicles. During one such opportunity I careened onto a side street and killed my headlamps. After I saw the DOJ vehicles pass on the main road, I doubled back to the highway and resumed my journey to New Hampshire.

I spent the night at the Barnett Roadside Motel in Concord. Saturday was a fine spring day; I selected a gray suit with a mauve tie and proceeded to the state capitol a little before noon. When I passed through the stone archway to the capitol lawn, several hundred agents had already arrived; clearly the conspiracy is much larger than we previously thought.

The agents were gathered in front of the capitol steps and around the statue of Daniel Webster. In a shocking breach of security, many of the agents carried signs advertising their plans. These included *Broil the Rich*, *Workers of New Hampshire unite—we have nowhere to go but the White*

House, and *Hey Billionaires—That's our money*. In one group, mostly female, the signage was of a different nature: *Abortion on Demand*, *Bedrooms over Boardrooms*, *It's my body—I'll do what I want with it*, and *I vote with my pussy*. The function of these women in the organization was unclear to me. While their slogans suggested that it had something to do with fornication, the women were exceedingly unattractive, so I'm not certain of this.

Two (2) signs were directed at Byte Yourself Software. One depicted male genitalia with the slogan *Hey Tina: Byte This!* On the other, the Byte Yourself logo was modified to resemble a woodscrew wearing a crown. The slogan on this one said, *We're getting screwed royal-LEE*.

Finally, an elderly woman in a multicolored crochet poncho and pink wig carried a sign that said, inexplicably, *Bossa Nova All Ovah*.

I should also mention that the costs of maintaining such a large organization appear to be putting considerable financial strain on the Department. Many of the agents had holes in their clothing, and some smelled as if they were unable to afford soap or antiperspirant.

In view of the resources that the Department has put into this operation, combined with the various slogans, it is my conclusion that the Department is planning a large-scale attack on Byte Yourself Software as the leading edge of a plan to steal the presidential election and undermine the entire capitalist system. Latin dance, and perhaps fornication, will play a role in the attack, although exactly what the role will be is uncertain.

The Attorney General arrived. He stood on the balcony of the capitol between two granite columns. His speech confirmed my suspicions about the Department's intent. I recorded it on my IQPhone, and I reproduce it here in its entirety.

FULL ASYLUM

"What a beautiful day. They say if you don't like the weather in New Hampshire, wait a minute." Some of the agents giggled. "I better make this a short speech so I'll be sure to finish before it starts snowing." After scattered applause, the Attorney General continued. "When I arrived here today, I did a little circuit shaking hands with some of you. Everyone asked me the same question. 'Bill, are you running for president?' Well, I have an announcement to make, and I want the people of New Hampshire to be the first to hear it. I have taken the first steps in that direction. This morning I formed an exploratory committee that will survey the political landscape and make a recommendation as to whether I should run for president of the United States!"

The applause was much louder this time.

"I am making this decision at time of grave national crisis. In the past four months, at National Airport and Boulder Dam, at Masonic Hall and on Main Streets across America, economic saboteurs have attacked the families and the businesses of this country. I pledge to you today that under my leadership the Department of Justice will find and arrest the cowardly sabos who were behind these attacks. They shall be tried by juries in the states where their crimes were committed and, if convicted, punished to the fullest extent of the law."

"Currently, the department is pursuing a lead linking one of America's leading companies to economic sabotage. To Corporate America, I have this message: you are not above the law. If we find evidence of an alliance between you and the sabo conspiracy, you will share the same fate as your sabo shills."

The cheers that greeted this verbal assault on Big Business abruptly turned to screams. A circle of bare pavement opened up around the statue of Daniel Webster like an expanding ripple on a pond—if pond ripples were powerful enough to shove people out of the way. "They're here," people shouted. "The sabos are here!" At the first sign of the disturbance, security officers grabbed hold of the Attorney General and shoved him back inside the building. Closer to the statue, Department agents prepared to meet the imminent sabo attack. A group of teachers formed a circle around a cluster of blue trash bins while urging others to "Protect the recyclables!" Nearby, a bearded man in a "Vegan for Peterson" t-shirt ran from agent to agent, desperately asking, "Did they bring meat with them? Does anyone know if the sabos brought meat with them? I need to be in a meat-free zone."

I got close enough to the statue to see what the fuss was about. A piece of paper was taped to the pedestal. At the edge of the circle, a beefy man in a plumbers' union jacket tried to remove it by poking it with a long stick. He was afraid to get too close. He eventually got the stick under the paper and pushed it off the pedestal, but before he did I got a photo of the text with my IQPhone camera. It began with a description of the spinning machines and power-looms that had made life so much easier in the old Massachusetts textile mills. Then it said:

> Such is the state of things actually existing in the country, and of which I have now given you a sample. And yet there are persons who constantly clamor against this state of things. They call it aristocracy. They beseech the poor to make war upon the rich, while, in truth, they know not who are either rich or poor. They complain of oppression, speculation, and the pernicious influence of accumulated wealth. They cry out loudly against all banks and corporations, and all the means by which small capitals become united, in order to produce important and beneficial results. They carry on a mad hostility against all established institutions. They would choke up the fountains of industry, and dry all its streams.

FULL ASYLUM

> In a country of unbounded liberty, they clamor against oppression. In a country of perfect equality, they would move heaven and earth against privilege and monopoly. In a country where property is more equally divided than anywhere else, they rend the air with the shouting of agrarian doctrines. In a country where the wages of labor are high beyond all parallel, and where lands are cheap, and the means of living low, they would teach the laborer that he is but an oppressed slave. Sir, what can such men want? What do they mean? They can want nothing, sir, but to enjoy the fruits of other men's labor."
> – Daniel Webster, March 12, 1838

"We have to fire him," Beverly said gleefully when she finished reading. "One of our resources stalked the attorney general of the United States. As a company, we can't condone that. I'll ask Van Dyke in HR the correct process. I should have seen this coming."

"Why was that?" Tina asked.

"Gimbel said some goofy things during last week's staff meeting. He has a fixation on Bill Peterson."

"Don't know that I blame him," Tina said. "I remember Gimbel from the Crypt Yourself team. I was going to promote him when Bill Peterson got the product banned. Peterson chucked a spanner into Gimbel's career."

"Peterson monkey wrenched a lot of careers around here," Beverly replied, "but Gimbel is the only one who responded by playing hide-and-seek with the Massachusetts State Police. He's obviously a risk to us."

Addison looked past Tina and studied the view through the wall of glass behind her. The sky was a clear blue. Down in the pond, the fountain was on for the season; rainbows danced in the spray. Addison tried to reconcile the beautiful spring day with the anxiety inside him.

"It's a joke," he said at last.

Beverly and Tina looked at him skeptically.

"Look at your calendars," he said. "April Fools."

"It's too elaborate for a joke," said Tina. "Gimbel must have really done the things he describes in his trip report—or most of them anyway."

"What makes you think that?" Addison asked.

She tapped the stack of papers on her desk. "He sent us his receipts."

"Gimbel wouldn't be the first software engineer to go to great lengths for a practical joke," said Addison. "I once heard about a young programmer at Consolidated Software who stole Isaac Ross's designer desk and spent the next six months mailing him photos of it in front of famous landmarks."

Tina laughed. "Good thing he never found out who did that or my career there would have ended a lot earlier."

"How did you get the desk to the top of the Eiffel Tower?"

"I didn't. The pictures were fake. The desk was in a janitor's closet the whole time."

"Anyway, I think you can see that Gimbel might not really think that the maid in his hotel room came to torture him or that the attorney general is a supervillain who sends secret messages over the Channel Five news. Like I said, April Fools. I'll have a talk with Mr. O'Hare about appropriate workplace behavior and that will be the end of it."

"What do you think, Beverly?"

Beverly looked at Addison. He was not only looking back, he was checking her out! "Well, now that Addison mentions it, it *is* April 1…"

"It's your division, Addison," said Tina. "I'll leave it up to you." She swiveled in her chair and faced the window. She was reluctant to share her next thought. "There is another aspect of this that concerns me," she said.

"What's that?" Addison asked.

Tina turned around and faced her executives again. As she spoke, she tallied her points on her fingers. "One, as you know, I got an anonymous e-mail a few weeks ago warning that Byte Yourself is under investigation by the Department of Justice. Two, the head of the department is now promising to prosecute a corporation that's linked to economic sabotage. Three, there were people at that rally protesting specifically against Byte Yourself. It all adds up to a threat to the company."

"I think you're reading too much into a couple of signs carried by some unglued fomenters," said Addison. He looked at Tina and Beverly; they seemed tired. There were cracks in Beverly's pancake makeup. The upcoming release of the business application software was taking its toll on the whole leadership team. "Gimbel's make-believe paranoia is rubbing off on us," he said. "We're not linked to economic sabotage. We have nothing to worry about."

"I'm not so sure," said Tina. "I'm going to do some due diligence and talk to the corporate counsel."

Before she could reach for the phone, it rang. She pressed the speaker button. "Ms. Lee," said her admin, "Your next appointment is here: Mr. Willow from Fox Hunt Apartments."

"Looking for an apartment?" asked Addison.

"Looking to *build* some," Tina replied. "Do you ever drive by Fox Hunt? They got a huge piece of undeveloped land. If I can get the permits, I'll invest in some construction. Could be a great showcase for our products."

"The county could use some more apartments," said Beverly. "I, for one, am dying to move out of my mother's house."

"Ms. Maxwell," said Tina to the speakerphone, "please ask Mr. Willow to wait ten minutes. Then get our lawyer on the phone."

"Tina," said Addison. "Go ahead and meet with Mr. Willow. I'll get with the corporate counsel."

β 1 1

The light was wrong. It reminded him of the time he came home and found Lacey in his bed. Gimbel rolled over under the sheet and squinted at his new clock radio. 6:03. That made it four hours sleep since Chris stopped pacing. That was Chris's new thing. Instead of listening to music, he paced. Every night, as Gimbel lay sleepless under the covers, his eyes followed Chris's heavy footsteps across the ceiling. Back. Forth. Back. Forth. Sometimes they didn't stop until sunrise. It was like listening to a metronome, or to the thumping of Captain Ahab's peg leg as he patrolled the decks of the *Pequod*. Captain Ahab was on a mission to obliterate Moby Dick. Gimbel had no illusions as to Chris's mission.

Gimbel tried to drift off again, but the shrieks of children playing by the pond prevented him. His eyes snapped open. *Did I send Tina a report about "infiltrating" the Department of Justice?* He felt around the night table until he found his IQPhone. Holding the device in his hand, he adjusted the distance until he could read the screen without his contact lenses. There it was in his outbox. E-mail to Tina Lee, Friday, April 1, 10:36 a.m. *How am I going to explain that?*

Gimbel stretched out his arm and dropped the phone, hoping it would land on the night table. A thud indicated it found its target. A few seconds later, it rang.

"Hello?"

"Hello, Gimbel?"

"This is Gimbel."

"Oh, hi. It's Lacey. I didn't recognize your voice. Why are you talking like you're the King of England?"

"Huh?"

"You have a British accent."

"I do?" He switched to Midwest newscaster English. "How's this?"

"You sound normal now."

"I feel normal for the first time since you left. Must be hearing your voice. How's life in Fort Wayne? What's on your mind so early on a Saturday morning?"

"Don't be a jackass fool, Gimbel O'Hare. It's 6:00 p.m."

"P.m.?" He sat up in the bed, pushed the slats apart on the Venetian blinds, and peered between them. "I wondered why the sun is rising in the west. I've been asleep for sixteen hours."

"You must have been dog tired. What have you been doing with yourself—besides following my boss to New Hampshire?"

"How did you know about that?" he asked as he got out of bed. He juggled the phone as he wrapped a silk bathrobe around himself.

"I saw you on TV. Nice suit. You blended right in." After a pause, she added, "Hey, Gimbel, you're breaking up a touch. Give me a holler on your other phone."

Gimbel's other phone was the computer in his spare bedroom. Cognizant as they were about the justice department's surveillance of Gimbel's domain, Lacey and Gimbel had arranged a commlink that was immune from cell phone eavesdropping and out of range of Chris's hidden microphones. Gimbel tied the belt on his robe as he walked to the next room. Sitting down at the desk, he opened a window on the computer. The words *Link Secured by Crypt Yourself* appeared. The software was left over from Gimbel's days on the Encryption Research Team; he never deleted it after the team disbanded. Before Lacey left for Indiana, he installed a copy on her laptop. The words on the screen became animated. They zipped into the window frame, shrinking as they traveled. A live video feed of Lacey sitting at a kitchen counter filled the frame. She wore a t-shirt that said, *Fort Wayne, Indiana. Where Johnny Appleseed came to die.*

"Tell me what you saw in New Hampshire," she said.

Gimbel told her the story he had written in his trip report, leaving out some of his more bizarre interpretations. "Did you see who taped the note to the base of that statue?" Lacey asked.

"No," Gimbel replied. "Am I a suspect?"

"You were smack dab in the middle of two of the attacks."

"And you were my alibi for two others."

"You're not a suspect. Don't get all tore up about it. I found someone more sinister than you."

"No one's more sinister than me, babe."

"It's a group of people actually," said Lacey.

"Who?" Gimbel asked.

"The UWL."

Gimbel studied Lacey's face on the screen and tried to figure out if she was serious. She was.

"The UWL *is* suspicious," he said. "It's just not normal for so many men to wear costumes in public. But aside from that, what makes you suspect them?"

"Data mining. I used the department computers to look for patterns. I found one." A click of her mouse brought up a map of the United States in a corner of Gimbel's screen. Colored dots covered selected cities. The dots were mostly, but not always, in groups of three.

"What's the pattern?"

"First, I figured out how the Betamaker recruited his agents. It turns out *Betamaker* is a misnomer. He didn't actually make them."

"Then how did he recruit them?"

"He advertised." She explained that just before each attack, with the exception of the first one, ads had appeared on SoshNet asking Beta Eleven to contact Alpha One in the targeted city to receive his orders.

"That's great," said Gimbel. "Now all you have to do is follow the money trail to whoever bought the ads."

"Already tried that. Ended up in a cul-de-sac. He went to one of those little third-party payment companies—you know, the ones that guys use to prevent their wives from seeing the Internet porn charges on their credit card bills."

"I thought those companies are illegal."

"They are, but it's hard to prevent them from operating offshore."

Gimbel chuckled. Much as he wanted Lacey to succeed, he found comfort in the notion that there were still some places in the world where a business could operate beyond the reach of the CREEPS.

"You haven't told me how the UWL is involved," he said.

"That's the second pattern. The Universal Wrestling League was nearby during almost all of the attacks. They were in Washington during the attack on the airport. In fact, they were sitting on a plane on the tarmac."

"I remember. I saw them board."

"Then they were in Las Vegas during the attack on Boulder Dam and in Boston during the chaos at the New Hampshire capitol."

"You said 'almost all of the attacks'. What was the exception?"

"The Academy Awards. Remember? We flipped over to the UWL during a commercial break, and they were in Seattle."

"Could the incident in Hollywood have been a copycat attack?"

"No, because of the last pattern I found. Almost every attack was directed at Consolidated Studios. National Airport and Boulder Dam both caused cancellation of UWL shows at considerable cost to Consolidated. The Academy Awards attack, of course, was aimed at Isaac Ross, who's head of the studio."

"Let me guess, there was one exception."

"New Hampshire. That attack was directed against the attorney general. I can't think of any link between him and Consolidated. That's why I called, really. I hoped you would have some ideas."

Gimbel pondered. Just over a week ago he had told Beverly that Bill Peterson was linked to the attack on Isaac Ross. But he couldn't remember why he thought that. It was as if someone else had been talking. Looking at the bottom of the videophone window, he saw the words *Link Secured by Crypt Yourself* embedded in the frame.

"There is a link," he said, "but I don't see how it ties to the attack. It's the software that's linking you and me. Bill Peterson wanted it banned, but it was Isaac Ross who made it happen. His support put it over the top."

"I didn't know that. I'll study on it. But even if there is a link between Ross and Peterson, the UWL was still a thousand miles away on Oscar Night. That blows a hole in my theory the size of the Space Needle."

"No, it doesn't. It's your lucky break."

"How's that now?"

"Dozens of wrestlers and crew members travel with the UWL. You don't know which one is the Betamaker. But if you find out who wasn't in Seattle, you'll know."

"I do believe you're on to something, Gimbel O'Hare. Looks like I need to phone up some folks and get me a recording of that Seattle show."

"I wish I could be there when you make the arrest. I bet there will be lots of headlines."

"'Attorney Lacey Briefs solves Betamaker case.' Thank you, sir. I'm beholden to you."

After she hung up, Gimbel realized he already knew what Lacey would find in that recording. There *was* a wrestler absent from Seattle on Oscar night. She was in Los Angeles, making a movie.

PART
III
Error of the Moon

It is the very error of the moon;
She comes more near the earth than she was wont,
And makes men mad.
    – William Shakespeare, *Othello*, 5.2

CHAPTER 10

SOUTHERN BREEZE

I am but mad north-northwest; when the wind is southerly I know a hawk from a handsaw.
   – William Shakespeare, *Hamlet*, 2.2

It was one of those mornings when the contact lenses didn't want to go in. When Gimbel tried to place them in his eyes, the lenses hurt, or stuck to his fingers, or fell in the sink.

There had been no response to his bizarre trip report. Beverly did tell him to expect a call from Addison. When he asked her what the topic was, all she would say was, "general discussion." Whether Addison wanted to reprimand him for his tour of New England or chat about the latest episode of *Sorry*, Gimbel had no idea. It didn't matter in any case. Addison hadn't contacted him yet.

After re-cleaning his lenses six times, Gimbel could see at last. Razor time. *Something is going on with Beverly*, he thought as he massaged the shaving gel into a white lather. She cancelled her staff meeting Monday. Since then she spent most of her time in her office with the door closed. Cindy, Andy, Bart, and Madame Butterfly were often in there with her, sometimes for three hours without a bio-break. Gimbel could see them through the glass pane next to the door. Beverly appeared in the cafeteria only long enough to grab a salad that she would eat at her desk. Yesterday, Gimbel was behind her at the register. He asked if there was a problem and if there was anything he could do to help. "You're doing exactly what I need you to do," was the reply. "Keep working on the disaster recovery plan." She took her change from the cashier, picked up her tray, and returned to the secrecy of her office.

A stubble-free Gimbel showered, dressed, and drove to the office. When he arrived at Test Nest II, Andy and Bart were already there. It was unusual for them to be in the lab before 'stenics, but a lot of things were unusual this week. "Hi, guys," Gimbel said as he hung his suit jacket on the back of his chair. They didn't look up from their screens. "Can't talk now," said Bart.

It was Cindy who finally breached the wall of silence. She came to the Test Nest late in the afternoon and looked over Bart's shoulder. "Gimbel knows this part of the code," she said. "Did you ask him about it?"

"No. Beverly said she wanted him to focus on disaster recovery."

"Man up, Bart," Cindy replied. "Do you want to make Beverly happy or do you want the code to work?"

She brought Gimbel up to speed on the last three days. The integration of the Toolbox with the application code had failed. When all the components came together, the software wouldn't start. Spreadsheets didn't open and documents concealed their contents. The team had tried the usual troubleshooting tricks—adding debug lines to the code, stepping through the commands one at a time—but when they did the problem went away. "Of course it did," said Gimbel. "Software is governed by Heisenberg uncertainty. The act of observing it changes it."

Cindy looked annoyed. "Do you have anything to offer besides nerd humor?"

"Actually I was serious," said Gimbel. "It's a timing problem. Something's happening out of sequence."

"I could put some delays in," Bart offered.

"Don't do that," Cindy said. "Aside from being a kluge, it will slow the application. We have to actually find the problem and fix it." She turned to Gimbel. "Can you do it?"

"Point me to the source code."

β 1 1

The Test Nest was a different place after the second shift left. The fluorescent lights seemed brighter. The two-dozen engineers who filled the room in daytime were asleep in their houses and their apartments, their technical discussions and pop culture jokes muted. Only Cindy was still up; she texted him from home every few hours to see how it was going. Around 2:00 a.m., he was able to tell her that he found the problem. The fix was easy, but it had to be duplicated in hundreds of places. He still had the macros that he wrote to replace the proprietary markings. He was modifying one of them to automate the fix. It would take the better part of a day, however, to feed all the code to it. It would go faster if he had some help. *b there in 15*, Cindy wrote.

She arrived dressed as she had been at home, in sweatpants and a tank top. Cindy and Gimbel divided the source code between them and got down to business. They worked silently; the hum of cooling fans was their only soundtrack. Indifferent to the scarcity of warm bodies, the air conditioner continued pushing chilled air through vents in the floor tiles. The room got cold. Cindy hugged her chest with goose bump covered arms. Gimbel offered his suit jacket. It was too big in the shoulders, too short in the sleeves, and it looked silly with sweats, but it kept Cindy warm.

Some early arrivals were already dribbling into the lab when Cindy and Gimbel finished their repairs. The newcomers were mainly middle-aged men whose workdays started right after dropping the kids off at school and ended promptly at 4:00 p.m., in time to pick them up from soccer practice. "Were you here all night?" one of them asked. When Cindy nodded, he smiled condescendingly. "It's nice to be young."

Gimbel typed some commands into his workstation to kick off a build. It would take several hours to run. "Caffeine?" he asked Cindy. "I'm cafeteria bound."

"Maybe later," she replied. "I'm going back to my office to e-mail Beverly."

They descended the ramp and pushed through the double doors that led out of the Test Nest. At the elevators, Cindy pushed the up button, Gimbel the down. When he arrived at the cafeteria, he found a metal grill blocking the entrance. It wasn't open yet. Beyond the grill, cafeteria workers mixed oatmeal and brewed coffee. Gimbel checked the placard with the hours. Half an hour still. He poked his nose through the steel mesh and inhaled. Did aromatherapy work with caffeine? The wool trousers of his suit itched. So did his eyes. What he needed even more than coffee was to go home, take a shower, and clean his contact lenses. He passed through the lobby and escaped into the sunshine. A light wind carried warmth and the scent of fresh mulch from the south. The splash of the fountain and the rapid-fire chirp of a cardinal sounded refreshingly natural after a night spent among mechanical fans.

As Gimbel strolled to his car, Brownie McCoy puttered into the parking lot. Brownie drove a two-door Hankuk subcompact painted like a relic of the 1960s. A rainbow and a fountain of stars decorated the hood. A multi-colored hippie font spelled *love* on the passenger-side door; the driver's side said *greed*. He pulled up next to Gimbel, rolled down his window, and said, "You're going the wrong way, man."

Gimbel leaned on the car door. "Brownie, I love you like a father," he said, "but of all your jokes, that one's the worst."

By mid-morning Gimbel was back in the Test Nest with fresh blue pinstripes and grit-free contacts. The build was still running. He checked his e-mail while he waited for it to finish. There was a meeting invitation from Addison for 4:00 and a reprimand from Beverly for missing 'stenics.

Shortly after 3:00 the build was finished, the software loaded, and the Toolbox team gathered around Gimbel's workstation. He clicked an icon and a spreadsheet opened. Neat rows of data arranged themselves on the screen.

"Success!" said Andy.

"Way to go, Gimbel!" Bart added.

"We lost four days on the schedule," said Beverly. "I'm going to need to give Addison a full report on what went wrong."

"You see in the fourth row, where it says 4.65?" Madame Butterfly said.

"Where?" asked Beverly.

"Over there." She pointed to the screen.

"I see it. 4.65," said Beverly. "Does that have to do with the problem?"

"No, but it's important," said Madame Butterfly.

"What's important about 4.65?"

"I was the one that typed it into the test data file."

Beverly's effort to control her temper was visible. "Will someone please tell me why the program wouldn't start up?"

"Timing," said Gimbel. "The program was trying to read the data while it was still opening the file."

"We put in a check to make sure the file was open first," Cindy added.

"Shouldn't there have been a check in there to begin with?" Beverly asked.

"Yes," said Gimbel.

"Why wasn't there?"

"I suppose the original programmer didn't think of it."

"And who was the original programmer?"

"I'd rather not say."

Madame Butterfly interrupted. "I typed 17.263 in the next cell, too."

Beverly ignored her. "I have to know who programmed this. We're almost a week behind schedule now and Addison is going to want to know who to...what happened."

Gimbel opened the source code and pointed to the screen. Cindy looked at where he was pointing. "Oh," she said. "Beverly, we should take this offline."

Beverly's IQPhone beeped. She looked at the screen. "Addison is waiting for me," she said. "I'm out of time. Give me the answer now."

"It's early code from before you were our manager."

"What does it say?" Beverly said very evenly.

Cindy read the name of the programmer out loud. "Beverly Dix."

β 1 1

Beverly's departure from the Test Nest was quite dramatic. She stomped down the ramp and slammed the double doors behind her.

The team hung out for a while after she left. It was Thursday afternoon and little work was getting done. Cindy told the team to plan on working the weekend to make up schedule. Everyone groaned, but promised to be there. For now, they decompressed after a week of software bugs, marathon meetings, and projectile blame, with a big turnaround at the end. Madame Butterfly experimented with the suction cups on the floor tile lifter; she wanted to see if they would stick to a desk, a wall, and a cardboard box. Bart talked about a paintball tournament coming up. He asked to borrow Gimbel's sniper rifle. "I gave it back to Brownie," Gimbel said. "You'll have to ask him."

Before long the soccer dads left. Andy and Bart weren't far behind. "Brewski time," they said. "We'll be at Kilkenny's."

Gimbel, Cindy, and Madame Butterfly were picking up their things when Cindy said, "Hey, Gimbel."

"Yeah. What?"

"Thanks." She said it like she meant it.

"You're welcome," he replied. Then he remembered something. "What time is it?"

"4:30."

"Crap. I was supposed to be in Addison's office at four."

"Don't worry about it. He's probably still got Beverly in there. Any bets on which one of us she's throwing under the bus?"

Gimbel ran down the ramp and reached for the doorknob. Just then Brownie burst into the room, nearly hitting Gimbel with the door. "The fuzz are all over this place," he said.

"I don't speak hippie," Cindy replied.

"The police. *Los Federales.* The CREEPS, man. They're searching the whole building."

"What are they looking for?" Gimbel asked.

"You."

β 1 1

It was cramped under the floor. Gimbel lay squeezed between the pedestals that held up the tiles. He twisted his neck uncomfortably; the alternative was to mash his face against the four-sided slab above him. Lengths of power conduits and coils of fiber optic cable reached out for him like man-eating vines in a horror movie. Apparently "Get Unwired" didn't apply below decks. But housing the strands of copper and glass was just one purpose of the crawl space. It doubled as the distribution system for the air conditioning. Gimbel shivered in the artificial wind that blew dust onto his suit and through his nostrils. Every tenth tile was perforated to discharge frigid air into the Test Nest. Pitiful imitation sunbeams filtered through the vents. Beneath them, patches of concrete glowed feebly, islands of light in a nighttime sea. *Good thing they're looking for me and not Brownie*, thought Gimbel. *There's no room down here for his belly.*

Brownie's announcement of the CREEPS impending arrival had been followed by inflamed deliberation about what to do. Cindy picked up the phone to call Tina Lee, but the landline was dead. She tried her IQPhone, but couldn't get a signal.

"Told you," said Brownie. "CREEPS jammers."

While he argued with Cindy about the best way for Gimbel to avoid capture, Madame Butterfly continued playing with the floor tile lifter. She pulled the epoxy-coated squares out of the floor in a carefully selected pattern and stacked them in a corner. When she had drawn most of a happy face this way, Cindy intervened. "That's not safe, Daphne. Someone could fall through the holes."

"Yeah, man," Brownie added. "They would disappear and we would never find them."

As his words sunk in, what was intended as a joke became a plan. Minutes later, Gimbel was concealed snugly beneath the center of the happy face. He watched the circle of lights around him go out one by one as Brownie and Cindy dropped each floor tile back into its slot with a thump.

Gimbel didn't know how long he had been there. His wrist was pinned between his hip and a pedestal and he couldn't move his arm to see the Chromega. He heard Brownie insist that Cindy go home. After a bit of protest, she did. Some time passed after that, but eventually Gimbel heard the door open and multiple sets of heavy footsteps fan out into the Test Nest. After so many nights spent listening to it, there was one step Gimbel easily picked out of the crowd. Chris Molson was leading the search team.

"Who's in charge here?" said Chris.

"That'd be me."

"Name?" another man asked in a bored voice. "Last name first."

"McCoy, Desmond. I'm the sysadmin."
"Please spell that."
"T-H-A-T."
"No, your name. Spell your name."
"Y-O-U-R N-A—"

Chris interrupted Brownie's display of orthography. "Never mind, Lieutenant," he said politely. "Mr. McCoy, we're looking for Gimbel O'Hare. Have you seen him?"

Brownie started to answer, but a soldier in the server area distracted him. "Hey, man," Brownie said. "Tell the SS wannabe over there to look out. He almost knocked over one of my racks."

"We'll knock over more than that if you don't tell us what we want to know, Mr. McCoy," said Chris, abruptly exposing the malice that lay beneath the polite veneer. "Where is Gimbel O'Hare?"

"Ain't here. See for yourself."

The stamping of boots echoed through the crawl space as Chris's men searched behind equipment racks and inside utility closets. Clots of dust shook loose from the tiles. Gimbel stifled a sneeze. After several minutes, the lieutenant said, "Mr. Molson, there's no one here but the beatnik. Should we take him in?"

"Not yet. You, McCoy, when was the last time you saw Gimbel O'Hare?"

"Hours ago."

"Where was he?"

"At that computer."

Captain Ahab circled Gimbel's workstation. "Pack up this machine," he ordered the lieutenant. Then he asked Brownie, "Is this the only computer he used?"

"I don't have to answer any more questions, man. I got a right to remain silent."

"Stomach," said Chris softly. Gimbel heard a muffled thud.

Brownie howled. "What's with the brutality, man? That's unconstitutional. Also bad karma."

"Did Gimbel O'Hare use any other computers?"

"Get off my case, man."

"Again," said Chris.

Another muffled thud, followed by a groan. Brownie's knees hit the epoxy near Gimbel's hiding place. Gimbel couldn't let the beating continue. He wrenched his arm free and pushed upward on the floor. Seeing a tile open slightly, Brownie scrambled to his feet and stood on top of it. "Sometimes Gimbel used other computers," he confessed.

"Lieutenant, pack them all up."

Gimbel heard racks pushed across the floor, computers and monitors dropped carelessly into boxes, and occasional protests from Brownie: "Watch it, man. You'll break that," or, "Use a screwdriver on that connector. Tools are what separate us from the hyenas."

The sneeze escaped so fast that Gimbel didn't have time to suppress it. Activity in the Test Nest froze. There were no voices and no footsteps. Then Brownie said, "Gesundheit."

"Who are you talking to?" Chris asked accusingly.

"To you. Didn't you sneeze?"

"No," said Chris.

"Then it must have been me," Brownie replied. "Aren't you going to say gesundheit?"

"You wanted the right to remain silent. Now's a good time to start," Chris replied, raising his voice for the first time. Gimbel heard him walk away from Brownie.

"Still waiting for that gesundheit, man."

"Lieutenant, if there's one more 'man' out of this hippie, put a gag on him. The '60s are over."

Commotion resumed as Chris's men continued their disassembly of the Test Nest. The lieutenant spoke into a walkie-talkie for a while, and then he walked over to Chris. "Mr. Molson," he said, "both buildings are secure. There's no sign of Gimbel O'Hare."

"He's here," Chris insisted. "His car is still in the parking lot. Find the subterranean nerd!"

"Should I call in the dogs to sniff him out?"

"No."

"It's the best way."

"The AG says no dogs. There's a boatload of TV cameras outside. Peterson doesn't want to lose the animal rights vote. Don't look so disappointed."

"I like calling in the dogs."

The sounds of footsteps, packing, and hand trucks went on for some time. Then all went quiet. After a while, Gimbel saw a panel open several feet away and Brownie's beard poke through the gap. "Where'd you go, man?"

"You're in the wrong place. Over here."

"Sorry." He pulled up the floor tiles directly above Gimbel. The fluorescent lights stung after the long game of hide-and-seek in the dark. Brownie helped him up. Gimbel brushed the dust off his suit and checked his watch. He had been under the floorboards for three hours.

He looked around at what remained of the lab. The raid had been pure pillage. The floor was nearly bare. Plastic cable ties and a few scraps of cardboard were the only litter. All the electronic equipment was now evidence. Every computer was gone. Unfaded patches of desktop marked the spots where monitors had rested. Stripped of their silicon guts, server racks resembled skeletons. Their coaxial sinews hung uselessly, connected to nothing.

"This is going to put us behind schedule," said Gimbel. "Beverly is going to be upset."

"She'll be more upset that you escaped."

Gimbel looked at Brownie and put a hand on his shoulder. "Thanks to you. You took a punch in the belly for me. Twice. I owe you."

Brownie patted his stomach. "Fortunately there was plenty of cushion to absorb the blows," he said. "Still, I should have left Cindy in charge. She's tougher than I am. She wouldn't have caved and we'd still have a lab."

"You recovered fast enough. I had to bite my lip to stop from laughing when you badgered Chris for a gesundheit."

Brownie turned serious. His elfin smile vanished as he removed his half-moon glasses. "Those CREEPS are on a real asshole trip. I wouldn't mind taking a few of those hosers down." Before Gimbel could remind him that kind of talk was dangerous, Brownie changed the subject. "They're watching the parking lot. You're going to need a disguise if you want any hope of getting out of here."

Gimbel looked around the lab for materials, but the CREEPS hadn't left much behind. "Unless I can weave a vest out of cable ties," he said, "I got nothing."

"No need for plastic ties," said Brownie. "I got leather." He opened a metal cabinet and removed a garment from a hook on the inside of the door. "Western-style vest," he said. "Circa 1967 or '68. Earth-tone buckskin, previously broken in. Two wood toggle-style buttons with leather loops. Fringe on front, naturally. Stretch out your arms." He slid the vest over Gimbel's suit jacket. It was big enough to wrap around him twice. "Be careful with that," Brownie said. "I expect you to bring it back intact."

"I knew you'd have something," said Gimbel. "But won't a fringe vest be conspicuous in an office parking lot?"

"Yeah, but it's got one big advantage."

"What's that?"

"No one's looking for a guy in a fringe vest. Now let's do something about your face." He produced a baseball cap from a desk drawer. A picture of a marijuana leaf decorated the front. He placed it on Gimbel's head and pulled the bill down low over his eyes.

"Won't the law-and-order types from the justice department be suspicious of a guy in a weed hat?"

"They might be, but they won't do anything about it. They're not looking for a guy in a weed hat. Next, your car: they're definitely watching it. Take mine." He tossed Gimbel a fob hanging from an oversized peace sign key chain. "Don't worry about *love* and *greed* on the doors."

"Because no one's looking for them?"

"You got it, man."

"How will you get home?"

"Don't worry about me. And don't go home—they'll be waiting for you. Don't use your credit cards either. Find a place to hide and I'll try to find out what's going on." He pointed to Gimbel's IQPhone. "Text me in a couple days," Brownie said. "We'll meet up."

"I'll use Crypt Yourself."

"Do you know where you're going to go?"

"I think I know a place."

β 1 1

It took a while to find the entrance. Gimbel left the hippie mobile in the Pentagon Palace garage and circled Gracie's Department Store on foot. Sheets of plywood blocked the doors. He tested for loose panels but they were nailed tight. Returning in the other direction, he checked lift doors and ventilation grates with no better luck. As he doubled back one more time, he looked for additional points of access, but found none. Reaching the front of the mall, he sat down on a curb and tried to figure out how to get in. He had a flashlight that he'd found in Brownie's glove compartment. He might be able to use it to find an opening he missed, but he was unwilling to accept the security risk. The CREEPS were still looking for him and the beam would advertise his presence. During business hours he could get into Gracie's through the paintball arena, but at this time of night it was closed. A cold wind blew leaves and pieces of litter along the gutter, past Gimbel's feet. He wrapped the leather vest around himself more tightly.

A car approached. The headlights expelled the darkness from the store across the street. In the window, a faded orange banner announced, "Going out of business. All books 75% off." One end of the banner had come loose; it dangled against the glass. Gimbel remembered when a row of trees lined the sidewalk in front of the bookstore. He wondered what happened to them. The car passed and Gimbel watched a pair of red taillights retreat at full speed; the driver was in a hurry to escape to a different neighborhood. Looking back at the bookstore, Gimbel thought he saw something move in the light of the three-quarter moon. When his eyes adjusted, he discerned the figure of a person walking down the sidewalk. The figure wore a bulky, gender-concealing overcoat. It shambled, as if it were painful to move and reaching its destination didn't matter anyway. It passed the bookstore and disappeared into the shadows.

Gimbel stood up from the curb and jogged across the street to the point where the figure had disappeared. He found himself at the entrance to the Pentagon Palace Metro station. Gimbel wondered why the figure had gone in there. It was after twelve o'clock and the trains had stopped running for the night. There would not be another until dawn.

He passed through the doors and began the walk down the stopped escalator just in time to see the figure reach the bottom. The figure turned and disappeared in the direction of the underground passageway that connected the station to Pentagon Palace Mall. Gimbel could hear footsteps on the terra cotta tiles. He leaped from the last step onto the tile and followed the figure to the passageway.

Two-by-fours were nailed diagonally across the entrance. Beyond them, the passage was dark. Gimbel turned on the flashlight and shone it down the length of the corridor.

There was no one there.

In front of him, at the opposite end of the corridor, *Pentagon Palace Mall* was stenciled on a transom window above a row of boarded doors. Gimbel slipped between the two-by-fours and walked the length of the corridor. The plywood over the doors was nailed tight, just like on the doors outside. Gimbel turned around to see if the figure was hiding in the shadows behind him. The spot of the flashlight bounced around the hallway. It pushed the dark aside like a hand dipped in water; as it moved, the dark poured back in behind it. The spot skimmed concrete walls and penetrated through cobwebs into corners but found no one. Wires protruded through the concrete where oversize LCD displays had once advertised women's lingerie and men's cologne. One display remained. A crack the length of the screen made it worthless to looters. It leaned against the wall, abandoned.

Gimbel turned off the flashlight and saw something glow. Grayish light traced the outline of the cracked display. He approached to see where the light came from. He grasped the side and tilted it forward. Behind it, a hole in the concrete provided access to a tunnel. The source of the light was at the other end.

Gimbel stepped through the hole carefully to avoid tearing his suit trousers on the jagged concrete edges. When he let go of the flat panel display, it tipped back into place behind him. The ceiling of the tunnel was low; Gimbel had to stoop slightly.

When he emerged at the other end, the stink of body odor and mildew invaded his nostrils. Gimbel bent over and retched. He had not eaten since lunchtime; the dry heaves convulsed his body. "Be quiet over there," someone growled.

After a minute, Gimbel recovered. He stood up and looked around. He already knew what he was going to see. He had known since his paintball days, when he tried to push the door to Gracie's open and someone on the other side pushed back. But it still amazed him.

The derelict store housed a city. All around Gimbel, the homeless slept on sheets of cardboard and soiled mats. Their belongings filled shopping carts and lay heaped on the floor. There were panhandlers and bag ladies. There were couples with wedding rings and couples without; it didn't matter here. There were families with children asleep in their parents' arms. The residents occupied the edges of the ground floor; a pyramid of rubble occupied the center. Since the roof collapsed two winters ago and crashed through nine floors of retail space, rebar weeds grew from a compost of concrete chunks, broken light fixtures, and dust. The moon colored the debris an unnatural shade of silvery gray. When Gimbel looked up, he realized what happened to the trees that had disappeared from in front of the bookstore. They had been chopped up for firewood. Necklaces of campfires circled what was left of the upper stories. No wonder the parking lot always smelled like burning wood. The cone above him resembled a tree house village in a fairy tale, but without heroes, magic, or a pine-fresh scent. The stars sucked smoke from the pit. Gimbel recalled reading Dante in high school. Nine floors. Nine circles of hell.

Gimbel switched on his flashlight and searched for a place to spend the night. People slept close together. There was barely enough room to walk between them, much less to sleep. Gimbel had to move carefully to avoid tripping on anyone. At one point his flashlight met the bloodshot eyes of a bearded man drinking a brand of whiskey that was definitely not Glenjohnnie. "Shut that off," the man called as he shaded his eyes with a gnarled talon.

There seemed to be some empty space near the elevators, but as Gimbel approached them he found out why. The denizens had removed the doors and converted the shafts into latrines. Gimbel gagged on the stench of excrement. He retreated back to the slightly less disgusting odor of human sweat. Unable to find a place to sleep on the ground floor, he headed to an escalator to search for a vacancy upstairs.

He found a space on the fourth floor just big enough for him to lie down. Gimbel rolled up Brownie's leather vest into a pillow and closed his eyes. He tried to remember everything that happened since he struggled to insert his contact lenses. That was two days ago. There was the software crisis. *Foolish of Beverly to try to read from a file without checking if it was open. I wonder what she said to Addison.* Then there was the vigil under the floor tiles during the CREEPS search. *Isaac Ross is obviously behind it. I told Lacey he was in with Peterson.*

He remembered the scene in *Bitterweed* where Double-G arranged a recognition signal for Dunn to know his contact in Monte Carlo. He gave Dunn one piece of a queen of spades that had been torn in half. Dunn's contact would be the man with the other half. *I only have half a playing card*, he thought. *Where's the other piece?*

He was just dozing off when another thought jerked him awake. *What's in it for Peterson?*

A boot kicked his leg. "This is my space," someone snarled. "Get the hell out of here." Gimbel opened his eyes and saw a tall, thin man standing over him. His hair hung in greasy strands and he sported three days of chin stubble. "Get gone." His neighbors raised their heads and looked around like wolves wondering what woke them. When they saw Gimbel, their eyes narrowed.

"Sorry," said Gimbel. "I didn't know." He picked up the leather vest and backed away.

As he continued his upward journey, Gimbel began to figure out the social order. The primo real estate went to the best fighters. On the sixth floor there was more open space, but it was better defended. On the eighth floor, a gang of UWL rejects guarded the top of the escalator. They wore open shirts with the sleeves cut off but they weren't cold. They had plenty of girls and firewood to keep them warm. The leader flirted with a pair of skanks whose fishnet stockings and caked mascara made Suzie Winsome look classy. They stroked his muscular chest and fingered his gold chains greedily.

When he saw Gimbel, the leader said, "No one gets by here unless I say so."

"Already gone," Gimbel replied as he started to turn back. It was just as well that he would never find out what was on the ninth floor.

"Hang on," said the leader. He approached Gimbel and took hold of the bill of his marijuana-logo cap. "I like this."

"You can't have it," Gimbel grunted. He grabbed the cap out of the man's hand and ran. The gang chased him, but only for one flight. Gimbel didn't stop until he got to the bottom floor. In this world, where the most violent rose to the top, instead of the most productive, the bottom was where Gimbel belonged.

The screams of an infant got his attention. Gimbel looked in the direction of the cries and, by the light of a nearby fire, saw three boys with dirty faces tormenting a squat woman in a black dress. In one hand, she held a squirming baby, in the other a can of soup. The oldest boy tried to steal the soup from her. The tug-of-war lurched back and forth across a blanket of plaid flannel; the combatants kicked over the woman's few possessions in the process. Stacks of rags toppled. Dishes crunched underfoot. In an effort to tilt the contest in his favor, the boy's minions poked the woman with sharpened sticks. In the firelight, they resembled runt demons with pitchforks.

Gimbel tried on the snarl he learned upstairs. "You're done here," he told the boys in his most authoritative voice. "Leave the lady alone." The woman's tormenters froze and looked at Gimbel with hostility. They had been bullying a middle-aged woman with a baby and now someone less defenseless suddenly confronted them.

The woman yanked the can free from the oldest boy's grasp. Remembering something he heard in a horror movie, Gimbel added, "I cast you out, unclean spirits." The boys ran off. *I'm moving up in this world*, Gimbel thought. *I now rank above the eight-year-olds. At this rate I'll be up to the second floor by Halloween.*

"Are you okay?" he asked the woman as gently as he could. When she didn't answer he moved closer to see if she was injured. That was when he realized he knew her.

"Mrs. Lazuli," said Gimbel. "It's me. It's Gimbel O'Hare."

"Gimbel," she said, looking at him suspiciously. Mrs. Lazuli wore the same dress—now torn—that she had worn on Thanksgiving; Mimi still wore her turkey costume. The red fabric neck wattles were filthy and one of the googly eyes was missing. Their frightened faces flickered in the firelight.

"Gimbel," Mrs. Lazuli repeated. For a moment she seemed to recognize him, but then she started screaming, "No! No! No!"

"Mrs. Lazuli, what's wrong? I'm not here to hurt you."

"No! I don't have your money."

"What money?"

"I told you, I don't have it. I gave it to Mr. Willow. Go away!"

At the mention of Mr. Willow, Gimbel understood what worried her: the money he had given her for her December rent. "Mrs. Lazuli, it's okay," he said. "I'm not here to take back the money."

Mrs. Lazuli relaxed, but only slightly. "Not here for money?" she asked.

"No money."

Mimi let out a cry. "Here," said Gimbel, holding out his arms, "let me help you."

Mrs. Lazuli recoiled from him at first, then slowly held out Mimi for him to take. He cradled the baby in his arms. Since Mimi continued to cry, Gimbel sang the closest thing to a lullaby he could think of: the theme from *The Future is Just Beginning*.

FULL ASYLUM

The future is just beginning.
The past was just chapter one.
Your kiss makes me feel
Like I'm finally real.
You're the best there is, Jon Dunn.

It was weirdly appropriate. Gimbel hoped that life in the ruins of Gracie's really would be just chapter one for Mimi, and that a new future would begin for her. Soothed by the music, and by a pair of arms that weren't completely exhausted, Mimi's cries trailed to whimpers. The gentle breath of sleep took over. Mimi's car seat sat on the blanket. Gimbel laid her in it. She was getting too big for the carrier. Her feet, wrapped in the footies of her Thanksgiving costume, hung over the edge. Gimbel watched the sleeping baby for several minutes and then turned to her mother.

"I came to see you before Christmas," he said. "I wanted to make sure you were all set for the January rent."

"They came for me. Mr. Willow—and some men. They said I had to leave."

"Did they say why?"

"They said they were evicting me. I told them I paid the rent, but they said I had to leave. They said I had ten minutes to pack. They only let me take one suitcase. And Mimi."

Gimbel looked around but saw no suitcase.

"I don't have it anymore," Mrs. Lazuli said. "I traded it for food."

As she talked, Mrs. Lazuli straightened her belongings, restoring the order that ruled her patch of floor before the boys attacked. She arranged two place settings of company china on the blanket. One of the plates was broken in half; she pushed the two pieces together so that the jigsaw edges meshed. A metal picture frame lay face down on the flannel. Mrs. Lazuli propped it up at one of the place settings, revealing a photograph of her husband. The serious eyes behind his round glasses brought dignity to his wife's table.

"Where is your car?" Gimbel asked.

"They wouldn't let me take it. They said it was evidence."

She set a pair of candles in brass holders and lit them with a match. The pilgrim woman centerpiece stood between them; her white bonnet was torn. Although Mrs. Lazuli had tried to fluff the honeycomb paper dress back into shape, she could not completely repair the dent where a federal agent had stepped on it. When he saw the pilgrim woman, Gimbel realized what Mrs. Lazuli was trying to do: reconstruct Thanksgiving dinner, relive her last moment of happiness before the CREEPS battered down her door. Gimbel wondered how many times she had repeated this ritual since November. This time would be different. This time Mr. and Mrs. Lazuli would finish the meal. But it always ended the same, with three demon boys standing in for the CREEPS.

Gimbel looked at the people around them. A pre-teen in a halter-top applied makeup by the light of a kerosene lamp. She would be on the eighth floor too soon. A man snored, a gray scarf around his neck, an empty hypodermic at his feet. Two children fought over a bag of tortilla chips.

"Gimbel," Mrs. Lazuli said suddenly, "do you know what 'optimize utility' means?"

"What?"

"Optimize utility. What does it mean?"

"It's a piece of software. It allows your computer to make the best possible use of disk space."

He wondered why Mrs. Lazuli was interested in disk space. She thought about his answer. "No, that doesn't make sense," she said. She turned to the photo of her husband. "Ricardo," she said, "you always told me 'markets optimize utility.' But I don't know what that means. Please explain it to Gimbel, dear."

"Oh, *markets* optimize utility," Gimbel repeated. "You mean utility in economics."

"Yes, economics. I think it has something to do with what happened to us, and," she gestured around her, "all of this."

Gimbel thought the abandoned department store was an odd setting for a symposium on the fundamentals of economics. But when he looked at the collapsed roof and the empty display cases and the sleeping people, he realized there was no place where the consequences of bad economic policies were more pertinent. In any case, Mrs. Lazuli seemed eager for an answer. "I took History of Economic Thought in college," he said. "The professor said it meant that if left to their own devices, people would apply their resources in such a way that as a group they would be as happy as possible. If they were rational, a free market would facilitate their happiness better than any other system. But economists no longer believe that the real world works that way."

"Why not?"

"They concluded people aren't rational."

Mrs. Lazuli shielded her mouth with one hand so she wouldn't be overheard. "They underestimate us," she whispered to her husband. Then she asked Gimbel, "What if people aren't left to their own devices?"

"You mean, what if the government decides for them what to spend their money on? If it tells them how much to spend for health insurance, and how much for retirement, and how much for National Government Radio?"

"Uh-huh."

"I suppose they'll be less happy. If people on their own pick the optimal outcome, then some other outcome the government picks for them has to be less than optimal. The government can't create wealth; all it can do is move wealth around. The more wealth it moves, the farther things get from the optimal distribution until…"

"Until you're here," Mrs. Lazuli said.

Suddenly she realized she hadn't eaten yet. She pulled the tab on the soup can, poured the contents into an enamel pot, and held it over the candle flame. While it heated, Mrs. Lazuli watched the moon through the breach in the ceiling. The three-quarter disk was just disappearing beyond the edge of the aperture. Mrs. Lazuli craned her neck and squinted, as if trying to find someone. "Are you still there?" she yelled.

"Who are you talking to?" Gimbel asked.

"The people on the roof."

"What people?"

"All the people that aren't down here."

"What do you mean?"

Mrs. Lazuli explained. "It's a story. Once upon a time, the whole country lived on the roof, and they had cocktails, and bathtubs, and Thanksgiving."

"Sounds nice."

"It was. Especially the bathtubs." Her thoughts lingered in the hot water for a moment. Then, remembering, she said, "Oh, but there was a hole in the roof. Some of the people fell in. The other people, the ones still on the roof, they were good people and they wanted to help. They took some bricks and concrete and cans of soup and dropped them in the hole to help the people down below."

"Did it work?" Gimbel asked. "Were their lives better, now that they had bricks and concrete and cans of soup?"

"No."

"Why not?"

"Because it made the hole bigger! The people on the roof pulled the bricks out of the edge of the hole and that's what made the hole bigger. Then the people that were standing on the edge fell in too. Now there were more people who needed help and the hole just got bigger and bigger and more and more people fell through."

"So what do you do to help the people in the hole?"

"I thought you were supposed to be smart, Gimbel. Don't you know?"

"I haven't slept in two days. I'm a little slow. What's the answer?"

"I'll give you a hint. It's like you said before. Moving bricks around just makes things worse."

"Got it," said Gimbel. "You have to make more bricks."

"And they lived happily ever after."

β 1 1

When Gimbel was a boy he had a cat. Some mornings when Gimbel opened his eyes, the cat was sitting on the bed staring at him, her face a few inches from his, willing him awake.

It was Mrs. Lazuli's face that he saw when he awoke in the department store that morning. She sat motionless, watching him. She held a sheaf of paper in one hand. The sunlight shining through the roof revealed how much recent months had aged her. Wisps of gray invaded her wiry black hair. Crevices flowed across her forehead and cascaded from the corners of her mouth. It occurred to Gimbel that "laugh lines" was one of the least appropriate phrases in the English language.

When she saw that Gimbel was awake, Mrs. Lazuli handed the sheaf of paper to him. "Mr. Willow gave this to me," she said. "I thought if you saw it, you might be able to help us."

Gimbel sat up and unfolded the pages. After reading a few lines he said, "Hmm."

"What is it?" Mrs. Lazuli asked.

"It says it's a warrant of seizure. It seems Mr. Willow lied. I'm not a lawyer, but I think it means he didn't actually evict you. That's why it didn't matter that you paid your rent. The government seized your car and apartment for evidence in the case against your husband." He continued reading out loud, "Whereas, on December

15 the United States filed an amended criminal complaint, verified by Attorney Christopher S. Molson of the United States Department of Justice…"

Gimbel lowered his hand. The pages dropped into his lap. Mrs. Lazuli retrieved them and held them up to Gimbel's eyes. "Keep reading," she said impatiently. "Why did you stop?"

"Because I found out all I needed to know."

She looked disappointed. "Does that mean you can't help us?"

"It means," Gimbel replied, "that I can help both of us."

CHAPTER 11

GETTING UNWIRED

To be one's self is to slay one's self.
 – Henrik Ibsen, *Peer Gynt*, 5.9

It was early morning on Friday when the tow truck barreled into the Byte Yourself parking lot. It leaned on two wheels as it took the curve into the driveway. The cab was painted solid red with no lettering to advertise the name of the towing company. Spinning into position, the truck backed up in front of the only car in the lot, a midnight blue Cheetah YK-9. The brakes sang a metallic C-sharp and the truck halted a few inches from its quarry.

The driver hopped out of the cab and yanked the tow hook. Roomy blue-striped coveralls accommodated his sizable belly. Above the belly, a white beard spread across his chest like a hairy bib; all it needed was a picture of a lobster. He reached under the car and hooked the towline to the chassis.

As he tugged on the line to test that the hook was secure, three CREEPS approached. Sunlight reflected off their black boot polish. Patches on their commando sweaters identified them as Sergeant Stasi, Corporal Savak, and Private Cheka. The last two men carried automatic rifles, pointed safely at the ground.

"Good morning, sir," said the sergeant. "You have entered a CREEPS surveillance area. Please step away from the vehicle and identify yourself."

"My name is Desmond McCoy."

"What are you doing here, Mr. McCoy?"

"The department sent me, man. They told me to tow this car to the evidence garage."

"I can't let you do that, Mr. McCoy. This car is under surveillance until the owner returns."

"Doesn't look like he's coming back, man," said Brownie.

"Sorry, the car stays here. Orders."

"Whoa! Déjà vu. I got orders, too." He reached for his chest pocket.

"That's far enough, Mr. McCoy. Please move your hands away from your pockets and raise them above your head."

"Can't do it, man. The pockets are sewn on."

"I meant your hands. Raise 'em."

Brownie curved his arms overhead and crossed his legs at the knees. Although this put him in a basic ballet position, he looked more like a beach ball than a ballerina. He curtseyed anyway.

The sergeant turned to Corporal Savak and gestured at Brownie with an over-the-shoulder thumb snap. No further instruction was needed. With Private Cheka eagle-eyeing for sudden movements, the corporal slung his rifle over his back and approached Brownie. Pulling open the snap on Brownie's chest pocket, he removed a piece of paper. He handed it to Sergeant Stasi and resumed his position behind his superior. The sergeant unfolded the paper and scanned its contents while Corporal Savak watched over his shoulder. "Need me to read that to you?" Brownie asked. The sergeant flashed Brownie his best shut-up-or-I'll-shut-you-up glare and resumed reading. "Looks like the bona fide, Sarge," said Corporal Savak. "It's got Mr. Molson's name on it."

"Then why don't we know anything about it?" the sergeant snapped. "Call in for confirmation." Corporal Savak removed a walkie-talkie from his belt, said a few words into the mike, and passed it to the sergeant. "Lieutenant, Sergeant Stasi reporting. We got a Desmond McCoy here with an order to tow O'Hare's vehicle to the evidence garage. Over.…That's right, McCoy, Desmond. Over." He listened as the lieutenant provided instructions. Halfway through, he gestured to Private Cheka, who raised his rifle and aimed it at Brownie. "Roger that, Lieutenant. Over and out."

Sergeant Stasi returned the walkie-talkie to the corporal. "Well, Mr. McCoy," he said, "the lieutenant asked me to congratulate you on finding a new job so quickly in this economy. He was wondering what you would do with yourself after he confiscated your computers. He also said, 'How's your stomach?'"

"Oops," Brownie replied.

"Mr. McCoy, I want you to listen to me very carefully and do exactly what I say. Drop slowly to your knees and clasp your hands on the top of your head. I'm sure I do not need to waste your time with any clichés about false moves. Private Cheka here has never shot a sabo and the guys have been giving him a hard time about it." He turned to the private. "You'd welcome an opportunity to get them off your back, wouldn't you, Cheka?"

"Yes, Sarge!"

Brownie followed the sergeant's instructions. He moved with uncharacteristic grace, as if he had done this before.

"Corporal, search the truck."

Corporal Stasi looked carefully through the passenger side window. "Hey!" he shouted. "He's got brownies!" He opened the door and removed a baking pan from the seat.

"Tell me, Mr. McCoy," the sergeant said as he took the pan from Corporal Stasi, "do you always bake brownies for stealing cars?"

"I like a snack, man."

"So do I, Mr. McCoy. So do I." The brownies were uncut. The sergeant tried to slip his fingers under them to free them from the pan.

"Leave those alone!"

"Or you'll do what?" the head CREEP asked.

"I got rights."

"What rights?"

"The Fifth Amendment, man. Private brownies shall not be taken for public use without just compensation."

The sergeant licked crumbs from his fingers. "Corporal," he said as he renewed his attack on the baking pan, "compensate Mr. McCoy."

Corporal Savak positioned himself behind Brownie. Taking his rifle in both hands, he swung the weapon back and then propelled it forward towards the kneeling hippie. Brownie grunted as the blow to his back from the rifle butt knocked him facedown on the asphalt.

Sergeant Stasi finally pried loose a hunk of chocolaty confection and shoved it whole into his mouth. "Moist!" he said, the word barely distinguishable through a mouthful of deliciousness. "You missed your true calling, Mr. McCoy." He paused to chew. "If I put in a good word I'm sure I can get you a job in the prison bakery." Then, to his men he said, "Guys, have some of this." As Private Cheka kept his weapon aimed at the prisoner, the sergeant tore another brownie out of the baking pan and placed it in the private's mouth. Then he brought the pan over to the tow truck and offered it to Corporal Savak, who had begun his search of the vehicle in earnest. The corporal ate a brownie with one hand while he ransacked the glove box with the other.

The tranquilizer acted fast. Within minutes, Sergeant Stasi and Private Cheka sprawled unconscious on the pavement, their faces blissful, an overturned pan of brownies beside them. Corporal Savak hung awkwardly through the door of the tow truck.

Brownie sat up on his haunches. Standing slowly, he groaned and massaged his back.

He approached the two men on the ground, pausing just beyond their reach. When they didn't respond to his presence, Brownie moved in closer. The private had dropped his rifle as he fell.

Brownie picked it up, removed the clip, and prodded the CREEPS with the muzzle. They remained motionless.

He was about to restore the rifle to the spot where he found it when he thought, "I might want this someday." Returning to the tow truck, he stowed the weapon and the clip behind the passenger seat.

He walked over to the driver's side and unhooked the walkie-talkie from Corporal Savak's belt. Speaking into the mouthpiece, he did his best impression of the sergeant. "Stasi reporting, again. Over."

"Go ahead, Sergeant."

"Lieutenant, I got tired of waiting for O'Hare. I gave McCoy the go-ahead to tow his car. Over."

Profanity poured from the speaker.

"Stop being a REMF, sir," said Brownie.

"I didn't hear that, Sergeant."

"Yes you did, sir. REMF. Want me to spell it out for you? Rear. Echelon. Mother—"

The lieutenant didn't let him get to the last word. Profanity turned to promises of physical violence.

"Lieutenant," said Brownie, "any time you want to come over here and make good on those threats, I'll be waiting. Stasi out."

He tossed the walkie-talkie towards the sergeant's sedated body. It rolled to a stop a few inches from the brownie pan. "If you think you're in trouble now," said Brownie, "wait until they analyze the leftovers in that pan. Don't worry. I'm sure your grandchildren will visit you in the stockade."

Turning his attention back to the truck, Brownie operated the lever to reel in the towline. The cable stiffened and the front end of the Cheetah rose off the pavement with great dignity. Brownie grabbed Corporal Savak by the collar and tried to pull him out of the cab, but his foot was caught under the brake petal. Brownie unhooked it. The corporal tumbled onto the asphalt.

Back in the driver's seat, Brownie lowered the window and waved goodbye to the three unconscious CREEPS. The truck started for the exit. The Cheetah YK-9 trundled behind.

β 1 1

Since Kilkenny's served neither lobster nor champagne, Gimbel settled for a hamburger with a Glenjohnnie chaser. He filled out the paperwork to get charbroiled Angus in place of government-approved soy. It arrived in a red plastic basket with wax paper and French fries. Gimbel took each bite slowly, enjoying the charbroil flavor. As he ate, he engaged in some rudimentary spycraft: he used the frosted-glass mirror behind the bar to surveil the entrance.

He hadn't eaten since yesterday's lunch. He hadn't gotten the chance: today's calendar had been completely booked. His first appointment was with Mrs. Lazuli. The crowd in Gracie's had thinned. Most of the homeless went out for the day to beg, or procure supplies, or work in offices. Gimbel and Mrs. Lazuli sat on concrete blocks halfway up the rubble pile. The warm sun and open sky above them reminded Gimbel of the time he visited the ruins of an ancient amphitheater in Italy. He asked Mrs. Lazuli to retell the story of her banishment from Fox Hunt Apartments. This time he took notes on his IQPhone, interrupting frequently with questions. When she finished her story and they returned to her blanket, Gimbel requested a photo of Mimi. Mrs. Lazuli produced one from under a pile of laundry and gave it to him. In return, he gave her the fringe vest. "Trade it for food," he said. Brownie could lecture him later about bringing supplies back from the field intact.

The hippie mobile was where he left it in the garage. After a stop at a pharmacy to stock up on contact lens solution, dental floss, and other essentials, he drove out to Fairfax. He washed as well as he could in the men's room of the public library. Then he logged on to one of the library's communal terminals and checked the news sites for info about the Byte Yourself raid. The Department of Justice had filed charges against the company under the Federal Economic Sabotage Act. Specifically, the department alleged that Byte Yourself conspired to reduce its employment level via unauthorized efficiencies enabled by a horizontal monopoly. The attorney general considered Gimbel's September 20 e-mail about eliminating the BAD Toolbox to be a smoking gun; there was a link to it on the DOJ website. Byte Yourself's stock had crashed; the board of directors planned to hold an emergency meeting on Sunday evening to consider its response. Gimbel O'Hare was still at large and had earned a spot on the CREEPS Ten Most Wanted List. Video of his *Sorry* appearance had gone viral and the *Washington Courier* website had posted a short bio of him next to an editorial demanding a solution to the problem of antisocial software engineers. After counting the number of factual errors in the bio (there were three), he took a quick look at SoshNet. An ad caught his attention. "Beta Eleven: report to Washington, DC, headquarters." He typed a response and then dedicated the rest of the afternoon to writing a SoshNet app. Mastering the APIs took some effort, but after a few hours the app was ready for prime time. Gimbel ended the session and headed over to Kilkenny's.

He was halfway through his burger when Chris arrived and met a friend at the pool table. While Chris racked the balls, his friend ordered a pitcher of beer from the bar. Gimbel waited for the game to get underway before he approached them.

The friend was talented. He got halfway to clearing the table while Chris stood by chalking his cue. Finally the friend scratched and Chris got his turn. As he lined up his first shot, nine ball in the corner pocket, a voice said, "I should play the twelve if I were you. It will leave you in a better position for your next shot—if you get one."

Still leaning over his cue, Chris looked up and saw his downstairs neighbor standing with a red basket at the other end of the table. "You're supposed to be in jail," he said as he lowered his head again. The cue ball smacked the nine dead center and knocked the striped ball into the pocket. The white sphere rolled to a stop behind a wall of three solid balls. Chris attempted a bank shot to liberate the cue ball from behind the opposing barrier and goad the ten into the side pocket.

"Oh, bad luck," said Gimbel. "You missed."

Chris lay the cue down on the table and removed his IQPhone from his belt. "Let's see what we can do about that jail thing," he said.

"Good. Maybe we'll share a cell."

"What's that supposed to mean?"

Gimbel put the red basket down on the rail. He removed a wad of paper from the inside pocket of his suit jacket and pushed the folded sheets across the pool table with a bridge.

Chris put his IQPhone down on the green felt. He unfolded the papers and read the heading.

"So what?" he said. "It's a warrant of seizure."

"It's evidence," replied Gimbel.

"Of what?"

"Of perjury. Of abuse of power. You told a judge that you needed the apartment for a criminal investigation, when you just wanted a place to live."

"That's a lie! I did need the apartment for a criminal investigation. I needed it for *two* criminal investigations. The department cleaned it out to search for evidence in US vs. Ricardo Lazuli. Then we used it to conduct surveillance of you in US vs. Byte Yourself Software."

Gimbel picked up the basket again and took a bite from his hamburger. "Tell me, Chris," he said as he licked his fingers, "is it customary in the DOJ to bring girlfriends and stereo equipment along on a stakeout?"

"It was my cover!"

"Try not to shout when you tell that to the press. You'll be more credible that way."

"The press?" said Chris before picking up his IQPhone again and punching in a phone number. "It doesn't matter. Where you're going, you'll never get close enough to the press to tell them anything."

"The thing is," Gimbel replied, "I'm the only one who can stop it from getting to the press."

Chris put the phone down again.

"I thought that would get your attention," Gimbel said. "I developed a little software application this afternoon. In one week, it will automatically post a copy of this warrant to SoshNet—with an appropriate explanation—unless I shut the app down. So if anything happens to me, the Department of Justice, the *Washington Courier*, and a billion others will know what you did."

"No one will believe you. You're an accused criminal."

"It will be easy enough for them to check it out. The warrant is in the public record."

"I didn't do anything wrong! It was for a case. *Two* cases!"

"Then you have nothing to worry about." Gimbel carried the red basket around to Chris's side of the table. "Did you know," Gimbel asked, "that the family you sent out into the street had a baby?"

"No."

"You didn't bother to find out." Gimbel took a photo out of his pocket and showed it to Chris, who recognized his own living room. A chubby baby, perhaps six months old, sat propped in an armchair. She wore a t-shirt featuring an American flag and the slogan *Star-Spangled Girl*. Underneath a jungle of black curls, her round face was adorable but serious as she concentrated on the buttons of a telephone.

"Her name is Mimi," Gimbel said. "Did they teach you anything in law school about the effect of cute babies on a jury?

Tell your side of the story in court if you think it will help. You had to evict her to protect the public. I bet the press nicknames you the Baby Evictor. But don't fret. The attorney general will back you up. Won't he?"

Chris looked around the pub. A group of women sat around a long table drinking Dublin Margaritas. They cooed as the woman at the head of the table, who didn't have a margarita, tore the floral paper off a gift box and held up a tiny one-piece sleep suit.

"What do you want?" Chris asked.

"Drop all charges against me and Byte Yourself. Release Ricardo Lazuli and return his apartment to him."

Chris thought for a moment. "I can get Lazuli off," he said. "You too, probably. But not Byte Yourself. Tina Lee is the one they're really after."

"Who are they?"

"Attorney General Peterson and his political advisor."

"Does this advisor have a name?"

"I don't know. I never met him."

"Never mind. I think I know who he is. Why do they want to take down Tina Lee?"

"I don't know. It has something to do with Peterson's White House bid. They'll never agree to drop the charges. The deal is too big."

"Then you and I don't have a deal at all."

"I told you I can't. Nothing I say will convince them."

"You have seven days to think of something."

"I *could* think of something," said Chris, grinning maliciously. "Or I could just do this." He grabbed the pool cue from the table and swung it like a baseball bat. It connected with Gimbel's knees, hard. Gimbel fell beside the pool table. The basket fell with him, spilling bun crust and shredded lettuce onto the linoleum. Gimbel grabbed his knees and grimaced.

"I thought that would get your attention," said Chris. "I'll do it again if you don't tell me how to shut down your SoshNet app."

"You're not going to torture me dressed like that, are you?" Gimbel replied.

Chris looked down at his clothes. He was dressed as he had been at the office, in a gray suit and red tie. "What's wrong with the way I'm dressed?"

"I heard you wear a black uniform when you want to play Gestapo."

"Subterranean nerd!" Chris yelled as he pulled back his cue and aimed it for Gimbel's head. He began his swing. Gimbel tucked his chin into his chest and shielded his head with his hands. His surroundings disappeared from his consciousness. There was no Kilkenny's, no bar, no pool table, no happy people eating and drinking and opening presents. There was only a wooden rod arcing towards his head in slow motion and the sound of his own heartbeat.

And something red. Gimbel waited for the impact. It never came. He turned his head and looked over his shoulder to the place where Chris was standing. No one was there.

His surroundings seeped back. A crowd was gathering. Their voices drowned out the sound of his heartbeat. Something slapped rhythmically. In front of him, he saw stiletto heels, six inches long, supporting a pair of muscular calves. Above him, a woman talked trash. "IF YOU WANT TO MESS WITH LITTLE 'N' CUDDLY YOU'LL HAVE TO GO THROUGH ME."

When Gimbel raised his head, Cheri Tarte was standing over him. He realized he had been foolish to confront Chris before he had some muscle to back himself up. Fortunately, the Crimson Crusher swooped in when she did, like a superheroine in a red sundress and matching headband. The black strap of her handbag separated her breasts, emphasizing their roundness. From Gimbel's perspective, she was a welcome sight in all sorts of ways.

She was more muscle than needed to dispatch Chris. The sinews of her arm barely strained as she held him by his belt six feet in the air—with one hand. His arms and legs thrashed as he tried to regain the floor. With her other hand, Cheri Tarte spanked him with his own pool cue.

When she saw Gimbel looking up at her, she greeted him. "Hello, Little 'n' Cuddly. Glad you're okay." She leaned the cue against the table and extended her arm to help him up.

"Thank you for the rescue," Gimbel said as he grasped her hand and pulled himself to his feet. "My still intact skull thanks you too."

He pointed to Chris, still dangling from her other hand. "You can let him go now."

"I forgot." She laughed and relaxed her grip. Chris dropped to the floor. Cheri Tarte picked up the pool cue and tapped it against her other palm like an oversized ruler.

Chris scrambled to his feet and went supersonic out of the bar.

"Well," said Gimbel, straightening his tie, "he left on cue."

β 1 1

After Chris left the bar, Cheri Tarte pulled Gimbel into a booth. She came right to the point. "I got your response to my SoshNet ad." She read from the screen of her IQPhone. "'I know who you are. Meet me tonight at Kilkenny's in Fairfax. Little 'n' Cuddly.' You want to tell me how much you know?"

"I know you're the Betamaker," Gimbel replied. "I know you're responsible for sabo attacks in Washington and Las Vegas and at least two other places."

She didn't bother to deny it. She just wanted to know the price for his silence.

"I'm not here to blackmail you," Gimbel replied. "I'm here to warn you."

Before he could explain, Pam came to the table with her order pad. "Gimbel!" she said. "You haven't been to paintball in forever. What can I get you two to drink?"

"I had a hamburger and a drink at the bar," he replied. "Please bring the check. We won't be staying." Pam went to the register. Cheri Tarte was puzzled. "We can't stay here," Gimbel explained. "I'm not the only one who knows about you. Or I won't be for long. The Department of Justice has all the pieces. If they haven't put them together yet, they will soon. The CREEPS won't be far behind."

"Why not let them come? You'd collect a nice reward. I'm first on their Ten Most Wanted List."

"I'm second."

Cheri Tarte looked impressed. "Way to go, Gimbel," she said. "What do we do now?"

"We get out of town."

"I have a car."

"Rental?"

"Yes."

"In your name?"

"Yes."

"The CREEPS will be looking for it. We'll take my car."

Pam came back and dropped a black plastic sleeve on the table. Gimbel opened it and placed some bills inside. When Pam was out of earshot, Cheri said, "I have to go back to my hotel first."

"It's too dangerous."

"I have papers there. Photos. Evidence. They prove that the UWL has been laundering illegal campaign contributions for Attorney General Peterson."

Gimbel whistled. Cheri Tarte had just conjured the other half of the torn playing card, the piece he had been looking for. "What hotel are you in?" he asked.

"Barnett Crystal City."

β 1 1

Getting Cheri Tarte into the hippie mobile required some coaxing. "Aren't we supposed to be inconspicuous?" she asked when she saw the rainbow painted on the hood and the words on the doors.

"It might not look like it," Gimbel replied, "but this car has a big advantage over yours in the inconspicuous department."

"What's that?"

"No one's looking for it."

They pushed the passenger seat as far back as it would go, but there still wasn't enough room in the subcompact for Cheri Tarte's legs. She squeezed in with her knees mashed against the glove box.

As they sped eastbound on I-66, Cheri wanted to know how Gimbel got on the CREEPS Ten Most Wanted List. He told her about his e-mail to Addison and the DOJ raid on Byte Yourself. Then it was her turn. Gimbel asked how she learned about the illegal campaign contributions.

"It was after we wrapped in Los Angeles," she said. "The *Error of the Moon* crew went on location in Geneva, but I didn't have any Swiss scenes so I returned to the UWL. My first show was in Orlando. I was driving to rehearsal when I realized I left my script at the hotel. I turned the car around. When I got back to my room, a bellboy was there for no apparent reason. He excused himself, but it was suspicious. There was an incident last year when a fan broke into my room and hid a camera there—he recorded some naughty video of me and posted it on the Internet. I thought the bellboy might be another amateur videographer. I searched everything. Picture frames, light fixtures, drawers, pillows…"

"Did you check the air vents?" Gimbel asked. "Sometimes they hide cameras in the air vents."

"No, nothing in the air vents. But when I felt up my suitcase I found a bulge where there shouldn't be one. It turned out there was a secret panel and an envelope full of cash inside. After that, it was a matter of recruiting a Beta and having him follow my luggage to see where the envelope ended up. It turned out to be a Peterson campaign office."

It started to rain. Not hard, but enough to blur the taillights of the other cars. Gimbel switched on the windshield wipers.

"Is that why you came to Washington?" he asked. "To confront the attorney general?"

"No," she replied. "I'm here for *Error of the Moon*. We're on location to film a car chase."

"What are you going to do with the evidence you gathered?"

"Wait for the right opportunity to go public. It isn't easy when everyone responsible for enforcing the law works for the criminal."

Gimbel thought. "I know a lawyer in the Department of Justice who may be honest," he said, "but she can't do us any good unless we get your file before the CREEPS do." He passed a slow moving car. "But here's the most important question of all."

"What that?"

"What's the URL for that naughty video?"

Cheri Tarte laughed and punched him in the shoulder. "You're not going to need a video," she said.

β 1 1

They parked in the underground garage at the Barnett Hotel. Although Cheri Tarte's room was on the twenty-sixth floor, Gimbel insisted on getting out of the elevator two floors below and stairing it the rest of the way. When they got to her floor, Gimbel opened the fire door a crack. He peered through the opening into the hallway. Cheri Tarte stood behind him and looked over his head.

CREEPS infested the hallway.

They tramped in and out of Cheri Tarte's room as their captain gave orders. A sergeant carried a file folder in one hand; he concealed his other hand behind his back. "We found this, sir," he said, handing the folder to the captain. The officer leafed through its contents. "Good work, sergeant," he said as he turned over a page. "This will go straight to the AG."

"Is that the money laundering evidence?" Gimbel whispered.

"Yes," Cheri Tarte replied. "We're too late."

The captain looked up from the folder. "Where did you find this, sergeant?"

"In her underwear drawer."

At the mention of underwear, the captain giggled unpleasantly, like a middle school boy who just heard genitals mentioned in sex ed class. "You went through her unmentionables?" he asked. "Why didn't you mention that?"

"I'll do better than mention it," the sergeant replied. "See for yourself." He showed his commanding officer what he was hiding behind his back. It was a white brassiere. The design was a marvel of structural engineering. There weren't actually steel girders or rivets, but they would not have been out of place. The CREEPS sergeant tossed the undergarment to the captain, who put it on his head. "Check it out," he laughed. "My whole head fits in one cup."

"Let's see how it fits around your neck," Cheri Tarte said.

She reached to open the door but Gimbel pushed it closed. "These guys are serfs," he said. "Scary serfs with guns, but still the cellar of the feudal system. It's the king we're after."

They descended the two flights of stairs and re-boarded the elevator for the return trip. Leaving town was out of the question now. They needed a place to hide until they could figure out how to recover the evidence folder. Gimbel thought of going back to Gracie's, but Cheri deserved a better title than Queen of the Dispossessed.

FULL ASYLUM

The elevator stopped on twenty-one and a bellman cart nosed through the door. Gimbel and Cheri Tarte moved to one side to make room for it. Someone followed it in, but Gimbel could not see him clearly. He only glimpsed a patch of red hair and a patch of red uniform through the barrier of suitcases and garment bags. The space between the cart and the wall was narrow. Cheri Tarte and Gimbel stood close together. Behind her, beyond the open doors of the elevator, a chain of mood lights traced the corridor. Through a picture window, Gimbel saw the metallic cylinder of an airplane on its final vector into National. A haze of landing lights washed out the night sky as the jet flew towards them. The elevator doors closed, squeezing the aircraft out of existence.

The walls of the elevator, the towers of luggage, and the tall woman beside him boxed Gimbel into a corner. When he stood next to Cheri Tarte on the floor of the Horizon Center, his eyes were level with her neck. Now she wore heels and he found himself face to face with her breasts. They slumbered in the soft cotton fabric of her dress. As he watched them rock in their cradle, Gimbel realized he had become conscious of her breathing. His eyes followed her red tresses over her bare shoulders and up to her face. They made eye contact. Her emerald-colored eyes displayed affection—and amusement. Her smile was so broad she seemed to struggle not to laugh out loud. Suddenly Gimbel felt a warm glow, as if he had waited a long time for something and it unexpectedly came to pass. But all that had happened was that Cheri Tarte's hand had brushed against his forearm. He inhaled her perfume. It smelled like cherries: not the artificial cherry flavoring found in sucking candy and lip gloss, but actual ripe cherries on a warm summer day. He wondered why he hadn't noticed it before. Was it the closed-in space or was she growing warm too?

As the elevator resumed its slide down the shaft, the bellboy stared at the doors for a few moments before he also noticed the perfume. He looked over his shoulder at the luggage cart and was surprised to see a woman standing on the other side. He was even more surprised to see her trademark red hair above the metal frame of the cart; he knew the UWL wasn't in town. The bellboy pulled a notepad and a pen from his jacket pocket and held it up for an autograph.

"I think you've mistaken me for someone else," the woman replied.

"I'm sorry, ma'am" said the bellboy. "I thought you were a different six-foot-three-inch woman with cherry-colored hair. My mistake."

"I can't believe he bought that," said a familiar voice on the other side of the cart.

"Is that Gimbel O'Hare?" the bellboy asked, peering between two garment bags.

"Yes, you paintball idiot savant," said Gimbel, smiling back through the gap. "She's pulling your leg. She is Cheri Tarte. So Joe, is this your big secret for getting UWL autographs? Moonlighting at the Barnett Hotel?"

"This is where I am when I'm not ducking paintballs. Hey, did you see the CREEPS all over the building? Maybe we'll be on the news."

"Cheri Tarte and I are the news," Gimbel replied. "The CREEPS are after us."

Joe pulled the emergency stop. The elevator hung in space between the third and fourth floors. "How can I help?" he asked.

"We need a place to hide," said Gimbel.

Joe thought. "There's no one in the Grand Suite this weekend," he said.

"Can you get us in without using our names?"

"Sure," said Joe. He pulled a key card from his belt on a retractable cord and held it up for Gimbel to see. "I can get you into any room in the hotel."

"What if someone tries to check into the Grand Suite while we're there?"

"I can check you in with fake names when I get back to my station. That will prevent anyone from walking in on you. You'll even be able order room service."

"Won't you need a credit card?"

"I can put it on the UWL account." He looked at Cheri Tarte. "Since you really do work for the UWL, it won't be stealing."

"Okay," said Gimbel. "We'll take the Grand Suite."

Joe pushed the emergency stop back into place and pressed the button for twenty-seven.

"This is one helpful friend you have," said Cheri Tarte, her face smiling above the bellman cart. She thrust her arms between the garment bags and gave Joe a big hug.

β 1 1

Gimbel closed the door to his bedroom and descended the steps to the salon of the Grand Suite. He wore a white bathrobe with an embroidered Barnett monogram. The one-size-fits-all garment was too big for him, but the pile of the terrycloth fabric was deep and luxurious. The rolled lapels muffled his neck like a fur collar.

Cheri's door was shut, but apparently she had already closed the deal with the room service waiter. Under the Louis XV chandelier, white linen draped a table just big enough for two. Flame-shaped light bulbs reflected off fine china and real silver. The baby grand piano had been converted into a makeshift sideboard. Four serving platters waited on the closed lid, their contents hidden under silver cloches. There were also glass beer mugs, an assortment of crystal tumblers, bottles of imported lager, and a fifth of Glenjohnnie.

Gimbel picked up the bottle of scotch and studied the label. Thirty years old, same as he was. He wondered if he would drink sixty-year-old scotch when he hit the threescore mark. He splashed the amber liquid into a glass and tasted it. It had noticeable smoothness compared to the pre-teen concoction served at Kilkenny's. Across the room, a row of windows overlooked the city. Gimbel walked over and admired the rain-swept view as he sipped from the cut crystal. The Capitol Dome was lit up. Traffic streamed across a bridge and entered the District near the Jefferson Memorial. To the left, the Washington Monument dominated the skyline.

Cheri Tarte came out of her room and stood next to him at the window. She wore a white terrycloth robe too. It was as small on her as it was large on Gimbel. Falling only to mid-thigh, it was open in front, displaying plenty of bra, panty, and quadriceps. Her wet hair hung tangled and wild. She exuded a fresh application of cherry scent. Without asking, she took the glass from Gimbel's hand. After a generous swallow of single malt, she returned the tumbler to him.

"Darling," he said. "Have you seen my suit? It disappeared from my room."

"It was filthy," she replied. "And wrinkled. And stinky. I sent it to be cleaned. Why do you ask? Are you going somewhere?"

"There's nowhere else I'd rather be."

"Good. Because until the valet comes back with your suit, you're my prisoner."

He pointed to the covered dishes on top of the piano. "Any bread and water over there?"

"I'll show you. Sit down."

He didn't sit. He waited until Cheri carried a pair of dishes over from the piano and then he pulled her gilded chair out for her. Once she was settled he sat opposite. She removed the cover from the first dish. "Ribs," she said. There was a full rack of them dripping sticky red barbecue sauce. "Those are mine." She slid the platter over to her side of the table. Then she raised the cover on the second plate. "You have to have salad. I don't date fat guys."

FULL ASYLUM

At least it was a good salad: mesclun greens, grape tomatoes, candied pecans, and slices of pear. There was just a hint of raspberry vinaigrette; a fine kitchen is distinguished by the garde manger's light hand with the dressing ladle.

Last summer Gimbel took a road trip with Liza and they ended up at a rib joint. When the food came, Liza carefully sliced each rib off the end of the rack and surgically removed the meat with a knife and fork. A few stubborn ribs resisted utensils; she held the ends of the bones daintily between her thumbs and forefingers and took delicate bites. As for the sauce, in case of accidental contact with skin, clean immediately with a moist towelette. She must have gone through two-dozen of the square packets.

Cheri Tarte employed a different technique. She picked up the rack with two hands and twisted each rib free as if it were a piece of bread. Holding it in a solid grip, she tore off chunks of meat with her teeth. Her lips attended to any morsels that clung to the bone. When the bone was sucked bare, she tossed it on a plate and ripped off another while she was still chewing. After a few ribs, a ring of barbecue sauce glistened on her upper lip and stained her chin like blood. A silver bowl of moist towelettes remained untouched on the lid of the piano.

Her green eyes told him that she enjoyed the ribs, that she knew he was fascinated by her enjoyment, and that she enjoyed that too. She held his gaze as she gnawed on a bone. Finally she said, "You can watch me eat, but if you'd rather look at my breasts, that's okay too. There may be some barbecue sauce on them."

"Don't you mind?"

"A little barbecue sauce never hurt anyone."

"No, I meant your breasts."

"They never hurt anyone either—except this one time when I pinned Suzie Winsome and—"

"You're not like other women, are you?"

Cheri Tarte took that as a compliment. "I certainly hope not," she said through a mouthful of pork. "Most women are afraid they won't measure up. I'm not. I'm definitely not like those feminists who object to being judged on their looks. They insist on being judged solely on their intellectual accomplishments, but their great intellects haven't figured out the truth about men and women."

"I'm handicapped with a good intellect myself," Gimbel replied. "What truth do you mean?"

"In spite of the claims of the feminists to the contrary, men and women are pretty evenly matched in intelligence. The war between them has to be fought with other weapons."

"Is it a war then?"

She liberated a piece of meat from her teeth with a fingernail. "War is the natural state in any relationship: man and woman, boss and employee, con man and sucker—it's always a fight to see who's in charge."

"If intellect doesn't decide the winner, what does?"

"Sex," she said.

Gimbel thought about it. "I need you to explain that."

"Your intellect really is a handicap, Gimbel. Don't you see how guys act around beautiful women?"

"When there's a beautiful woman around, I'm not paying attention to other guys."

"See what I mean? A sexy jiggle or a sinful pair of legs and the rest of the world fades to black. We have something you want. That makes us powerful."

"Some women don't have a sexy jiggle or a sinful pair of legs. Aren't you being unfair to them?"

"*Nature* is being unfair to them; she distributes her gifts unevenly. But every woman gets something—she should use it. Instead, the feminists hide their assets under bulky sweaters and prison haircuts. You know the type. While the rest of us have fun watching Jon Dunn, all they do is complain that the movies don't respect women."

"I'm sure I never met that type."

"You can find them in wealthy suburban living rooms nibbling *petits fours* and whining that they're oppressed. Of course they're oppressed. What do they expect, when they throw away their most potent weapon? They convince themselves they're victims, so that is what they become."

She had a point; Gimbel thought about Beverly's Addison obsession. "I believe you," he said. "But there are other kinds of feminists out there. They would say you're the real liberated woman: empowered, in charge."

Cheri Tarte was unimpressed. "They should speak up," she said. "Their buzzcut sisters are getting all the headlines."

"Don't the buzzcut sisters have a point? Shouldn't a woman use her intellect?"

"Of course she should. She should use *all* her assets."

"What assets does my side have?"

"Normally, your side has physical strength."

"You managed to neutralize that advantage. You don't believe in a balance of power, do you?"

"I believe in power. Just not balance. It prolongs the conflict unnecessarily. When I'm with a guy, I want him to do what he's told and thank me for the privilege. I get away with it because, unlike the feminists, I know how the world works. It's easy to figure out. You can see it in any high school classroom. Students work hard, they do their homework, they participate in class discussions. But a girl with a really spectacular rack walks into the room and she's the one the teacher falls in love with. Sometimes there's a scandal."

She reached over to the serving platter for another rib and discovered there weren't any. "Gimbel," she said. "Bring one of those other plates over here." He walked to the piano. "Bring some beer too," she yelled after him. He filled a mug and brought it back to the table along with one of the covered dishes. He thanked her for the privilege and pulled the cover off the dish. Another rack of ribs.

As Cheri tore off the first rib, Gimbel asked, "What happened to the teacher that fell in love with you? Did it end in scandal?"

"I didn't say I was talking about me."

"That's right, you didn't." He took a bite of salad. "So what happened to him?"

"It was Mr. Kenner. Eleventh-grade English. He just gave me better grades than I deserved. Much better than the girls in the Suburban Women's Grievance Society. He also gave me books to read for extra credit. That way I'd stay after class and discuss them with him. That was all. There was no scandal."

Eschewing the handle, she picked up the beer mug and drained it. Gimbel refilled it for her while she chomped another rib.

"What books?" he asked.

"Huh?" said Cheri Tarte.

"You said Mr. Kenner assigned books for extra credit. What books?"

"Nietzche. Ibsen. Camille Paglia."

"Mr. Kenner made you the woman you are today."

"*I* made me the woman I am today. Mr. Kenner just gave the reading assignments."

"Which author was your favorite?"

"Ibsen. I liked *Peer Gynt*."

"I never read it. What's it about?"

"It's about using all your assets."

"I didn't know Ibsen wrote about…assets," said Gimbel. "I didn't think he was into soft core."

"Very funny," said Cheri. "Peer Gynt was a man who was destined for greatness, but didn't get there."

"Why not?"

"Because of what happened in the Hall of the Troll King."

"There's a Troll King?"

"Sometimes it's translated 'Mountain King.'"

"That sounds familiar."

"It should. Grieg wrote music for it. You'd recognize it if you heard it. They use it in cartoons and commercials when they want something that sounds creepy. Peer wants to marry the Troll King's daughter, but the king doesn't believe in mixed marriages. He tells Peer he has to become a troll. He has to wear a tail, and drink cow piss, and live by the troll motto."

"What's the troll motto?"

"The king explains it. Humans have an expression, he says, 'To thine own self be true.' But for trolls it's 'To thine own self be enough.' Peer accepts that. Next he has to have his eyes cut so he can see the world in Troll-vision. That's where Peer draws the line. The trolls take it badly. They attack Peer. He has to fight to escape.

"He has many adventures after that. He makes a fortune and loses it. He becomes a prophet, a scholar, and the Emperor of the Self, but none of these gigs last. At the end of a wasted life he returns to his native country an old man. A button maker shows up to explain the afterlife to him. Heaven is for those who are true to themselves, but there aren't many of them. Genuine assholes go to hell. There aren't many of them either. Most souls, the great mass of the mediocre, are melted down like defective buttons. They fuse together and get recast. God is very frugal with souls and buttons. No asset should be wasted. The Button Maker has orders to collect Peer's soul for the casting ladle. Peer begs for a chance to prove that he deserves heaven or hell. He doesn't care which. Loss of self is what terrifies him."

She finished the second rack of ribs. Without waiting to be asked, Gimbel brought her the third one. She continued the story between bites. "Peer goes off in search of witnesses to his greatness or to his evil. As luck would have it, he finds his old nemesis the Troll King wandering in the mountains. Peer asks him to testify to the Button Maker about the great thing he did in refusing to become a troll. The Troll King replies that he can't do it; it would be a lie. Peer reminds him that he refused to have his eyes cut. True, replied the king, you turned down the physical trappings of trollness. 'But you took away my motto graven on your heart. That compelling word that distinguishes Troll from Mankind: Enough! And, ever since, with all the energy you have, you've lived according to that motto.' You see, his whole life, Peer was self-satisfied. He was enough. Even though he was talented, he didn't use his talent. He was too lazy to become anything worthwhile. He wasn't true to himself."

"That's profoundly metaphysical," said Gimbel. "Peer didn't become something, so now he'll become nothing. I take it he gets melted down."

"Ibsen doesn't say. In the last scene Peer earns a reprieve from the casting ladle as he buries his tears in the lap of a woman who loves him. The Button Maker tells him they'll meet again.

"Actually, when I got to college, I took a class in Scandinavian literature and the professor told me I had the play all wrong. When Ibsen said that your self isn't enough, he meant that you should serve other people and carry out God's purpose for you. I reread the play and the professor was probably right. But I didn't care. I liked my interpretation better. Does any of that make sense?"

"I think it's why people keep going to see Jon Dunn movies," said Gimbel. "He demonstrates what's possible to them, if only they were true to themselves. Do you remember when Grant Casey told me I wouldn't want to know Jon Dunn in real life? He said I wouldn't want to know a man who blows up every building he walks into. He missed the point." He swirled his whiskey in the glass. "Beta Eleven isn't about drinking Glenjohnnie or blowing up buildings. It's about being the best at everything you set out to do."

As he said it, he realized he understood something about her. "Alas," he said, "poor Cheri."

"Why do you say that?"

"Because you must hate the speeches they write for you. Recycling and toilet flushes."

She nodded.

"You're an indoor cat. You were bred to hunt. But the UWL locked you in the house. You see a robin hopping outside the window, but there's a glass barrier keeping you from him. He mocks you with his singing. You're a prisoner of people whom you consider your inferiors. But you're watching them. Someday they'll hold the door open just a little too long. Then you'll rush to freedom and annihilate your prey."

At first Cheri Tarte said nothing. Then, "IS LITTLE 'N' CUDDLY TRYING TO SAY THAT CHERI TARTE IS A PUSSYCAT?"

He reached across the table and brushed a tear from her cheek. "I promise not to tell anyone," he said.

They ate in silence for a while. When she finished, Cheri Tarte licked barbeque sauce off her fingers. "There is one thing I'm built for—besides annihilating my prey," she said. "Eating."

"That way you'll grow up big and strong," Gimbel replied.

"Apparently I'm not big enough. I'm still hungry."

"We're out of ribs."

"You didn't finish your salad. Shove it over here."

He slid the plate across the table. She finished the mesclun and pear slices while Gimbel watched. When the plate was empty, Cheri Tarte said, "You're not like other guys, are you?"

"I certainly hope not. Why do you ask?"

"Most guys get upset when I tell them what to do. Or eat them under the table. You seem to be enjoying it."

"Most guys are trying to compete with you for who will be in charge. I already know."

"Glad you got that straight."

"I didn't say it was you."

She opened her mouth to reply, but nothing came out. Then she slammed her elbow down on the table. "We're going to settle this," she said. "I'll arm wrestle you. I'll even use my weak arm."

"To make it fair?"

"No, to make your loss more demoralizing."

"I can't lose," he replied.

"What do you mean, you can't lose?" She pushed the terrycloth sleeve up her arm and pointed to her flexed bicep. "*That* says you can lose."

"I can't lose because I want you to be true to your self. I want you to be strong and independent. It's an if-then-else-block. *If*, by some miracle, I slam your arm down on the table, *then* I beat you and I win. *Else*, in the more likely scenario where it's my arm that's eating tablecloth, you did what I wanted. I still win."

"So no one has to lose? How will we know who's in charge?"

"I don't think nature intended for one person to be in charge. Not between equals."

She straightened her elbow to extend her hand across the table. "Equals," she said. They shook on it.

"Equals," Gimbel repeated. Then he shook out his hand at the wrist and added in a voice higher than normal, "but not in grip strength."

Gimbel looked at the plate piled with greasy white bones. He wondered whatever happened to Mr. Kenner.

"Time for dessert," she said.

"There's no food left."

"You're going to eat cherry tart."

She stood and walked away from the table. Pausing, she looked back at him over her shoulder and held out her hand for his.

In the agony of the days that followed, Gimbel often remembered what she looked like standing in the salon of the Grand Suite: her tousled red hair, her coy expression, her open robe, her bare feet on the parquet.

He took her hand. They looked at each other as she led him up the stairs to her bedroom.

β 1 1

The CREEPS were waiting for Lacey at the gate.

"Welcome back to DC, Miss Briefs," said the captain. He took her carry-on bag by the strap and gave it to a private to carry.

The flight was the last to arrive at National that night. The jetway discharged its passengers into the dimly lit concourse. They gave the CREEPS a wide berth and hurried to the exit, past closed snack bars and deserted waiting areas.

"What did I miss while I was in the air?" Lacey asked. She swore she would never fly in the middle of a search-and-capture again. Ninety minutes without the use of her IQPhone had provided too many opportunities to imagine things going wrong. Somewhere over Pittsburgh the woman in the next seat had looked at Lacey and offered her an aspirin.

"We completed the search of her hotel room," said the captain.

"Did you all find anything?"

"Clothing. Toilet articles. Some fashion magazines."

"What about papers, computer files, and such?"

"No, ma'am."

"Where is the suspect at?"

"She didn't return to her room. We reviewed the hotel security video and identified her leaving the Barnett by automobile at 1830 hours. She headed north, towards Route 66. I put out an APB and a little while later the Fairfax Police reported finding her car at a pub. I sent in a retrieval team, but there was no sign of her. Evidently the car had been abandoned."

Lacey forced herself to stand straight. It had been two weeks since Gimbel suggested investigating who was absent from Seattle. Since then she had worked non-stop. The UWL cooperated. The front office provided access to video archives and employee travel records. Only one League member was in Los Angeles on the night of the Academy Awards. Stuck in Fort Wayne, Lacey struggled with long-distance coordination of court orders and CREEPS. When word came this afternoon that Cheri Tarte had checked into the Barnett, there were last-minute travel plans, a sprint to Fort Wayne International, and hours on the ground waiting for a connecting flight in Detroit. Everything was finally in place for an arrest. If they lost the suspect now...

"That just beats all. Then what did you do?" she asked the captain.

"The retrieval team combed the area while the video techs continued to review hotel security footage."

"And?"

"And we found her. She returned to the hotel and entered the Grand Suite just after 2100 hours. A short man in a suit accompanied her."

"Got an ID on the man?"

"We don't have a clear shot of his face. He was wearing a cap."

"Then you haven't moved in on them yet?"

"No, ma'am. We waited for you. I posted guards in the corridor. They're not going anywhere."

"Fine work, Captain. Let's move out."

β 1 1

Cheri Tarte was always revved afterwards. It was as if she took a man's strength away from him and added it to her own. Gimbel had hidden reserves of it that she had not suspected when he first scurried onto the set of *Sorry*.

Dressed in her underwear, she propped one leg on a coffee table for hamstring stretches. What she really wanted was some heavy lifting, but there was no way she could get past the CREEPS and reach the fitness center. She looked around the salon for anything resembling a dumbbell. There was an alabaster lamp shaped like a Greek column. She lifted it off the end table. About twenty pounds. Not enough, but it seemed to be her only choice.

She removed the shade for a set of arm curls. It had been fun telling Gimbel about *Peer Gynt*. The play had been her bible for a decade, but somehow it had never come up in any of her previous dates. Maybe it came up tonight because she enjoyed being around Gimbel. Or maybe it came up tonight because Gimbel was the first guy who asked.

She stretched out on the floor and bench-pressed the lamp. Strong pecs put the wallop in her punch. When Cheri Tarte was fourteen, she dated an older boy with a car. She was a little rounder then, less cut; her hair was light brown. Her boyfriend promised to take her to the mall one Saturday afternoon so she could buy a tank top on sale at Gracie's. When he didn't show, she went to his house and found him playing video games with two of his friends. "Sorry, babe," he said, "I decided to hang with the guys." She really wanted that tank top. The three boys never did live down what happened next. Half the school saw their black eyes as they followed Cheri Tarte around the mall. That was the day she decided she would always dominate the guy she was with; the alternative was to submit. She used punches then. When she got older, she discovered there were less violent, but equally effective tools of subjugation.

Twenty-five reps. Keep going. Little 'n' Cuddly had some strange ideas. He thought neither of them had to be the boss. He couldn't be right. Could he? Maybe after this business with the CREEPS was over, she would spend some time with him and find out.

She completed fifty reps without feeling the burn; the lamp wasn't getting the job done. It didn't help that, lying on the floor, she couldn't lower her arms far enough. She put the lamp back on the table and looked around. There had to be something in the Grand Suite that could challenge her.

When she saw it, her first reaction was, "No. Effing. Way." Then she remembered something Kong told her once, downstairs in the bar. "You're stronger than you think." The worst that could happen is she'd have to pay the hotel for damages. She inspected the underside. The case seemed solid enough. She removed the remaining glasses and bottles from the lid, along with the untouched bowl of moist towelettes. Crawling underneath the piano, she crouched behind the pedals and pressed her back muscles against the case. She raised one knee, kneeling on the other as if proposing marriage. The piano jerked upward. She held the legs to steady it and tilted the case slightly backwards to make room for her head. Then she straightened her legs.

She glanced in the mirror and saw herself standing with a baby grand on her back. She pushed her butt out to begin the squat. Checking her reflection, she verified that the weight did not cramp her form. Boobs thrust forward, thighs parallel to the floor. She pressed upwards. Quads flexed, calves bulged, and the piano rose slowly. Her legs quaked but they kept going. When she was standing again, she took a pair of deep breaths. She felt good. One more rep.

The crash that followed was *not* the sound of a piano hitting the floor. It was the sound of double doors battered off their hinges. Five CREEPS dressed in black body armor somersaulted into the room and landed in positions around Cheri Tarte. A semicircle of rifle barrels formed a barrier between her and the exit. Lacey Briefs, dressed in a slightly wrinkled gray business suit, followed the CREEPS into the Grand Suite and took her place next to their commander. "Lady," the captain said, "put down the piano and clasp your hands on your head." Counting the number of automatic weapons arrayed against her, Cheri Tarte calculated the odds. She found them slightly unfavorable and did as she was told.

"You are under arrest for violations of the Federal Economic Sabotage Act," said Lacey. Approaching Cheri Tarte, the captain ordered her to put her hands behind her back. He was a big man, but Cheri Tarte was a little bigger. She smirked at him as he slipped the handcuffs over her wrists.

With the Crimson Crusher restrained, the CREEPS relaxed. They fanned into search mode, opening drawers and checking under sofa cushions. Pointing to the bedroom doors, the captain asked, "Where's the little guy?"

She nodded to her own room. "That one." The captain signaled two of his men. They jogged to Cheri Tarte's bedroom. "No need to hurry," she said. "He's not going anywhere."

A few minutes later, one of the CREEPS descended the steps from Cheri's room and reentered the salon. "He's secure," he said. "Says his name is Jon Dunn."

"Let's find some ID," Lacey said.

β 1 1

"Hello, darling," said Gimbel. His British accent had returned. He sat up in the king-sized bed, naked to the waist. The earth-tone bedspread covered the rest of him. A pair of handcuffs shackled his right wrist to the brass headboard. "Sorry if I don't hug you."

"Do you know me?" Lacey asked.

"Of course, darling. You're Lacey Briefs of the Department. You have an affinity for classical music, Volta Cola, and—"

She interrupted him before he could get to her more intimate predilections. "Do you know who you are?"

"Dunn," he said. "Associated Industries."

Lacey shielded her eyes with one hand and sighed. When Gimbel set her on the trail that led to this hotel suite, she had no way of knowing he would be at the end of it. She looked up and scanned the room. A pair of terrycloth bathrobes was draped over the back of a chair. The picture window, with its vista of nighttime Washington, seemed peculiarly bare, and then Lacey realized why. The curtains had been pulled down and lay in a heap on the floor, along with most of the pillows and several condom wrappers. A woman's handbag was open on the night table.

"Unchain him," she told the CREEPS. "Put a robe on him and get ready to go."

"Miss Briefs?" asked one of the soldiers, tentatively.

"Yes, Corporal, what is it?"

"We don't have the key."

"Why not?"

"Because those handcuffs...they're not ours."

"Find the key," she ordered wearily.

It was inside Cheri Tarte's handbag. A few minutes later, Lacey and the CREEPS led Gimbel down the stairs to the salon.

"What do we do with him?" the captain asked.

"Take him to the judge," said Lacey. "Recommend that we put him with the others."

"That place is getting full."

"There's no place better equipped."

"What happens now?" Cheri Tarte asked. "Off to jail?"

"That's the formula," Lacey replied.

Reporters and cameramen filled the corridor. A pair of CREEPS cleared the way, followed by the two handcuffed suspects. Cheri Tarte was shameless in her red bra and panties, thanks to months of practice appearing in front of cameras with minimal clothing. Gimbel swaggered like a nerd prizefighter. His open robe hung over his shoulders, revealing boxer shorts adorned with math equations. With each step, the terrycloth swayed like a cape. An armed CREEP was assigned to each of them. Lacey and the captain made up the rear guard. It was her big moment, the one every prosecutor works for: the perp walk. Why did it feel like she was the perp?

Microphones and flashbulbs intruded on the procession. "Cheri Tarte," yelled a reporter, "what do you have to say for yourself?"

"THE DOJ IS GOING TO BE SORRY THEY MESSED WITH THE CRIMSON CRUSHER!"

"Are you guilty?" yelled another.

"WHENEVER POSSIBLE!"

The reporters had their sound bite; Cheri Tarte was of no further interest. They shifted to Lacey.

"Miss Briefs, how does it feel to have caught the Betamaker?"

Lacey didn't answer.

"Miss Briefs, when will the arraignment be?"

She remained silent.

"Miss Briefs…Miss Briefs…Miss Briefs…"

When they reached the end of the hallway, the two CREEPS in the lead peeled smartly off to the sides and pivoted to guard the waiting elevator. Lacey and the others passed between them into the car. She turned around and saw the cameras staring at her with their glassy eyes. Then the metal doors slid shut. She stood in the front; the others couldn't see the tear that dropped from her eye and slid down her cheek. Whether she cried because of Gimbel's condition, or because he was in the Grand Suite in the first place, she couldn't have said.

CHAPTER 12

FULL ASYLUM

That he is mad, 'tis true; 'tis true 'tis pity; and pity 'tis 'tis true.
– William Shakespeare, *Hamlet*, 2.2

The O'Hares watched their son through the one-way glass. He sat in a circle with the other patients. The ten men and two women wore blue hospital gowns with hospital-issue slipper-socks. The cinderblock walls were blue as well. The doctor explained that blue was a soothing color. On one side of the room, a door labeled *Exit* separated the Jon Dunn ward from the outside world. Nearby, a sad-looking geranium decorated the nurses' station. The harsh fluorescent lights of industrial medicine overwhelmed the attempt at cheerfulness. A pair of muscular orderlies in white uniforms sat with their feet on the desk playing video games on their IQPhones. Opposite the nurses' station, a hallway led to the sleeping area. The patients spoke softly among themselves. Gimbel seemed uninterested in the conversation. He stared at the window. Sheets of rain slid down the glass. Beyond the windowpanes, the universe was limited to iron bars and gray sky.

"I have examined your son and come to a preliminary diagnosis," said the gray-haired man in the lab coat who introduced himself as Dr. Pollan. He sat at the table in the darkened observation room, stroking his beard contemplatively. The only illumination filtered in from the ward on the other side of the one-way glass. Lacey's phone call had wakened the O'Hares at 3:00 a.m. the previous day; they booked the first flight they could get. Air Traffic Control had slowed flights into National because of the rain; the trip was interminable. When they finally landed in Washington, they came straight to the psychiatric unit at Walter Reed Army Medical Center, where they were told their son was still being processed. They came back after a restless night in a hotel room and Dr. Pollan greeted them.

The doctor gestured for Gimbel's parents to join him at the table. Mr. O'Hare was a short bald man with a bulbous nose. His pants were pulled up high to prevent them from wrinkling. They covered his small paunch, but left a gap above his shoes. In one hand, he held an unlit pipe, which he had removed from between his teeth to speak. "I'm very eager to hear your diagnosis, Doctor. Please go ahead."

"Mr. and Mrs. O'Hare," said Dr. Pollan, "to give you the whole history of psychiatry, why Freud said this, why Jung said that, and how we reconcile the two here at Walter Reed, would be a great waste of time. So since brevity is the soul of wit, I'll come straight to the point. Your young son is suffering from an unbalanced mental state. I call it an unbalanced mental state because his mental state is unbalanced, and how else can you define an unbalanced mental state but by an absence of balance mentally?"

"We've had a long trip and a miserable night," Mrs. O'Hare said wearily. "Our tolerance for psycho-babble is low. Please come to the point."

"I assure you," the doctor continued, "I use no psycho-babble. It's true that he's suffering from a cognitive disorder, and more's the pity. The medical term is *spynusitis*."

"Sinusitis?" asked Mr. O'Hare. "What do his sinuses have to do with—?"

"Not sinusitis. *Spy*nusitis: the erroneous belief that one is a spy. I coined the term myself. It's unlike anything I've encountered before. Completely resistant to drugs, you know."

"Then how do you plan to treat him?" asked Mr. O'Hare.

"I am going to engage your son in cognitive therapy. This form of treatment involves establishing a relationship with your son—a therapeutic alliance—and helping him explore his beliefs. The objective is to change his thought patterns by altering the way he feels. The group setting is somewhat experimental; I hope to enhance the usual therapy by giving similar patients an opportunity to explore each others' beliefs as well."

Mr. O'Hare was skeptical. "Has this therapy actually worked on any of the other patients?"

"Your son is in good hands," Dr. Pollan assured him. "Ask around the hospital. Ask if I ever said, 'This is the course of treatment,' and then had it proved otherwise. Have me fired if I'm wrong."

"But does it work?"

"We're getting there, we're getting there."

"Getting where?"

"To the root of their problem. It seems to be a number of factors in various combinations—stress, lack of sleep, an obsession with spy movies—but there is one factor all the patients have in common."

"What's that?"

"Unfulfilled potential."

Mrs. O'Hare stood up and walked back to the observation window. "He's not making friends," she said. She turned to her husband. "I always told you, George, he's too shy."

"That's perfectly normal at this stage," said the doctor. "He's been through a lot since Friday night: a court appearance, a preliminary psychiatric evaluation, his first night in new surroundings. I'm sure he'll interact with the other patients in a day or so. You'll see. I'll retire and grow zucchini if he doesn't."

"Doctor," said Mrs. O'Hare, "when can we talk to him?"

"I'm headed into group now. I don't see any reason why you can't meet with your son after the session. No reason at all. In the meantime, make yourselves comfortable here. Conceal yourselves behind the observation window and watch the proceedings. There's a vending machine down the hall if you get hungry."

When the doctor left, Mrs. O'Hare turned back to the one-way glass to see what Gimbel was doing. He had stopped staring out the window. Now he stared at the exit.

β 1 1

"Dunn, Associated Industries."

"It's a pleasure to meet you, Mr. Dunn, a genuine pleasure. My name is Dr. Pollan." He checked his notes on the screen of the notepad computer. "Now, Mr. Dunn," he went on, "it says here you got yourself into a bit of a scrape on the twenty-first of December. Can you tell us what happened that day?"

"I was on a mission. Economic saboteurs planned to blow up a commercial airliner. Our sources told us that a handoff of the plans was going to occur in the lobby of the Barnett Crystal City. My assignment was to intercept the communication and avert the attack."

Gimbel stared at the door. This interrogation had nothing to do with him. The people in the hospital gowns were crazy. Every one of them claimed to be Jon Dunn. That was not possible. There was only one.

The door was painted the same shade of blue as walls. It appeared to be solid metal. An electronic lock, similar to the ones in the Test Nest, ensured that no one could get in or out without entering a PIN on a numeric keypad. A label in one corner said *Secured by Byte Yourself IROSS.*

The make-believe Beta Eleven was still telling his story. He described his discovery of the dead drop location in the hotel gift shop. He talked about his ride to National Airport as if it were an exciting race against a ticking time bomb, rather than what it was: five minutes on city streets to find a bomb that didn't exist. He covered every detail of his activities at the terminal, including the shove he gave Gimbel at the inspection station. For a man who claimed to be a secret agent, Airport-Dunn seemed unconcerned with secrecy.

Dr. Pollan reached into the pocket of his lab coat and removed a plastic card. "This was found in your hotel room," he said. "It's an Indiana driver's license with your picture on it. According to this, your name is Victor Shepherd and you live in Fort Wayne, Indiana." He handed it to Airport-Dunn, who studied the picture, read the address, and flipped it over several times. "It's a cover story," he said.

"So you're not really Victor Shepherd of Fort Wayne, Indiana?"

"No, Doctor."

"Do you live in Fort Wayne?"

"No, I live in the Mayfair section of London."

"Have you ever been to Fort Wayne?"

"No."

"Tell me, Mr. Dunn," said the doctor, "before you found the secret plans in the gift shop at the Barnett, did you have any suspicions that a sabo plot was in the works?"

"I did."

"What gave it away?"

"Jackets."

"Jackets?"

"Yes, my son kept losing jackets. Sabos stole them. I suspect they used them to clothe a terrorist army."

"You said 'son,' Mr. Dunn," said the doctor. "Do you have a son? I'm just wondering because there was no mention of one in any of your movies. Not one of your movies at all."

"He was part of my cover."

"It's a fine thing to have a son, a fine thing indeed. Where does he live?"

"Oh, he lives in Fort Wayne."

"Does he live with his mother?"

"Yes."

"Do they have a house or an apartment?"

"A house."

"Is it nice?"

"Oh, yes."

"What's it like?"

"There's an old-fashioned oak banister. It reminds me of a country store."

"Have you ever been in the house?"

"No."

"But it's a real house, and your wife and son live there."

"Oh yes, the Crown Security Service is very thorough in providing a cover."

The doctor turned to the rest of the group. "Did the CSS provide a cover to anyone else here?"

A slim man with wire-rim glasses raised his hand. Dr. Pollan said, "Go ahead, Mr....?"

"Dunn," replied the man. "Associated Industries."

"Go ahead, Mr. Dunn. What was your cover?"

"I taught American History at a public high school in Lowell, Massachusetts."

"That's very unusual. No supervillains in high schools. None at all."

"You'd be surprised how much villainy can be found in secondary education. I found a major cover-up."

"What cover-up was that?"

"A massive conspiracy."

"A conspiracy to do what exactly?"

"To cover up America's past."

The Dunns were impressed by the magnitude of this revelation. The doctor asked Teacher-Dunn how he discovered it.

"I first learned about the conspiracy while my class was studying the Industrial Revolution. I wanted my students to understand that it had both costs and benefits. In Lowell, industrialization wasn't something distant; it occurred right there in town. I searched the Internet for firsthand accounts of the city's textile mills. Nearly the entire staff were women, you know, the so-called Mill Girls. I found testimony in which some of the Mill Girls complained to the state legislature about fourteen-hour days and outbreaks of tuberculosis caused by the 'unwholesome' atmosphere. But others thought the conditions were quite good. They claimed the average workday was closer to twelve hours. A doctor testified that, even though there were many cases of TB, the Mill Girls were in better health than the average citizen of Lowell. I also found glowing reports from famous visitors like Andrew Jackson and Davy Crockett. Even that perennial critic of the factory system, Charles Dickens, popped in. He said, 'there was as much fresh air, cleanliness, and comfort, as the nature of the occupation would possibly admit of.' I gave the reading material to my students and divided them into two teams. After they read it, the plan was to hold a debate about whether the women who left their farms to work in the Lowell Mills were better off than those who stayed behind to work the land."

"Well, Mr. Dunn, you certainly worked like a dog on your cover story," said Dr. Pollan. "You sound like a real teacher."

"Living one's cover keeps one alive," replied Teacher-Dunn.

"It certainly does. How did the debate turn out?"

"It didn't. One of my students—his father was a professor of labor relations—complained that the positive portrayal of the mills in some of the accounts offended him. I was sent to the principal's office. I got a two-week suspension for use of an unauthorized lesson plan. Apparently the only book about factory conditions approved by the Commonwealth of Massachusetts is *The Jungle*."

"As one of CSS's top agents, it must have been very disappointing to you to fail in a mission like that. Very disappointing indeed."

"Oh, I completed my mission."

"But there was no debate."

"That was just my cover. The mission was to deliver a secret message to the New Hampshire State Capitol."

Dr. Pollan removed a piece of paper from his pocket and unfolded it. "Is this the message?" he asked. The patients passed it around the circle to Teacher-Dunn. As it passed Gimbel, he recognized the page he had seen taped to the statue of Daniel Webster.

"Yes, that's the message," replied Teacher-Dunn.

"It's a quote from Daniel Webster," said Dr. Pollan. "Mr. Webster was the greatest American orator since sliced bread—a towering figure in our history, towering. Why did his words have to be delivered in secret?"

"Daniel Webster isn't on the approved reading list either."

The other patients thought this was a plausible explanation. Murmurs of approval went around the circle. "Thank you, Mr. Dunn," said the doctor. "Can anyone else tell me about their cover story?"

The man next to Gimbel raised his hand. Gimbel recognized him as the would-be commando who tried to kidnap Isaac Ross during the Academy Awards. Although hospital gowns made all the Jon Dunns in the ward equal in dress, they were not equal in dentistry. A missing tooth suggested that Oscar-Dunn was a man of limited income. "Please introduce yourself," said the doctor.

"Dunn," he said. "Associated Industries."

"What was your cover?"

"I was CEO of a jitney service in the Compton section of Los Angeles County. The poverty level in Compton is well above the average for the United States. One day I was sharing some beers with my friends and we started talking about why it was so hard for the residents to find employment. One of my friends said that finding employment wasn't difficult. The problem was getting to work—few of us had cars. After some discussion, we decided to buy some used mini-buses and offer a shared-taxi service to our neighbors. We could assist them with transportation and bring some profit to ourselves.

"Everything went swimmingly at first. We built a strong customer base in Compton, strong enough to expand to other areas. Soon our customers started requesting rides to the airport. That's when our trouble started, with the airport. One of our drivers was waiting for a passenger to arrive at LAX when the chauffer of a large limousine accosted him. He accused us of siphoning his passengers by undercutting his prices. A short time after that, a gentleman from the government visited our offices, accompanied by a CREEPS unit. He informed us that we were in violation of various safety regulations, in addition to the laws concerning minimum wages. The CREEPS troops removed our mini-buses from the premises, effectively eliminating our transport provisioning capability. Regrettably, six of our clients lost their jobs the following week due to absenteeism."

"I'm sorry the government shut you down," said Dr. Pollan. "Very sorry. But you weren't doing your clients any favors by driving them around in unsafe mini-buses."

"The mini-buses were perfectly safe," replied Oscar-Dunn. "We had state inspection stickers for all of them. It was our office that was considered dangerous. The government inspector cited us for stacks of papers higher than the official limit and for lack of a written procedure for safely putting paper in the copy machine."

"What about the other charge? Surely your drivers are entitled to a living wage."

"Maybe so. But now they don't have any wage."

"What happened next?"

"I wanted to learn who was behind the attack on our business. So I conducted reconnaissance of area limousines."

"What did you find out?"

"Not much, at first. But then I got a tip that a large number of limos were converging on a building called Masonic Hall. I determined that this must be their secret headquarters. I infiltrated the facility to take down the mastermind behind the operation."

"There must have been a lot of people there, Mr. Dunn. How did you identify the mastermind?"

"I was able to identify him based on the surveillance photos that I received from Alpha One."

"Alpha One? Who's that?"

"The director of the Crown Security Service."

The doctor pressed some icons on a notepad computer and handed it to Oscar-Dunn. "Is that Alpha One?" asked Dr. Pollan.

"Yes. That's her."

"And that's the person who authorized the attack on Masonic Hall?"

"Yes, sir."

"Pass it around," said the doctor.

As the pad traveled around the circle, the other patients confirmed that the picture on the screen was indeed Alpha One. Gimbel was last. When the pad finally reached him, he recognized a picture he had once seen on the web: Cheri Tarte giving the finger.

"One more question," said Dr. Pollan. "After the operation at Masonic Hall, did you report back to headquarters?"

Oscar-Dunn fidgeted. "Not yet," he said.

"Why not? Reporting back to headquarters must be very important."

"I just haven't."

"Do you know where headquarters is located?" The other patients showed a great deal of interest in the question. One, who had been staring out the window, suddenly paid attention. Another, who had been slumping, abruptly sat up straight upon hearing the talk of headquarters.

"Of course I know where headquarters is located!" said Oscar-Dunn. "I have the highest possible security clearance."

Vegas-Dunn blurted out, "I need to report back to headquarters too!"

The doctor continued to address Oscar-Dunn. "Can you tell me where headquarters is located?"

"Of course not. That information is classified far above your level."

"You can tell me," said Airport-Dunn. "I have the highest level too!"

"Me too!" said Teacher-Dunn.

The talk of headquarters agitated the patients. The two orderlies at the nurse's station looked up from their video games.

Airport-Dunn got up from his chair and approached Oscar-Dunn. "Dunn," he said, "Associated Industries. It's okay for me to know the location of headquarters. You can whisper it to me, so these imposters don't hear."

"Get away from me," said Oscar-Dunn. He stood up and pushed Airport-Dunn away from him. "I am Jon Dunn. You're the imposter."

Dr. Pollan nodded to the orderlies. They rushed over and took Oscar-Dunn by the arms. Just then, Vegas-Dunn ran over and attempted to give one of the orderlies a karate chop. The orderly had to let go of Oscar-Dunn to block the hit. Oscar-Dunn twisted free from the second orderly. The other Jon Dunns jumped out of their chairs and joined the melee, all except Gimbel, who sat alone in the circle pressing icons on the notepad computer. A list of wireless networks came up on the screen. The first entry read:

    Beta11Ward   Unsecured Wireless Network

"They made this too easy," he said. As Gimbel slipped the notepad under his hospital gown, Dr. Pollan and the two orderlies dodged punches and pleaded with the patients to see reason.

β 1 1

"What happened to your conference table?" asked the vice chairman.

The airplane wing table was nowhere to be seen. A mismatched collection of folding tables took its place in the Executive Conference Room. The board of directors sat around it, Tina at one end. Next to her, Addison Reed leaned back in his swivel chair and stretched his legs. His pink dress shirt and color-coordinated tie were crisp, in defiance of the rainy evening.

"I don't know where my conference table disappeared to," Tina replied. "Someone seems to have stolen it." She poked Addison. "I hope I'm not going to get pictures of it on top of the Eiffel Tower. Unfortunately, this is not the time for practical jokes."

"I didn't have anything to do with it," Addison replied.

Tina called the meeting to order and asked the corporate counsel to report on his discussions with the Department of Justice. He was a prim man in a gray three-piece suit. "The settlement proposed by the DOJ is quite reasonable," he said. "I got off the phone with the chief of staff half an hour ago. He's offering a plea agreement. If we plead guilty to the charge of economic sabotage, the AG guarantees no jail time for any Byte Yourself executive. But he wants Tina to appear on *Sorry* to apologize for the breach of the public trust. She also has to pay a fine, and the AG wants her to pay it personally—regardless of the indemnification clause in her contract. He said the public demands accountability."

Tina asked the size of the fine. Consulting his yellow legal pad, the counsel read a number from the neat lines of handwritten text. The number was large. It wouldn't knock her off the 500 Richest Americans list, but combined with the drop in the stock price, it would push her noticeably further from the top.

She moved on. "What about the antitrust charge?"

"The AG is willing to drop it, but there's a catch."

"What is it?"

"We have to break up the company."

He paused to let that sink in. Shocked expressions and angry exclamations traveled around the table.

"The AG says that to make the antitrust charge go away, we need to spin off the Business Automation Division. BAD will become an independent corporation."

The vice chairman sat opposite Tina. He had a large, bald head and an authoritative manner. "If we spin off BAD," he said, "and I emphasize 'if,' Addison Reed would be the logical candidate to head the new entity. Mr. Reed, are you willing and able to do this?"

Addison was diplomatic. "I would miss the friendships I made at Byte Yourself," he said. "However, if there's something I can do to maintain continuity of leadership at BAD, I feel I have an obligation to the stockholders, and to all of you, to do it."

"What about IP?" asked the corporate counsel. "Can we divide intellectual property between the two companies? Can we make a clean separation between the OSD code and the BAD code?"

"It's ironic," said Addison. "We can separate them, but only because we're innocent of the charges against us. If I had taken Mr. O'Hare's suggestion—if I had, per the DOJ's charges, leveraged the horizontal monopoly power of Byte Yourself Software to use the

OSD Toolbox in the BAD product—then separating the code would have been a nightmare. Funny how it worked out."

"If we're innocent of the charges against us," Tina asked, "do you think we should fight them?"

"I didn't say that," Addison replied. "But I did say we need to consider the best interest of the stockholders. Wall Street gave our shares a beating after the raid. If we fight the charges we'll face a lengthy trial that we could lose. Then Tina and I would go to jail and the fate of the company would be up to the DOJ. We'd be playing courtroom roulette with Byte Yourself Software as the stake. Taking the plea deal will eliminate the risk of losing everything. It's also the fastest way to get this behind us and see the stock price return to a fair valuation. I think we should take it. But then, I'm biased. I get BAD out of the deal." He flashed a smile as he said the last part.

A gray-haired woman wearing a pearl choker spoke up. "Is BAD even a viable business at this point? The DOJ raid and the confiscation of the equipment in Test Nest II seriously compromised its capacity to deliver software."

"My foresight worked in our favor," said Addison. "About a month ago, I directed my team to update the disaster recovery plan. Gimbel O'Hare drew the assignment and did an excellent job. The BAD team has been working all weekend to implement his plan. I sent the resources to the electronics superstore yesterday with a shopping list and a stack of prepaid debit cards. They're in the lab as we speak stringing the equipment together and loading data from our offsite back up."

"Is there anything we can do to help?" asked the gray-haired woman.

"Only if you can cure Mr. O'Hare by tomorrow," said Addison. "As you know, he's in the psychiatric unit at Walter Reed. In addition, we haven't been able to get in touch with either Cindy Valence or Desmond McCoy. Without the plan author, the team lead, or the sysadmin, it's been slow going. I had been hoping to have Test Nest II up and running by COB tomorrow but it now looks more like Tuesday or Wednesday."

Several of the directors expressed concern about Cindy and Brownie. "We don't know where they are," said Addison. "Beverly Dix and I both talked to Mrs. McCoy several times, but all she would tell us is that her husband was busy and that she had given him our messages. Beverly talked to Ms. Valence on the phone. Ms. Valence told her she was busy too. When Beverly pressed her to come in anyway, she told Beverly to 'get bent.'"

"Call Ms. Valence yourself," Tina said.

"I did, but I couldn't reach her. Her voice mailbox was full and no one answered the door when I went to her apartment." The gray-haired woman wondered if perhaps Cindy had been arrested sometime after she had talked to Beverly. The corporate counsel said he had assurances from the DOJ that Gimbel O'Hare was the only Byte Yourself employee who had been taken in to custody.

"What about Mr. O'Hare?" asked the vice chairman. "I pulled his personnel file. Until last September, he was an exemplary employee. Then we had a charge of sexual harassment, an incident with the cafeteria cam, irregularity with an expense report, and now one of his e-mails is the main piece of evidence against us. If he had been fired at the first sign of trouble, we wouldn't be in this situation now."

The implied criticism didn't ruffle Addison. He even conceded that the vice chairman might be right. "But every decision seemed like the right one at the time. We did put Mr. O'Hare on a performance improvement plan after the sexual harassment incident. He completed the plan successfully. I had a meeting scheduled to reprimand him regarding the expense report, but the DOJ raid interfered. As for the e-mail, like I said, since we didn't implement his suggestion, I didn't think we did anything wrong."

FULL ASYLUM

"The AG is willing to drop the charges against him as part of the settlement," said the corporate counsel. "Although in my opinion, the question is academic since Mr. O'Hare is in no condition to stand trial."

"What do we know about his condition?" asked the gray-haired lady.

"I spoke to his parents this afternoon," said Tina. "It was a short conversation. Needless to say, they're devastated. They said Gimbel is suffering from spynusitis—he thinks he's a spy. They met with him briefly, but it will be a couple more days before the doctor has a definite prognosis. I assured them if there was anything Byte Yourself Software could do for them they should let me know."

"Any word on how he got that way?"

"Sometimes I'm amazed that we're not all in the asylum."

"Why do you say that?"

"Since I talked to the O'Hares," Tina said, "I've been trying to figure something out. Psychiatric patients sometimes think they're Napoleon. Sometimes they think God is talking to them. Sometimes they think they're God themselves. Why does this one think he's Jon Dunn? I think I know why.

"Most of us like Jon Dunn because it's fun to watch someone drink heavily, get the girl, and blow stuff up. But what appeals to Gimbel goes much deeper. Jon Dunn excels."

The directors watched their reflections in Tina's oversized glasses and in the picture windows behind her. Beyond the large rectangular panes, only the white floodlights of the pond interrupted the black night sky. They illuminated the streaks of rain that fell into the water and the jet of the fountain that shot perversely in the opposite direction. The storm tried to blow it from its upward course, but the watery plume persevered. It twisted in the wind. Occasionally it broke. But it never stopped trying to reach the sky.

"You know the theme song from *The Future is Just Beginning*," said Tina. "'You're the best there is, Jon Dunn.' Dunn is the best agent, the best stunt driver, even the best comedian—with a quip for every near-death experience. He's the best lover. His skills in the bedroom are so formidable that evil women switch sides mid-kiss. Even his enemies think he's the best—and usually tell him so during a coronary-to-coronary talk around twenty minutes from the end of the movie.

"That's what Gimbel O'Hare wanted: to be the best at something. He wanted to take his talents for cryptanalysis, which are considerable, put them to good use, and see a finished product at the end of the day.

"The only thing he needed from the rest of us was to stay out of his way, to give him the freedom to excel. Because there is no excellence without freedom. Do you know where the word *excellence* comes from? It's Latin. *Ex-cellere*. It means *to rise above*. By definition, you can't excel, you can't rise above, by doing the same thing as everybody else. You have to have the freedom to do something different. You have to have the freedom to take the risk that something that hasn't been tried before will work. Sometimes you have to have the freedom to be the fool that rushes in where angels fear to tread. Excellence isn't just risky, though. It's also time-consuming. You better have the freedom to put in long hours.

"Observe that Jon Dunn's boss doesn't expect him to excel without freedom. Every Dunn movie starts the same way. Beta Eleven goes to Alpha One to get his orders. Alpha One tells Dunn, 'We think so-and-so is up to no good. Go find out about him.' And then Alpha One goes away. We hardly see him again until the end of the movie.

"But it's only a movie. In real life, we abolished freedom and replaced it with Isaac Ross's cooperative society. It sounds good, 'cooperative society.' We're all in business; we all know how important it is to cooperate. But when Isaac uses the phrase, it has a darker meaning. It means society tells you what to do, and you will cooperate. The cooperative society tells you what to eat. It tells you what to do with your garbage. It tells you what health insurance you have to buy. It tells you how much to pay your employees. It tells you what jokes you may tell. As we learned the hard way, the cooperative society tells you what you can do with your software library. If you consider doing something different, a team of CREEPS is standing by to set you straight.

"Where in the cooperative society is there a place for Gimbel O'Hare, and all the other would-be Jon Dunns with an inclination to excel? After attending 'stenics, and defending themselves on *Sorry*, and paying their National Health Quarterly Supplemental Premium, and hiding from the CREEPS, they're free to devote their time and energy and resources—if they have any left—to turning their vision into reality. Unless of course, the cooperative society decides to outlaw their vision entirely, as it did to Gimbel O'Hare when it put Crypt Yourself in the Index of Forbidden Software.

"Anyone who manages to overcome all the obstacles that the cooperative society places in his path and still aspires to excellence is so unusual, so far from the norm, that his behavior looks like insanity to the rest of us. But we have a place for people like that. Gimbel O'Hare is already there. We built a society where there is no place to excel except the lunatic asylum."

The rain pattered on the windows. All the members of the board were in the conference room on the top floor because at some point in their careers they excelled. But they had all started their careers in the age of competition. They had risen to the top before the Financial Crises and the Federal Economic Sabotage Act. They thought about the decisions they had made which were considered good business at the time, but which now would be crimes. They tried to imagine what their careers would be like if they had to start again in the cooperative society.

Finally the woman with the pearls said, "Tina, I've been struggling with how to vote on the DOJ offer. Do we plead guilty, spin off BAD, and guarantee that we stay out of jail? Or do we fight against a charge that has no merit? But you convinced me. The DOJ has been pushing this company around for years for the sole reason that we excel. We had an encryption program that was better than anyone else's so it had to be banned. One of our programmers came up with a way to save money—he's supposed to do that—so we had to be charged with a crime. It's resistance time. Spurning this deal is a great way to start."

Addison shook his head.

The debate went late into the night. Many directors agreed with the gray-haired lady: the DOJ was attempting to perpetrate an enormous injustice and it was important to fight back. Others, including Addison, pointed out that the stockholders paid the board of directors to make money, not fight injustice. Most of the directors resented the need to choose between the two.

It was 2:00 a.m. when Tina called for a show of hands and directed the secretary to record the vote.

β 1 1

Gimbel sat in the plastic chair with his hands folded in his lap. The hospital gown hung from his relaxed shoulders, blue fabric draped neatly over his legs. His voice was calm as he answered Dr. Pollan's questions.

"Do you know who I am, Mr. Dunn?"

"Of course I do, sir. You are a stenographer. You were sent here to take down my report about my investigation of the Attorney General."

While Dr. Pollan did not seem to find Gimbel's surveillance of Bill Peterson to be particularly unusual, there was one aspect of Gimbel's response that concerned him deeply. He made a note on a pad of paper (he had lost his notepad computer). *Thinks I'm a stenographer. Clearly unhinged.*

In contrast to Gimbel, the other Dunns were tense. Several exhibited nervous tics, jerking their heads or scratching the backs of their hands. Dr. Pollan was cognizant of the change in mood since yesterday's fracas. In response, he had assigned two additional orderlies to the ward, bringing the total to four. They no longer lounged at the nurse's station playing video games on their IQPhones. Instead they staked out tactical positions and scanned for signs of trouble. Their phones remained on their belts, untouched.

Oscar-Dunn watched the orderlies carefully; his eyes spun from one to another. Every few minutes, when he thought they weren't looking, he left his chair and tiptoed towards the exit. His stealth was ineffective: the spectacle of a large man fluttering like a ballerina while his butt stuck out the back of his hospital gown was difficult to miss in the brightly lit room. Each of his excursions ended with a pair of orderlies escorting him back to his chair.

The doctor continued questioning Gimbel. "What if I told you I was not a stenographer?"

"I would say that is unfortunate. It's an honest profession. It consists entirely of recording the truth. In any case, may I use your phone? I need to alert headquarters that they sent the wrong man."

The mention of headquarters set the circle in motion. Heads jerked repeatedly and Oscar-Dunn made another attempt to reach the door. As the orderlies brought him back, Dr. Pollan tried to change the subject to one that would not agitate his charges. "What was the last thing you read, Mr. Dunn?"

"A book, sir."

"What was it about?"

"About three hundred pages."

"I mean what did it say in the book?"

"It said that psychiatry is not a true science, that its practitioners are charlatans, and that they spend their lives trying to convince healthy people that they're sick. While that may or may not be true, it was very impolite of the author to say so. If a psychiatrist read the book, how would that make him feel? He could read it you know, if only he could return to his childhood, and learn his ABCs like I did."

The doctor wrote in his pad again, *How would psychiatrist feel? Psychiatrist's problem—not patient's—rooted in childhood. Sometimes one encounters a more acute sense of irony in the asylum than in the outside world. Method to his madness.* He underlined the last sentence and then said out loud, "As it happens, I know my ABCs."

"That's a fine quality in a stenographer."

"Also convenient for reading books. Very convenient, indeed. Tell me, Mr. Dunn. Where could I get a copy of this magnum opus?"

"I just returned mine to the library. You could get it from there if no one else learns the alphabet and checks it out first."

"Which library would that be, Mr. Dunn?"

"The library at headquarters."

Two more Dunns were out of their chairs. The doctor attempted a more direct approach. "Perhaps it would be best if you refrained from mentioning headquarters," he said. "We wouldn't want to risk a security breach by accidentally revealing its location."

"I'm sure there's no danger of that," Gimbel replied. "Everyone here is cleared." The Dunns nodded eagerly. "There would be no breach of security if I were to say that headquarters is located at 950 Pennsylvania Avenue. Corner of 10th."

Chaos erupted. Dunns jumped out of their chairs. Dr. Pollan stood and ordered them to return; they knocked him over as they rushed to the door. Outnumbered by a factor of three, the orderlies were unable to hold them back. Vegas-Dunn twisted the door handle. It didn't move. The door was locked. Teacher-Dunn tried to unlock it by typing random numbers on the keypad. "Hurry up," yelled Oscar-Dunn. "I have to report to headquarters immediately."

Gimbel remained in his seat. He removed the notepad computer from under his hospital gown. On the screen, an e-mail he had written earlier awaited transmission:

> To: DMccoy@ByteYourself.com
> From: GOhare@ByteYourself.com
> Date: 18 April
> Subject: Rendezvous
>
> Brownie:
>
> Pentagon Palace garage. One hour. Please bring me a change of clothes.
>
> Gimbel

He pressed the icon for *Encrypt and Send*. Then he stepped over Dr. Pollan and joined the other Dunns at the door. "Remember," he told them, "that's 950 Pennsylvania Avenue. Look for the entrance that says 'The Palace of Justice is a Hallowed Place.'" He pressed several more icons on the notepad. There was a metallic click. "What are you waiting for?" he asked the Dunns. "The door's unlocked."

This time when Vegas-Dunn turned the handle, the door opened. Twelve psychiatric patients in hospital gowns and slipper-socks, each one believing he or she was Jon Dunn, escaped through the doorway and headed for the streets of Washington, DC.

β 1 1

He found the back seat of his car before he found Brownie. It lay on the pavement near the delivery entrance, next to an unmarked semi-trailer truck.

During the trip from Walter Reed, Gimbel was self-conscious about his hospital gown. He had to walk almost a mile in it from the medical facility to the Takoma Metro station. The rain had stopped but water still coated the concrete sidewalks and dripped from the weeds growing between the cracks. Gimbel's slipper-socks soon became saturated with moisture. Since his wallet had been confiscated as evidence at the Barnett, he had no money to pay for train fare. He jumped the turnstile to board the train. At Gallery Place he changed to the Yellow Line for the journey across the Potomac and out of the city. Although afternoon commuters crowded the outbound train, they kept their distance. Three rows of orange upholstered seats separated Gimbel from his nearest neighbors. They glanced surreptitiously at the man dressed for the psychiatric ward. They whispered to each other. Gimbel distinctly heard a pudgy bald man in a suit say "Betamaker." At Pentagon Palace, Gimbel jumped the turnstile again to exit the subway. He was grateful for one thing. Thanks to his slim build, the one-size-fits-all gown covered his backside—at least when he wasn't jumping a turnstile.

When he didn't find Brownie in the Pentagon Palace garage, he IM'ed him using the notepad computer he took from the hospital: *Where r u?* A moment later, the reply popped up: *Truck court.*

Gimbel approached the semi. A ramp extended to the back door of the trailer, which was open. Bright fluorescent light shone inside, along with intermittent blue flashes. "Brownie?" Gimbel called.

Brownie appeared in the doorway wearing blue-striped coveralls. "Gimbel," he said, "you're late."

"I lost my watch," Gimbel yelled back, holding up his bare wrist as proof. "What's the back seat of my car doing down here?"

"The trunk wasn't big enough for the flywheel," Brownie replied. "I had to break through to the back seat to make room."

"Flywheel? What are you doing to my car?"

"Come on up and take a look."

FULL ASYLUM

Gimbel climbed the ramp to the trailer. Brownie wiped the grease off his hands with a rag and shook hands with Gimbel. "Glad to see you, man," he said.

The midnight blue Cheetah YK-9 was inside the trailer, along with most of the equipment from Brownie's basement workshop. Red metal tool carts were stowed against the walls with half the drawers open. Tools were scattered on the tops of the carts and spread out on the floor. The blue flashes came from under the car. Someone down there was welding.

"Who's your friend?" asked Gimbel.

Brownie switched off the weld power supply and knocked backhanded on the car's rear bumper. "Come on out," he said. "We have company."

A pair of blue coveralls shot out from the back of the car. The person inside them lay on a rolling mechanic's creeper and held a welding electrode. The coveralls appeared to be Brownie's extra set. They hung loose on the welder's thin figure. Brownie removed the welder's mask, uncovering the brown tresses and beaming face of Cindy Valence. "Hi, Gimbel!" she said. "Nice outfit."

"You too," he replied.

"I brought some threads like you asked," said Brownie. "Over there."

He pointed to the far end of the trailer. A full-length mirror was attached to the wall. Next to it a tuxedo on a hanger dangled from a coat rack. "It's a bit formal for covert action, isn't it?" Gimbel asked.

"It's all I had in your size. My son wore it to his prom."

Gimbel took Brownie's wrist and looked at his watch. "It's okay," said Gimbel. "It's after 6:00."

"Get dressed while we finish with the car," said Brownie. "Then we'll show you the mods."

"Change behind a tool cart," Cindy joked. "I don't want to see your output cable."

313

Brownie had remembered everything—shirt, studs, cummerbund, patent leather shoes, IQPhone with Gimbel's data preloaded, new Chromega timepiece, even a replacement driver's license. Gimbel thought it best not to ask too many questions about where the last item came from. He stood in front of the mirror and knotted the black bow tie. Stepping back, he saw the tuxedo fit quite well. The jacket even gave him the illusion of shoulders. He had to say it: "Dunn, Associated Industries."

Brownie and Cindy spent twenty minutes showing him the modifications to the Cheetah. They had installed a gun rack on the underside of the trunk lid. It offered a choice of several weapons while keeping them clear of the flywheel. A new LCD display had been added to the dashboard; labels in Arial font described the functions of the various icons. "Keep the angle low or you'll drop like a rock," Brownie warned. Then he helped Gimbel onto the creeper and gave him a look at what Cindy had been welding under the chassis. When Gimbel emerged, he straightened the tuxedo jacket and asked, "Won't Tina notice her conference table is missing?"

"I'm sure Tina has bigger things to deal with," Brownie replied. "Like keeping herself out of jail."

The prospect of Tina going to jail reminded Gimbel what was at stake. This was not merely a matter of clearing his own name. Tina, Brownie, Cindy, Cheri Tarte, even Joe—all their futures depended on what Gimbel did now. He thought about how well Tina had treated him when he was on the Encryption Research Team, about Brownie's Thanksgiving Day lecture about capitalism, about learning the strategy of paintball at Joe's picnic table, about working through the night in the Test Nest with Cindy, about clowning with Cheri Tarte during her entrance into the Horizon Center. He also remembered that Brownie took a punch in the gut for him, that Cindy thought Gimbel's software talents were more important than Beverly's wall of silence, that Cheri Tarte rescued him from an imminent blow from a pool cue, that Joe had given him and Cheri Tarte a place to hide without asking any questions. They had all been great, great friends to him.

"Time to do this," he said. He lowered himself into the driver's seat.

Brownie closed the door for him and leaned toward the open window. The aperture framed his grinning face, half moon glasses, and white beard. "I expect you to bring this car back intact, man," he said. Gimbel gave him the thumbs up and rolled up the glass. He checked his bow tie one last time in the rearview mirror. He clenched his jaw and pressed the ignition button. The sound of the motor reverberated inside the trailer. Gimbel backed slowly down the ramp. When he reached the pavement, he circled in reverse until the car faced the exit. He stopped. He shifted into drive and pressed the gas pedal. The midnight blue Cheetah YK-9 sped out of the truck court and accelerated towards the city of Washington.

CHAPTER 13

GEORGE WASHINGTON SHOWS THE WAY

Dr. Arsenic stirred the contents of the demitasse with a tiny silver spoon. "We have a great deal in common, Mr. Dunn," he said. "We are both men of extraordinary talents, yet for too long those talents have gone unrecognized by the world. I had thought you would be the one man capable of appreciating my vision of the future. I am troubled by your lack of imagination."
    Dunn sipped his espresso. "I appreciate your myopia," he said. "And I have no trouble imagining you in a jail cell."
    – Ethan Fielding, *The Future is Just Beginning*

The time is now near at hand which must probably determine whether Americans are to be freemen or slaves.
    – George Washington, Address to the Continental Army, August 27, 1776

The telephone buzzed. Attorney General Peterson looked at the LCD display. It identified the caller as *Becker, T.* He pressed the speaker button. "Peterson," he said.

He heard the voice of his chief of staff through the speakerphone. "Byte Yourself called," said Becker. "The board voted early this morning. They agreed to our terms."

Peterson exchanged a congratulatory look with his visitor. Isaac Ross sat in one of the black Harvard Alumni chairs on the other side of the desk. A gold medallion with the university seal decorated the top rails of the seat backs. Isaac's gray suit made him look dignified. The news from Tim Becker made him look smug. He whispered to Peterson, "Make sure they agreed to everything."

"Tim," Peterson said, "did they agree to plead guilty to the E.S. charge?"

"Yes," Becker replied. "They will also spin off the Business Applications Division. Tina Lee will cover the fine personally, per our terms. She wants to know when she will appear on *Sorry*."

Peterson looked at Isaac. "Why wait?" said Isaac. "The show airs Tuesday nights. That's tomorrow."

"Did you get that, Tim?" Peterson asked.

"Yes, sir. I'll tell Byte Yourself we're on for tomorrow night, Tuesday, April 19."

"Thanks, Tim," said Peterson. "That was a good day's work." He looked over to the fireplace on his right. The antique clock on the mantel—it had once belonged to Robert Kennedy, whose portrait hung above it—showed it was already past 7:30. "You headed home, Tim?"

"In a bit, sir, but there's one other thing I need to discuss with you first. Chris Molson came to see me this afternoon."

"I hope you congratulated him on a successful raid."

"I did, but that's not what he wanted to see me about. He's being blackmailed."

"Blackmailed! By whom?"

"By Gimbel O'Hare."

Peterson was annoyed. For the second time today, Gimbel's name had come up. Becker had already briefed him on the escape from Walter Reed. Gimbel was supposed to be a bit player in this political theater, but he persisted in upstaging the leads. Becker explained about the warrant of seizure for the Lazuli apartment and the threat to expose Chris for seizing an apartment for personal use.

"We have four days until the evidence is automatically posted to SoshNet."

"How do we get Mr. O'Hare off center stage without dropping the charges against Byte Yourself?"

"Counteroffer," Becker replied. "We tell him that Byte Yourself's agreement to cop a plea changed the situation. Dropping the charges against the company is no longer on the table. However, we'll drop the charges against him—we're doing that anyway—and we'll get Ricardo Lazuli off the hook. We'll even give Lazuli his apartment back."

"Mr. O'Hare is still at large. How do we get in touch with him?"

"E-mail. He sent a message before he escaped from the asylum. I got the Cryptanalysis Unit working to decode it. They haven't succeeded yet, but it proves he's using his account. Once we convince him we're dropping the charges against him, he'll come out of hiding."

A slashing motion on the other side of the desk got Peterson's attention. Isaac was gesturing for him to put Becker on hold. "Hang on, Tim," said Peterson. He pressed the mute button.

"Why are you going to all this trouble?" said Isaac. "Fire Molson and be done with it."

"Isaac, it wouldn't be right. I was the one that suggested Chris use the Lazuli apartment for himself."

"Does Mr. Molson have any proof of that?"

"No, but…"

"Then throw him under the bus!"

Peterson thought of something to tell Becker and then unmuted the phone. "Tim, if there's one thing I learned at Harvard Law School, it was the importance of being ethical. This department does not tolerate unethical behavior in the warrant application process—or in anything else. Tell Mr. Molson he's terminated, effective immediately."

"Yes, sir. Goodnight."

"Wait, Tim—one more thing. I want to interrogate the prisoner in the Betamaker case."

"I'll contact Lacey Briefs."

Peterson looked over at Isaac, who was shaking his head. "Don't bother Miss Briefs," Peterson said into the speakerphone.

"It's her case, sir."

"It's my case, Tim. I'm the attorney general. Every case is my case. Have Cheri Tarte brought to my office right away."

"As you wish." Peterson ended the call.

As twilight fell on the city of Washington, the light from the window behind the attorney general grew dim. Gray shadows enveloped the office. Peterson picked up a Byte Yourself control pad from his desk and slid his finger across the screen. The art deco sconce lamps that flanked the window glowed. Color returned to the luxurious wood paneling and the autographed photographs of Peterson with his arm around presidents and actors. Above the fireplace, RFK looked thoughtful in his dark jacket, which may or may not have been leather. With his windswept hair and upturned collar, he resembled James Dean.

"It's ironic," said Peterson.

"What's that?" Isaac asked.

"We got our boot on the neck of Byte Yourself, but I can't turn on the lights without their help."

Isaac laughed. It was a guttural, unpleasant sound—more cough than laugh. "That is as it should be," he said. "Byte Yourself must take its assigned place in the cooperative society."

"Tina Lee goes on *Sorry* tomorrow. Then what happens?"

"You arrest her, of course."

Peterson hesitated. "We made a deal with her. No jail time."

"Why should she get off with a slap on the wrist after such a stunning and public confession? No, you arrest her and take the credit. Bill Peterson, the crusading attorney general, who exposed the corrupt alliance between Big Business and the sabo conspiracy and freed America from the threat of enslavement to the corporations. I went over your speech. It's fine, just take out the quote from George Washington."

Peterson protested. "It's a good quote—one of the best in the speech. Listen." He started to read from a piece of paper. "The time is now near at hand which must probably determine—"

Isaac interrupted. "Forget it. You can't be associated with a man who owned slaves."

"I'm not going to defend George Washington's ownership of slaves. It was a blot on his character. But it doesn't change that the things he said about freedom still inspire millions, especially those members of the public still attached to the Founding Fathers."

Isaac's irritation grew. "Take it out," he said angrily. "You can throw a bone to the sentimental Right by pointing out the date: April 19, Concord and Lexington. You can call the prosecution of Byte Yourself the shot heard 'round the corporate world. The story should be good for four or five news cycles. Then the announcement of your presidential candidacy will put you right back in the news."

Peterson contemplated two weeks of favorable press coverage. A knock on the door interrupted his meditation. "Come in."

A CREEPS captain, the one who had led the operation at the Barnett, shoved Cheri Tarte into the office. She wore an XXL prison jumpsuit. The sleeves had been too tight for her arms and had been cut off. The chest was still too tight; the zipper wouldn't close. The cleavage visible through the open neckline transformed the prison garb into haute couture.

When she saw Isaac Ross, she asked, "What's he doing here?"

"My dear," Isaac replied smoothly. "I am disappointed that you need to ask. I am your employer, after all. I'm concerned about you. At Consolidated Studios, people are our most important resource. Naturally I became personally involved when I learned you had been arrested. I told Mr. Peterson that I am confident we can get to the bottom of this in no time and that you will be cleared of all charges."

The captain carried a manila folder. "Are those the papers from her hotel room?" Peterson asked, reaching for the folder.

"Yes, sir." The captain handed the folder to him. Peterson opened it and began reading. "Put her over there," he said, pointing to the empty Harvard chair without looking up.

The CREEPS captain proceeded to secure Cheri Tarte to the chair. He laid two pairs of handcuffs and two pairs of leg irons on the desk, like an inquisitor showing the instruments of torture to an accused heretic. With the handcuffs, he shackled her wrists to the arms of the chair. Cheri Tarte pursed her lips at him. "I love it when you're kinky," she said, "but you're going to miss out on some amazing things I do with my hands." The captain ignored her and chained her ankles to the chair legs.

Peterson handed the folder across the desk to Isaac. While Isaac leafed through it, Peterson asked the captain, "Has anyone besides you seen this folder?"

"Just the sergeant who found it."

"Does Miss Briefs know about it?"

"No, sir. I thought you would want me to bring it to you directly."

"Quite right, Captain. Good work."

Isaac finished scanning the dossier and placed it on the desk. "That's quite a collection," he said. "ND, places, photos of couriers exchanging cash, even signed confessions from some of them."

"I will get out of here," Cheri Tarte replied. "Then I'll make sure that dossier gets into the hands of the public."

"Oh, the public doesn't need to know about this. All that talk about transparency in government is just a myth to promote job security for high school civics teachers. After a century of political reforms, the only thing that's changed about the smoke-filled rooms where the real deals are made is that smoking is no longer allowed. Now, there's something I must ask you. Is this the only copy?"

Cheri Tarte said nothing. The attorney general nodded to the captain, who slapped Cheri Tarte across the face.

"I'd like to see you do that when I'm not handcuffed to a chair," she said.

"I ask you again," said the attorney general. "Are there any other copies?"

"Blow it out your barracks bag."

Another slap to the face. A drop of blood appeared at the corner of her mouth. "Is this the part where you say, 'We have ways of making you talk'?" she asked.

"No," replied Peterson. "We just go ahead and use them."

Isaac reached over and put his hand on her thigh. "Really, my dear," he said. "If you would only answer Mr. Peterson's questions, I'm sure you'll be back at your hotel in no time."

Cheri Tarte looked skeptically at Isaac's hand. "Copping a feel, Isaac?" she asked contemptuously. He removed his hand. "I knew all that respect for woman stuff was just talk," she said.

Without warning she lunged forward toward the desk. Her biceps grew harder and more defined as they strained against the handcuffs. A web of angry veins pushed up against her skin. Her arms trembled with the effort. Peterson flinched, but the handcuffs held. Cheri Tarte laughed and relaxed. "You guys ought to switch," she said.

"What do you mean, switch?" Peterson asked.

"I mean the two of you are miscast as good cop and bad cop. In the first place, Mr. Attorney General, the bad cop shouldn't be afraid of the prisoner. As for you, Isaac, have you ever thought of casting me in the role of Tinker Bell?"

Isaac was clearly puzzled. "Tinker Bell?" he said. "Of course not. For starters, Consolidated will never film the story of Peter Pan while I'm at the helm. Every boy needs to grow up. But even if we did, you'd be thoroughly unconvincing in the role of the diminutive fairy sidekick. You're not the right physical type. Perhaps you could be Mr. Smee. Why do you ask?"

"Because I'd be about as convincing as Tinker Bell as you are as the good cop."

The buzzing of the telephone probably saved her from another slap in the face.

"Peterson," said the attorney general into the speaker.

A woman's voice was on the phone. She was barely audible above the sound of shouting in the background. "Sir, this is Dora Jarr," she said. "I'm a security guard at the main entrance."

"Yes, Ms. Jarr. I remember you from the airport. What can I do for you?"

"We're having some trouble here that I thought you should know about."

She was obviously upset. Peterson asked her to take her time and tell him what happened from the beginning.

"I was just doing my job—you know, my job of *not* confiscating dangerous items from people's luggage. It was pretty quiet, like it usually is this time of night. Then they started showing up."

"Who?"

"Jon Dunn."

"Jon Dunn?"

"Well that's the name they're giving. There are about a dozen of them. They're wearing hospital gowns and demanding to be admitted to the building. They keep asking to see Alpha One. I checked on the computer, but there's no Alpha One in the system."

Isaac whispered across the desk. "They must be the ones who escaped from Walter Reed with O'Hare." Cheri Tarte looked relieved. This was the first she had heard that Gimbel was out of the asylum. Peterson swiveled in his chair and typed on his computer. A moment later he turned back to the speakerphone. "Ms. Jarr," he said. "I just sent you an e-mail with a picture. Can you tell me if the man in the photograph is in the lobby?"

A moment later, Dora replied, "No."

"O'Hare's not with them," Peterson said to Isaac. Over the speakerphone, they heard Dora Jarr confront the intruders. "Step away from the desk," she shouted. "If you don't cooperate with the security procedures I'm going to call the police!" Then there were only the background voices.

"Ms. Jarr, are you still there?" Peterson yelled into the speaker.

After a pause, Dora Jarr came back on the line. "I'm here, sir."

"Are you okay?"

"Yes, sir. They're not trying to hurt me."

"What *are* they trying to do?"

"Report crimes."

The head of the nation's primary federal criminal investigation and enforcement agency should hardly be surprised that visitors to his building wish to report crimes. Nevertheless, all he could do was repeat "Crimes?"

"Yes, sir. Crimes. One man says there's a massive conspiracy of limo drivers. A guy with glasses is complaining that Daniel Webster is being repressed. The guy from the airport is here too. He wants to tell us about a stolen jacket."

Someone in the background yelled about envelopes full of cash.

"What did he say?" asked Peterson.

"He said he followed the envelopes to a campaign office."

Peterson and Isaac looked at each other. Then Peterson said, "Listen, Ms. Jarr. Just hold tight. We're going to send you some help."

"Thank you, sir."

Suddenly Cheri Tarte leaned forward in her chair and spoke authoritatively into the speakerphone. "This is Alpha One," she said. "Do you recognize my voice?" At the other end of the line there were cries of "Yes!" and "It's her!"

"I'm in the building," said Cheri Tarte. "Come on in!"

The noise coming from the lobby intensified and then the call ended abruptly. Peterson stared at the speakerphone as if it would come back to life of its own accord.

"Captain," he said at last, "get your men. Go down to the lobby and restore order. And find Gimbel O'Hare!"

The captain pointed to Cheri Tarte. "What about her?" he asked.

Attorney General Peterson visually inspected the handcuffs that bound Cheri Tarte to the chair. "She's not going anywhere," he said. "She still has a lot to tell us."

β 1 1

The statue stood at attention. The bronze spy held his head up, his boyish face unafraid of the sparse traffic on Constitution Avenue. His open coat and untied scarf provided scant protection for his thin body. The British soldiers and Loyalists who were his captors and who would soon be his executioners had bound his ankles with a cord to prevent his escape. Nathan Hale was twenty-one years old when he was hanged. According to the inscription on the pedestal of his statue, "he resigned his life, a sacrifice to his country's liberty."

Near the statue, Gimbel took cover behind a magnolia tree. Its perfume scented the night air. The white blossoms looked like full moons floating in a sky of broad, dark leaves. The foliage concealed Gimbel from the occasional car that cruised along Constitution Avenue. Headlights shone through the spindly flowers of a nearby coggygria, producing creepy moving shadows on the limestone walls of the justice department. In the intervals between cars, crickets provided background music for the spring evening. The ground floor window was too high above the pavement for Gimbel to see inside. He scrambled up to a narrow ledge and clung to the window shelf with his fingers, a rifle strapped to his back. Aluminum mullions divided the casement into an array of glass rectangles.

Gimbel pressed his face against a pane in the bottom row and spied the interior of the building. Through the slats of a Venetian blind he saw a dark office—close of business had been hours ago. Beyond the open office door, a string of hanging lamps projected yellowish circles onto a marble floor. The frosted glass hemispheres guided a CREEPS private as he patrolled the long hallway.

Gimbel wondered whether his diversion with the Jon Dunns had worked. There was no sign of it from here. The soldier walked casually as he moved deeper into the building, as if nothing out of the ordinary was going on. Gimbel hoped that when the CREEP reached the end of the corridor, he would turn off into a connecting hallway. Instead the black-clad figure reversed course and started back towards Gimbel, who crouched lower to avoid detection. If the soldier did not move out of the hallway soon, Gimbel would try another window, or perhaps reconnoiter the Pennsylvania Avenue side of the building.

Then he saw a flutter of blue cloth and a familiar face with glasses. Teacher-Dunn appeared at the far end of the corridor. He snuck up behind the soldier with his hands stretched out in front of him. Reaching for his adversary, Teacher-Dunn placed his hands around the private's neck and squeezed. The high black collar of the standard issue bulletproof vest protected the CREEPS soldier. Teacher-Dunn's attempt to strangle him was ineffective. The soldier flipped Teacher-Dunn over his shoulder and onto the floor. As the soldier fumbled with his rifle, Teacher-Dunn scrambled to his feet and ran back the way he came. He mooned the soldier through the open hospital gown as the fabric flapped in his wake. The soldier took off after him. The trail of water left on the floor by Teacher-

Dunn's soggy footwear caused the soldier to slide along the corridor. He flapped his arms and jerked gracelessly to avoid falling. At the end of the hallway, Teacher-Dunn disappeared around the corner with the CREEPS soldier in pursuit. A long empty corridor stretched in front of Gimbel.

Gimbel saluted Nathan Hale. He removed the rifle from his back, aimed the butt of the weapon at the windowpane, and said, "I only regret that I have but one window to break for my country."

β 1 1

It didn't take long to find Peterson's office. Gimbel already knew the room number, 5111. He had looked it up on the Internet while he was still at Walter Reed. Peeking through the double doors, Gimbel found the outer office deserted and the lights out. The carpet appeared black in the dark. Only one patch, on the other side of the room, revealed the blue color it assumed during business hours. That's where a quadrangle of light shone through the partly open door of the inner office.

Gimbel crossed the anteroom and crouched behind the attorney general's door. The rich wood paneling, brightly lit sconces, and Cheri Tarte's orange jumpsuit contrasted with the gloom on Gimbel's side of the portal. He was happy to see her. He wasn't concerned about the handcuffs; he was certain she could break out of her chair if she wanted to. But the patch of blood at the corner of her mouth angered him. He wished she would say something. He wanted to hear in her voice that she wasn't badly hurt—and he wanted to hear her voice. The door hid the other occupants of the room from him. On the plus side, they couldn't see him either.

"Very well," said a man. "We'll come back to that question. But before you leave here you will tell us whether you made a copy of this folder."

Gimbel was not surprised to recognize the voice of Isaac Ross. He had figured out weeks ago that Peterson was drawn to Ross like a mosquito to swamp water. Now Gimbel had an opportunity to prove it. He took the IQPhone from his pocket and started the voice recorder app. Every word spoken in the attorney general's office would be captured in the phone's memory.

Peterson took over the interrogation. "The economic sabotage committed by the Jon Dunns is, of course, at the heart of the case against you. All the perps were pillars of society: good jobs, strong families, no sabo connections—perfectly normal in every respect— until they met you. What did you do to them? What made them think they were Jon Dunn? How did you turn them into the instruments of your revenge against Consolidated Studios and against me? Isaac and I would like to know."

"I'll bet you would," Cheri Tarte replied contemptuously. When she spoke, Gimbel felt excitement—and relief. She sounded okay.

"Of course we would like to know, my dear," said Isaac. "It's a mystery that has consumed the taxpayers' resources for months. In addition, you seem to have discovered a secret, quite by accident, I'm sure, that has eluded kings and emperors for millennia: how to get people to cooperate. We know you advertised for all the Betas except the first one. How did it start?"

"It was after the show where you made me demonstrate the recycle bins. I was in the bar at the hotel. Kong and the others had gone to bed and I was by myself. A man came in and introduced himself. 'Dunn, Associated Industries.'"

"That was Mr. Shepherd, from Fort Wayne?"

"I found that out later, on the news. When I was with him, he stuck to his story about being Jon Dunn. I played along. I said, 'Okay, then I have a mission for you. Your instructions will be dead dropped to the gift shop tomorrow morning. Look for a copy of *Blueprint for Terror.*'"

"You told Mr. Shepherd that a work of fiction was an actual blueprint for terror and he believed you?"

She smirked at Isaac. "What can I say, I have a way of being very persuasive."

For a moment, the men shifted uncomfortably in their chairs. Isaac spoke first. "What about the others? Did they all think they were Jon Dunn before they met you?"

"Yes."

"Are you telling me that, without any intervention from you, our cities are teeming with unbalanced individuals who think they are a secret agent famous for wrecking cars and blowing up buildings?"

"Sorry, Isaac. There are people out there who aren't eager to take their assigned places in your cooperative society."

The plush carpet muffled the footsteps. Gimbel never heard the intruder enter the outer office. He was unaware another person was in the room with him until it was too late. Someone kicked him in the back, causing him to spill through the door and sprawl on the floor of the attorney general's office.

Bill Peterson looked down at him from behind his desk. "Mr. O'Hare," he said cheerfully, "it's very kind of you to drop in."

Gimbel picked himself up from the floor and groaned. It was unclear whether he was groaning because of the blow to his back or because of Peterson's tired cliché. "You had to say it, didn't you?" Gimbel said.

"I'm delighted by your visit. You saved me the trouble of instituting a second search for you. Or is it the third? I lost track. Permit me to introduce myself. My name is Bill Peterson. I believe you've met everyone else here. My political advisor, Mr. Ross—" Gimbel nodded to Isaac. "Ms. Tarte—"

"Little 'n' Cuddly! I never knew you looked so good in a tux."

"I always knew you looked good sleeveless."

"—and of course, Mr. Reed."

Gimbel turned around to face the man who had kicked him. "Glad to see you dressed for the occasion," said Addison. As always, he was dressed impeccably. His matching tie and handkerchief were a rich burgundy today, his blond hair stylishly moussed. He didn't take any chances that the advantage he had in height would be sufficient to intimidate Gimbel. For that purpose he relied on a nine-millimeter automatic.

"I should have known it would be you," said Gimbel. "Inviting me to your office at the exact time of the raid on Byte Yourself couldn't have been a coincidence."

"If you had shown up," Addison replied, "Mr. Peterson would have been saved the trouble of looking for you. To ensure that he doesn't have to look for you again, please remove that rifle from your back and hand it very carefully to Mr. Ross."

Isaac received the weapon with distaste. He walked around the attorney general's desk, placed the rifle gingerly on the credenza, and returned to his seat. "I do hate firearms," he said. With Gimbel disarmed, Addison relaxed. He reclined in the wingback chair in the corner and laid his nine-millimeter on the armrest.

Gimbel walked up behind Cheri Tarte. She tilted her head back; he leaned forward and kissed her on the mouth. "How are they treating you, darling?" he asked.

"I'm so happy here, I can't leave my chair."

He stroked her hair. "How's the food?"

"They won't let me have seconds and ribs aren't on the menu at all."

Gimbel glared at Peterson. "I watched your confirmation hearing. I distinctly recall you saying that constitutional shortcuts are not the American way. Does that not apply to the Eighth Amendment?"

"I did speak out against constitutional shortcuts," Peterson replied. "But omitting ribs from the prisoners' diet hardly comes under the heading of cruel and unusual punishment."

FULL ASYLUM

"Excuse me, Mr. O'Hare," said Isaac, "you interrupted an interrogation. We would like to get back to it. We can discuss your own situation when we're through. Now then, Ms. Tarte, you were telling us about the influence you have over the Jon Dunns."

Gimbel ignored him. He massaged Cheri Tarte's neck and shoulders. She looked up at him and purred. "That feels good."

"I've been wanting to do that for days," Gimbel replied.

"So you've been thinking about me?"

"Of course I thought about you. I thought about you the whole time I was in the asylum."

"That's sweet. It's nice to be remembered by crazy people."

Peterson looked on as Gimbel and Cheri Tarte gazed into each other's eyes. The attorney general was uncertain what to do. Isaac tried to interrupt again. "Mr. O'Hare—"

"I thought of you too," Cheri Tarte said to Gimbel. "I want us to take a trip together."

"Mr. O'Hare—"

"That would be nice. Where would you like to go?"

"I haven't decided. Either Hawaii or Aspen."

"Mr. O'Hare—"

"Definitely Hawaii. Skiing is too much exertion. We'll want to save our energy for...other things."

They talked about which islands to include on their itinerary. Isaac shouted, "Mr. O'Hare! The interrogation!"

Gimbel finally noticed that Isaac was trying to get his attention. "I wouldn't bother with the interrogation," he said. "You'll be too busy preparing your defense to make use of anything Cheri Tarte tells you."

"What's that supposed to mean?"

"It means," replied Gimbel, "that you're going to jail. I put the pieces together. I know what this is about."

Peterson stood up and sat down again. Addison yawned. Isaac looked concerned for a moment. But then his face relaxed and he said smoothly, "This young lady might have planted an idea or two in your head, completely without proof. Beyond that, you couldn't possibly know a thing."

"This young lady did plant an idea in my head, Isaac. The proof is in the manila folder in front of you."

Isaac looked over to the file on the desk. "Who told you that, Mr. O'Hare?"

"You just did. Cheri told me about the illegal campaign contributions with which you're funding Bill Peterson's presidential ambitions. It was rather brilliant to use the UWL to launder the money. With the league constantly on the road, you could transport fresh currency anyplace in the country. When it arrived, there was always a friendly unionized bellboy standing by to pass it on to the campaign. But what Cheri Tarte didn't know was the price Peterson paid for your help: the investigation of Byte Yourself Software and the charges of economic sabotage. It was an ingenious scheme, really. You got to take an irritating competitor down a peg while Peterson got on the fast track to the White House.

"But there was an obstacle, Isaac. To build the prosecution, Peterson needed a man on the inside. That's why you encouraged one of your top honchos to accept the job offer he had received from Tina Lee."

Gimbel turned to the man stretched out in the wingback chair. "Once ensconced in the Byte Yourself executive suite, Addison, you provided Isaac with a steady stream of proprietary information, including my infamous e-mail. Now you're supposed to get the Business Automation Division as your reward for betraying Tina. The hard part must have been keeping her off guard in the days leading up to the raid."

Addison spoke up from the corner. "Actually, that was the easy part. When your trip report made her suspicious, I promised to take care of it. I told her I would get together with the corporate counsel. Then I did nothing. Doing nothing is easy. What was hard was ensuring you were still on the payroll when the raid went down. I had to intervene twice to prevent you from getting fired. You should thank me, really. I was your fairy godmother."

"I am grateful to you—I needed the paycheck. It was fortunate that Beverly is in love with you. That must have made the intervention easier."

"That did work to my advantage. I had no intention of requiting her love—pancake makeup and pencil brows are a turnoff for me—so the situation could continue indefinitely."

"Why did you put me on *Sorry*? Was that my audition for the role of sabo?"

"Isaac wanted to get a look at you. He had to make sure you were sufficiently unlikable."

"I'm glad I didn't disappoint him."

Cheri Tarte grinned. "I liked you."

"Thank you, darling." He kissed her again.

Peterson clapped four times, slowly and only a little sarcastically. "Correct on all counts, Mr. O'Hare, a very impressive performance. It's usually easy for me to neutralize those who got in the way of the Department. Thanks to the Federal Economic Sabotage Act, the jails are full of them. But you were different. I don't suppose you went to Harvard."

"UVa."

"Pity. You showed the persistence of a Harvard man. You took up my time and my personnel. You caused me to lose trust in two dedicated line lawyers. You tied up the CREEPS while they searched for you—twice. You're still tying them up while they round up the psychiatric patients that you let out of the asylum. On top of that, I've got three soldiers in the stockade on drug charges and a Cryptanalysis Unit working overtime to decode the e-mail you sent this afternoon."

"Tell your cryptanalysts to go home," said Gimbel. "They won't be able to decode it. Also, it's OBE."

Shakespeare may have called envy the green-eyed monster, but the sin that beamed from Cheri Tarte's emerald irises was pride. "You did all that?" she asked. "And I thought you were just a computer geek."

"I can't take credit for the three CREEPS in the stockade. But the rest..."

"You should get in trouble more often. Hot water is your element."

"Indeed," Peterson said. "You have proven yourself quite resourceful in hot water. There may even be a position for you in a Peterson administration."

Isaac tried to interrupt. The interrogation was out of control. Gimbel took a deep breath and tried to act serious. He pointed out that Peterson's move to the Oval Office would create a vacancy in Room 5111. "Count me in for attorney general," said Gimbel. "With the resources of the Department, I could prosecute the men who punched Brownie McCoy in the stomach." Isaac turned red. "I could also prosecute whoever was responsible for that." He pointed to the dried blood at the corner of Cheri Tarte's mouth. "Then there's the business of the illegal campaign contributions."

"I wouldn't think you would care about that," said Peterson. "You just talked about the Constitution. Don't you think Isaac has the right to throw as much financial support as he wants behind the candidate of his choice? First Amendment and all that."

"I think everyone has that right. But if Isaac's the only one, while everyone else is forced to observe the legal limits, well it's just not on, old boy. Sorry, when I'm on the other side of that desk, there will have to be a full investigation."

The notion of Gimbel O'Hare as the nation's top cop pushed Isaac over the edge. "Enough with the hero–villain mutual admiration crap," he shouted at Peterson. "This isn't a Jon Dunn movie. I own Jon Dunn! Jon Dunn is getting a makeover. When I'm finished with him, he'll learn his place in the cooperative society.

Just like you, Mr. O'Hare. I don't care what you think you figured out. You're legally insane. A judge certified you the day before yesterday. Make your accusations. No one will believe you."

"Isaac, you're a troll," said Gimbel. He turned to Cheri Tarte. "We're in the Hall of the Troll King."

"Good thing we know the way out," she replied.

She went from zero to sixty in a quarter of a second. Standing and swinging her hips, Cheri Tarte smashed her chair against the desk. The Harvard alumni chair collapsed like furniture from a doll's house, freeing her from her restraints. A heap of spindles, legs, and armrests buried the university seal. She selected a chair leg from the pile. What had been her cage was now her weapon. She stood in her orange prison uniform, her muscular arms holding the chair leg over her head, handcuffs hanging uselessly from both wrists. Looking down at Addison and Isaac, she gleefully anticipated her next move. It was one she had practiced many times with Suzie Winsome and Brenda Biggs. As she brought the chair leg down over Isaac's head, she simultaneously kicked Addison in the jaw.

While Cheri Tarte engaged the Troll King and his minion, Gimbel scrambled over the top of the attorney general's desk. He snatched his rifle from the credenza and aimed it at Peterson. "Please stand and put your hands over your head," he said. Peterson obeyed. The two men stood in front of the darkened window, Gimbel in his tuxedo looking along the rifle barrel, the taller Peterson in gray pants and a white shirt, flattening his styled hair under his clasped hands. With his hostage secure, Gimbel glanced over to see how Cheri Tarte was doing. She had taken Addison out of the game entirely; he slumped unconscious in his armchair, his chin resting against his chest. Isaac was in a chokehold. The ogre who terrified the business world appeared small and vulnerable as Cheri Tarte pressed the chair leg firmly across his throat.

"You're sexy when you take prisoners," said Gimbel.

"I'm sexy when I do everything," Cheri Tarte replied.

Keeping his rifle aimed at Peterson, Gimbel walked around the desk. He removed one hand from the weapon long enough to retrieve the manila folder and shove the sheaf of papers into his cummerbund. "Now," he said, "you two are going to make sure that Cheri and I have no trouble getting out of the building. Let's go for a walk."

"We're not going anywhere," Isaac replied. His voice was hoarse, due to the pressure of a chair leg against his throat. He pointed at the rifle. "You won't dare use that thing."

"Are you sure?" asked Gimbel. "I'm legally insane."

Peterson went first; Gimbel propelled him forward with the rifle. Behind them, Isaac staggered as Cheri Tarte continued to apply pressure to his throat. They traversed the outer office and exited to the hallway.

They passed a brightly colored New Deal mural. The focal point of the Depression-era allegory was Lady Justice, blindfolded and wrapped in a flowing Greek gown. A villain in a black tailcoat lay on the ground. He had a thin mustache that curled at the ends. Lady Justice was crushing his windpipe with one foot. "Reminds me of you," Gimbel commented to Cheri Tarte. Around the central figures, citizens worked happily in a land freed from crime and tyranny. Some tilled the fields. Others manned machinery in a factory. A pale man in a smock inspected the contents of a test tube. In one corner, three Founding Fathers in bright blue coats and powdered wigs studied a large parchment that might have been the Bill of Rights.

Gimbel and the others proceeded to the elevator at the end of the hall and waited for it to arrive. Suddenly, the CREEPS captain emerged from a stairwell. The glass panel tinkled faintly as the door shut behind him. When he saw Peterson and Isaac held hostage, he removed his pistol from its holster. He circled to get a better shot at Gimbel and said, "I was just coming to see if the attorney general needed anything. Looks like he did." He released the safety. "I'm an expert marksman, Mr. O'Hare. If Mr. Peterson gives me the word, you and your girlfriend will both be dead before any harm can come to these two gentlemen. Now, put that rifle down on the floor and raise your hands above your head."

Gimbel pushed the rifle harder against Peterson's back and said, "Tell the nice captain that you're not willing to take that chance."

"But I *am*," said Peterson. "Goodbye, Mr. O'Hare. You have interfered with my plans for the last time."

The CREEPS captain tightened his finger on the trigger of his pistol. Gimbel dropped his rifle and reached out for Peterson. But he knew that shielding himself by swinging the hostage into the line of fire only worked in the movies; in real life, the bullet would kill both of them.

The stairwell door burst open a second time. Two Jon Dunns in hospital gowns ran out. In their hurry, they bumped into the CREEPS captain, sending him sprawling backwards. His gun fired, propelling a bullet harmlessly into the ceiling. As he fell, the captain hit his head on a fire extinguisher. He sank to the floor, out cold. The Jon Dunns scrambled down the hallway and vanished into the stairwell at the other end.

"Looks like I'll be interfering with your plans a few minutes longer," said Gimbel.

Peterson lunged towards Gimbel's rifle, but a growl from Cheri Tarte made him think better of it. Gimbel casually picked up the rifle and then removed a ring of keys from the captain's belt.

The art deco aluminum doors slid open. Gimbel, Cheri Tarte, Peterson, and Isaac stepped into the dusty elevator. When the doors closed again, they began their descent to the ground floor.

β 1 1

The sky was still dark, the half moon only midway through its journey. The streetlamps put out a sickly blue light that combined with red flashes from the traffic signal at the end of the block. The overbearing stone structures of the DOJ and the IRS turned 10th Street into a claustrophobic trench. But the birds were undeterred by their grim surroundings. They perched in the lacebark elms and tweeted a promise of approaching daylight.

Gimbel, Cheri Tarte, and their hostages emerged from the justice department into the cool, predawn air. Gimbel prodded Peterson with his rifle. Cheri Tarte had released her chokehold on Isaac; she periodically shoved his back to keep him moving. They squeezed between the concrete planters that protected the DOJ from car-borne explosives. Then they stepped off the curb and crossed the street halfway to the red brick sidewalk that ran along the median.

A dozen parking spaces were painted alongside the median. Gimbel and the others walked down the sidewalk until they reached the one that was occupied. The Cheetah YK-9 was a small defiant piece of the private sector in the midst of Federal Triangle. "Much nicer than the hippie mobile," said Cheri Tarte.

"I'd open the door for you," said Gimbel, "but..." He nodded to the rifle that he held with both hands.

"Let me open the door for *you*," Cheri Tarte replied.

"Right hip pocket," said Gimbel.

She came up behind him, reached into his pocket, and removed his key fob. Then she kissed the top of his head. Gimbel continued to guard Ross and Peterson, who stood side by side on the sidewalk with their hands in the air. After Cheri Tarte opened the driver side door, she walked around the car and took her place on the passenger side. Gimbel heard her close her door and start the ignition. It was *sayonara* time. As he backed into the driver's seat, Gimbel kept his eyes, and his rifle, on the prisoners.

"You won't get away," said Peterson. "Every policeman and CREEP in Washington will be chasing you the moment you leave the curb."

"We'll see about that," Gimbel replied. Peterson had tried to have him killed at the elevator. Revenge is a dish best served with a laser sight. The red dot shined brightly on Peterson's thin white shirt. "Goodnight, sweet prince," said Gimbel. He squeezed the trigger.

There was a rush of air. Peterson felt something sting his chest. He clutched his hands to the point of impact and fell backwards.

Gimbel showed no remorse. He swung his legs into the car, closed the door, and drove away. At a break in the median, the YK-9 executed a barely controlled high speed U-turn. Lying on his back, Peterson watched the car pass.

On his right he heard the tramp of army boots. He turned his head and saw a team of CREEPS jogging over from the building. The leader called to him. "Mr. Peterson, are you all right?"

He felt a knobby hand cradle his head. Isaac knelt at his side. "You will not die," he said. "I have spent too much on you."

Prick, thought Peterson. *I'm dying and he's worried about the return on investment for his campaign contributions.*

He felt something sticky where his hands pressed against his shirt. He tilted his head forward to take a look. The greasy liquid oozing between his fingers wasn't blood. It wasn't even red. It was clear, and somewhat reminiscent of egg white.

Peterson leaped to his feet. "Frigging paintball!" he shouted.

β 1 1

The director cursed. "What do you mean, Cheri Tarte isn't here? We sent a lawyer to bail her out three days ago!"

The production of *Error of the Moon* had encountered its share of obstacles—interference from Isaac, a lackluster car chase, technical glitches with the 3-D equipment—but this was the first time anyone had seen the director get mad. His assistant tried to explain the situation. "The DOJ invoked the Economic Sabotage Act and convinced the judge to issue an indefinite continuance of the bail hearing."

"I'm trying to make a movie to warn the public about sabos. Are you telling me the laws against sabos are getting in my way?"

"We're working on it, sir. We filed an appeal and there's a hearing scheduled first thing this morning. It's just that…"

"Spit it out!"

"The lawyer…he's not optimistic."

"Tell him to get optimistic!" the director shouted. "We need Cheri Tarte on location now!"

"I'm on it." The assistant removed a cell phone from his pocket. The lawyer was on speed dial.

The two men stood in the middle of the George Mason Memorial Bridge. The monument to the author of the Virginia Declaration of Rights was closed to traffic. At one end, the Washington Police rerouted cars bound south across the Potomac River. The activity on the bridge rivaled the preparations for a space flight. Technicians unloaded equipment and assembled it by the light of portable arc lamps. Those with a moment to spare dashed into the commissary tent to grab a doughnut or a cup of coffee. Others set up cameras at the railing to capture long shots of Jon Dunn's Cheetah YK-9 as it cruised along the shore, pursued by a cavalcade of fast-moving cars.

While his assistant coaxed the lawyer out of bed, the director went to scout the car chase route. It started at the Jefferson Memorial, a short distance from the bridge. The rotund white structure squatted on the banks of the clover-shaped Tidal Basin. Floodlights illuminated the white dome and shone on the marble steps that spilled from the portico. The YK-9 was ready to go; it waited at the base of a ramp beside the monument. The ramp led to a specially built platform that overlooked the top of the stairs.

The director and the stunt coordinator had finally agreed on twenty-five pursuit vehicles. They were parked on the circular road that enclosed the monument. *Police* and *KDS* were stenciled in large block letters on car doors. Mechanics performed final adjustments. They darted like sandpipers among the parked cars.

The team never did come up with the one simple and fun stunt that the director had asked for. Each draft of the chase rehashed the one before, with fewer cars in pursuit and fewer monuments blown up. Finally, time ran out and the director had to go with what they had. In the end, they targeted the Jefferson Memorial for destruction by computer graphics and spared the Washington Monument; they had to redub the hotel scene for consistency. If the director had his way, he would spare both structures, but Isaac insisted on blowing up at least one slave-owning Founding Father.

The director looked in briefly on the interior of the monument, which had been converted into an ad hoc dressing room. Makeup chairs had been installed at the base of the colossal statue of Thomas Jefferson. Finding Grant Casey in one of them, the director exchanged a few words with him, and then went back outside. He verified that the fences around the monument were open and the security barriers lowered to allow cars to move freely during filming. He crossed the Tidal Reservoir Inlet Bridge, a short concrete structure that spanned the narrow channel connecting the Tidal Basin to the Potomac River. Proceeding through West Potomac Park, he inspected the cherry blossoms with a flashlight. Their condition disappointed him. They had been agonizingly late this year. The director had burned money for weeks to keep the cast and crew on the payroll while he waited for the pink blooms to fill out. When the peak finally arrived, three days of rain pounded the nation's capital, destroying the delicate flowers and confining the film crews to their hotels. The rain stopped yesterday afternoon. Blossoms remained, but they were past their prime.

Disappointed, the director returned to the George Mason Bridge. Stepping over the cables that connected the current-hungry equipment to noisy electric generators, he found his way to an isolated spot. He stood at the railing, beyond the glare of the arc lights, and gazed out at the Potomac. When his eyes adjusted, he saw the sky was gray with the first glow of dawn. The glass-smooth water reflected the brightening sky. Upstream, the office and apartment towers of Rosslyn served as backdrop for the graceful arches of the Arlington Memorial Bridge. A boat chugged past. A pair of wild ducks paddled near the shore, stopping occasionally to poke their heads under the surface of the water.

Looking back at his crew, the director watched a team of electricians wire up the military-grade comms system. The cables had already been laid. Each length had been measured and cut in advance; when they arrived on location they fit into place perfectly. One of the electricians was a big man with a shaved head and a full mustache. He looked like a wrestler, circa 1890. He verified the operation of the handset, speaking confidently into the mouthpiece. His competence had a calming effect on the director.

The director returned to his assistant. "What did the lawyer say?"

"I got cut off. I lost the signal."

"Get him back. But first—is Cheri Tarte's stunt driver here?"

"Of course."

"Fine. We'll shoot the wide-angle shots first. The close-ups can wait until Cheri Tarte gets here. The comms system is up. Call the guard at the entrance to the park. Tell him that if Cheri Tarte arrives, he should send her up here immediately. I don't want any delays."

"Yes, sir."

"We film as soon as the sun comes up."

FULL ASYLUM

β 1 1

"I'm sorry, sir, the park is closed." The guard said it for the fiftieth time this morning. "They're filming here. No one can enter without a pass." The jogger turned around and ran back towards the Kennedy Memorial. At least this one didn't say, "I pay taxes for this park."

Blue sawhorses barricaded the road. To prevent trespassers from going around them, the studio had erected red snow fencing across the grass on both sides of the pavement, cutting off access to the thin peninsula between the Tidal Basin and the Potomac River. A dozen onlookers stood behind the barrier, hoping for a glimpse of Grant Casey or Lana Wong. The guard tried to keep the spectators on the grass. The road needed to be clear for official traffic.

The comms system buzzed. The guard picked up the handset. It was the director's assistant. "I understand, sir," said the guard. "If Cheri Tarte arrives, I'll let her right through." He returned the handset to the base. That's when he noticed the elderly couple walking in the park a short distance away. The husband wore a sports jacket, the wife a green tracksuit. They must have slipped past while the guard was on the phone. They moved slowly away from the barricade, towards the river.

"Come back here," yelled the guard. "The park is closed. No one can enter without a pass!"

β 1 1

"Did he say something?" asked Mr. Bentel.

Mrs. Bentel looked over her shoulder. "I think he's just waving," she said. She waved back at the guard and smiled.

They stopped at the edge of the water, next to a green and white sign that said, *Feeding the birds is strictly prohibited*. Mrs. Bentel opened her purse and removed a plastic bag containing stale bread. She tore off a few pieces, tossed them in the water, and waited for the ducks to notice.

"I don't know why they have to have a guard," said Mr. Bentel. "We pay taxes for this park."

β 1 1

Gimbel checked the rearview mirror. He chuckled as he watched Peterson stomp on the sidewalk and shout angrily. Clearly Peterson now realized that Gimbel had held him hostage with a paintball gun.

The midnight blue Cheetah YK-9 turned right on Constitution Avenue. Gimbel drove quickly in the sparse predawn traffic.

He reached into the pocket of his tuxedo jacket and removed the key ring he had taken from the CREEPS captain. Keys jingled as he handed them to Cheri Tarte. "One of these should open those handcuffs," he said.

As Cheri Tarte removed the pairs of handcuffs that dangled from each wrist, the car passed another overbearing government building. This one housed the Environmental Protection Agency. Concrete planters lined the sidewalk in front. They were full of dirt and bare of foliage. "It's just my opinion," said Gimbel, "but the environment should be protected by people who can grow something."

Cheri Tarte started on the leg irons. "I'm sorry about the asylum," she said. "If you hadn't been with me you wouldn't have been taken there."

"It was worth it," Gimbel replied.

"Are you better now?" she asked.

"I don't know. I hope not. You heard the attorney general. In a moment, every policeman and CREEP in Washington will be chasing us. We're going to need Jon Dunn."

FULL ASYLUM

Under the semicircular south portico, the White House windows showed no signs of activity. The flag on the roof hung straight down, motionless in the lack of breeze. Gimbel wondered whether the president was awake and how he would react to the cabinet vacancy that Gimbel was about to engineer.

He asked Cheri how many pals she had on SoshNet.

"About a million," she said. "Why do you ask?"

"That should be enough." Keeping one hand on the wheel, he removed his IQPhone from his pocket. He held it up in front of the windshield and looked at the screen long enough to turn off the voice recorder. "I wave-filed the whole conversation in Peterson's office," he said. "We have a recording of Isaac acknowledging your file folder. We have Addison's confession. We have Peterson saying that my accusations are correct on all counts. We even have him encouraging that CREEPS captain to kill us." He handed the phone to Cheri Tarte. "Peterson wants publicity. Let's give him some. Upload the file and post it to SoshNet."

Cheri Tarte leaned over the screen and typed. Something was wrong. She frowned and typed some more. "I got zero bars," she said at last. "No signal." She looked out the windows, turning her head in all directions. No one looked back except the slightly supercilious stone eagle perched above the entrance to the Federal Reserve.

"What are you looking for?" Gimbel asked.

"CREEPS. They always jam cell phones when they conduct an operation."

"That's what Brownie told me. How did you know about it?"

"Kong said so."

"The guy with the monkey fur?"

"He's really very sophisticated. You should see him with a tux and a martini glass."

"We should fix him up with our friend Lacey. Sounds like her type."

"What about the CREEPS?"

"Let them get their own dates."

Cheri Tarte told him to be serious. He looked out the window to get his bearings.

"The Franklin Roosevelt Bridge is coming up," he said. "The only thing we have to fear is getting through the next two blocks."

"You had to say it, didn't you?"

He explained that the highways on the other side of the river were like spaghetti. Once Gimbel and Cheri reached the Virginia shore, the CREEPS would never find them. "Also, we should be out of jamming range."

The checkpoint was at 23rd Street. Three CREEPS Humvees barricaded the way ahead, cutting access to the bridge. The road to Virginia was blocked. Gimbel stopped. The vehicles faced each other across the intersection. Finally, a CREEPS sergeant emerged from one of the Humvees. As the sergeant approached, Gimbel put the car in park and punched up a map on the Cheetah's GPS display. An icon popped up, indicating the location of the Cheetah. Gimbel looked for a way out of the city. "Arlington Memorial Bridge is the best bet."

The black-uniformed sergeant stood by the car, gesturing for Gimbel to roll down the window. "Hold on to something," Gimbel said to Cheri. He jerked the gearshift into drive and slammed his foot on the gas pedal. As soon as he cleared the CREEPS sergeant, he cranked the steering wheel sharply to the left. The car slued into the turn; Gimbel and Cheri leaned into the three g force that pushed them in the opposite direction. A siren started up. Blue lights flashed in the rearview mirror. The CREEPS were going to chase them.

The rectangular block of the Kennedy Memorial emerged from the trees ahead of them. The marble pillars alternated blue and white as they reflected the lights of the CREEPS vehicles. "Ask not what your Cheetah can do for you," said Gimbel as he pressed down on the accelerator. "But I'm asking." The needle on the speedometer settled between eighty-five and ninety. The gap between the Cheetah and the black Humvees grew longer. Gimbel changed lanes to end run a slow-moving car.

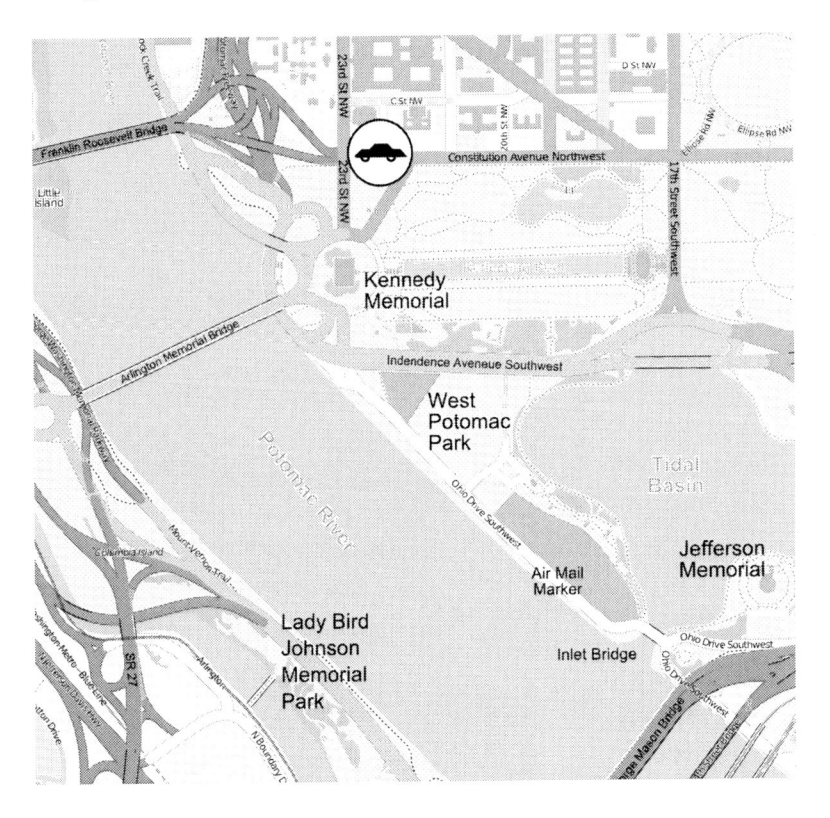

Kennedy Memorial Circle looped behind the monument and fed Arlington Bridge. Gimbel had to slow as he made the turn into the circle. The entrance to the bridge emerged between the gilded statues of Valor and Sacrifice, the Arts of War. "We'll escape the feds yet," Gimbel said. Twin columns of streetlights converged on Arlington House across the river. Their elongated glass globes, reminiscent of gas lamps, were still lit. But the path to Arlington was closed. Just beyond the statues, five Washington Police cars blocked the road. Beyond them, early commuters packed the inbound lanes. They honked at the stopped cars in front of them. A few got out of their vehicles to see what was going on.

Ignoring the no U-turn sign, Gimbel swerved to the left, crossed three lanes, and doubled back over the tip of the traffic island. As he reentered the circle, four of the police cars joined the chase. The fifth remained behind in case Gimbel tried to circumnavigate the Kennedy Memorial and return to the bridge. The CREEPS Humvees sped into sight just as the police cars pulled out. The lead vehicles collided and skidded into the base of one of the statues. The golden figure of Valor gazed ahead impassively as he rode on the back of a golden horse. Marching beside them, Valor's Amazonian sidekick also had her sights fixed on the road ahead. Only the horse condescended to look down at the mayhem below.

Three patrol cars and two Humvees were still operational. They slowed to avoid broken glass and bits of police cruiser; one of the Humvees drove over the traffic island. Gimbel took advantage of the opportunity to increase his lead. He exited Kennedy Memorial Circle and approached Ohio Drive. Once again on a straightaway, he accelerated to one hundred miles per hour. The flashing blue lights in the rearview mirror were far behind.

Welcome to West Potomac Park. Just as the Cheetah passed the brown-and-white National Park Service sign, the sun appeared over the woods to the east. It turned the sky to a cold sapphire blue. The Potomac River sped by on the right. In the calm waters near the Virginia shore, the reflections of the trees were in sharp focus.

The blue wooden sawhorses came up on them suddenly. Gimbel had to brake hard to avoid hitting them. The guard approached and looked through the windshield. Seeing Cheri Tarte in the passenger seat, he followed his orders. Without asking for IDs, he removed the wooden barrier, waved the car through, and closed the barrier behind it. Onlookers raised their cell phone cameras over the snow fences and tried to get pictures of the midnight blue Cheetah YK-9 and the tuxedo-clad driver. Gimbel stopped just inside the barricade, opened his window, and called the guard over. "Some more cars will be along in a couple minutes," he said. "I expect them to crash the barricade. You may want to take cover in a safe place."

He floored the accelerator. They passed a half dozen baseball diamonds on their left. Dense woods marked the boundaries of the outfields and hid the Tidal Basin. The tall white spire of the Washington Monument rose above the evergreens. Up ahead, the dome of the Jefferson Memorial was visible through a gap in the trees. The south end of the Inlet Bridge came into view just beyond an S-curve. As Gimbel and Cheri approached the curve, they saw, at the water's edge, a pair of elderly tourists studying a stone marker.

β 1 1

"What does it say?" asked Mrs. Bentel.

Her husband put on his magnifying spectacles and bent over the bronze plaque affixed to the stone. "Air Mail," he read. "The world's first airplane mail to be operated as a continuously scheduled public service started from this field May 15, 1918. The route connected Washington, Philadelphia, and New York."

"I bet in those days, the TSA didn't steal your compact."

β 1 1

The midnight blue Cheetah YK-9 soared past the portico of the Jefferson Memorial. Jon Dunn, Secret Agent Beta Eleven, sat in the driver's seat, wearing an expensive gray business suit on his body and a look of determination on his face. The car sailed through the air, cutting a trajectory across the columns. On the marble steps below, a surprised tourist fought to hold onto his hat while his wife took pictures of the car's underbelly.

At ground level, Cheri Tarte maintained a parallel course. She sped along the road in front of the monument, driving a black sedan with the KDS logo on the door. Sitting in the passenger seat, a man in the uniform of a security guard operated the sunroof. He stood through the aperture, wrestled a rocket launcher out of the car, and rested the cylinder on his shoulder. He squeezed the trigger. A cloud of smoke puffed out from the back of the launcher while a projectile popped out the front. The projectile seemed to hover for a moment. Then it ignited and zoomed towards the YK-9. The missile flew under the car, missing it by inches. It passed between a pair of Ionic columns and skidded across the floor of the portico, into the interior of the Jefferson Memorial. "All monuments are destroyed equally," said Dunn.

An instant later the YK-9 landed on the marble steps with a bump. Dunn shook as the car bounced down the stairs. When it reached the bottom, he steered onto the road, narrowly edging out the KDS car.

Dunn sped away from the memorial. Cheri Tarte followed close behind. Backlit by the sun, two streams of pursuit vehicles flowed dramatically around the foundation of the monument. White police cruisers and black KDS sedans emerged from both sides and fell into formation. The cars embraced the shoreline. Steering wheels revolved as drivers struggled to stay on a narrow strip of pavement that had been intended for pedestrians. One policeman miscalculated and sent his cruiser tumbling into the Tidal Basin. Water poured from the driver's seat as he emerged from the car into the knee-deep reservoir. Leaving him behind, the convoy passed under a row of cherry trees. Pink blossoms swirled in the slipstream.

As he approached the Inlet Bridge, Dunn accelerated into the curve. He hoped that Cheri Tarte would either fail to keep up or carom off the guardrail trying. But she negotiated the turn expertly. With Cheri still in scorching pursuit, Dunn drove onto the bridge. To his surprise, a *second* midnight blue Cheetah YK-9 was heading straight towards him, speeding across the bridge from the other end. In the driver's seat of the second car, Jon Dunn, dressed in a tuxedo, looked equally surprised. Cheri Tarte sat next to him, her red hair falling over the shoulders of an orange jumpsuit.

β 1 1

The movie stunt car was headed straight at Gimbel. Through the windshield, he could see the driver, who looked like, but wasn't, Grant Casey. A pickup truck kept pace alongside. Two cameras were mounted in the box. One of them, in the rear of the truck, pointed backwards to film the dozens of vehicles now streaming onto the two-lane bridge. In front of it, the second camera aimed at the YK-9, recording the stunt driver's horrified expression through the side window. The cameraman glanced over his shoulder to see what the driver was looking at. When he saw Gimbel driving towards him, he responded professionally. He rotated the camera forward to capture the imminent crash.

Gimbel clobbered the brake pedal. He yanked the gearshift into reverse and backed away from the onrushing armada at full speed. At the end of the bridge, the road widened to four lanes, giving Gimbel room to turn around. He saluted the cameraman with two fingers and tugged the steering wheel. The car spun until it moved forward again. Gimbel headed back in the direction he had come from, towards the Kennedy Memorial.

On the road ahead he saw a familiar set of flashing blue lights. The vehicles that had escaped the accident at the statue of Valor had finally caught up with their target. The three Washington Police cars and two CREEPS Humvees closed the gap. Behind him, the film crew continued its pursuit. The opposing waves of speeding vehicles were about to crush Gimbel and Cheri between them. Gimbel looked around for an escape.

On his left, the waters of the Potomac River flowed placidly towards the George Mason Bridge. On his right, the obelisk of the

Washington Monument supervised a baseball diamond. The newly risen sun was behind the monument. It cast a long shadow across the outfield, like an arrow pointing towards the river. "The father of our country," said Gimbel. "First in war, first in peace, and first in giving directions." He steered in the direction indicated by the arrow.

There was a jolt as the YK-9 drove over the curb. The car passed between a pair of trees, picking up speed as it bumped down the incline and crossed the grass towards the embankment. Gimbel reached for the new display that Brownie had installed on his dashboard. He pressed a large red icon labeled *Engage*.

"What are you doing?" Cheri asked.

"Going air mail."

β 1 1

Mr. and Mrs. Bentel stood by the Air Mail marker and watched the two clusters of vehicles speed towards each other. "They're driving like crazy people," said Mrs. Bentel.

"The police are never around when you need them," her husband replied.

"I think they *are* the police."

A dark blue car broke away from the pack and jumped the curb. The others followed. They headed dangerously close to the elderly couple.

As the cars gained speed, Mrs. Bentel's eyes rolled up and she fell to the ground.

β 1 1

The second Cheetah YK-9 flew off the embankment and out over the Potomac.

Behind it, police cruisers, KDS sedans, CREEPS Humvees, and the first Cheetah YK-9 all tried to stop at once. They slipped on the wet grass and collided like bumper cars. The Humvees, which had muscled their way to the front, were pushed into the river from behind. Miraculously, not one vehicle hit the white-haired woman lying on the ground beside the Air Mail marker. Her husband was also spared as he crouched over her, patting her hands to revive her from her faint.

All eyes, or at least those that were still open, turned to watch the YK-9 as it soared over the river. Several segments of what looked like an airplane wing unfolded from underneath the car. The segments joined together and locked into place, creating a shield between the YK-9 and the river.

The car arced downwards towards the water. The wing partially submerged and glided along the surface.

Then the car bounced.

It skipped across the river like a stone on a pond.

As the car approached the Virginia shore, the wing tilted, hitting the water at a slightly steeper angle. The final bounce was higher than the previous ones, allowing the car to clear the embankment. It sailed over a tangle of porcelainberry and landed on the grass.

Back on the Washington side, a dozen CREEPS stood by the river's edge. They watched helplessly as the YK-9 crossed the grass, turned onto a road, and disappeared into Lady Bird Johnson Park.

At the railing of the George Mason Bridge, the director yelled cut. "*That's* the stunt I was looking for!"

EPILOGUE

INDEPENDENCE DAY

[Independence Day] ought to be solemnized with pomp and parade, with shows, games, sports, guns, bells, bonfires, and illuminations, from one end of this continent to the other, from this time forward forevermore.
– John Adams, Letter to Abigail Adams, July 3, 1776

If Gimbel's life were a movie, his escape from Washington would have been followed by a tiresome race by car to New York City, where he would have arrived on the set of *Sorry* just in time to stop Tina Lee from giving away half the company. Then he would have made a speech on national television about the important lesson he learned: be yourself.

None of these things happened.

Although his British accent went away, for the rest of his life there was a part of Gimbel that continued to believe he was Jon Dunn. That part of him kept striving to fulfill his potential and excel. He was quite open about this, much to the concern of his parents. They urged him to return to Walter Reed and finish the treatment that had been interrupted when he escaped the asylum. "I'm grateful that you worry about me," he told them, "but I caught the bad guys and won the girl because of my supposed illness. I'm not looking for a cure."

FULL ASYLUM

As for stopping Tina, Gimbel hadn't forgotten the teasing that Brownie once gave him for trying every form of communication except the old-fashioned telephone call. As soon as Gimbel got out of range of the CREEPS jammers, he called Tina on his IQPhone and told her about the conspiracy between Ross and Peterson. Then he sent her, via e-mail, the recording of the conversation in Peterson's office, cc: Lacey Briefs. Tina immediately cancelled her appearance on *Sorry* and politely backed out of Byte Yourself's plea agreement. After Gimbel got off the phone with Tina, he passed it to Cheri Tarte who logged into SoshNet and posted the recording on her fan page to an instant audience of one million. Gimbel logged into SoshNet as well. He checked the application he had written to publish the evidence against Chris Molson. It still counted down to Friday. Gimbel shut it down. It was no longer needed.

Attorney General Peterson tried to deny everything. He assembled a press conference in the Great Hall of the DOJ building. Behind him, an enormous pair of art deco aluminum statues made him look small as he read his prepared statement from a teleprompter.

"I'm sure you all heard the recording that went viral today on the Internet. It appears to be a conversation between Isaac Ross of Consolidated Industries and myself, in which we openly discuss a conspiracy to steal the presidential election. I came here to say that the FBI laboratories have examined the recording and determined that it is completely fabricated."

The text stopped rolling across the teleprompter, the usual cue for a dramatic pause. After a couple seconds, it resumed. "But if I said that," Peterson continued, "it would be a big lie. The recording is genuine. It was made in my office early this morning and every word in it is true."

Disorder swept the hall as reporters made calls and typed messages on IQPhones. An FBI detail, led by Lacey Briefs, approached the podium. Peterson stared at the teleprompter. The words displayed were not the speech he had approved. In one corner of the screen, he noticed a sticker with the words *Secured by Byte Yourself IROSS*.

After depositing the attorney general securely in a holding cell, the FBI detail's next stop was National Airport. Isaac was trying to flee the country on his private jet. Unfortunately for him, Lacey had quickly obtained a court order freezing all of his accounts. When he tried to purchase jet fuel, he was told that he had no credit. Without a source of energy, his escape vehicle was an expensive sitting room. The FBI detail surrounded the immobilized plane on the ground. The news photos showed Isaac being escorted down the steps of the airplane, his hands cuffed behind his back. He looked furious.

As the philosopher-king of Consolidated Industries, Isaac had always viewed his executives as organs for carrying out his decisions. Unaccustomed to working without coordination by a central brain, they foundered in his absence. Consolidated's stock crashed. The simultaneous recovery of Byte Yourself and the change in the political climate put Tina Lee in an excellent position to buy out a competitor. Consolidated's board of directors was relieved to make a deal.

The following weeks were busy ones for Tina. Identifying the right team to lead the combined company required dozens of personnel decisions. Among them was finding a replacement for Addison at the helm of the Business Automation Division. She was impressed that, in spite of the destruction of their lab, the BAD team had met its May 1 delivery date. Tina was determined to promote from within. With that object in mind, she visited Beverly's office one afternoon in mid-May.

"I never trusted Addison," Beverly said. "I'm not the least bit surprised he was working for Isaac Ross."

"His job is yours now," Tina replied. "We'll go public with it as soon as it's cleared by HR."

There was a commotion in the hallway. Cindy Valence shouted, "Daphne, don't go in there. She's meeting with Tina."

The door opened and Madame Butterfly fluttered into the office. Cindy followed a few steps behind, looking apologetic.

Beverly tried to be polite in front of her boss. "Daphne, I'm in an important meeting now. Please come back later."

"But it's important," Madame Butterfly said breathlessly.

"I haven't got time right now."

Tina interrupted. "There's always time for the people who work for you," she said. "Besides, I think you and I are done here. Go ahead, Daphne. What did you want to say to Beverly?"

Madame Butterfly took a moment to compose her thoughts. "Beverly, I'm worried about Cindy. She told me we should be nice to Gimbel O'Hare now that he's a big hero and all. I don't want her to get into trouble."

Tina raised an eyebrow behind her oversized glasses. "Why would being nice to Gimbel get Cindy into trouble?"

"Because Beverly said to be mean to him."

Beverly feigned ignorance. "What are you talking about? I never said any such thing."

"That's okay, I forget things sometimes too. Remember when we were at Kilkenny's? It was because of what happened with Gimbel and Cindy. You proposed a toast to dragging Gimbel down to hell."

She spoke so candidly that it was hard to doubt her. Tina sighed. "It looks like you and I weren't done," she said to Beverly. "Daphne, Cindy, is there anything else?"

They shook their heads.

"Then I need to talk to Beverly alone. Please close the door on your way out."

MICHAEL ISENBERG

β 1 1

The chairman banged his gavel. "This hearing on S.56, A Bill to Repeal the Federal Economic Sabotage Act, is hereby called to order. Our first witness is Lacey Briefs. Miss Briefs is the lead attorney on the DOJ Task Force for the Review of Economic Sabotage Prosecutions. Welcome back to Washington, Miss Briefs. I understand you're here to stay this time."

"Thank you, Senator. Yes, it is my intention to make Washington my home now." Lacey sat at the witness table and read her opening statement. "The Task Force recommends passage of this bill and repeal of FESA.

"To date, we have reviewed over two hundred prosecutions. Nearly every one of them has proven to be without merit. In most cases, the alleged sabos have been released from custody.

"The case against the wrestler Cheri Tarte was one of the first under review. After she discovered that Isaac Ross was laundering illegal contributions for the Peterson campaign, there were few legal options open to her, due to the corruption in the Department of Justice. In view of this, and in view of the role she played in exposing that corruption, the department has dropped all charges against her.

"The charges against Byte Yourself Software and Gimbel O'Hare have been dropped as well. As we now know, Isaac Ross and Bill Peterson fabricated these charges to further their own agenda.

"The findings of the Task Force demonstrate that the government used FESA primarily as a political weapon. It was directed at people who were innocent of wrongdoing, other than offending those in power. While this finding reveals the lack of effective safeguards in FESA, there is also reason to question whether FESA was ever necessary in the first place. You will hear testimony later today from two Nobel laureates in economics recently released from federal prison. They subsequently served on a panel that studied the policies implemented by the government in the wake of the Financial Crises. The panel concluded that these policies caused needless suffering by siphoning resources away from their optimal uses, thereby distorting markets. It was these policies, and not so-called economic sabotage, that prolonged the crisis. The sabo conspiracy never existed."

After the hearing, the chairman took Lacey aside. "Is it true what I read about you?" he asked. "Are you really dating Kong?"

Lacey was taken aback. She had gotten used to the question ever since the fan blogs started publishing photos of her and Kong in restaurants and concert halls. But coming from an elderly man in the United States Senate, the question was just creepy. She replied warily. "Yes, sir. I am dating a wrestling man."

"Good," said the senator. His big ears made his grin seem wider. "Can you get me his autograph?"

β 1 1

Mrs. Bentel examined the plastic jug through her reading glasses. Something was embossed on the bottom, but she couldn't tell if it was a recycling symbol or some other marking. She moved to the kitchen window to view it in better light, but the glyph remained stubbornly illegible.

"Screw it," she said. She bypassed the recycling bin and threw the jug in the trash.

β 1 1

"Welcome back," said Tina. "How was Hawaii?"

The grin on Gimbel's face and his suntanned skin told her all she needed to know. His beige linen suit complemented his post-island complexion.

Gimbel and Cindy joined Tina in her conference room. The airplane wing table had been restored to its place following its dip in the Potomac. The seams where Cindy and Brownie had cut it into segments were only visible to someone who looked for them. A pair of manila envelopes lay on the table in front of Tina.

She explained the reason for the meeting. "I still haven't found a new director for the Business Automation Division. In the meantime, I decided to appoint myself acting director and manage BAD personally. Cindy, I've been talking to some of your team members and they told me it was your leadership that made the on-time delivery possible. I want you to be my deputy."

Cindy was grateful to Tina for her confidence, and a little embarrassed. After playing ball with Beverly for half a year, it turned out that old-fashioned results were the key to advancement at Byte Yourself Software.

Tina discussed the division of labor. "Obviously, I have other responsibilities besides BAD. I'll mentor you, but you're going to have to take charge of day-to-day operations on your own. Eventually we'll name a permanent director. Your performance as deputy will determine whether you will be in the running for that position.

"The first thing you need to do is hire a new sysadmin. Brownie McCoy is moving to the Entertainment Division—assuming you approve his transfer. After the director of *Error of the Moon* saw that car you and Brownie put together, he declared that Brownie was a master builder and he put on a full court lobby to get him to head the FX department."

"Transfer approved."

Tina moved on to the next topic. "Speaking of lobbying," she said, "our friends on the Hill assure me they got the votes to repeal FESA." She turned to Gimbel. "That makes Crypt Yourself legal again. We're going to re-launch the product and I want you to be tech lead."

Gimbel welcomed the opportunity to once again exercise his cyber breaking-and-entering skills.

"You'll report to OSD, but you're going to have to work with Cindy to integrate Crypt Yourself with the business software. I know the two of you had some history. Are you going to be able to work together?"

Cindy and Gimbel smiled at each other. "I think we can get along," said Gimbel.

Tina remembered another concern. "You have a gig of your own with the Entertainment Division," she said to Gimbel. "Will you have any trouble juggling that with your new responsibilities?"

"No," he replied, without hesitation. "The Entertainment Division assures me that it will only be an occasional cameo with minimal impact on my time. They're even going to send a private jet to Reagan National."

"Now for the good part," said Tina. "Obviously if you take these assignments, there will be changes to your compensation." She picked up the two manila envelopes from the table and handed one to each of her visitors. "This is my starting offer."

Gimbel and Cindy opened the flaps and glimpsed at the pages inside. There would not be much need for negotiations.

β 1 1

Gimbel slept nine hours that night. He dreamed about cherry tarts until the alarm went off. He was already starting his second egg when the high-pitched whine of power saws and the rapid pounding of hammers began to echo across the parking lot. He went out to his balcony and stood at the railing to watch the construction. The wooden frames of future buildings dotted the ground. Around them, yellow bulldozers barreled over mounds of earth. "Looks like I'll have some new neighbors soon," he said. He bit into a buttery slice of toast. "I hope they're quiet."

β 1 1

Upstairs, the Lazulis had already finished breakfast. Mr. Lazuli knelt on the living room carpet as he unpacked his accounting books. He quietly lined them up on the shelves by topic, in order of increasing complexity.

Mrs. Lazuli entered the room, holding Mimi by the hand. "Look who's ready for Saturday," she said cheerfully. Her husband raised his head from the carton of books and saw that his daughter had tried on her Independence Day costume. Behind his round glasses, his stern expression softened. Mimi wore the long coat, ruffles, and knee breeches of a Founding Father. Her black curls emerged from a tiny three-corner hat.

"Don't forget what I taught you to say," he told her. "Happy Fourth of July!"

"'Pea Fuff 'Lie!"

Still kneeling on the floor, Mr. Lazuli conducted with his arms. "Happy Fourth of July!"

"'Pea Fuff 'Lie!" Mimi yelled gleefully as she ran across the room into the waiting arms of her father. The American Dream was back on.

β 1 1

He did not look forward to the conversation.

The director turned on the flat panel display that hung on the wall of his conference room. The black bowl haircut and oversized glasses of Tina Lee filled the screen.

He skipped the greetings and came right to the point. "I take it you're pulling the plug on *Error of the Moon*," he said.

"Why would I do that?" Tina asked.

"Iona Klimt. We turned you into a villain."

"I don't have a problem being a villain. I just don't like being a lame one."

"On top of that, my storyline is about to go OBE. As soon as Congress repeals FESA, my movie will be yesterday's blog entry."

"Here's the one projectile that will assassinate both avians," said Tina. She held up a paperback copy of *Error of the Moon*. "Have you read this?" she asked. "The original novel?"

"Of course."

"Then you know that the villain had a much more diabolical plan than conspiring to lay people off. Use it."

"It's too late. The movie is already in the can."

"That can be fixed. A few new scenes, a little dubbing, some stock footage from NASA, and you're there. You'll need one new set. And money—let me know how much by COB."

"Will do." The director sounded happy.

"One more thing," said Tina. "What's with the spring water in Iona Klimt's office? It's Jon Dunn. Give him a real drink."

β 1 1

"Goodnight, sweet princess."

The black and camo mound on the floor was the motionless body of Cheri Tarte. The puddle of blood expanded beside her. It seeped under the door and into the control room.

Jon Dunn still wore the blue cotton flight suit that he had stripped from the astronaut back at the launch site. No doubt the astronaut's unconscious body had been found by now. The guards who discovered it would have alerted Iona Klimt that Dunn had escaped from his cell. She would be expecting him. He inserted a new dart into the air pistol. Holding the gun out in front of him, he approached the entrance and pressed the button beside it. The door slid open instantly. He stepped over Cheri Tarte and invaded the control room. The door swished shut behind him.

Iona Klimt sat at the control console, smoking a cigarette in a long black holder. Behind her, large sheets of space-age plastic afforded a view of the moon's surface. Dunn had anticipated the windows when he substituted an air pistol for his usual .45 caliber Glückenspiel. If a stray bullet punctured the clear polymer, the contents of the room, including any people, would be swept up in the tempest as the air rushed out through the opening. Without spacesuits, they would die in the frigid vacuum outside.

Beyond the windows, the Stars and Stripes and the base of a lunar lander stood where Apollo astronauts had left them over half a century ago. The sun and the earth shone brightly above them. On the horizon, a string of craters marked the limits of the dusty gray landscape. Just as Dunn entered the control room, bright light and a billow of smoke erupted from one of the craters. Then a missile rose majestically from the opening. It cleared the crater, turned in the direction of the earth, and disappeared into the star-filled sky.

"You're too late," said Iona Klimt. "The bird has, how do you say, flown the coop." Although the missile was no longer visible through the windows, Mrs. Klimt monitored its progress on the three overhead screens built into the wall in front of her. The left-hand screen provided video coverage. It showed the first stage of the missile complete its burn and separate from the kinetic warhead. The right-hand screen displayed a diagram of both the earth and the moon. An S-shaped curve connected them, indicating the planned trajectory of the missile. A flashing light near the moon showed the missile's current position. The center display was larger than the other two. On the screen, the earth appeared, blue and peaceful, blissfully unaware that an instrument of death headed its way.

"You must issue the self-destruct code," said Dunn. "Seven million people will die if you don't."

"Eight million," replied Iona Klimt. "To put that into perspective, there are seven *billion* people on earth. I am willing to sacrifice eight seventieths of one percent to achieve my objective. It is a small fraction."

"Unless you're one of the people involved."

"Please take a seat, Mr. Dunn. My missile has a long way to travel. Neither of us is going to do anything until it reaches Washington."

"We'll see about that." He aimed the dart gun at Iona Klimt. Just then, he felt the tip of a metal barb pressed against the side of his head. He had not seen Su Mi hiding just inside the door, holding a dart gun of her own. "Please lower your weapon, Jon," she said.

He raised his hands. The dart gun dangled from his trigger finger. As Su Mi took it away from him, he said, "Hello, darling. Fancy meeting you here."

"Are you surprised to see Miss Mi?" said Iona Klimt. She continued matter-of-factly. "The peoples of the East have always been more practical than you Westerners. Our utilitarian approach accounts for the longevity of our civilizations. Miss Mi recognized that a new power would soon emerge on Earth. She made a practical decision to align herself with it. We in the East don't allow ourselves to be transported by our passions."

Dunn looked at the monitors. The missile had already completed a quarter of its journey.

"You'd be surprised," he said. "At our last encounter, Miss Mi was quite transported by her passions."

The reminder of her last encounter with Dunn had a sudden and transformative effect on Su Mi. Iona Klimt's shining vision of the future conflicted with Su Mi's memory of a night by the fireside in a snow-covered Swiss chalet. The conflict was visible in her expression. Then, just as suddenly, she resolved the conflict. Her face hardened into a look of determination. She turned her air gun away from Dunn's head, aimed, and squeezed the trigger. The dart sped over the top of the console and lodged in the center of Iona Klimt's forehead.

Iona's eyes grew wide. Her last word was barely audible. "Why?"

"Because he's the best."

Dunn dashed around the console and pushed the corpse of Iona Klimt out of the command chair. She tumbled to the floor. Taking the high-backed chair, Dunn began to type. There was a knock at the door. "Lock it," he ordered. Su Mi pressed some buttons on a keypad by the entrance. "That should slow them down," she said. As Dunn continued typing, he looked alternately at the overhead displays and the screen in the console. Suddenly there was a flash of light on the left-hand display. The missile exploded loudly into a yellow and orange fireball. White-hot streaks raced outward as burning pieces of metal were expelled into space. The position indicator disappeared from the right-hand display. In the center, the blue orb of the earth hung peacefully in space, unharmed and out of danger.

The knocking on the door turned into hammering. "Mrs. Klimt," someone shouted, "are you all right?"

A pair of space suits stood ready by an airlock. Dunn ran over to them. He picked up one of the helmets and tossed it to Su Mi. "Time to go," he said.

An automatic weapon sounded. Someone outside the door was firing at the lock. He wasn't using an air gun.

β 1 1

To mark the six-month anniversary of their escape from the asylum, the Jon Dunns returned to Washington for a reunion. They rented a meeting room at the Barnett Crystal City to enjoy bacon-wrapped scallops and an open bar stocked with Glenjohnnie. Gimbel learned that the other patients' experiences were similar to his own. They had returned to their jobs and families. Oscar-Dunn had hired a lawyer to fight the citations for safety violations. The charges were dropped, he got his vans back, and the jitney business flourished. Teacher-Dunn had persuaded the Lowell school board to let him begin the school year with a great debate on industrialization. It was a big hit and now he was developing the curriculum for use across the school system. Airport-Dunn was very busy: Congress planned to restore funding for the F-38 fighter and his company had appointed him proposal manager.

The Dunns invited Dr. Pollan to join them. Having no hard feelings, he accepted. He even proposed the first toast. "To spynusitis patients, wherever you may be. You were right about everything. It was the rest of us who were mixed up. I hereby certify that you are all perfectly sane. Perfectly sane, indeed. I'll retire and grow zucchini if you're not."

β 1 1

"Eight...nine...ten. The winner: Cheri Tarte, the Crimson Crusher." The referee held up Cheri's arm in triumph. Kong lay defeated at her feet, an expression of pain on his face. When Cheri looked down at him, the pain disappeared for an instant. He grinned and winked at her.

Pumping her fists, Cheri did a victory lap around the ring. The audience cheered wildly. Signs waved and flashbulbs popped. Cheri Tarte was no longer a target for nacho cheese and soda bottles. She was the crowd's favorite again.

"HEY! CHERI TARTE! I GOT SOMETHING OF YOURS."

Cheri Tarte stopped in the middle of the ring and looked around to see who called her. Joy stood under the archway at the entrance to the arena. Her Christmas sweater was nowhere in sight. Perhaps she had burned it, as she once promised. Instead she wore the stretch fabric and gold lamé of a full-fledged Vixen. The muscles of her bare arms weren't big, certainly not in Cheri's league, but they were lean and well defined. She draped one arm over the shoulders of Gimbel O'Hare.

Gimbel wore a black tuxedo and a neutral expression. It was unclear whether his association with Joy was entirely voluntarily. They made a cute couple, though. Equal in height, they seemed well matched.

Cheri Tarte leaped over the ropes, her red hair flying behind her. "GET YOUR SKANKY HANDS OFF OF MY SPY," she yelled.

She ran down the aisle to fight for her man.

Acknowledgments

Like Isaac Newton, I stood on the shoulders of giants.

First and foremost, Ian Fleming. His invention of James Bond, and the James Bond movies, gave me many hours of entertainment and inspired this parody.

I'm sure that Shakespeare doesn't mind that I stole some lines from his plays, along with some situations and characters: after I wrote the scene in chapter 12 in which a doctor explains to concerned parents the cause of their son's madness, it occurred to me that the situation was so reminiscent of Act 2, Scene 2 of *Hamlet* that I couldn't *not* rewrite (and rename) Dr. Pollan based on Polonius.

I attempted to make the story as accurate scientifically as possible (at least outside of the Jon Dunn sequences, which contain many impossibilities). Although there's no such disease as spynusitis, Licensed Clinical Social Worker and psychotherapist Eric Leventhal provided me with crucial background on the workings of the psychiatric ward. Deborah Barber identified much of the DC area flora that I mention and Dr. Robert Wickham of the University of Guelph Department of Physics advised me on the mechanics of stone skipping. Any mistakes on these topics are my sole responsibility.

Another source on the behavior of stones on pond surfaces is Lydéric Bocquet's article, "The Physics of Stone Skipping," *American Journal of Physics*, volume 71, issue 2, pages 150–155, published in February 2003. The Bocquet article draws on the first edition of L.D. Landau and E.M. Lifshitz's *Fluid Mechanics*, which is the source of the equation for the lift force that appears on Brownie McCoy's whiteboard in chapter 4.

Dr. James Feigenbaum of the Utah State University Department of Economics and Finance explained the fine points of utility optimization to me, and for the record, disagrees most emphatically with some of what I say on the subject.

Accounts of working conditions in the Lowell Mills can be found in Maury Klein's "The Lords and the Mill Girls" in *American History Illustrated*, October–November 1981; Charles Dickens's *American Notes*, chapter 4, 1850; Davy Crockett's "A Tour of the Lowell Mills" (1835); *The Lowell Offering* (1840–1845); and "Investigation of Labor Conditions," Massachusetts House Document, no. 50, March 1845.

All quotations from Sun Tzu's *Art of War* are from the 1910 translation by Lionel Giles. The quotations from *Peer Gynt* and *An Enemy of the People* are from the translations in Random House's Modern Library Edition of *Eleven Plays of Henrik Ibsen*. The quotation from Daniel Webster in chapter 9 is from his "Second Speech on the Sub-Treasury Bill." The entire speech can be found in the fourth volume of Little, Brown and Company's 1860 collection *The Works of Daniel Webster*.

The language Jon Dunn used in chapter 3 to justify the constitutionality of suppressing free speech is nearly identical to the language the US Supreme Court used in *Buckley v. Valeo* (1976). I merely substituted "interstate commerce" for "the electoral process." Not only can it happen here, it's already happening.

Darko Tomic was great to work with and provided a wonderful cover design. He put up with all the changes I asked for—including one after I had already signed off on the proofs. My copy editor, Kristy Stewart also put up with a lot—I dug in my heels regarding capitalizing the wrestlers' trash talk—but she drilled into me the difference between a hyphen, an en dash, and an em dash.

Finally, I would like to thank Piet Barber, David Boxenhorn, May Chin, Cris Crawford, Peter Everett, Peter Gruenbaum, Bill Hees, Irwin Jungreis, Adam Rasmussen, and Robin Reich for helpful discussions, advice on the manuscript, and letting me steal jokes. Their criticisms and suggestions made this a better book.

Discover the Full Asylum Store
http://store.FullAsylum.com

T-shirts – Coffee Mugs – Mouse Pads – Greeting Cards
Refrigerator Magnets – Coasters

Fun and practical gifts for all the freedom lovers on your list — including yourself! Save with frequent special offers.

Powered by
zazzle

The Zazzle Guarantee: If you don't love it, we'll take it back. If you are not 100% satisfied, you can return it for a replacement or refund within 30 days of receipt.

Merchandise, vendor, and terms subject to change without notice. Computer mouse and glass of scotch sold separately. By someone else. You probably figured that out.